A WOMAN NAMED DEFIANCE

SELECTED WORKS BY MARY FAITH FLOYD WITH HER NOVEL, EAGLE BEND

Edited by
Douglas Stuart McDaniel
and Tyler Dippel

Illustrations by
Patricia Grace

STORYHAUS MEDIA, LLC
Knoxville, Tennessee USA
2019

Names: Floyd, Mary Faith, McDaniel, Douglas and Dippel, Tyler. | Floyd, Mary Faith, McDaniel, Douglas and Dippel, Tyler, A Woman Named Defiance.
Title: A Woman Named Defiance / Mary Faith Floyd, Douglas McDaniel and Tyler Dippel.
Description: First Edition. | Knoxville : Storyhaus Media, 2019.
Identifiers: LCCN 2019952697 | ISBN 978-0-9800553-5-1 (paperback)
Subjects: Regional History–Nonfiction. | Appalachia–Social life and customs–19th century–Nonfiction. | BISAC: NONFICTION / Historical. | NONFICTION / Historical.
GSAFD: Regional nonfiction. | Nonfiction. | Appalachia.

A WORD
FROM THE PUBLISHER

This project began nearly 14 years ago when the late Becky French Brewer and I were working on a book about historic Park City, an independent streetcar city in East Knoxville, Tennessee.

As we gathered notes about important figures from Park City's past, I stumbled across a fascinating family by the name of McAdoo, but they lived a suburb over in the historic town of Old North Knoxville, and so I set aside those notes—another project for another day.

Six years later, as I was working on my third book, *Historic North Knoxville*, I retrieved my notes about Mary Faith Floyd, her husband William Gibbs McAdoo, and two of their children, William Gibbs McAdoo Jr. and Laura Julia Sterette McAdoo. I included essays about each of these family members in that book.

During the course of that research, I reached out to Brooke Clagett in Friendship, Maryland, the daughter of Brice McAdoo Clagett and the great, great granddaughter of William Gibbs McAdoo and Mary Faith Floyd McAdoo.

My mother, Betsy Chandler Drake, was helping me at the time with initial research. Betsy and I visited Brooke at her historic estate, Holly Hill, the circa-1698 Clagett family home in Friendship and one of the oldest homes existing in America. Brooke provided us direct access to the original diaries of Mary Faith Floyd, William Gibbs McAdoo, and Charles Rinaldo Floyd, which, because of her father's gift, are also available on microfilm at the Library of Congress, where we did additional primary research.

It was during this period that I first envisioned a book about Mary Faith Floyd, and fell in love with its tentative title, *A Woman Named Defiance.*

While numerous 20th century references presented this as a fact, I had not yet found primary research evidence that she was indeed named "Defiance."

Knowing that Mary Faith Floyd was born in September, 1832, Betsy and I zeroed in on the diaries of her father, Charles Rinaldo Floyd in the fall of that year. Through this, we were able to definitively prove from his diary that after returning to his plantation several weeks after Mary's birth, that he did indeed name her Mary Malinda Defiance Floyd.

This proud woman, born of noble roots in the antebellum south, maintained a standing in two worlds, the quintessential Old South with the conflicts and betrayals of the early Indian wars and the Indian removals of the 1830 and 1840s as well as the conflicts and turmoils of the Civil War.

She addresses these contradictions in her novel, *Eagle Bend*, describing early white occupants as being as "savage" as the natives themselves.

> *"The earliest white occupants of the soil were, in their habits, almost as hardy and nearly as savage as the Indians themselves. Indeed, the fierce and relentless hostility of the red man had compelled the resolute pioneer to adopt in great measure the same mode of life and style of warfare as those of their foes for their own preservation."*

As rumors of civil war increased, she married William Gibbs McAdoo in 1857, then attorney general for the Knoxville circuit. McAdoo would serve in the Confederate army in the Georgia campaign as a judge, placing the family in obscure poverty in Milledgeville, Georgia until their eventual return to Knoxville in 1877. As her husband, a bit of a hypochondriac, brooded on strolls through Old Gray cemetery and wrote sonnets to lovely young Knoxville women, Mary Faith Floyd managed the family budget, sewed for neighbors for small amounts of money, while simultaneously challenging the status quo by submitting essays, literary criticism, poetry and two complete novels to publishers in the southeast and New England—all while witnessing the pain and tragedy of street shootings during the Reconstruction era in Milledgeville and in Knoxville.

In her novel, *Eagle Bend*, Mary Faith Floyd embues in her young protagonist, Minona Dearing, the feminist entrepreneur qualities that seem more autobiographical as Minona, like Mary Faith Floyd herself, struggled to gain the attention of editors and publishers in Boston, New York, and Savannah.

A woman challenged with her place in society and within her family, Mary Faith Floyd spoke with an intellect and a keen, progressive new vision that she shared with her children and her grandchildren.

Her essay on equal pay for women was published in Southern newspapers in 1873. Her essay on child abuse appeared in her 1885 literary journal, the *Southern Head-Light*, which she published with her husband upon his retirement from the East Tennessee University—now the University of Tennessee.

She inspired her daughter Laura, who later became Madame Gagey, the Parisian solonierre, to host, in 1910, salons in fluent French in Paris on the rights of women and blacks in the southern United States—strong political statements published as far away from Paris as newspapers in Atlanta, Georgia.

Madame Gagey tragically died in novelist Anatole France's bed of a barbiturate overdose only a year later—a story worthy of a Somerset Maugham novel. These two women, largely overlooked by history for reasons we may never understand—perhaps because of their Confederate roots, or perhaps because, as a critic of literature, Mary Faith Floyd may have crossed paths with those far more favored by history.

It is notable that neither woman is depicted today on the suffragist statue on Market Square in downtown Knoxville.

Mary Faith Floyd's son, William Gibbs McAdoo Jr.—Laura's brother—became far more well-known as Secretary of the Treasury under President Wilson. He was instrumental in the development of the Federal Reserve, and married Wilson's daughter, Eleanor, in the White House. McAdoo Jr. would also run for president of the United States twice—in 1920 and 1924—but this book is not about the McAdoo men.

This book is about the McAdoo women—in particular, one woman named Defiance.

Douglas Stuart McDaniel
President and Creative Director
Storyhaus Media, LLC

TABLE OF CONTENTS

ABOUT
THIS BOOK

While digital copies of Mary Faith Floyd's 1872 novel, *The Nereid*, are accessible, the search for her other novel, "set in East Tennessee" would prove elusive. Was it titled *Eagle Bend*, as I surmised, or was it alternatively titled *Antethusia*, as hints on the Internet had suggested for years?

Visits to dozens of university libraries, obscure historical societies, and even the Victorian library at Historic Rugby, Tennessee, all proved fruitless. A conversation with the curator of the Library of Congress was equally frustrating.

"Yes," he said. "We have it registered. No, we don't have a copy of the book. I'm sorry."

I would periodically search historic databases for what would become my own personal southern literary grail. Small clues would keep me going. In January, 2019, I was frustrated to learn that the Georgia Historical Society would be closed for a year for renovation. But I would often start over in my search for her novel.

I sighed, and launched yet another quixotic Internet search, when, to my surprise, up popped an 1882 newspaper advertisement for Mary Faith Floyd's new novel, *Eagle Bend*.

A newer, online database of historic Georgia newspapers was now available at the University of Georgia library in Athens. Advertisement after advertisement appeared in the *Savannah Morning News* for her forthcoming book through 1882 and 1883. But I searched the expected dates and still did not see her words appear. I was convinced the Internet would continue to tease me.

I finally realized that the weekday editions of the *Savannah Morning News* were online, but the Sunday editions were not. Our business partner, Stephen Zimmerman and I planned a trip to Athens, spending a Sunday afternoon amidst reels of microfilm. I took the reels of weekday editions, cross-checking each month through 1882 and 1883. Stephen, fortunately, took the Sunday edition reel, and within minutes, discovered Chapter 1 of her novel, serialized in the *Savannah Morning News* beginning in February, 1883, and running for

12 consecutive Sundays. We PDF'd each page, emailing them to ourselves.

We finally had a copy of her novel—a volume, it turns out, that may never have been published in book form. If you find one, know that you have found something exceedingly rare.

Our work had just begun. The 1883 typesetting would prove impossible to transfer through optical character recognition, or OCR. But our team of digital savants were tenacious. We printed oversized posters of each page at Office Depot so that we could read the tiny print, and then, using a podcasting microphone, would read each chapter slowly, recording them as audio files. We then uploaded these files over weeks to an online transcription service, downloading the transcripts and then turning the work over to our other business partner, Tyler Dippel, who copiously edited and formatted the resulting raw text over more weeks.

There are three or four words that have proven untranslatable from the original, largely due to creases in the original newsprint. These are noted with asterisks.

As I stood waiting on the poster printouts, I caught myself in a moment, imagining on what paper Mary Faith Floyd wrote her original words 136 years ago, then envisioning her negotiations with her publisher, Colonel John Holbrook Estill, a survivor of the first battle of Manassas and an early board member of the Bonaventure Cemetery in Savannah, where he is buried.

I stood still in the moment, considering the typesetters at work at the *Savannah Morning News,* putting her words to press. I glimpsed in my mind's eye the men and women of Savannah, on their porches, reading her words with their tea on a sunny Sunday after church.

I then considered the considerable work many years ago to store copies of these newspaper in musty basements. The technicians preparing the pages for their first preservation on microfilm. The librarians cataloging the reels. The decades of storage, the wonder of where these pages might be. To the moment of our rediscovery, and our own digital transformation process back to the printed pages you now hold in your hand.

Douglas Stuart McDaniel
President and Creative Director
Storyhaus Media, LLC

AN INTRODUCTION
TO THE SELECTED WORKS
OF MARY FAITH FLOYD

BY DOUGLAS STUART MCDANIEL

The Floyd and McAdoo Families

Mary Faith Floyd was born at Fairfield Plantation near St. Marys, Georgia on September 9, 1832, the daughter of Charles Rinaldo Floyd and Julia Ross (Boog) Floyd. From her father's diary:

Monday, 1st October, 1832. Election Day. B. Hopkins and Mech.d (sic) rode to Jefferson and I rode to St Marys on my stallion Ruffian, and arrived there before 12 o'clock. After stopping a short time at the Gen l's, I went to Mrs. Kings and for the first time saw my little daughter, Mary Melinda Defiance, who is a beauty with beautiful hair and sparkling eyes.

According to the Georgia Historical Society, Charles Rinaldo Floyd (October 14, 1797-March 22, 1845) was a noted duelist, soldier, and plein air painter. He was the son of General John Floyd, who commanded the Georgia forces in the War of 1812 and fought with General Andrew Jackson in the Creek Indian War of 1813-1814.

It is believed that Mary's middle name, Defiance, was in honor of Camp Defiance, a battle encampment her grandfather, General John Floyd, had established during the Battle of Calabee Creek in Macon County, Alabama. According to the *Encyclopedia of Alabama*, John Floyd's Georgia troops were caught off guard as Red Stick leader Paddy Walsh and his 1,300 Creek warriors charged Floyd's two cannons. Floyd's militia narrowly averted defeat by quickly securing the cannons and returning fire on the charging warriors.

Charles Rinaldo Floyd followed in his father's footsteps as commander of Georgia forces in the Seminole Indian wars in Florida, and, according to Mary

Faith Floyd's own 1913 obituary, was ignominiously commissioned by General Winfield Scott to support the Indian removals from Georgia, Florida, and Alabama as part of the Trail of Tears.

Mary Faith Floyd first married Randolph Gillis McDonald (1826-1854) of St. Marys, Georgia. He died only two years after their marriage of yellow fever. They had one son, also named Randolph McDonald, who died in Knoxville, Tennessee in 1902.

Her depiction of the yellow fever epidemic in coastal Georgia in her first novel, *The Nereid,* is so accurate that it is referenced in modern medical journals about the disease, including the book *Yellow Fever Years: An Epidemiology of Nineteenth-Century American Literature and Culture.*

In 1857, Mary Faith Floyd met and married William Gibbs McAdoo at the Montvale Springs Resort in Blount County Tennessee. A debutante ball at this resort is portrayed in her novel, *Eagle Bend.*

Also a widower, McAdoo was born in 1820 at the McAdoo family home at Island Ford, in Anderson County, Tennessee, the scene and setting of much of *Eagle Bend.*

At the time of their marriage, McAdoo was attorney general for the Knoxville circuit and a prominent member of the Knoxville bar association. He had been a soldier in the Mexican War under General Winfield Scott, served as a Tennessee legislator, and was a professor of geology at the East Tennessee University in Knoxville.

The McAdoos had seven children in the tumultuous years just before and after the Civil War. Caroline Blackshear McAdoo (1859-1905), John Floyd McAdoo (1860-1888), Rosalie Floyd McAdoo (1861-1920), William Gibbs McAdoo Jr. (1863-1941), Malcolm Ross McAdoo (1865-1932), Nona Howard McAdoo (1868-unknown), and Laura Julia Sterrete McAdoo (1870-1911). They also lost an infant son, Charles Lane McAdoo, in 1873.

At the time of this publication, the McAdoo home still stands in Milledgeville, where they had remained through the Reconstruction period until 1877. The family then returned to Knoxville, where Mr. McAdoo resumed his duties at the university, renamed the University of Tennessee in 1879.

Mary Faith Floyd continued to write after returning to Knoxville. First living on State Street, the family soon moved to the town of North Knoxville, and frequented the Market House at Emory Place. They were an extremely well-read, but also ecumenical family, and often went week by week to different churches—Methodist, Baptist, Presbyterian, and Lutheran, according to her diaries. In Victorian Knoxville, churches were the place to be seen, to be noticed, to establish social connections that one could follow up through the week with calling cards and teas, as she would note.

Her husband, on the other hand, turned out to be quite the hypochondriac. According to both of their diaries, he passed his days contemplating death while strolling through Old Gray Cemetery, as he wrote sonnets to half the women in Knoxville.

Sonnet to Sara in Acknowledgment of a Gift of Fragrant Violet Flowers Knoxville, August 10, 1889

Dear Gleam of sunshine in this world of gloom!
An inspiration and a light art thou
Such, or diffusing that the wrinkled brow
Relaxed to a smile which doth illume
Most gladly the worn heart, and freshened bloom
As with an artist's pencil-touch, can throw
O'er heart and feature an angelic glow
Exalting life above sad human doom.
Refreshing to my senses and my soul—
All my true soul of admiration made
All what is lovely in this world of ours—
Charmed life of bliss throughout thy life's full whole
Deservest thou for her perfumes rich arrayed—
One profuse posy of sweet violet flowers.

W.G.M., Sr.

And then sometimes he would write innocent sonnets to mountains.

Sonnet to Unicoy Mountain When She Concealed Herself in Clouds

And hast thou veiled thy face from me O Queen
Of thine imperial realm half earth, half sky?
The sunshine is around me, but mine eye
In loving quest of thee, of all the scene
Most loved, as far from my childhood thou hast been,
Sees naught but morning drapery, and a sigh
Breathes in the breeze that from thee whispers by—
O, dost thou still abide behind thy screen?
Or art thou fled like Egypt's queen of old,

From Anthony's cause? Or like the Austrian wife
Who quit the Corsican when Fortune frowned?
O Unicoy, loved with a love untold!
Smile from thy heights serene, and my sore strife
'Gainst cruel foes, with victory shall be crowned!

> *W. G. McAdoo*
> *Knoxville, Tennessee*
> *August, 1887*

It was Mary who largely held the family together through their post-war poverty, and despite her wealthy family having owned the Fairfield and Bellvue plantations in Georgia, she was a breadwinner for the family as much as her husband, if not more.

Their children were fascinating in their own right. Three daughters—Laura, Nona, and Rosalie, each taught school at the Girls High School in Knoxville, and Laura may have also taught school in Clinton, Tennessee, according to the 1987 book, *Anderson County: Historical Sketches*, by Katherine Baker Hoskins.

Nona also wrote sonnets—to a girl named Fannie.

Sonnet To Fannie Nishel

Thou dearest of dear friends! So young and fair,
Oh art thee gone forever from my sight?
For thee warmth and cloudless morning bright,
And hope's glad rainbow spanning all the air,
No thought that thou coulds't die did ever dare
Nurse the dread thought that all my love's delight
In Thee, O Paragon of Friendships might,
E'er could be dead and leave me in despair.
No more on earth thy noblest spirit, where
In all the universe thy blest abode
Shall I behold? In yonder star the brightest
Beyond our solar realm, in loftiest sphere
Eternal sure thou art, and on that road,
Thither, let me pursue with footsteps lightest!

> *Nona Howard McAdoo*
> *Knoxville, Tennessee*
> *January 21, 1887*

Sonnet To Fanny Nishel

I know t'was more folly and madness and I missed
Thy padded bust unto my throbbing heart,
And strove some warmth and life and love t' impart
Unto its rounded and voluptuous breast;
But still unmoved it proved, and when caressed
Most fondly, with a cold coquettish art,
Repulsed each touch of Cupid's vanquished dart;
And left fond love by love's neglect, distressed.
Ah, were this RACHEL—not her counterfeit—
Were this HER glorious frame of flesh and blood,
And life and soul—with love's resistless might,
Her heart with throb responsive, well I wit,
And passion's eager and delicious flood,
Would bear us to the islands of delight.

While Mary may have been more stern toward the children than her husband, she deeply loved her children, according to her diaries, and frequently did extra sewing and needlework to make sure that the boys, especially Will (William Gibbs McAdoo Jr.), and Ross (Malcolm Ross McAdoo), had what they needed. But she doted on the girls as well, frequently giving Nona or Rosalie the money from her sewing.

Their father seemed equally affectionate, especially with the boys. At Christmas, in 1871, while they were still in Milledgeville, he would write sonnets back and forth to the boys as a challenge both from a literary and educational perspective. The boys called him Dr. Old Rat, and he would reply to Will, the future Secretary of the Treasury and two-time presidential candidate as "Sharp Wit," while he addressed Ross, in couplets, as "Little Pink."

Dr. Old Rat promised, in these numerous rhyming couplets, that if the boys were good to their mother, and brought in the light wood, that Santa would sail on a ship from the Azores, bringing them candy and firecrackers.

Hole in the Wall, Dec 14, 1871

Dear little boys! I saw you yesterday
Frolicking all about the house in play.
And watched you as you trudged away
To go to Milledgeville with steps not loath or slow.
I heard you say you wished for me to write;
Therefore this line I pen to you tonight.

I should have written last night, but your cat,
Seemed bent on swallowing a dish of rat.
And as I could not willingly agree,
To make his feast, it was my lot to be.
Penned in my hole all night—the live-long night,
And that's the reason I did not write.
You must keep up your cat, or sure as fate,
Far from such peril I must emigrate.
But if I go, I hope you'll not forge my good advice;
And you must never let
Your face and hands grow filthy, or tell lies,
Or disobey your Mother's counsel's wise,
Or violate the Sabbath, quarrel or fight,
Unless in fighting you're extremely right.
And if you are, first thump your foeman soundly,
But cease whenever he surrenders roundly.
And never strike a sister or a brother,
No matter what you may do to another.
In short, you owe God for your gentle birth,
All rarest traits of excellence and worth.
And you must pay, and be of boys the best,
And being such, I shall most-sure request.

Dr. Old Rat

In the privations of post-Civil War Milledgeville, however, Dr. Old Rat
sadly had to write the boys that Santa's ship had sunk, the candy and
firecrackers were spoiled, and the boys would only be getting sturdy boots.

Meanwhile, Mary Faith Floyd's early diaries documented her struggles with
her literary submissions, her frustrations with editors and publishers, and her
observations about neighbors getting shot in the street during Reconstruction,
her sewing, and the family's lack of money and status. Her later diary entries
in Knoxville contained mild disdain for what she deemed to be vapid society
parties, often specifically directed toward one Mary Boyce Temple, the spinster
daughter of Knoxville industrialist Oliver Perry Temple. Miss Temple was also
an author and part of the women's suffrage movement in East Tennessee.

Mary Boyce Temple's soirées were legendary, and with the McAdoo family's
post-war poverty and her husband's paltry University salary, Mary knew they

just couldn't keep up. We see this sentiment poignantly in *Eagle Bend* in the character of Minona Dearing's Savannah-born mother, Eriginia Dearing.

> *Mrs. Dearing was not a heartless. She was a voluptuary—a fair specimen of a wife in fashionable society. Between her husband and herself there existed a perfect state of amity, a sort of quasi happiness. She performed all her duty to him as far as her knowledge of that phantom went. Mingling with her circle, balls, parties and dress were essential parts of existence. Accustomed from childhood to the giddy whirl of a city, she had no idea that the extreme pursuit of pleasure became a dissipation—labor—a sin. She was sympathetic with the poor, gave much in charity, and was foremost on committees for inspecting and mitigating the abuses of orphan asylums and other philanthropic institutions. Of that higher type of love, of perfect self-abnegation. Mrs Dearing knew nothing; therefore she felt guilty of no breach of kindness when she withheld her presence from the languishing couch of her afflicted spouse. Perhaps those are most fortunate in life who feel only this theoretical love and enjoy only a negative happiness. They live longer, carry youth beyond the meridian plentitude of existence, and while they experience less felicity, they avoid many ways that wear away heart and life together.*

In her later years, Mary would witness monumental changes in society and within her family. She became one of the leading members of Ossoli Circle, a women's literary and cultural organization in Knoxville, and was the second president after Miss Mary Boyce Temple. According to her 1913 obituary, Mary Faith Floyd McAdoo was a "decided progressive in all political, social and industrial problems, and had a profound grasp of these questions. She was a believer in women's suffrage, because she believed that it would do more than any other one thing to destroy the social and economic injustices to which women were subjected."

Her son, Will, or William Gibbs McAdoo Jr., would go on to build early street car lines in Knoxville, but would soon leave for the financial markets of New York, helping secure the financing for the Hudson River tunnels, while her son Ross would manage streetcar railways in Atlanta, Georgia and Patterson, New Jersey according to Issue 4 of the *University of Tennessee Record*.

It seems from the diaries that Nona and Rosalie stayed close to their mother, especially after their father's death in 1894. But it would be daughter Laura that seemed to closely follow her mother's literary footsteps, if not on an even grander, but more tragic scale.

An Equally Defiant Daughter

While she didn't have Defiance as her middle name, Mary Faith Floyd's youngest daughter, Laura Julia Sterette McAdoo, was a force of nature equal to her mother. How she ended up married to Oscar Trigg, we may never know. Perhaps partially a result of the literary birthright influence of her parents, she became a published intellectual on the international stage, rivaling her financially successful brother, William Gibbs McAdoo Jr., the Secretary of the Treasury under President Wilson and who presided over the establishment of the Federal Reserve System, and to whom she was predictably compared to in her obituary in the *Atlanta Constitution*.

Laura had a stormy marriage to Oscar Trigg, the socialist friend of Jack London, Frank Lloyd Wright, Upton Sinclair, and Clarence Darrow. Trigg was an 1890s believer in free love, and according to newspaper reports, guest lectured at the Spencer-Whitman Institute in Chicago, located on Calumet Avenue. The center was named for Herbert Spencer and Walt Whitman, but it was apparently also a free love colony, and according to the newspaper headlines that appeared during their 1907 divorce, it is where Trigg had been caught *"in flagrante delictu."*

While in Chicago, before she married Trigg, some of her works included an article in Volume 21 of The Arena, published in 1899, entitled *Woman's Economic Status in the South*.

Laura Sterette McAdoo writes in *The Arena*:

"My attention has been recently called to the subject of woman's relation to labor by the many magazine and book discussions bearing upon that theme. That economics should present a new problem in these better days—the problem of woman—is but another proof of the invasion of democratic ideas into every field of human science. Exemption on grounds of sex is a product of feudal conditions. With the general democratization of views following in the wake of scientific disclosures, no class nor caste can be excluded from adjudgment upon equal terms. If "the word of the modern is the word en masse," the corresponding implications invest into every field of social endeavor. It has been the misfortune of woman, as, alas, it has been her chief pride, to be regarded from the emotional standpoint. But science is impartial and refuses to yield preferential sentiment.

It is, however, safe to say that most masculine verdicts upon this theme are even yet biased by tradition—and this is true even of those which claim to be scientific."

In 1898, as Laura Sterette McAdoo, she writes a poem on Altruism for Volume I., No 5 of *The Mind,* a "Magazine of Liberal and Advanced Thought, Science, Philosophy, Religion, Psychology, Metaphysics, Occultism." John Emery McLean, editor.

In October, 1901, first writing as Laura McAdoo Trigg, she reviews Elia W. Peattie's romance, *The Beleaguered Forest,* for *The National Magazine,* under the title, *A Woman's Book and Its Characteristics.*

In 1903, she writes, as Laura McAdoo Trigg, in Volume 13 of *the Monist,* by the Hegeler Institute, a review of Lester Ward's *Pure Sociology: A Treatise on the Origin and Spontaneous Development of Society,* where she analyses evolutionary aspects of sociology.

Despite having been writing such important essays on major topics of the day, Laura would flee from her marriage to Trigg, move to Paris, France in an effort to reinvent herself and find a new audience for her ideas.

According to an article in the August 28, 1910 edition of the *Atlanta Constitution,* Laura managed to successfully redefine herself in very little time.

"Of Intellectual Paris Southern Woman Writes," the article is headlined.

"M. Paul Margueritte has just published a romance under the title of 'Human Weakness;' M. Marguerite is one of those writers whom one cannot read without a certain tenderness,' writes Madame Julie Gagey-McAdoo (Laura McAdoo Gagey) in the second of her series of letters on Intellectual Paris."

Laura had quickly remarried—this time to a noted cardiologist, Dr. Pierre Julien Gagey. She continued writing essays, and hosting salons in Paris, speaking in fluent French on the rights of women and blacks in the southern United States, known only as the solonierre known as "Madame Gagey."

Sadly, she soon caught Dr. Gagey with a mistress as well, and she abandoned him for the French novelist Anatole France. As the septegenarian France worked on his new book, *The Gods Will Have Blood,* the thirty-something Laura Gagey became his muse and his audience as he wrote. When it was finished, she wrote him plaintively, claiming the work was hers as well, and France scorned her. So Madame Gagey killed herself with an overdose of sleeping pills.

Late to the game, the April 12, 1914 edition of the *Atlanta Constitution* finally documents Laura's tragedy.

Georgia Woman Who Died in Paris

A beautiful Georgia woman who died in Paris a little over a year ago (it was three years) and who, if she had lived, would have, in time, been recognized there for her intellect and literary talents, was Laura McAdoo Gayez (Gagey), sister of the secretary of the treasury. Beautiful and brilliant in her youth, and a student of French literature, she first wrote short stories for the American magazines; then finished literary critics. Her first husband was a professor in the Chicago university. She was a part of the intellectual life there until her residence in Paris and her marriage to Dr. Gayez (Gagey) a French scientist of marked attainment. She was studying with him, and attending a course of lectures in the academy, when one of the speakers touched upon certain social phases of the southern states of the United States.

He misrepresented facts in statements he made pertaining to the negro race problem when the young American woman arose and in the most fluent French corrected the speaker, and instructed her learned listeners in the question about which she knew so much and they knew so little.

She was at once sought for by the intellectual element of that great city. She became a regular speaker at their conferences, and a contributor to French magazines, one of her last articles being a very brilliant one pertaining to the feminist movement as she saw it in France. Madame Gayez (Gagey) in her thought and attitude, her fearlessness and directness of utterance, had very much the spirit of her distinguished brother, now one of the most marked men in the world of affairs. With her knowledge and seriousness of viewpoint, her sense of personal conviction in her activities, she had that social gift and that love of life in its pleasures that made her home a delightful one.

Miss Emily Harrison of Atlanta visited Madame Gayez (Gagey) but a few moments previous to the latter's death and described as one of the interesting incidents of the visit that Madame Gayez's (Gagey) little boy knew all of the Uncle Remus stories and could repeat them in French.

Laura Julia Sterette McAdoo Gagey was buried in Paris at Batignolle Cemetery. Her mother, Mary Faith Floyd McAdoo, died two years later, February 6, 1913. Mary would not live to see her son William run for President of the United States in 1920 and again in 1924.

The Selected Works of Mary Faith Floyd

During the Victorian period, many female writers often hid their gender to appeal more broadly to editors, publishers, and readers. From the Brontë sisters writing as Currer, Acton, and Ellis Bell, to Louisa May Alcott often appearing as A.M. Barnard to produce her gothic thrillers, here we have a twice married southern female writer proudly and perhaps shockingly using her maiden name as her nom de plume.

Compare, perhaps, this boldness in Mary Faith Floyd to the distinct fearlessness of French romance writer of the same period, Amantine Lucile Aurore Dupin (1804-1876), who published under the pseudonym of George Sand, and was one of France's most prolific writers of the 19th century. She was a woman not only with a male name, but a woman who notably dressed frequently in male attire.

At the funeral of George Sand, the *less* popular Victor Hugo spoke fondly of her.

"George Sand was an idea. She has a unique place in our age. Others are great men... she was a great woman."

One could argue that Mary Faith Floyd rejected this notion of *femininism in obscura*, choosing a path that bridged literature and commerce as a woman in full. During the Reconstruction period, her main body of work were essays and literary criticism, often of male authors and the role of women in society, before she penned her first novel, *The Nereid,* in 1872.

Finding an audience for her poetry, essays and short stories in southern newspapers and magazines as early as 1870, Mary Faith Floyd never steered clear of feminist topics, even 50 years before women would earn the right to vote.

The works selected for this volume were painstakingly rediscovered over a period of 14 years, and illuminate Mary Faith Floyd as a progressive voice that has long been overlooked by history.

Let us begin with her 1873 review of a book on domestic hygiene entitled *The Ways of Women,* where she goes out of her way to summon ancient goddesses in a sarcastic broadside.

She quickly discards the author's work as a treatise on therapeutics, and launches into her own well-formed opinions on solving the knotty problems of women being able to sustain themselves in society honorably and successfully.

This essay only gathers steam as Mary Faith Floyd makes light of society's perception of woman.

"No aristocratic 'golden lily' of the Celestial empire values her little foot," she writes, "nor more persistently compresses it into diminutive boots, than does our modern crop of young ladies; and alas, be it spoken, many old ones too are addicted to this folly! The Flathead Indians do not endeavor more systematically to fashion their heads into abnormal form then do our modern esquisites of the "fair sex" by continued lacing, to shape their waists into waspish slenderness. As well tell a woman to give up life as to urge her to relinquish these unhealthy styles of fashion and appear in the proportions nature gave her."

Move over, Margaret Mitchell. Mary Faith Floyd just popped your Scarlet O'Hara whalebone corset 60 years before you penned her, right up the road from Milledgeville in Atlanta.

Well *fiddle dee dee*, Miss Scarlet. Mary Faith Floyd isn't done yet, even within this one essay.

"Any attempt in women, particularly Southern women, to go beyond the specified callings enumerated (teacher, seamstress, as Floyd herself was, or boarding house keeper) are considered encroachments on masculine territory," she writes. "A dependent woman is almost forced into servile occupation and often where these fail, into vice, for bread and existence."

She returns to the author's work briefly to compliment him on his admirable dissertation upon health laws, and the educational and industrial wants of women, but not before firing one more salvo toward society:

"Even should she (a dependent woman) be blessed by obtaining employment, for the reason that she is a woman she receives only a third or a fourth the sum for a given amount of labor that is paid to a man," she begins.

"This is gross injustice; and in no respect does society need a reform so much as in opening modest and suitable avenues to female industry, making these honest labors respectable, and giving the same wages to either sex for the same amount of well performed work."

According to *Time* Magazine, one of the earliest references to advocacy for equal pay for women was a February 1869 letter to the editor of the New York Times that questioned why female government employees were not paid the same as male ones.

Mary Faith Floyd was not far behind that letter writer, but she was far ahead of many other progressive thinkers, especially in the southern United States.

Her other essays are imbued with the need for education as the great leveler of society, from reviews of books on penmanship, drawing of objects, laws of light, of shade and of shadow.

In her 1875 review of "Witched," a story appearing in the noteworthy *Southern Magazine*, she castigates northern writers for their mischaracterization of "negro" dialect, writing, "As a class," she writes, "Negroes, except those on remote and isolated plantations, speak very much as unlettered white people. They have acquired much correctness of expression by domestic communion with the white race and do express themselves in the broken gibberish attributed to them by many fiction caterers."

She continues, "We wish the author of 'Witched' would make a tour to the Sunny South and observe how our real negroes talk, or if the writer is a Southron, we advise her to make an excursion beyond her own neighborhood to learn how negros do really talk elsewhere.

Later in her writing career, back in Knoxville, Mary Faith Floyd briefly published a literary journal called *The Southern Head-Light* with her husband. In it, one particular essay stands out. Titled "Cruelty to Children," she cautions that corporal punishment should be seldom used, and that "few people remember that children are free and independent creatures, given to us to foster and train in the straight and narrow way."

She notes a sweet young teacher who connects with "rough boys in her department," and that the teacher was in despair.

"There are many children entrusted to my care that no reproof can reach. They are brutalized at home. Fierceness and coercion won't do. I tried kindness. It was a new voice to them. It acted like a charm. Think of this. There are hundreds of children among the laboring classes who are looked upon as brutes of burden by their owners to be cuffed and kicked, with never a kind word. They are ill clad, ill fed, poorly housed. Is there any wonder that they grow brutalized with scarce a humanized characteristic in their beings?"

Mary Faith Floyd finishes this essay, written in 1885, with a call for good men and women to organize a society for the prevention of cruelty to children.

Lavish Depictions of the Natural World and Human Interactions

In her much earlier 1871 review of Prime Minister Benjamin Disraeli's novel, *Lothair*, we see her admiration for his "handsome descriptions of scenery, its individualization of characters, and its sarcasm upon some of the follies of the age—especially that hard grapple of church after the wealth of individuals for the extension of each particular sect and its control over political opinions."

Her love of scenery and individualization of character is evident in her novel, *Eagle Bend*.

Mary Faith Floyd's writing style is lavish "but very readable," Crystal Huskey writes in 2019 in the *Clinton Courier News*. "The writing brings to mind novels by Anthony Trollope and even Thomas Hardy in its description of the natural world and human interactions."

Chapter IV of *Eagle Bend* opens with a stroll over the hillsides and bluffs around Clinton.

Weeks fell from the gigantic tree of time, as leaves drop in autumn, ere Mr. Dearing was sufficiently recovered to stroll around the neighboring hills.

Mr. Portwood's rustic residence was situated upon an abrupt bluff hundred feet above the level of the river, short distance below two picturesque islands which divide the stream above into three channels. The bluff is made up wholly of limestone, arranged in thin strata, dipping to the southeast at an angle of about forty-five degrees. In this limestone is found fossil shells, both univalves and bivalves, small in size (not more than an inch in length), and occasionally a trilobite and an ammonite.

On the topmost pinnacle of this bluff, and within a dozen yards of the country house, are many Indian graves. The bodies were deposited in shallow cells which the natives countless ages ago, had excavated in this friable limestone; and each tomb was bordered by a hedging of thin stones set up edgewise marking its boundary. From some of these the bones of the nameless aborigines had been disinterred, and amid the small heaps of yellow clay and fragments of limestone, could be seen fossil shells of a million of years ago when an ocean rolled it's billows over the scene, and the shattered bits of human bones and here and there and undecayed human tooth of far more modern origin—probably only a thousand years of age.

Wherever the white man's axe had spared the native vegetation of this upheaval of limestone, a dense forest of cedars held complete possession of the earth's surface. These huge shrubs, sometimes rising to the dignity of trees, spread out they're stiff branches so low as almost a rest upon the ground, and rose in regular cones to a pointed apex of foliage occasionally thirty or forty feet in height. Beyond this narrow ridge of limestone an alluvial soil occupied the earth's surface. There the gigantic oak and hickory, and the still mightier or tulip trees which botanists, from its peculiar leaf, have aptly styled the Liriodendron, send far up toward heaven their lofty summits. Slender papaw trees put forth their delicate stems, sometimes burdened with golden fruit; and under all the soil is carpeted thickly with the fallen leaves of former years.

By way of introduction, but without overt spoilers, we encourage the reader to dive into the Victorian Appalachian world of Mary Faith Floyd's *Eagle Bend,* set in East Tennessee and Georgia in the late Reconstruction period of the late 1870s. The novel was serialized in the *Savannah Morning News* over twelve Sundays in 1883 and has quite frankly been lost to history ever since.

Her novel opens with a tragic carriage accident on a river bank near Clinton, Tennessee. Clarek Dearing, a Savannah merchant touring East Tennessee with his hard-drinking horseman, Jock Hethrington, is injured, and must spend months recovering in a rural mountain cabin. Dearing finds the mountain people fascinating, and soon purchases the old Eagle Bend estate so that his family may summer there from the oppressive heat of Savannah.

It must be added that the Eagle Bend mansion, like many scenes in Mary Faith Floyd's novel, were actual places. She weaves into her storylines places like Lea Springs Resort in Grainger County, Mann's Cave, Black Oak Ridge, the Jacksboro Stage Road, and the Holston River Ferry in Knox County, as well as Montvale Springs Resort in Blount County and Tallulah Falls Gorge in north Georgia. Sadly, the old Eagle Bend estate was torn down in 1962 by the Tennessee Valley Authority.

It is Clarek Dearing's daughter, Minona Dearing, however, who is the main protagonist of this novel. Only 16 but already an aspiring writer, we see much of the author in the character of Minona. Her efforts to convince the book and newspaper editors, including Messrs. "Wary & Wirey," of New York, to consider her works as a woman in the 1870s feels almost autobiographical at times, as she challenges the male-dominated establishment of the literary worlds of Savannah, New York, and Boston while discovering for herself the nobility of the mountain people of East Tennessee.

The novel offers surprising twists and turns, from highway robberies and murder trials in rural Anderson County to descriptions of debutante balls at Montvale Springs Resort and weddings and Christmas balls in wealthy Savannah. *Eagle Bend* provides a rich tapestry of scene and character that dispels any preconceived notions about hillbillies or 19th century southern female writers.

Writes Tyler Dippel, one of the editors of this book, "Have you ever imagined what it would be like to be a debutante in East Tennessee during the late 19th century? I never did, but *Eagle Bend* captivated me in ways I didn't know possible."

"As her words cascade across the page like a flowing river from rural cabins in Clinton, Tennessee to the seacoast of Georgia, you will soon discover that you have already drifted out to sea. From her richly descriptive accounts of the Tennessee mountains and surrounding area, to the simultaneously uplifting and heartbreaking emotions evoked from her layered characters, Mary Faith Floyd's novel immediately transports the reader to the time period."

Dippel continues, "*Eagle Bend* offers the modern reader a glimpse into life in Victorian-era East Tennessee as you embark on a journey with surprisingly more twists than an old Appalachian road."

POETRY

BY MARY FAITH FLOYD

LETTERS OF THE DEAD
A POEM

BY MARY FAITH FLOYD

Slight links that bind us unto death,
More frail than dying infants' breath,
What hopes, what fears, do you contain
Of Times departed lengthening chain?

Those hands that traced these loving lines,
The hearts that throbbed with life's designs,
In ruthless Death's cold frost lie still,
Congealed life's ruddy quickening rill.

Canst thou, poor perishing papers frail,
Which fly before the passing gale,
Outlast angelic man, and rise
His phantom from the mystic skies,

And teach us that the weakest thing,
A feather on the breeze's wing,
A leaf, a flower, can longer stand
Than man, made monarch by God's hand?

They can, alas! a solemn thrill,
Pangs which life's pulses strangely chill,
Coil round the heart as to our gaze
Come forth these relics of past days.

Drift wood are we, swift floating o'er
The sea of Time to Heavenly shore:
Celestial fields! O, happy those
Who first attain thy blessed repose!

Beyond the tyrant Sorrow's sway,
Care cloud's not the eternal day;
But, with the loved and lost, is won
The crown of glory through God's son.

November, 1870

Published in THE FEDERAL UNION.
Milledgeville, Georgia, January 3, 1871.

GOLDEN VOICES
A POEM

BY MARY FAITH FLOYD

When sunshine o'er earth's verdant breast,
Pours out its radiant gold,
And gilds the hills, and paints the trees
With magic touches bold,
My soul drinks draughts of calm delight,
That all my senses fill:
Then nature's golden voices deep
My quivering pulses thrill.

When winds are stirred with angry howls,
With tumults loud and hoarse,
Wrapping the sun in clouds of gloom.
Loosing the lightning's force
In gleaming, forked tongues of flame—
When maddened oceans reel,
Then wild sublimely-golden tones
Through coral soul-depths peal.

When ebon night hangs o'er the world,
Her wondrous starry fold,
And Diana pale through rushing clouds
Walks like a huntress bold,
Sad Memory walks, and opens the door,
And waves her phantom hand;
Oh! then the golden voices dear
Sweep from the spirit land!

Voices that speak from friends who once
Were treasured jewels here
In earth's rich perishing cabinet;
But now, in loftier sphere,
Swell out in heavenlier tones than earth's
Most charmed symphonies,
And forge, with golden music's bars,
Links lifting us to skies.

October, 1871

THE FEDERAL UNION.
Milledgeville, Georgia, June 12, 1872.
From the Southern Recorder.

THE RAINBOW OF PROMISE
A POEM

BY MARY FAITH FLOYD

Respectfully dedicated to the Parents and Relatives of the late George C. Harris, of Milledgeville.

I saw the sunrise on last Sabbath morn
Flesh into glory all the clouded West,
Spanning it with a rainbow to adorn
The white tombs underneath it, where did rest
The quiet dead; the well beloved and lost
Gone on before us to the Future Land.
O Glorious rainbow! Type of the bridge they crossed
How soon shall we cross too, and with them stand?

The purple-golden arch did seem to spring
From one new grave made but on Friday last,
To which a sudden Providence did bring
One manly form from us forever passed!
One week ago, in life and health he stood,
Youth bade him hope for three score years and ten—
Loved fondly by the wise, the brave, the good,
Now gone forever from the walks of men!

O thank Thee, our Almighty Father, who,
Whether all laden with the weight of years,
Or in bright youth to the dark tomb we go,
Thy mercy all abounds and wipes our tears;
And true repentance, e'en at the last hour,
Suffices to remove the stain of sin,
And Faith in Thee still works with marvelous power
To ope the pearly gates and let us in!

Not for the dead and realms of endless light,
Not for the early dead, escaped life's woes
Shall flow our tears, but for the desolate blight
That falls upon the loving breasts of those
Left here behind, in whose rent hearts a void
The world can never fill, an anguish makes,
Which cannot, but with life, be all destroyed,
And which, while we bless God, still throbs and aches!

He doeth all things well—our Father doth—
In His vast wisdom, His eternal ken,
His will is best for dead and living both;
He willeth best the lives and deaths of men;
He biddeth some remain to work some end;
He taketh some to 'scape some dreadful doom:
O ever, He our Father, wisest Friend,
On both sides of his gate to Heaven, the tomb!

Milledgeville, Georgia, December 22, 1874.

UNION & RECORDER.
Wednesday, December 23, 1874.

Fatal Accident

On Wednesday morning, 16th, Mr. George C. Harris, youngest son of Judge Iverson L. Harris, was preparing to go hunting. With his gun in his hand, he lingered to talk with some of the family, leaned on his gun, the muzzle under his arm, thoughtlessly threw his foot around striking the hammer, exploding the cap and discharging the contents, inflicting a fearful wound which he survived only about 24 hours. Thus in bloom and vigor of early manhood, full of hope and promise, was his bright young life extinquished. The sad accident was not only a terrible shock to the aged parents, but cast a gloom over the community.

UNION & RECORDER.
Wednesday, December 23, 1874.

THE TALMAGE SCHOOL BELL
A POEM

BY MARY FAITH FLOYD

Affectionately dedicated to Mrs. R. W. Talmage.

Bell, sweet bell,
Thy soft tones tell
Of many a passing hour
Old Time's remorseless power
Hath driven across the world,
And into darkness hurled,
Freighted with hopes that perished;
Yet time thy sweet tones cherished.

Bell, proud bell,
Thy deep tones tell
Of busy hearts that best
Of eager hurrying feet,
Of souls that did aspire
To grasp Promethean fire
On the high hill of science,
Bidding all toil defiance!

Bell, sad bell.
Thy mournful swell
Recalls the loved and lost
Who the dark river crossed
Beyond the shores of Time,
And on the heights sublime,
With raptures that are Aidenn's*,
List to thy earthly cadence.

Bell, dear bell,
Once more thy swell
Floats on the passing gale,
Telling the gladsome tale
That young ambition stirs,
Whene'er his eager ears.
Hear thy glad strokes that urge ambition
To grasp proud Leaning's grand fruition!

Bell, loved bell,
Long, loud and well,
Thy silvery, call shall swell,
And cast a magic spell
O'er toilers of the mind,
Who shall rich treasures find,
Vast as the realm empyrean,
Deep in the Spring Pierian!

UNION & RECORDER.
Wednesday, December 2, 1874.

* Arabic term for *Paradise*. Ed.

EPITHILAMIUM
A POEM

BY MARY FAITH FLOYD

Respectfully dedicated to the Rev. and Mrs. G. T. G. of Milledgeville.

In the gloom of life's dark places
Clouded by misfortune's skies,
Light breaks through celestial spaces;
Paved with joy the pathway lies
All the blissful future through;
And fragrant as the flowers, the dew
Of morning hath besprinkled, life
Is lifted from its darkening strife.

O Hymen! Happy art thou, when
The good, the virtuous, find in thee
The bliss that angels, rarely men,
And loveliest women, sometimes see
And feel in life's sad thrall of care!
Such bliss, the grandest and most rare
Be yours, my friends, through longest span
By God vouchsafed to mortal man!

The Georgia Weekly Telegraph and Journal & Messenger.
Macon, June 1, 1875

[For the Telegraph and Messenger]

ESSAYS, CRITICAL NOTICES, AND BOOK REVIEWS

BY MARY FAITH FLOYD

CRUELTY TO CHILDREN
AN ESSAY

BY MARY FAITH FLOYD

Published in her 1885 journal, *The Southern Head-Light*

The world has given much and just applause to Henry Bergh, Miss Lou King and other philanthropists in the work of prevention of cruelty to dumb animals. This is all very laudable; but there is another and a very large class of animals subject to cruelties and gross injustice of which no one takes heed. We speak of children; sentient beings, but helpless to defend themselves against the tyranny and violence often exerted against them.

Few people remember that children are free and independent creatures, given to us to foster and train in the straight and narrow way. That we should restrain and guide them is perfectly proper; nay, that we may go beyond and punish them, passes without question; for the good Book says, spare the rod and spoil the child. Corporal punishment should be resorted to seldom, and then with extreme calmness and in a very dispassionate state of mind, administered for very grave faults only. Observation has led me to the conclusion that parents generally deal in this method of correction when they are angry and unaware how severe they can be with the little culprits trembling in their hands. If this can be said against educated, Christian, parents, what shall we think of the million brutes who maltreat these helpless babes God has given them to shelter and train for truth and right?

A very young teacher said to me that she was accused of showing partiality to some of the rough boys in her department. Probably her kindness to these degraded children was put to the score of cowardice on her part, by the youths who are quick to observe every act of a teacher with jealous care.

Said this sweet young teacher, "I was in despair. There are many children entrusted to my care that no reproof can reach. They are brutalized at home. Fierceness and coercion won't do. I tried kindness. It was a new voice to them. It acted like a charm. Think of this. There are hundreds of children among the laboring classes who are looked upon as brutes of burden by their owners to be cuffed and kicked, with never a kind word. They are ill clad, ill fed, poorly housed. Is there any wonder that they grow brutalized with scarce a humanized characteristic in their beings?"

Some good men and women ought to organize a society for the prevention of cruelty to children.

A small child has no way to express its wants or its disapprobation except by its cries. This is called crossness and the little one is often punished therefore.

A healthy, vigorous child needs occupation. His ideas are growing. His investigating proclivities are without limit. He dips into everything within reach to discover its use, and to occupy and divert his expanding mind. He is called bad and often injudiciously punished because he gets into "mischief" when he really has no thought but that of enterprise and learning the uses of things.

I was once acquainted with an old lady who reared fifteen children. Seven of these were boys and they all grew up to be sober men of integrity. Said she, "I always trusted them. They never told me lies, for I never made them fear me to a degree of concealment. I made a rule when they were young that they should tell me where they were going. I said to them, 'Boys, you have it in your power to visit vicious and disreputable places when you are away from me; but I believe you are honorable. I trust to your integrity to go nowhere that I should disapprove.' They grew upright, home-loving men with pure healthy minds and the girls are model women, noble wives without reproach. They all have their weaknesses and foibles of course; but a wise mother gave them all the license of free-born citizens, restraining them only in such matters as every child soon learns to feel is proper for its well being."

There are many lovely, judicious mothers in our midst. There are honorable, dignified, reasonable fathers who set glorious examples of well spent lives, devoted to duty, who daily lead the way their sons should go. We thank God for this. But the fact still remains that there are hundreds of maltreated little ones whose parents are oppressors either from the caprice of the moment, ignorance or intolerance of other's rights; and worse because they lack humanity, and are unfit to own or train these helpless babes endowed with immortal souls— entrusted to their care in the period of juvenility when the character is plastic and quick to take the impressions made upon it by the guiding hand of parents. How important, therefore, that parents should act wisely, justly, and dispassionately in the administration of reproofs and punishments, and in leading their children quietly, yet firmly up toward the high standard of Christian character!

THE HISTORY OF THE FAIRCHILD FAMILY
A REVIEW

BY MARY FAITH FLOYD

Sir John Herschell beautifully remarks, "Were I to pray for a taste which should stand me in stead under every variety of circumstances, and be a source of happiness and cheerfulness through life, it would be a taste for reading. You make a man a denizen of all nations, a contemporary of all ages. The world has been created for him."

Every reflective person must admit the justice and truth of this quotation. How essential then is it for this taste in the young to be fed with wholesome food! Books are silent companions which influenced our characters for good or ill almost as powerfully as pernicious or moral acquaintance among our fellow beings. Amid the immense mass of works of fiction that fill the libraries of the 19th century, none are more prolific of good than the writings of Mrs. (Mary Martha) Sherwood and Miss (Elizabeth Missing) Sewell. Mrs. Sherwood is of English birth and spent some years of her life in India, a zealous aid and the religious enterprises of Henry Martyn and Dr. Corrie, late Bishop of Madras. Her works are numerous and occupy a high station in the religious and moral world war for purity of thought and elevation of tone. None are more beautiful than "The History of the Fairchild Family," a touching little story for young people. This book is full of interest and inculcates the highest ideal of Christian conduct as the only sure rule of life.

Miss Sewell is the sister of the Rev. William Sewell, and a native of the Isle of Wight. She has also devoted a large portion of her time to the composition of books especially directed for the entertainment and instruction of growing minds. Amy Herbert is the most interesting narrative. The character of Amy Herbert is one of the most religious and self-sacrificing we ever read of, and shows how much influence even a child can wield who sets out in life to tread the narrow path of duty, and how truly sublime is the beauty of holiness.

Both of these authors inculcate the necessity of a practical use of the Fifth Commandment. Hence we fear that their works will be considered rather old-fashioned in this age when this injunction has been well nigh obliterated by the fast manners of Young America, and the demoralizing effects of the late war. About thirty-five years ago implicit obedience to parental government, and obligation to a higher law in the conduct of the young, were essentials in every person's training. Now-a days self-opinion has expanded to such large dimensions that each urchin has a will, and takes the reins in his own hands, feeling quite competent to reach the goal without the extrinsic aid of more experienced minds.

A modern author has pertinently said "a woman without religion is like a flower without odor." In this day when one sees so many of these inodorous blossoms along the by-paths of life, it is really refreshing to meet an occasional flower shedding the delicious aroma of piety distilled from Heaven in addition to its gorgeous coloring. We trust that the works of such authors as Mrs. Sherwood and Miss Sewell will become more popular. If read with an earnest desire to exalt, they cannot fail to infuse a sweet essence into those natures who emulate the pure characters therein portrayed.

It is to be hoped that the car-wheels of Time may be checked and the good old rate of progress restored, when in the language of Descartes, the youths of the country shall again feel that parents are sure guides to enable them to "learn what is true in order to do what is right."

These books can be ordered from Messrs. Harper & Brothers, Franklin Square, N.Y. Price, sent by mail, of Amy Herbert 50 cts: of Hist. Fairchild Family, $1.50.

THE FEDERAL UNION.
Tuesday Morning, November 1, 1870.

LOTHAIR
A REVIEW OF BENJAMIN DISRAELI'S NOVEL

BY MARY FAITH FLOYD

Lothair is the last novel of Hon. Benj. Disraeli, Ex-Premier of Great Britain. Mr. Disraeli comes by his literary proclivities very honestly. His father, Isaac Disraeli, is the author of numerous popular and valuable works. He was the only son of parents of Italian descent, from one of those Hebrew families forced by the Inquisition to emigrate from the Spanish Peninsular at the end of the Fifteenth Century. His ancestors dropped their gothic surname, and in gratitude to God for preserving them through many dangerous vicissitudes selected the name of Disraeli, never before or since borne by any other family, in order that their race might ever be recognized.

Our author's father (Mr. Isaac Disraeli) met much opposition from his parents at embarking on his literary career. Being an only child, they naturally desired he should be reared with a view to mercantile employments hitherto so profitable to their race. The young poet was sent from home, and every method was used to vary the bent of his inclination. When nineteen years of age he returned to London about the time John Wolcot reveled in the height of his fame as a satiric poet. Young Disraeli wrote anonymously, a poem "On the abuse of Satire." It created great eclat, and whatsoever doubt was entertained of its authorship was dissipated by Wolcot. Like all literary tomahawkists Wolcot dreaded the faintest sight of the scalping knife when directed against himself. He assailed a popular poet in a virulent pasquinade, rashly supposing him the guilty satirist. This gave more celebrity to Mr. Disraeli who returned to Enfield, with the journals disclosing to his parents that he was an author, and a successful one. They wisely interposed no further objection to the young man's literary career, seeing that the instinct of genius was too deeply rooted within for successful extirpation.

The present Mr. Disraeli, doubtless had no thwartings in his struggles after the lofty and beautiful in the ideal world of an author. He is represented in his early life, by a contemporary as very flashy and exquisite in his dress; "a joyous dandy," the pride of his old father, and possessed of a flood of extraordinary eloquence. Says a writer of thirty-five years ago, "Mr. Disraeli talks like a race horse approaching the winning-post; at least five words in every sentence must have been much astonished at the use they were put to, and yet no others, apparently, could so well have expressed his idea." In his earlier novels this raciness of language is very observable, and a sparkling wit courses through them.

Lothair is the work of mature age. As Max Muller says, there is exhibited a "fresh breeze of thought" in it; and as was said of many of the German writers of the fourteenth century, Mr. Disraeli is a "man of creative genius, who looks at life with his own eyes and is able to express what he has seen, and thought, and felt, in language which must fascinate his contemporaries."

The plot of Lothair is nothing. Its merits lie in the handsome descriptions of scenery, its individualization of characters, and its sarcasm upon some of the follies of the age—especially that hard grapple of church after the wealth of individuals for the extension of each particular sect and its control over political opinions.

The character of the Oxford professor is a fine comment upon modern pedantry—that shallow book-learning and overflowing conceit so common in our day, which must ever flinch under the silver probe of solid acquirements.

The Cardinal is depicted with such verisimilitude that it is impossible to divest the mind of the opinion that he is a portraiture from real life, and not a creation of fancy. Lothair, although a British peer, has much of verdancy about him, and suffers himself to become the sport of intriguantes to which fact he does not awaken until he is under the espionage of the constant companionship of interested friends when he is in the hospital of Rome. How life is frittered away by continued publicity! The best mental capacity is quickly dissipated, and happiness itself put to flight if we are never, for a moment, allowed the enjoyment of solitude, or left alone to reflect upon one's inner self and call up from the depths whatever there may be good or great within us. How many obscure individuals in everyday life walk, like Lothair, under constant companionship and feel the need of that "mighty and essential solitude" De Quincey describes, so beautifully, in some of his unparalleled writings.

Lothair is published by the elegant house D. Appleton & Co., 90, 92 & 94, Grand street, New York.

THE FEDERAL UNION.
Tuesday Morning, January 10, 1871

THE WAYS OF WOMEN
IN THEIR PHYSICAL, MORAL, AND INTELLECTUAL RELATIONS.
BY A MEDICAL MAN.

A REVIEW

BY MARY FAITH FLOYD

"The Ways of Women!" What a tantalizing title to those grave chroniclers and deep-thinking dissertators who attribute all the great movements of history to woman's influence! How eager will be this large portion of mankind to plunge into the pages of this handsome and fascinating volume! Helen, Aspasia, Zenobia, Cleopatra, Maria, Theresa, and the long catalogue of illustrious women's "ways" of modern times, who impressed their genius indelibly on mankind; and the "ways" of the stirringly famous women of our extremely modern days—all these pass in review before our vision at the very title of this book.

But the volume is not such as these imaginings would conjure up. It is far more interesting, and far more useful than any romance of the history, or history of the romance of woman!

The work before us is no treatise on therapeutics; but as the learned author affirms, the object of it is to explain in a lucid manner how women may improve their condition. First, by conforming to the laws of health: Next, how they may best be qualified for sustaining themselves honorably and successfully in their various new relations to society. How to arrive at a clear elucidation of these too knotty problems, and obtain a successful result, is a difficult question to answer.

In all ages, women have been devoted votaries of fashion in violation of all hygienic laws. The love of adornment may justly be termed the ruling passion of the female sex. With all our boasted civilization in this thermal period of scientific light, women still cling to many of the practices of savages and semi-civilized nations. No aristocratic "golden lily" of the Celestial empire values her little foot, nor more persistently compresses it into diminutive boots, than does our modern crop of young ladies; and alas, be it spoken, many old ones too are addicted to this folly! The Flathead Indians do not endeavor more systematically to fashion their heads into an abnormal form then do our modern esquisites of the "fair sex" by continued lacing, to shape their waists into waspish slenderness. As well tell a woman to give up life as to urge her to relinquish these unhealthy styles of fashion and appear in the proportions nature gave her.

Few women have moral courage to brave the ridicule attendant upon an unfashionable appearance. It is admitted that the sex has wondrous fortitude to endure suffering, and this capacity gives power to the most delicate ladies to bear without murmur the tortures of prolonged ill health brought on by the demands of custom.

"Style" almost always runs counter to comfort and health. American women are celebrated for their early beauty, early fading and short lives. Certainly there is no reason why they should not live healthfully to the allotted three score years and ten. There must be some 'rot' in the system of dress and of self-management in its enlarged sense, that needs reform. It is to be hoped that the day will soon dawn when a few sensible women will begin this reform by discarding everything in fashion which is pernicious to health. Then youth, beauty, good temper, and good health will take the place of lassitude, premature decrepitude and faded visages.

Perhaps very many of the foibles and mal-practices of women are traceable to their want of advantages and status in society. Dr. Johnson, in his great dictionary of the English language gives the definition to the word "lexicographer," as "a harmless drudge." Had he given this meaning to the word woman, he would have been nearer right. In law, a married woman is a nobody. Widows and spinsters are required to pay debts, support families, pay the same rates of taxation and other legalized robberies, or just debts, as men all over the world. But custom debars them from any avenues for self-support, if they be poor, except in the over-crowded tracks of teacher, seamstress or boarding house-keeper. Unfortunately these three time-honored avenues to daily breath are crowded with half famished needy seekers. Not only in the South, but in every city in the North, may be witnessed the picture of impoverished woman which the fiendish Freedman-Bureau Agent J.W. deForrest, portrayed a few years since in Harper's Magazine. "Imagine," he says exultingly, "the indignation of a 'fine lady' who must keep boarders; of another who must go out to service a little less than menial; of another who must beg rations with low-downers and negroes!" How well the envenomed words fit, also, the unfortunate of the sex of "harmless drudges" in Mr. DeForrest's own native land!

Any attempt in women, particularly Southern women, to go beyond the specified callings enumerated are considered encroachments on masculine territory. A dependent woman is almost forced into servile occupation and often where these fail, into vice, for bread and existence. She must either starve or consider herself fortunate to remain a "harmless drudge." Even should she be blessed by obtaining employment, for the reason that she is a woman she receives only a third or a fourth the sum for a given amount of labor that is paid to a man.

This is gross injustice; and in no respect does society need a reform so much as in opening modest and suitable avenues to female industry, making these honest labors respectable, and giving the same wages to either sex for the same amount of well performed work.

"The Ways of Women" is an admirable dissertation upon health laws, and the educational and industrial wants of women. Every mother of a family, every woman should obtain the work, read it carefully and observe the hygienic rules therein explained. Many sensible women violate health-laws in their own and their children's training from ignorance; and we recommend the "Ways of Women" to their earnest consideration. We quote words of a most celebrated writer who says: "Some books are to be tasted, others to be swallowed, and some few to be chewed and digested." This work contains 491 handsome pages on tinted paper, published by John P. Jewett & Co., No. 5 Dey St., New York. Every one should read it for "there is wisdom in it beyond the rules of Physic," to quote a most apposite expression of Lord Bacon.

UNION & RECORDER.
Milledgeville, Georgia, August 20, 1873.

LIVING FEMALE WRITERS
A REVIEW

BY MARY FAITH FLOYD

"Mind is the great lever of all things!" exclaimed Daniel Webster in one of his eloquent speeches.

Prior to the so-called recent rebellion the Southern people in general appeared content with the lighter adornments of refinement, accomplishments and courtliness of manner, without the exertion of more potent charms to recommend them. But the war developed a deeper, sterner, undertone of thought—a kind of introspective searching which has led them to grasp this "great lever," and use it energetically, as may be seen in numerous literary productions, of no mean merit, from Southern authors.

Ida Raymond's Living Female Writers, and Professor Davidson's Living Writers of the South display a brilliant galaxy of literary stars of both sexes.

Among these is Mrs. Eliza Lofton Pugh, a lady of distinguished ancestry and reared in all the surroundings of luxury in Louisiana. During early childhood Mrs. Pugh wrote articles of merit giving promise of future excellence.

Recently Claxton, Remsen & Haffelfinger issued, in extremely handsome style, a work from Mrs. Pugh's pen, entitled "In a Crucible," a novel of the early stage of the recent war. In the opening chapters the author portrays the conscientious scruples of a clergyman of the Protestant Episcopal church against a change in the ritual, although he was warmly Southern in sentiment. She has described the combat between duty and his affection for his flock with much skill. Some of the characters are drawn with a great deal of the 'old Adam' in them, and display humanity very naturally. Others are somewhat too ideal to accord with that vraisemblance to real life, so charming in a work of fiction.

The Greek artists were justly considered adepts in ideality. Their creations were masterpieces of beauty; every posture betrayed a studied elegance above the abandon and careless grace of natural figures. To attain this ideal was a perfection of art, beautiful and fascinating, but too elevated for mortal mediocrity to look upon with a feeling of homogeneity. Humanity gazes at such creations with a serene pleasure–a distant delight, such as is felt on seeing a quiet sunset behind clouds edged with silver and golden brilliancy, lovely to behold, but not of this lower world.

A still higher order of art is found in a just combination of the idealistic with the realistic; and therein consists the wonderful genius of Michaelangelo. In sculptures and in paintings his figures possessed all the beauty and elegance of the Greek artists, and in addition, all the careless grace, the magical suppleness, the wonderful expression of feature, the nameless variety of slight touches which dissever the identity of one person from that of another, and make each one an individual being, whether that being be represented on canvas or in time enduring stone.

This is the true perfection of art. We feel while in rapturous gaze at such, that there is magical beauty, genuine perfection; and yet that a kindred tie exists between them and us.

This mingling of ideal and real is the secret of success with all artists; the key to the attainment of the highest excellence in authors as well as to all other artists; and although the possibility of this art can be reached in practice, it is more difficult in writing than perhaps in any other department.

Mrs. Pugh's style is easy and her work emanates from a mind rich in culture. There are some fine descriptions of natural scenery in Louisiana; and to those versed in psychology and pathognomy the book is a study.

As the title suggests, the characters are taken through a crucible of trials potent in their power of purification. This book can be had at Messrs. Hunt, Rankin & Lamar's store in this city.

THE FEDERAL UNION.
March 6, 1872.

BARTHOLOMEW'S DRAWING BOOK
A REVIEW

BY MARY FAITH FLOYD

Among the recent improvements of the age for the instruction and gratification of young people is Bartholomew's Drawing Book, New Series. The Series consists of twelve numbers. Each number contains twelve plates, executed in the highest style of art, and twenty-four pages of drawing paper of superior quality.

Each book is progressive: from the first and most difficult of all steps, the drawing with accuracy and firmness straight lines of each kind, to the ornamental curves, and ornate figures so pleasing to the artistic eye.

In each lesson the principles of drawing are made manifest to the comprehension of children, and require only their diligent attention to memorize them.

These books impart a thorough insight into innitiatory perspective, the method of drawing from objects; the laws of light; of shade and shadow. They fill a want hitherto sadly felt in the series of drawing cards used by schools; that of combining the principles of drawing with the imitation of models.

A very current idea prevails, even with educated persons, that only a few talented people can acquire the art of drawing. We beg leave to deny this supposition. While all who make the effort may not become great artists, just as all who read and write do not make great authors, still, all who are educated to a true perception of form, and the charms of light and shadow, can attain excellence sufficient to give from delightful occupation, and a double pleasure in viewing Nature's glories.

Professor Huxley, one of the most renowned modern physicists, is a great advocate for the introduction of science into schools, so far as pertains to the development of the thinking faculties of boys and girls, and thereby preparing them to "face the scientific discussions and scientific problems" now current.

This he terms "earth-knowledge, or a knowledge of the earth, and what is on it, in it, and about it."

We heartily commend this idea of the great scientist to the thinking public, and at the same time suggest that every child be taught to draw. If drawing be only a fine art it is so intimately connected with the great science of mathematics that they may be considered Siamese Twins.

Bartholomew's Drawing Book, New Series, is published by Woolworth, Ainsworth & Co., 51, 53 & 55 John St., New York.

THE FEDERAL UNION.
Wednesday, May 8, 1872.

WILLIAMS & PACKARD'S SYSTEM OF PENMANSHIP
A REVIEW

BY MARY FAITH FLOYD

Guide to Williams & Packard's System of Penmanship is an elegant volume fully illustrative of the Art of Writing. It contains many handsome specimens of pen-drawing, and an amplified lucid explanation of the principles of chirography.

This art is reduced to a practical science which embodies a principle in every stroke of the pen. Nothing is so common in child-nature as to ask a reason for everything taught. If a good one be given, which can be put into forms that grow before the eye by every stroke of the pen, interest is awakened. There is method apparent in these lines and strokes, and the child no longer dozes over pot-hooks and straight marks, but feels that he knows something of what he is doing. Gain the attention of children, and the teacher acquires a potent leverage toward developing their unfolding faculties.

The science and the art of writing are two distinct departments. The science is a well defined system, which should be photographed upon the mind in indelible tracing, so that the curves and shades of each letter are formed mentally, and are transferable to paper without models. The art is the practical muscular ability to shape these principles into beautifully rounded, smoothly shaded letters, growing into uniform sentences, and constituting a harmonious whole.

All the highest perfection of penmanship is exhibited in Williams & Packard's Guide, reduced to a simplicity comprehensible to children from ten years and upwards. We heartily commend the work to the notice of the public. This book can be had from Slote, Woodman & Co., Publishers, 119 and 121 William street, New York.

THE FEDERAL UNION.
Wednesday Morning, May 22, 1872.

VIOLETTA AND I;
BY COUSIN KATE
A REVIEW

BY MARY FAITH FLOYD

Violetta and I; By Cousin Kate, edited by M.J. McIntosh, is a pathetic little story, written with a pen dipped in "the sources of tears." There is no plot to entangle the reader in its labyrinthic mazes; there are no sudden surprises to startle by their lightning flashes; but there is touching simplicity mingled with graphic suggestiveness which light up a whole scene before the mind's eye, as the fiery figures gleam upon the sombre back ground of the magic lantern.

The writer possesses that plastic skill which "turns to shape the forms of things unknown," and the lonely and suffering Violetta with the "great dread frozen" in her soft blue eyes seems figured before us, as she looks through the window, mourning for the loved who had "drifted out on the waves to the harbor of a better world."

The style is simple and quaint, and there are peculiar turns of thought and expression which add a charm to the story. The very simplicity of the book is one of the main levers of power, and exhibits no ordinary intellectual development and artistic skill in the author.

We hope, from the success of the volume, that she may be induced in her next effort to elaborate slightly her thoughts and scenes. They are handsomely drawn, but would have been faultless had she dwelt upon each more fully.

Most young writers tire of their creations and push them aside before they have chiseled out all the finer tracings which make a literary as well as a marble statue perfect.

The description of the gales, and the rising of the ocean's white capped waves is fine. It reminds one of a passage rendered by De Quincey from Æschylus:

"O multitudinous laughter of the ocean billows!"

Who, that has looked upon the tempest tossed sea, or listened to the fearful "music in its roar," has not felt its sublimity, and imagined the terror of being exposed to the mercy of the relentless waves? Who has not felt the magic beauty of the calm ocean, blue by imitation of the cerulean dome vaulted above? Those alone, who have looked on the ocean can appreciate the "multitudinous laughter" of its billows, and testify to the powers of graphic description.

We lament that so many writers wear the garb of pseudonyms instead of the genuine dress of their true names. We confess a desire to become acquainted with "Cousin Kate," and see other works from her pen.

The little volume before us is edited by M.J. McIntosh, a name frequently entered as a contestant for fame in the literary jousts of the world's tourney–and one eminently successful for purity of thought and elevation of moral tone. Miss McIntosh is a descendant of those hardy and daring Scottish heroes who emigrated early to this country and settled near Darien, Ga. Her works are many, and have been received in high favor both in America and Europe. Well may the South be proud to claim her name among its children of genius, and herald her as the prototype of what many of its gifted daughters may do.

Violetta and I, is published by Loring: Boston; Price 25 cts

THE FEDERAL UNION.
Tuesday Morning, February 14, 1871.

WITCHED
A REVIEW

BY MARY FAITH FLOYD

The Southern Magazine for December has its usual attractions as stories and poems. Among a number of articles, our eyes light on a brief story entitled "Witched," a tale of negro superstition ending in the tragic death of a bewitched negro. The story is well told with a copious overflow of negro lingo. We have lived at the South a lifetime and observe a curious difference of dialect between real live negroes, and those who figure in books—especially northern books. As a class, negroes, except those on remote and isolated plantations, speak very much as unlettered white people. They have acquired much correctness of expression by domestic communion with the white race and do not express themselves in the broken gibberish attributed to them by many fiction caterers. Even the gross superstitions of plantation days are being much modified and are seldom apparent in our section. We wish the author of "Witched" would make a tour to the Sunny South and observe how our real negroes talk, or if the writer is a Southron, we advise her to make an excursion beyond her own neighborhood to learn how negros do really talk elsewhere.

The other articles in this magazine are as usual, interesting, and we do not hesitate to pronounce the Southern Magazine as the best literary journal of the South. One important advantage it has over other publications is being the official organ of the Southern Historical Society. Every number contains publications of high value as historical records of the Lost Cause.

UNION & RECORDER.
Milledgeville, Georgia, January 12, 1875.

SHORT STORIES

BY MARY FAITH FLOYD

McCLINTOCK
A SHORT STORY

BY MARY FAITH FLOYD

Lucy Ashbie was at her first ball. She was a girl of fine appearance and looked remarkably well attired in a pale blue dress fashioned to display her handsome throat, neck and arms to their best advantage. She was whirling in the waltz with a young beau of fair pretensions, and the exercise gave sparkle to her eyes and color to her cheeks.

In one end of the room a group of gentlemen stood gazing idly at the waltzers.

"Who is that girl in the blue dress?" asked Maj. Reno McClintock of a friend beside him. "By Jove! she is the finest formed woman I have seen in a long time, and her movements are grace itself."

"That is Miss Lucy Ashbie."

"Does she live here?"

"Certainly, her mother is a widow, and you ought to know who they are."

"Why have I not seen Miss Ashbie before?"

"She has been away to school, and then on a long visit to some friends."

"I should like to hear her talk, though I do not usually care to converse with girls, they are such a silly lot."

"She is a sharp one, I can tell you," answered Carlton. "There, she has stopped waltzing, shall I introduce you?"

They crossed the room.

"My friend Maj. McClintock, Miss Ashbie," said Carlton.

"Will you promenade, Miss Ashbie?" offering his arm, and Carlton was left behind to observe the progress of the new acquaintance.

"I think I have seen you before Maj. McClintock. Were you not driving a span of fine horses a few days since? I see you know how to manage wild animals."

"My horses are only spirited, Miss Ashbie, but thanks for the implied compliment."

"I do admire wild horses, and were I a man, I should feel no interest in driving any other?"

McClintock smiled. "You have not been here long, I believe."

"No, have not long escaped from the thraldom of the schools, but this is my native place, you are the stranger."

"True, I have been here six months."

"Do you like the place?"

"Very much."

"Ah! here comes Mr. Carlton to claim me for the next set; do you dance?"

"No, and I am sorry you do, as it deprives me of your company. Console me by consenting to ride with me to-morrow afternoon."

"With the greatest pleasure, if you promise not to upset me. Good night," and Lucy bestowed a sweet smile which gave McClintock a pleasant sensation for the rest of the evening.

Maj. McClintock was a fine looking, intelligent man of considerable wealth. He was alone in the world at the time of his appearance in this story. His mother died when he was a small boy; his father before he was of age, leaving him with a very good property. Soon after he finished his education, he was persuaded by an old friend, a very pious member of a church, to join business and enter into partnership with him. McClintock being a man of integrity himself, artless of the world's ways, full of sympathy and enthusiasm, in the freshness of guilelessness, judged all men by his own standard and believed in the pious professions of his fellows. He permitted his business associate to arrange matters, form a contract between them, which he supposed all right, and paid very little attention to its technicalities. For sometime all went smoothly, and while McClintock had less to do than he wished, he congratulated himself on the great advantage he had secured in the partnership of an upright, experienced man, who would be an example and a guide to restrain the exuberance of youth, and mould both his moral and business qualifications. Ah! the blind confidence and infatuation of youth! It was not long before clouds began to lower. McClintock soon awoke to find his hands tied, his means cramped and while no man dared offer him an open insult or a broad impertinence, he was subjected to a thousand covert slights and innuendos, which cut like a dirk into the soul of a proud man, yet were such that they could not be grasped and the perpetrator punished by a sound thrashing. At the end of a few years McClintock came to the knowledge that his partner was a scoundrel; merciless and unscrupulous, and that he had been genteelly swindled out of all he had. Yet he lived in a law abiding, Christian country. Alas! alas!

The shock to his warm and generous nature was terrific and long, and he emerged from its blasting effects to become a misanthrope, alone in his misfortunes, but with a fixed determination to conquer and bring the god Pluto to his feet. He laid aside his broad-cloth, folded away his gentility, forgot he was born a gentleman of the bluest blood of the land, bought a suit of common clothes and drifted out west. No need here to tell of his difficulties and adventures to get to a mining region. Arrived there, he smoked his pipe with the roughest, ate his rasher of bacon with a relish born of vigorous exercise, worked abreast of the strongest regardless of blistered hands, and by perseverance and a lucky venture became a rich man. He served as legislator, had gubernatorial and senatorial opportunities thrown in his way and friends as thick as blackberries gathered about him ready to do his bidding,

Being of a sensitive turn, and having had his sympathies thrown back on him and his integrity and confidence cruelly abused, he allowed the first characteristic to seize possession of him to a morbid degree, and while he smiled with an elegant grace over proffered courtesies, he believed that all attentions were paid to his wealth, and the man was something apart, a machine, valued as long as it ground out gold; thrown aside as worthless when it ceased to increase its money. In early youth he had had his favorites, and a flame or two among the fair, as boys will. In his manhood, while his heart was fresh and open to impressions, he was not in a situation to think of marriage, and now, with his experiences, he doubted the existence of genuine love, believed that women, as well as men, were tinctured with self-interest, and he kept aloof for fear that the fair ones favors would be accorded to his wealth, and not to his excellencies as a man. At the moment that our story opens he was enjoying a rest, drifting idly with his associates, and waiting to see what fortune's wheel would turn up for him in the way of pleasure and happiness.

"McClintock," said Carlton, as they went along the street one day, "you have made yourself quite famous in the village."

"Ah! how so?" asked the Major puffin vigorously at his cigar.

"By your ride with Miss Ashbie."

"Is it then so rare for a gentleman to offer any attention to a lady?"

"Not exactly, but you are an exclusive fellow, and—you are rich. Don't you see you are sort of a lion to be stared at? Besides, people have little to amuse them and a small thing gets up an excitement."

"It must be very unpleasant to the girl. I'll tell you what you do, Carlton, go to ride with her yourself, and that will, at least, divide the sensation. The gossips will say the lady has two strings to her bow."

"I can't. First; I have no horses, and at this time I do not feel able to expend a cent in amusements, and next, I believe it is best for me not to cultivate the fair Lucy."

McClintock looked keenly at his friend.

"Anything against her?" he asked sharply.

"No she's all right, and fascinating—by George!—the danger is all on my side."

"Why don't you enter the field and carry off the prize?"

"Why? Ah!" with a harsh laugh, "the long and short is, I'm too poor to marry."

"A very good reason," said McClintock meditatively, a slight frown contracting his brow. "I must go," looking at his watch.

Carlton was a slender built young fellow with a pleasant face. A long, light brown, down-drooping moustache covered his mouth and his chin, although well turned, gave the idea of weakness. The eyes were inexpressive and heavy-lidded, but the man was amiable, kind, honest, and struggling against difficulties, to earn a living. He had, as yet, not found many helping hands to aid in the career he had mapped out for himself, but he was still striving, in a small way, after success. Lucy was his particular admiration, but the sense of his utter inability to sustain a wife, kept him aloof.

The cruel wrongs McClintock had endured, from his unprincipled friend had not entirely suppressed his warm, sympathetic nature. Perhaps the injustice he had suffered accelerated his kind feelings for poor young men endeavoring to acquire a support, without aid. He had made a promise to himself in his dark days, that if ever he gained a fortune, he would assist worthy comrades. Soon after his recent conversation with Carlton, he made some inquiries about his affairs, and satisfied himself as to his friend's needs

"Carlton," he said, when they met at the post-office, "come to my room this afternoon, I wish to see you."

It was summer time, and the dull cloudy day gave the little railroad village any other than a cheerful outlook, as Carlton walked along to keep his engagement, curious to know for what McClintock could wish to see him. He found McClintock solacing himself with a cigar in the office of the hotel, which building was the most prominent piece of architecture in the town, except the court house, and they went together to the latter's room. This room looked out on the front colonnade. Coats, pantaloons, and vests hung about the chairs, bed and trunks. The bureau was strewn with tumbled collars, cravats, gloves, comb, brushes, et cetera. Upon the mantel lay cigars, meerschaums razors and other trifles in comfortable confusion. The table displayed books, papers, pamphlets, in orderly disorder, and some fancy slippers lay in one corner, near a pair of high-in-step boots, and a forked boot-jack.

All these lent an air of comfort to the apartment, and suggested the beautiful systematic arrangement which characterizes the habitations of the lordly sex. Carlton accepted the proffered seat, and awaited, amid clouds of smoke, to hear McClintock's business. This young gentleman possessed very little talent for circumvention so he struck out at once into his subject.

"Carlton, I have some money I wish to put out at interest, say two thousand, and it occurred to me, after our recent conversation, that you are the right man, being a merchant, and you know the busy season will soon open."

"What securities will I have to give?"

"None, I will take your note. You need pay no interest the first year; after that, you can pay the principal in installments until the note is cancelled."

"You are very kind. I could then become a partner in the firm."

"Better open a small stock of goods for yourself I do not like partnerships," an ugly frown corrugating his brow.

"Perhaps you are right," said Carlton after a pause, "but I have one very great weakness that it is right to mention. I cannot say no to those who ask credit."

McClintock smiled and blew a long puff of smoke from his mouth.

"Why do you laugh?" asked Carlton, a shade of impatience in his voice. "Is it easy to say no to people who come and ask help, and appeal to your humanity to aid them in their efforts to make a living?"

"It is very difficult to do, but I can only remind you that charity begins at home, and if you do not learn to refuse credit then you'll soon have nothing left for yourself. I smiled because your words reflected one of my own weaknesses which I have fought hard to suppress."

"I believe you, old fellow, for while you are urging me to a stringent course, you are offering to lend me money with no securities."

"Begin right, Carlton," said McClintock not noticing this last remark, "purchase for cash, and advertise that you sell for cash, and hold strictly to your rule."

"I shall make the effort."

"I trust you will prosper," answered McClintock.

"Have you seen Miss Lucy recently?"

"No, but I promised to call very soon."

Carlton sighed, and soon after rose to go.

Lucy Ashbie's most intimate friend was Mary Powers, a plain unattractive girl of an envious disposition, but possessed of some good qualities. She had long desired the acquaintance of Maj. McClintock, and felt piqued that Lucy should have that pleasure. She was of an inquisitive turn of mind consequently always knew to the utmost minuteness, all that was going on in the town, and could more keep out of mischief than a pig could avoid rooting in a turnip patch.

"Well, Lucy," she said, meeting her friend on the street one fair afternoon, "how did you enjoy your ride?"

"Oh! very much. We went like the wind."

"Tell me about Maj. McClintock. Is he nice? He looks splendid."

"He is an incorrigible, interesting bachelor, who cares little for ladies, I imagine. I like his horses ever so well and mean to flirt with him just to keep in practice," she said laughing.

"I'm afraid you won't have a chance, Lucy."

"Trust me for that, Mary. He has promised to call and then I shall begin."

"I shall tell him. Forewarned, forearmed you know."

"That would be mean of you, Mary, to spoil my fun," and they parted, Lucy forgetting her light words as soon as uttered.

As the weeks rolled by and Maj. McClintock saw more of his new acquaintance his fancy was pleased, and he did not quite understand himself. His former cynicism was superseded by a good humored philanthropy, through which medium everything was seen couleur de rose. He had hitherto claimed an entire absence of weaknesses of any kind, and prided himself on his magnificent physique, and moral strength. His present mood was silly, in short he was a fool, and heartily despised himself for it. He caught himself sometimes watching on the street corners for a glimpse of a certain graceful form; indeed, one afternoon he went so far as to escort Miss Ashbie home which was nothing more than the courtesy due from a gentleman to a lady.

"I have not seen much of you lately," said Lucy to her companion.

"No, but I have seen you sometimes, as distant as the spheres in your dignity."

"Was I? I am glad some body thinks me dignified."

A smile flitted over his face.

"What is it, that you smile? Is not dignity commendable?"

"I suppose it is," not noticing the first question. "My horses have been idle for some time awaiting your pleasure. Shall we have another ride soon?"

"Yes, if you will promise to let me drive. Will you?" looking up in his face, eagerness expressed in every feature.

"Ah! I'm afraid you would upset me," he answered, laughing at the double meaning the words conveyed to himself.

"Oh! no, I promise, I will not. You can teach me how to drive, and I'm not one bit afraid."

"Very well, young lady, say Wednesday afternoon, I will call."

"I shall be ready," she said as they separated at her door,

"P'shaw!" he said to himself as he turned away. "What am I doing—meddling with another man's sweetheart. Well I'm in for this ride, and after I will go to Nevada and see about my lands, and come back cured of all follies." He lighted a cigar and went back to his hotel in the peaceful gloaming, while the silent stars lit their twinkling lamps on high to light this nether world of ours, and give delight to the worshipers of nature's works.

Lucy Ashbie was looking very pretty as Maj. McClintock handed her in his buggy on Wednesday. The excitement of the occasion quickened the rose hue on her cheek and added lustre to her brown eyes. The rich gold tints of her hair caught a glimmer from the sun and shone like burnished metal. The trees cast long shadows across the road giving grateful shade, and a cool breeze moderated the summer heat. Nature seemed to be resting and enjoying perfect repose. Indifferent topics engaged the couple in conversation until they had ridden some distance.

"Here is a straight stretch of road, Miss Ashbie, and I think the horses have been driven long enough to have some of their mettle subdued so that you can drive. There, hold the reins in this way," placing them in her hand.

"Oh! I have driven before. Now smoke a cigar, I am fond of the odor."

"Must I really?"

"Yes."

"There goes—over one stump. I am a poor driver, but I shall strive not to overturn you."

Presently the horses gave a plunge on the side of the road taking fright at a basket hung on the fence which run parallel to the road. Lucy dropped the reins and closed her eyes, as they darted forward.

"Foolish child! are you mad?" said McClintock, as he succeeded in catching them up before they fell between the horses feet. It required all of his strength, for some minutes, before he could rein in the animals, and then he turned to his companion. Her face was pale, her eyes closed, and her head drooped as if in a faint. He placed his arm around her and rested her head against his shoulder.

"Miss Ashbie there is no danger, you are quite safe."

She opened her eyes slowly. "Don't feel contempt for me, after all my boasted courage. My nerves have been much tried lately and I could not help it."

"Contempt for you," repeating her words, "why I—" he bit his lip, "Are you better," removing his arm from her waist. "I should have had more judgment than to have trusted the reins in weak hands."

"Oh! I am so sorry, Maj. McClintock," said poor Lucy in her mortification. "I do wonder if there are any brave women in the world!"

"I don't know," he answered with a short laugh. "Are you quite recovered from your fright?"

"Yes, it was very foolish of me, and I do not wonder you are angry."

"I am not angry," he replied, smiling, "you must not think that."

On their return ride, McClintock was preoccupied and taciturn, and Lucy marveled at his changed demeanor.

McClintock was an honorable, fair-dealing man. Not a word of understanding had passed between himself and Carlton on the subject of his real sentiments from Miss Ashbie, but from inadvertent remarks McClintock imagined Carlton was attached to the girl, and kept from a declaration of it by his poverty. When McClintock offered his friend a sum of money to begin business, he had a two-fold purpose, to aid him pecuniarily, and to enable him to prosecute his suit with Miss Ashbie, if he desired. At that time McClintock's fancy alone was pleased by the lady. His ride had suddenly startled him into a revelation that he loved her, and nothing prevented the betrayal of his feelings but the opportune remembrance of what was due to his friend. He determined to go away for sometime, and leave the field open to Carlton.

Carlton, on his part, felt that he would not interfere with the man to whom he owed obligation and so kept away from the fascination of the fair Lucy also, and she was left to wonder what suddenly deprived her of her two friends

When the autumn drew near Carlton left the village and went to the North to purchase his winter stock of goods. On his return trip he met a young lady on the cars to whom he offered some trifling courtesy, discovered that she was going on a visit to a friend living in the same village of which he was a resident and in a short time he became perfectly infatuated with her charms. His devotion to this stranger offered a new and tempting morsel of "news" in the little town, and visions of orange blossoms, wedding cake, &c., rose in the near future, before the eyes of the delighted gossips.

McClintock, having completed his business, arrived at home and the tide of excitement was at its flood. He dropped in on his friend one day, and looked about the neat store and assortment of notions spread out for customers.

"What is all this good news I hear of you, old fellow," he asked of Carlton; "is it true?"

"Can't say yet, I'm afraid to venture," he answered with a laugh.

"I wish I had known all this sooner. It would have saved me a journey, and much loss of time."

"What do you mean?" asked Carlton.

"I thought you were partial to Miss Ashbie, and I went away to avoid interfering with you."

"I'm sorry Mac, but I imagined you were 'struck' in that quarter yourself, so, I kept aloof to give you fair play."

"I suppose I need not fear you any longer," said McClintock laughing.

"You need never have done that even had I tried to rival you," answered Carlton, looking at the finely proportioned man before him.

"I wish you success, Carlton," said McClintock grasping his hand.

"The same to you."

Is there any Eden in this world without its serpent? A week or two of bliss and then–well! we'll go on with our story.

Major McClintock was returning from a visit to his betrothed to whom he had just given a costly engagement ring, when he chanced to overtake Mary Powers. Knowing her to be Lucy's friend, and feeling in a very amiable mood, he joined her.

"Why Major, where have you been? What a recluse you make of yourself, I have not seen you riding of late."

"I have been busy, and, at best, I am not a very sociable man."

"I believe the remark, I once heard a lady make, is pretty true."

"Let me hear it. I like compliments," he said laughing.

"She said you were an incorrigible and uninteresting old bachelor, that she liked your horses better than she did you."

"Is that all? Very flattering indeed."

"She also said she meant to marry you for your money, if she got the chance."

"And who is this lady who avows her sentiments so publicly?" asked he, while an angry flush swept over his face in swift torrent,

"Lucy Ashbie, of course," laughed Mary, half terrified, as she observed the fiery gleam in his eyes. "I must turn this corner, good-day, Major."

"I am much obliged," said McClintock, as he touched his hat in adieu.

He walked on slowly, his heart throbbing with a dull pain. Was it his Lucy who had so fully canvassed him, and avowed such indelicate sentiments? Could it be possible? Mary was her intimate friend and must know. He had not been acquainted with Miss Ashbie long and had suffered himself to be enthralled by a pretty face. Suddenly all the shine left the sun, and he seemed groping in deep clouds of disappointment and despair.

Days passed, and Lucy saw nothing of her lover. Her mother, always an invalid, was now quite ill, and she was too much engaged to analyse the strangeness of his conduct. She imagined that he had been called away suddenly, but then the malls were open, and he might have written.

One day Mr. Carlton called and mentioned in conversation that Major McClintock would leave the next week for Nevada, where he owned property.

"Has he been here all the time?" asked Lucy.

"Certainly, I have met him almost every day. I saw him out riding yesterday. He told me his business needed attention in Nevada, and he would be absent for some time."

"Mr. Carlton, I have a small box of Maj. McClintock's which it is important he should receive before he goes. Will you drop it in the post for me, and say nothing about it?"

"With pleasure, or I can hand it to him."

"Oh no: just drop it to the office, please. If you will excuse me, I will go and get it for you."

It was late afternoon. The trees cast long shadows athwart the earth, and the breeze soughing through their boughs, sounded melancholy and weird. A gentleman walking through the cemetery heard a low moan, followed by sobs, and on a nearer approach to the spot, saw a girlish form prostrate beside a new made grave. He paused, and removed his hat out of respect for such deep grief as the black-robed figure exhibited. Seeing no abatement of the young creature's sorrow, he, at last, touched her shoulder, intending to offer some word of consolation.

"Heavens! is it you, Lucy. Poor child lean on me and let me see you home!"

"I was not strong enough to bear it, but I could not go away without seeing my mother's grave," she said sadly, as if in apology.

"Going away!" said the gentleman, echoing her words.

"Yes, to-morrow. I have an engagement to teach for a year."

"You must not, you are mine. Take back the ring, Lucy. I love you and cannot live without you. Hold on to my arm, and we can go to yonder stone, where we can sit a few moments. There, lean on me. You remember our last day together? After leaving you, I met Miss Powers, and feeling in the happiest mood, I joined her. My joy was soon turned to gall, for she told me that you had said to her you meant to marry me for my money."

"And you believed her? Ah! you were right to stay away. I should have done the same," in a voice made harsh by contending emotions.

"Wait, Lucy, do not judge me too harshly. All of my life I have had a horror of being sought or accepted from any other motive than sincere affection. These feelings became accelerated and morbid from cruel outside circumstances. Miss Powers is your intimate friend. When she mentioned your remark, I was stung with mortification and anger, and I thought, if you so shamelessly avowed your intention, you had no love for me. Had I gone to you, I should have been too harsh, and have said many things ungenerous, for my pain was bitter. I took refuge in silence, and while awaiting a calmer moment you returned my ring, which left me no alternative."

"Poor Mary! she always exaggerated, I pity her."

"Pity! I could curse her," he said between his set teeth

"Don't," said the girl laying her hand upon his arm. "I did say I meant to flirt with you, in response to some of her badinage, after our first ride. It was an idle speech, and I have been deeply repaid for it."

"Lucy, say you forgive me, and let us be married at once, that I may share your grief."

"Ah! I cannot, I must go to-morrow and meet my engagement to teach my cousin's children for a year. By that time my affairs will be arranged and I hope to have enough for a support."

"You do not love me! You do not think of me in your independent programme," he said bitterly.

"I have passed my word, you would not have me break it, would you?"

McClintock was a man of honor, and to every honorable man his word is his bond, is it not? He was silent over his defeat for a moment, and then a sudden thought came, "I will find a competent person to fill your place, my love. If I do, will you agree?"

"No."

"Then you do not love me."

"I could die to serve you," said the girl, "but I am young and giddy. At present all your sympathies are aroused for me. Were I assent to your wish, you might regret it, in your calmer moments. It is better that I go to my cousin. The year's discipline will make me more worthy to be your wife. If, at that period, you have not changed your mind, I shall be ready to do as you wish."

"You are cruel, Lucy, and I do not see the force of your reasoning. Will you write to me, and wear the ring, since I am forced to bear your hard terms?"

"Yes, I must have something to console me. Let us go."

"May I visit you?"

"It will be best not. Don't part with me in anger," seeing a frown sweep over his brow.

"One good-by kiss, ah! love me, darling," he said gathering her in close embrace. "I shall be very desolate, after you have left me for a long year."

"It will soon end," uttered poor Lucy, striving to drive back the rushing tide of emotions which came sweeping over her at the dreary outlook, and making a brave fight to show a cheerful face to her lover. "Forgive me, and be reconciled for my sake. Good-by."

Eight months subsequent to Miss Ashbie's departure from her home, she received intelligence that Maj. McClintock had become bankrupt. She wrote to him immediately offering to fulfill her engagement at any time he desired. On receiving the letter McClintock felt in the well known words of Shakespeare, "sweet are the uses of adversity," and he was not slow in availing himself of the privilege accorded.

In a small city stood a handsome, imposing dwelling, with elegantly furnished apartments. In one of these is a gentleman near a slender lady, attired in deep mourning. Evidently they have just arrived from a journey, for the girl's hat is on her head, and she is removing her gloves.

"Welcome home. Lucy, I trust you will be happy here," drawing her tenderly toward him.

"Home!" echoed Lucy, opening wide her eyes, "I thought–"

"You thought I had failed," he interrupted smiling, "and that gave me my wife, God bless her!"

"How was it, Reno? I am quite bewildered. Mary wrote to me that you had lost everything."

"Only a few thousands. Mary always exaggerated you remember. Thank God for it this time."

End.

UNION & RECORDER.
Milledgeville, January 31, 1882.
Written for the Union & Recorder.

THE HATCHET ON THE MANTEL
A SHORT STORY

BY MARY FAITH FLOYD

From the Southern Farm & Home.
(Dedicated to Mr. and Mrs. C. W. Lane.)

I lived in a quiet straggling village where I was poor, obscure and unknown. I enjoyed all the vexing cares that usually attend that situation; but such cares, it may well be imagined, were not much in unison with my taste. I did not resemble Dean Swift or his ancestors in regarding "labor as pain." I had a love for all kinds of work; and unfortunately for myself, and for the world, I differed from the learned doctor in all other respects. I was neither learned nor witty. Unfortunately; because wit and learning are both pleasing when not intermingled with arrogance and pedantry. I consoled myself for these defects by the reflection that my industry would compensate, in some measure, for the absence of other qualities, and hoped I might get through life with this meed of praise—that I was a useful member of society.

There was one happiness I had, which I was fond of enjoying as often as my numerous duties would allow.

Not far from my house there resided a sprightly, tidy little lady. Facetious and intelligent, with many of those nameless graces that adorn woman, she never failed to fascinate all whom she met. I had the honor of calling this lady friend; and although I sometimes reflected that an uninteresting companion like myself must annoy by such frequent visitations, so selfish was I that I could not relinquish the comfort and pleasure I experienced in repeating the offence of thrusting my company upon her.

Her home was essentially the opposite of mine. Without being wealthy, she owned all the comforts of life; and the pleasing aspect of her well arranged parlor with its white walls, its simple furniture, and tasteful ornaments, delighted me. I felt no envy that my possessions were of more meagre dimensions than hers. I rejoiced that my friend was exempt from the privations I daily experienced.

Upon the mantel of my friend's parlor was an unsightly stone hatchet, made after the fashion of the red man before his ideas were modified by contact with European civilization. I wondered what freak induced my friend to keep this disfiguring ornament for such ostentatious display among her otherwise tastefully selected articles. I did not like to make any inquiries, fearing I should appear prying and impertinent. Being a woman, curiosity repressed became more wide-awake the more I struggled to lull it to sleep by those anodynes, good manners, reserve and non-intermeddling. Every time I beheld the broken, rude tomahawk, the edge of my investigating qualities grew far more keen than that of the mysterious weapon itself, cutting deep incisions into all those weak shields of defence with which I had enveloped myself.

Time, the great modifier, might have enabled me to triumph over temptation but for one circumstance. I called one afternoon and found my friend sweeping and arranging her room. She looked very charming, with her saucy little white apron, her sleeves rolled up, displaying a finely moulded pair of white arms. Her delicate hands wielded the broom with inimitable grace. Her face was flushed from the exercise, and I paused at the doorway to admire the domestic picture, saying inwardly, "Mr. Whitmarsh indeed has a treasure in his wife."

My friend greeted me kindly and accepted my offer of aid, saying that I might dust and arrange the mantel. My eye fell on the grim, battered stone hatchet, and instantly my curiosity quivered with a lively and irrepressible desire to learn the history of the horrible relic. I could not avoid remarking that the stone was a queer one, and added no beauty to the effect in the mantel arrangement. My friend's face blanched, and her voice trembled as she mentioned that it was an Indian relic of some antiquity connected with De Soto's expedition.

I ventured the statement that I was not sufficiently antiquarian in my taste to treasure ugly broken stones; and that the mantel would be much improved if the relic was discarded.

My friend with much embarrassment said it was valuable in her eyes; and there ensued an awkward pause.

I felt that I had been led into unwarrantable impertinence. Arranging the ornaments, I bade adieu to my neighbor, and returned to my solitary home; but my peace was gone.

I was a prey to torturing curiosity. My friend's mysterious deportment was gunpowder that had exploded all my investiture of self-control.

The wild desire to penetrate the secret pushed aside all other considerations. I could not sleep. How to elucidate the mystery was the tantalizing question.

I dared not approach my friend on the subject again; and I was sure I could not enter her house and restrain myself. I kept closely at home; but the hatchet haunted me like a spectre. My brain sprang into the most torturing activity.

"Tired nature's sweet restorer."

Notwithstanding all the coaxings in my power, persistently refused her balm I no sooner closed my weary eyelids than shapes of hideous savages with cleft and gory heads appeared, traced in fiery lines, and gibbered at me. I could almost hear the rattle of their skeleton jaws as they opened and closed with a snap in their pantomimic efforts to speak to me.

I became so timid that the thought of being alone at night was intolerable. I lost my appetite and felt as if my sanity was fast departing. It had been a week or two since I saw my friend, when I received a note inquiring why I had deserted her, and expressing a hope that I was well and would visit her very soon. I replied to the billet, saying I was ill, and would call ere long.

The weather was inclement, imprisoning me at home for several succeeding days. Then came a vernal day. Forest trees and flowers smiled in bright colors beneath their weight of rain drops, as children sometimes laugh with tear-dewed eyes. Twittering birds sung in the branches, and flew from twig to twig in their abandon of happiness. The air was soft with delicate odors. I was weary of home and of myself. A sudden inclination seized me to visit my friend. I had slept but little for several nights, and I thought a walk in the air might prove an anodyne.

I threw on my hat under this impulse, and hastened to my friend's mansion. Rapping quickly at her door I was annoyed at no response. I waited a few moments and concluded to enter the dwelling unannounced. Again I rapped, and walked into the parlor, hoping my friend would soon make her appearance. I glanced around at the familiar objects with delight, and was beginning to feel some of my old lightness of heart, when my eye fell upon the unfortunate stone hatchet. I shuddered, placed my hands upon my temples to press back the horrible sensations the object called forth, and threw myself upon the sofa to await my friend.

I knew not whether I fell into a slumber or a trance; but a lethargy seemed to steal over me, imprisoning every limb in motionless bondage. The walls of the white painted room expanded into a lengthened vista bordered on either side by primeval forest trees of gigantic height, their vast trunks hidden from view by a thicket of tangled vines and umbrageous shrubs.

By some strange and unfelt transportation I found myself in an open space in this dense wood; and as I gazed in wonderment, a stalwart savage, grim-visaged, and war-painted, emerged from behind a sheltering tree. His brawny breast was uncovered; but a tunic of gaudy colors was belted around the waist. From his shoulders hung a quiver of arrows, and upon his feet were bright-trimmed moccasins. In the left hand he held a bow of great length, and in his belt was thrust the tomahawk. With a bound he alighted near my feet, causing the welkin's echo to answer to the frightful war-whoop.

"Daughter of the pale face, be not alarmed! I mean thee no harm. Those who give way to idle curiosity must sometimes submit to suffer terrors. I have seen thy struggle to restrain thy eagerness to penetrate the mystery of the broken hatchet. The Great Spirit often rewards in this life those who strive to suppress evil or idle desires; and I have been sent from the happy hunting grounds to sate thy curiosity."

I had been so terrified by the war-whoop and the savage's startling proximity that my knees trembled, and I came near falling; but by a powerful effort, I calmed my fears and the speech of the savage re-assured me. I took a survey of my companion while listening to his words, which were delivered with precision and a deep, clear, bell-like tone. Upon his head tall gaily colored plumes waved in the soft spring breeze. His form was athletic and elegantly proportioned. About him clustered unmistakable graces of nobility and heroic traits.

While I gazed in rapt wonder and deep interest, the lordly savage again spoke:

"Know, then, that I am a nephew of Melora, the mighty and beautiful cacique and princess of Cofachiqui, and the remote ancestor of thy friend who is of far more distinguished pedigree than are the boasted descendants of Pocahontas. My illustrious aunt and I hover constantly in spirit around our pale-faced kindred, shielding them from harm and aiding them to perform great deeds.

"Among the followers of De Soto in his march to our village, was a proud handsome cavalier, Juan Vasquez de Gallegos, who became enamored of my sister, the beautiful Mochifa. So blinded was he by his attachment that he forgot his insatiate hunger after gold, laid aside his sword and buckler, and deserted his post as a warrior to become the husband of the red maiden of the forest.

"For a time the simple inhabitants of Cofachiqui were elated with the conquest Mochifa had made. Juan smoked the pipe of peace, mingled in the dances and joined in the chase; but the bright noon-day of happiness was soon beclouded, and dense curtains of doubt hung about the minds of the Indians. The treacherous De Soto rewarded the trusting hospitality of his red brothers by taking their beautiful queen Melora into captivity. Suspicion was aroused against Juan, and the grim warriors sought his life. But all their efforts were eluded by the watchful care of Mochifa. At one time, Juan was bound and secured to a spit before burning coals, that he might be slowly roasted alive, while his tormentors mocked his agony by cruel and insulting words. Juan's shrieks brought the poor wife to the spot, and her entreaties procured his liberation. Mochifa redoubled her vigilance after this warning, seldom suffering Juan to leave her presence. In time she became the mother of a daughter more beautiful than herself. When this child was a few weeks old, Mochifa sat in her wigwam observing Juan who was fashioning some arrow-heads out of the horn of a stag he had slain the day before.

"Her face was full of contentment, and her thoughts were far away, fancying the skill Juan would show in sending his polished arrows through the hearts of the fleet deer. Stealthy steps disturbed her reflections, and ere she could articulate an entreaty, a party of savages fell upon Juan and his head was cleft almost in twain, the stone tomahawk remaining so firmly fixed in the victim's skull that the assassin fled without detaching it. Mochifa sprung forward and clasped her babe to her bosom as her husband sank bleeding at her feet. The bereaved wife named her daughter Nithlee, which in the Indian tongue signifies night, in token of the darkness that fell upon her heart when she beheld her beloved partner murdered in her presence.

"Revenge is sweet incense to the nostrils of the red man; and Mochifa treasured her wrong, swearing by the bloody hatchet she withdrew from Juan's gory head to preserve it as a relic to be handed down to her posterity, who should event her husband's death.

"Mochifa died of a broken heart, and Nithlee became the wife of a young chief of her own tribe. Sons and daughters were born unto them, and the gory hatchet wreaked vengeance upon the savage murderers of Juan Vasquez de Gallegos, and did good service among the foes of their tribe.

"As the white settlers located in the country hunting the simple Indian like deer, and wresting his land from him, the village of Cofachiqui took the name of Silver Bluff from the tradition that De Soto and his followers searched for silver in the bed of the river, and among the strata of the bluff, some of which resembled silver ore.

"Nithlee's oldest daughter married a pale-faced resident of Silver Bluff; and to her the stone hatchet was intrusted with a solid injunction that it should be sacredly preserved, and the horrible incident of which it was a mute but lasting memento, should be related to each new possessor. In the contentions between the white and red man for several centuries, this hatchet figured in various deeds of blood, avenging alike the butchery of poor Juan Vasquez de Gallegos and the wrongs of the children of the forest.

"From this race of warriors of the house of the illustrious Princes of Cofachiqui, thy friend is descended in a direct line; and the hatchet on the mantel is the ancient and gory emblem of the cruel murder of Don Juan Vasquez de Gallegos.

"Daughter of the pale-face! Dost thou wonder that thy friend's countenance blanches at the mention of this bloody memento of a past age? My tale is done. Henceforth beware of the indulgence of idle curiosity!"

With a graceful inflexion of his body, and lordly wave of his hand, the savage turned and disappeared in the dense forest.

I opened my eyes, and with a start, sat upright. I was upon the sofa in Mr. Whitmarsh's parlor and my friend stood smiling beside me.

In my enthusiasm, I fell upon one knee exclaiming:

"All hail! illustrious scion of the regal house of the most beautiful Melora, Princess of Cofachiqui! Happy and honored I am to claim thee as friend!

"No longer do I wonder at the store set upon the 'Hatchet on the Mantel!'"

THE FEDERAL UNION.
Milledgeville, Georgia, November 15, 1870.

From the Southern Farm & Home.
THE HATCHET ON THE MANTEL.
(Dedicated to Mr. and Mrs. C. W. Lane.)

NOVELS

BY MARY FAITH FLOYD

THE LIGHT OF THE HOUSEHOLD
A NOVEL

BY MARY FAITH FLOYD

We find, in the *Daily New Era* of Atlanta, reference to the expected publication of a book with the above title, written by a lady of Georgia; and the inquiry is suggested whether she is a resident of Taylor county. We take pleasure in informing our contemporary that the writer of the "Light of the Household" is a resident of our good county of Baldwin—"Mary Faith Floyd"—and that she is a daughter of the late Gen. Chas. R. Floyd of Camden county of this State. We hope we shall soon have the pleasure of reading her book.

THE FEDERAL UNION.
Tuesday Morning, February 8, 1870.

EDITOR'S NOTE: This delightful teaser for her forthcoming novel leaves more questions than answers. It is uncertain whether her novel, *The Light of the Household,* was ever published, or if it indeed became her 1872 novel, *The Nereid,* which was serialized in Southern Farm and Home Magazine.

We look forward to republishing *The Nereid* in a future volume, should our readers find this volume enjoyable.

THE NEREID
A REVIEW

BY A. H. STEPHENS

This is a highly entertaining novelette, by a Georgia lady, under the nome de plume of Mary Faith Floyd. It is published in neat form by J W Burke & Co., of Macon, in this state. Price 50 cents.

Mary Faith Floyd is already extensively known to all readers in literary circles–in the Southern States at least–as one of the most classic writers of the times.

Heretofore her chief essays have been directed to Reviews and critical notices of the productions of others. It is in this field she has, by her great good taste and just discrimination, attained that merited distinction which she enjoys.

The Nereid, we believe, is her first attempt at anything in the form of a Book of her own. In it she has exhibited all her peculiarities of purity of style and chasteness of diction, accompanied with the most ennobling thoughts and sentiments.

The general scope and design of this book may also be very clearly understood, from the first lines of the Preface. In these she informs the public that the author's object was to present "a picture of life on the Atlantic seaboard of the Southern United States," anterior to the late war.

While the "author" gives us these pictures under the apparent "nome de plume," as we have said, of Mary Faith Floyd, yet there is, after all, not much fiction in this; for we believe it is generally known that the writer is Mrs. Mary Faith Floyd McAdoo, wife of Col. W. G. McAdoo, who is himself not unknown in the "republic of letters."

Mary Faith Floyd is the full maiden name of the author of *The Nereid*. She is a regular descendant of those Floyds on the sea coast of Georgia who have for nearly a century so signally illustrated the character of the State in the field of Art, as well as in the arena of Arms.

THE SOUTHERN RECORDER.
Tuesday, May 21, 1872.

Chapter I. As the lightning played wantonly around the wounded master, the man was enabled to see that one foot had been crushed by the falling vehicle. Ever and anon the coachman gave a loud shout, which was lost amid the roar of the elements.

EAGLE BEND
A NOVEL

BY MARY FAITH FLOYD

Published in the Savannah Morning News, 1883.

CHAPTER I.

Every author has his pet phrases, clauses, and adjuncts, which by constant usage become trite. Reader, I may have mine: if so, forgive me, and let the sublimity of the night, when the storm giant stalks abroad, tempt thee to step out and admire nature's wildest aspects. If thou be a man, lend me thine arm to steady my tottering footsteps as they plough through the plastic mud, or slip on the loose stones, and lead me, if not to witness a tragedy, at least to behold a tragic scene. If a woman, then give me thy gentle hand and I will support thee while we walk up a lonely road, startled as we go by angry nature's terrific frowns.

List to the wail of the winds, to the liquid lisp of the rain, the roars of the river. See the triple-tongued lightning. Hark to that crashing, crackling, crushing noise; then a fall; a hoarse sound that reverberates from hill to hill with multiplying tone. Hist! a plunge, a wild shriek, a low moan of agony. Let us hasten to the scene. Another dazzling flash out of the gloom, and there revealed is a carriage overturned with madly-plunging horses on a narrow ledge of road. A new-fallen tree impedes the way. See! they drag the carriage, another piercing scream. Look! they will go into the river below one more frantic leap. Thank God, they are freed! Hear their clanking feet; see the fiery sparks fly from their hoofs as they strike the rocks in their mad career onward.

Let us look into the carriage and see the sufferers. At this moment another gleam of electric light glanced athwart hill and dale, making visible again the fallen vehicle.

A man arose from the ground, his features rendered pale from fright and the lightning's lurid glare. Limping, he rubbed his hands nervously, then stretched his arms as if to assure himself that his limbs were whole and his safety complete. With a long-drawn sigh of intense satisfaction he groped his way to the carriage, awaiting another flash to show him his master locked in the slumber of a deep swoon. Exerting his lungs, the coachman gave several prolonged sonorous shouts, hoping that some habitation was near where he could get aid.

As the lightning played wantonly around the wounded master, the man was enabled to see that one foot had been crushed by the falling vehicle. Ever and anon the coachman gave a loud shout, which was lost amid the roar of the elements.

What could be done? Must he leave the wounded man in the drenching rain? If so, where could be a stranger in the darkness find assistance? In a last effort of despair he once more raised his voice in one prolonged, hoarse shout.

God be praised! Was it at an answering echo? No! Following the halloo a faint, flickering light gleaned in the unsteady air, then died out for a moment and again appeared nearer. Once more the coachman called and was answered. A man approached with a lantern. Just then nature, tired of her passion, as if in pity to the sufferer, withheld her frowns, suppressed her tears, and ceased her mutterings for a short time.

"Hold your lantern for God's sake! Here is a man killed, for aught I know, by this fallen carriage. Curse the night when the very devil from below is let loose!"

The new-comer held the light, whilst the coachman, with his help, extricated the wounded man from the wreck, and laid him on the coach cushions and a traveling blanket.

"My house isn't far away. I reckon you had better wait here until I bring my boys to help. I can get a litter, and with your help this gentleman can be carried to my house."

The coachman was again left in the darkness, while the stranger went in search of aid. In the space of a half hour he reappeared, followed by two stalwart youths bearing a rude litter. With care and steadiness the gentleman was lifted upon it and the party set forward.

The jostling of the litter, by the uncertain steps of the bearers on the water-soaked soil, seemed to rouse the injured man from his torpor. Several groans escaped his pallid lips. Then a faint voice said:

"Where am I, Jock? Did the horses leap into the river?"

The person addressed ordered a halt, and explained briefly that the coach was over turned, the horses gone the Lord knew where.

"And you, sir," he continued, "are badly hurt, I fear. The men are helping you to a house near by. You had better keep still and not talk."

Slowly the men proceeded along a narrow, ascending path for nearly a quarter of a mile, during which time few words were spoken, and no sound disturbed the solemn stillness save the noise of the river, and the sigh of the wind as it swept in fitful gusts down the hollow ravines along the way.

The quick bark of the house dog, and the stream of light from an open window indicated the approach to the house of the farmer.

The good woman of the mansion, apprised of the catastrophe by her husband, had prepared her own room for the reception of the stranger. The house was small; the accommodations poor; the arrangement hasty; but with that generous hospitality which is inherent among Southerners, the kind hostess had yielded her own apartment as the most comfortable in her establishment for the use of a suffering fellow-being.

Mr. Dearing, for such was the name of the traveler, was carefully placed upon a snowy white bed in a large, log cabin room, and such remedies as every "old wife" knows applied to his foot. The storm had now ceased, though the clouds still looked black and heavy; and Hugh Portwood, the second son of the family, was dispatched to the neighboring village of Clinton for a physician.

Mr. Dearing had recovered from his swoon and lay comparatively quiet, though any careful observer might have seen from the constant contraction of the muscles of the forehead that his agony was intense.

Apparently, he was in the plenitude of manhood; tall, slender, well-built, and in form approximating to symmetry. His face was fine without being very handsome. A broad, open forehead around which clustered thick wavy hair of a very dark brown, and well-defined brows shaded to a deeper hue a pair of dark, sympathetic blue eyes. The nose was straight; of a size too delicate for the other features. The lower portion of the face was concealed by thick, glossy beard which rendered the skin fairer by contrast to its dark color.

Mr. Dearing was wealthy. He had inherited a large property which he had increased by judicious care and attention to the business. By birth he was a Virginian, belonging to that genuine aristocracy which, although decried by others, constituted a characteristic and charming feature of society throughout the length and breadth that noble old commonwealth—the great parent of America's wisest men.

Soon after his marriage he had removed to Savannah and embarked in the mercantile business with great success. Fortune seemed to single him out as a particular favorite, and everything around him smiled and bloomed as a beautiful garden under the genial rays of a vernal son.

Mr. Dearing was journeying in a leisurely manner toward one of the mountain counties beyond Clinton, Tenn., where he owned large tracts of land;

when, by reason of the storm and the intoxication of his coachman, the wrong road was pursued, the carriage overturned and his foot injured.

After more than an hour had elapsed, Hugh Portwood returned to his father's residence, the Cedar Bluff, accompanied by a physician. The limb was examined and dressed. The foot was badly hurt, and Dr. Crandon, after administering an anodyne, urged upon Mr. Dearing, the necessity of perfect quiet and rest. At best, a month or two must pass before he could have perfect use of his wounded foot.

The restless nature of the wounded man did not relish this interdict upon motion; but in this case patience and endurance were the better parts of philosophy, and he resolved to close his eyes to the prospect of two months sojourn in a log cabin in the wilds of Tennessee, doomed to the everyday companionship of uncongenial, illiterate people.

Hugh Portwood, a youth of fifteen, volunteered to remain with the stranger during the night and minister to his wants. Mr. Dearing's fortitude under suffering had inspired Hugh with much admiration, and he resolved to do all in his power to alleviate the miseries of the guest.

After a time the soothing effects of the opiate began to be felt by the patient, and he insisted upon Hugh's seeking his couch, assuring him that he would be called if his services were needed.

Reluctantly Hugh threw himself upon a small bed on the opposite side of the room, resolving to remain awake: but Somnus holds absolute sway over youth, and ere long the boy lay in a sound, dreamless slumber, forgetful of the anguish of the stranger in whom he felt so much interest.

The night traveled surely and slowly through the hours leading to the gorgeous rosy-hued palace of the bright day-god. The sufferer, after tossing wearily upon his bed of pain, lay in a light slumber, alike deaf to the monotonous tone moan of the flowing river and the deep, healthy, breathings of his boy-nurse. It was the hour Bulwer so beautifully terms "that grey, indistinct, struggling interval between the night and the dawn," when Mr. Dearing was awakened from his dreaming, opium sleep by the light touch a fairy fingers upon his face. He unclosed his eyes and beside him, in the twilight dawn, stood a tiny figure in white raiment falling in loose folds to her feet. The hair was light, soft and fleecy, hanging in négligé curls about delicate face from which gleamed a pair of large, lustrous black eyes. For an instant the intrepid heart of Mr. Dearing, which had never cowered in the presence of mortal man, stood still. Was it an airy visitant from the eternal realms come, like Lord Lyttleton's ghost, to warn him of his speedy demise?

As his heart slowly regained its motion, and throbbed painfully in scale of fear, the little sprite against stretched out its soft fingers, stroked lovingly his cheek, and a bird-like voice exclaimed:

"Pa!"

At the sound of this tender and familiar epithet a thrill of delight coursed through the invalid's veins. How vividly it reminded him of the home, or the cheerful fireside, and the associations connected with absent loved ones of the "long ago."

The touch of the warm fingers assured him that the beauteous child beside him was no spirit from another world, but a creature of clay like unto himself.

Putting forth his hand he passed it lightly over the head of the child, who returned his caress with a glad smile.

"Beautiful babe, have you come to ease my pain?" exclaimed the gentleman.

At the sound of a strange voice the child cried out, awakening Hugh, who sprang up, rubbed his eyes, and walked toward Mr. Dearing's bed. His features expressed pleasure as his eye rested upon the little form.

"Sweet sister, you here?" he exclaimed, as he stooped and lifted the babe in his arms. "Naughty child to awake the gentleman," and he pressed the little girl to his heart.

"Nay," said Mr. Dearing, "do not chide her. She did no harm. I love children, and hope to make her acquaintance."

"She is shy of strangers," replied Hugh. "This was mother's room, and she, doubtless, thought you were father in the darkened room."

Kindly inquiring how Mr. Dearing felt after his sleep, Hugh left the room with his sister, and the gentleman had time to look about in the increasing light and observe his surroundings, as well as to reflect on the last night's accident and his subsequent escape.

He felt much curiosity concerning his new acquaintances. Evidently they were people beneath him in station and polish; but there was something in the department of Hugh—a native grace, despite his rude garb, which told of nobility of soul, and inherent refinement that shines and makes itself visible amid the most depressing circumstances.

Thought fatigued him; and giving way to the languor of the still potent anodyne, he again fell into that delicious, dreamy, half-waking sleep—the opium spell which plays such heavenly strains upon the strings of fancy.

Chapter II. At this juncture the little nameless, who had been amusing herself on the floor, approached Mr. Dearing and caught the watch which he still held, talking some unintelligible jargon expressive of her admiration, and interrupted the train of conversation.

CHAPTER II.

The sun had reached his meridian when Mr. Dearing awaked from his prolonged slumber. He felt all that sensation of strangeness which accompanies the beholding of new objects. Recollection was tardy in defining distinctly where he was, how he became an inmate of a rude cabin surrounded with coarse scanty furniture instead of the costly appurtenances which adorned his own stately residence in the busy hum of a populous city.

A twinge from the injured foot touched rudely the chords of memory. The wild storm—the hiatus of oblivion and nothingness, the subsequent agony—came clearly to his mind.

Pain is a wonderful vivifier of recollection. His head ached, and he experienced a feverish restlessness—a desire for companionship. Where was Hugh? And as mind unfolded her magic panorama, the little spirit, with its snowy, shroud-like garment, moved in the rapidly shifting scene. Again in fancy he felt the gentle touch of the baby fingers; again the musical voice with its soft intonation addressed him by the loving parental appellation.

His reflections were interrupted by a rap at the door, and a middle-aged woman plainly attired, entered and approached the bed.

"Good morning, sir. Hugh peeped in once or twice, but you were asleep, and the doctor said you must get all the rest you could. Will you eat some breakfast now?"

"Thank you. Perhaps I can. Are you Hugh's mother?"

"Yes, sir. He is my second son. My name's Portwood. I hope you had some sleep in our poor cabin and feel better. Our accommodations is sorry."

"I have a headache; but the foot is not so painful just now. I believe I slept, and this bed is very comfortable. I fear I trespass on your kindness."

"Such as we has, you're welcome to."

Saying this, Mrs. Portwood left the room, and soon returned with a waiter with coffee, chicken, biscuits, milk cold from the dairy located in the cool waters of the fountain at the foot of the hill, and fresh, golden butter kept cold and firm in the same place.

Mr. Dearing endeavored to partake of this tempting meal, but appetite was wanting; and, without rude scrutiny, he glanced carefully at Hugh's mother, occasionally engaging her in conversation.

Mrs. Portwood possessed an open, honest face somewhat worn by time. Her eyes were larger, dark, and had a benign expression. Her hair was black and glossy, drawn smoothly from the forehead and confined with a comb, with no effort at adornment. In height she exceeded the middle stature, with more athletic squareness than conformed to beautiful proportion. Her department was unassuming—her manner kind to the stranger, yet there was a something which indicated that her mind was preoccupied—engrossed with some master sentiment dominant in her own bosom.

Her appearance, her air, her self-absorption, her kind attention to himself, all interested Mr. Dearing. He felt a curiosity to learn all connected with her history. Knowing that to a mother her children are a never-failing theme of delight. Mr. Dearing remarked that Hugh appeared to be a promising boy.

"Yes, sir; he's the most likely of our boys."

"I had the pleasure of seeing one of your little girls this morning," continued the gentleman.

"Hugh told me about it. I'm sorry she disturbed you. You must excuse her, sir. She is our youngest, and the only girl, and we spoil her. She is only four years old."

In speaking of her daughter, Mrs. Portwood's face became animated, her eyes glistened with a light that made them beautiful.

"I shall be glad to form the acquaintance of the little fairy."

"Hugh can bring her in when you're better," and Mrs. Portwood rose and took the waiter, expressing regret that her guest could not eat of the homely fare.

Late in the afternoon, Dr. Crandon called and found his patient with much fever, suffering greatly with the injured foot. Although a country physician—a resident of an obscure mountain village—the doctor had studied closely his profession, and was by nature gifted with a goodly share of that rare article known as common sense. This combination of nature and art enabled him to discriminate quickly, from the wide field of remedies the science of medicine offers, which would be the most efficacious in affording present relief and effecting a speedy cure. After applying a soothing lotion to the swollen foot, he spent some time with a wounded man, knowing that a kind physician's presence in a sick room is a balm to a wound. Administering some mitigant for the fever, and leaving directions for the patient to be kept from excitement, Dr. Crandon departed, promising to call the ensuing morning.

For several days Mr. Dearing had high fevers, and was unable to make inquiries about the fate of his coachman, carriage and horses.

Mr. Portwood had inquired of the redoubtable Jock the name of his master, and whether his family, if he had any, would be apprised of the accident.

"The master will write hisself," replied Jock. "The doctor told me he would be better in a short while."

With this reply, Mr. Portwood was satisfied, feeling that it would be presumption in him to interfere with another's business. Mr. Portwood was an athletic mountaineer, with a finely shaped head, massive forehead, rather delicately moulded features, and an expression of total indifference alike to the joys or woes of mankind. His complexion, originally white, was tanned a rich brown by long exposure to the sun's rays and the rough weather of the mountains of Tennessee.

Once he had been a prosperous farmer, not so much from hard work as a combination of fortuitous circumstances. Marrying early a wife with a fair inheritance, above him a degree in station, he set out on life's journey with what is called a "good start." He was a very industrious, energetic man, but was not a prudent manager; and diligence without frugality is like a watch without a regulator.

As years passed and his family increased, Mr. Portwood found that his means for adequate support were left far in the rear, and no endeavors could bring them forward to the required point. One hope he cherished for improving his circumstances. He looked forward to the time when his boys, six in number, would be producers, as well as consumers; and then he hoped to retrieve his losses. He did not reflect that as a family increases in years so expenses multiply, and that without contrivance and prudence on the part of the head of the house, the aid of assistants would go as nothing. Of late, this startling fact began to dawn upon him, and he fell into an apathetic indifference, intermingled with spells of gloomy misanthropy, such as often possess half-enlightened minds—nay, too often hold control over the most intelligent.

Like himself, Mr. Portwood's sons were farmers, with the merest rudiments of education gleaned from the country schools in session during those months of each year when the cultivation of the crops was perfected and the harvest not yet begun. Apparently, they were not discontented with their lot, except Hugh. He was of a bookish turn, hungered and thirsted after knowledge—that mighty source of power—and secretly cherished a hope of getting a collegiate education. He devoured with avidity all the literature which fell in his way and, for an obscure mountain lad, was well informed; perhaps he would have been found, on close examination, to excel in learning most boys of his own years with far superior advantages. It is a weakness of humanity to undervalue things within our grasp, while we yearn even for evils which seem unattainable, imagining them blessings.

The wheels of time moved forward on rusty axles to the impatient, suffering, sick man; but all things disagreeable or pleasant must have a termination, and after ten days, Mr. Dearing summoned his coachman, called for writing materials, and wrote to his wife. He did not urge her to come to him, knowing her delicacy of health, but suggested that her presence would add to his happiness and aid his recovery. He scarcely expected that his letter would call her to him. In the solar system of their conjugal life they indeed revolved very near to each other around the great central sun of affection. But their orbits, like those of the asteroids, were wholly independent of each other. One was not planet, the other satellite. Many happy marriages are of this order.

"What became of the horses, Jock?" asked the gentleman, after completing his letter.

"Safe, sir, and well tended," replied Jock, fidgeting from one foot to the other as if uneasy about the result of the mishap's bearing on his own agency in it.

"And the carriage?" continued Mr. Dearing, looking steadfastly at him.

"Two wheels is broken, sir. I got Mr. Portwood and his boys to help me get it here. The wheels I took to a blacksmith in Clinton."

"Very thoughtful and very right, Jock."

Jock's face brightened, but the cloud again encompassed it as the master continued:

"And to what am I indebted for this severe hurt and all this expense of broken wheels? Out with it, Jock; you know the saying, 'An honest confession, etc.'"

"I think nothing would ha' happened if that cursed storm hadn't come on and made the lightning strike them trees right afore the horses' heads. I am glad, sir, you were not worse hurt."

"Was the storm all the cause? How came you to go the wrong road?" asked Mr. Dearing, looking sternly at the delinquent. "No trifling, Jock, or you may lose your place."

Jock became still more embarrassed, twirled his hat nervously from one hand to the other, and his weight apparently tired each separate foot from the frequent changes made from one to the other.

"The truth is, Mr. Dearing, I did taste a small glass of strong water to keep out the damp. Not enough to hurt. The dark night and the storm caused the mishap. I am sorry, sir, you was hurt." and Jock inflated his lungs with a long draught of air after easing his conscience by this forced confession.

Mr. Dearing was secretly amused, in spite of provocation to anger, but still wearing a threatening expression, he said:

"You deserve the fate of your namesake of Leydon. If you were not promise proof I would require a pledge from you to abstain from tasting your 'strong water' for a year. Your wages may pay the bill for the carriage repairs."

At this threat Jock made a tremendous swallow, looked frightened and abashed, and stammering acquiesced.

"See my letter put into the post, and beware of any more of your 'small glasses' or all will not be well."

Jock bowed respectfully, took the letter and left, and Mr. Dearing burst into a hearty fit of laughter, the first mirth he had felt since his sojourn at the cottage.

Jock Hethrington had been in Mr. Dearing's employment for many years. He was a mixture of Irish and American blood, a native of Virginia, and had been in the service, when a boy, of Clarek Dearing's father, and was given a common education. He was grateful, honest and trustworthy, with the one failing—too great fondness for spirituous potations, which, however, made him usually only more plausible and obsequious. Between him and his employer there existed a strong bond of friendship, which had taken root in early youth. Hethrington was older than Mr. Dearing by several years, always traveled with him, received good wages, and felt no allegiance to any one else. He both feared and loved the master, and bore has reprimands in good part. And although his drinking habit was very annoying, Mr. Dearing tolerated it for the sake of his many good qualities.

A few days subsequent to the interview between Mr. Dearing and his serving man, Hugh Portwood sought admittance into the invalid's room accompanied by his little sister.

"I have brought the child to see you according to promise. You were too ill to be disturbed before," he said.

She was neatly attired, with her hair nicely curled, and her beauty was not made less by the strong light of day. She was a delicate little creature, with regular features, soft black eyes and flaxen hair, Mr. Dearing showed his watch, endeavoring to gain acquaintance with the shy visitor.

"She is very pretty. What is her name?" he asked.

A slight look of embarrassment flitted over Hugh's face as he replied:

"She has no name."

"No name! That is strange! Is she not old enough?"

"Oh, yes, sir," replied the boy, "but mother has the notion, very common in this country, that children best remain nameless until they get old enough to name themselves."

"Queer idea, certainly. And did you select your name?"

"No, sir. Mother's great grandfather was a Scotchman, and I was called Hugh for him."

"If I may be excused for such curiosity, may I ask if you are pleased with your name?"

"I like it because it is the name of a favorite author of mine."

"Will you tell me who?" again asked Mr. Dearing.

"The great Scotch geologist, Hugh Miller. Ah, sir, he was an obscure boy as I am, and yet he has left a name always to be remembered."

Hugh's eyes kindled, and then suddenly recollecting that he was speaking to a stranger, a faint flush overspread his face, and he cast his eyes in an abashed manner to the floor.

"He is a great light towering high, showing how genius can elevate itself above every adverse circumstance. Moore beautifully expresses this in his line:

"'A light, a landmark on the cliffs of fame.'"

"I have not Moore's works, but would like to read them," said Hugh, with something of a sigh.

At this juncture the little nameless, who had been amusing herself on the floor, approached Mr. Dearing and caught the watch which he still held, talking some unintelligible jargon expressive of her admiration, and interrupted the train of conversation.

Mr. Dearing was a dignified, reserved man, holding everyone at a distance and a little in awe of him, yet he combined with this caution a very affectionate, gentle disposition.

Hugh had been the stranger's special nurse amongst a family that was very kind to him, and he felt peculiarly drawn to this youth who appeared to have read and thought much for his years. He determined to encourage Hugh to confide in him and discuss what he had read.

"Mother said I must not stay long with you, because we might tire you while you are weak," said Hugh.

"Oh, no! I cannot read. I weary of thinking about my mishaps, and shall be glad to see you and the spirit—for such she appeared to me. I have been here two weeks. Does Dr. Crandon think I can leave soon?"

"He says you must lie in bed several weeks longer, and then get about on crutches," replied Hugh, reluctantly.

"Delightful prospect!" said Mr. Dearing, impatiently. "You will be troubled with a fretful invalid longer than I imagined."

"I am sorry, sir, we cannot offer you better lodgings." So saying, Hugh and his little sister left the room.

CHAPTER III.

"Genista, where is the invitation to Miss Nathan's wedding? I have the note for Mrs. Ofel's party," said a lady to a tidy little quadroon with Caucasian features, ruddy cheeks, black eyes and hair oiled, brushed and tightly twisted from the temples in an eager desire to transmute natural curls into straight locks.

"I haven't seen it ma'am, but it may be in your dressing room."

"Search for it then and arrange my room. Everything is in miserable confusion."

"I didn't like to meddle with the table until you told me," said the girl, by way of excuse.

"Very right; but now put things in order. Bring the wedding cards, and lay my blue silk on the bed with the French flowers. I shall go to this wedding and disappoint Mrs Ofel's anxiety to have me at her house."

This last remark was made rather as a soliloquy, with something of a triumphant smile lighting the face of the speaker. The lady was slight in person and good looking. There was still the remnant of a childish, wax-doll beauty in the pale face, upon which ill health and fashionable life–those potent and too often successful rivals of old age–had traced a few readable hieroglyphics. There was an expression of patient apathy upon the countenance, which bespoke the monotony of desires and gratified by the magic wand of wealth. The speaker leaned languidly back in a light straw rocking chair toying with a silk tassel, the court of which confined the folds of a thin morning robe, and listlessly watched the motion of the maid in her labor of restoring order to the chaos of a lady's dressing room.

Her thoughts had strayed into her neighbors parlor, and fancy peopled it with the assembled guests, the timid bride, the triumphant bridegroom, herself, the magnet of attraction, all mellowed by the soft yellow light of the gas jets.

At this point there was a rap at the door. "Come in," said the lady with a slight frown of annoyance at the disturbance to her reveries.

"A letter, madame, from master," said the butler with a bow.

The lady received the letter and read it hastily, the shadow of annoyance deepening.

Chapter III. Her thoughts had strayed into her neighbors parlor, and fancy peopled it with the assembled guests, the timid bride, the triumphant bridegroom, herself, the magnet of attraction, all mellowed by the soft yellow light of the gas jets.

"Just like Mr Dearing! The most unfortunate of men, carriage overturned and his foot badly hurt. Confined to a country house a month or two, and I must go to him. That will do Horace; you can go." and she looked at the servant who was intently observing her.

With another bow. The waiter left the apartment. Mrs Dearing again perused the letter, and again, relieved the burden of thought by word utterance:

"What can Clarek mean by requesting me to go on this long journey? I always had an abhorrence to the mountain wilds of Tennessee. How could I exist among the barbarians he is with? Then I know he exaggerates everything. When he was ill in Columbus and I went there, I passed him on road and had to return alone to find him almost well at home. No! I will write and await an answer. If Clarek is no better, then I will go to him, even at the risk of my health. Poor fellow! I wonder what men would do without wives—more properly called nurses, in my opinion.

"Genista, I will go to the wedding tomorrow night. Have everything in readiness. It will be a brilliant affair, at Christ church, and the select party at the house. I cannot miss it. Order my phaeton to be at the door at 3:30 o'clock. I have some calls to return. I do not wish to be disturbed."

Genista acquiesced respectfully and continued her search after the cards.

Mrs. Dearing rose, reached her portfolio and began a reply to her absent lord. The letter was, doubtless short and sweet from the brief time consumed in its composition. The task done, she again summoned Genista, who brought the missing note.

"Place it upon the table, and give this letter to Horace to post at once."

Mrs. Dearing, provided with a book the two invitations, threw herself upon a lounge for a morning nap, while Genista went to deliver the letter and gossip with Horace over the news of the master's injury.

Mrs. Dearing was not a heartless. She was a voluptuary—a fair specimen of a wife in fashionable society. Between her husband and herself there existed a perfect state of amity, a sort of quasi happiness. She performed all her duty to him as far as her knowledge of that phantom went. Mingling with her circle, balls, parties and dress were essential parts of existence. Accustomed from childhood to the giddy whirl of a city, she had no idea that the extreme pursuit of pleasure became a dissipation—labor—a sin. She was sympathetic with the poor, gave much in charity, and was foremost on committees for inspecting and mitigating the abuses of orphan asylums and other philanthropic institutions. Of that higher type of love, of perfect self-abnegation. Mrs Dearing knew nothing; therefore she felt guilty of no breach of kindness when she withheld her presence from the languishing couch of her afflicted spouse. Perhaps those are most fortunate in life who feel only, this theoretical love and enjoy only a negative happiness. They live longer, carry youth beyond the meridian plentitude of existence, and while they experience less felicity, they avoid many was that wear away heart and life together.

The interval between the reception of her husband's letter and the hour of preparation for attendance on Miss Nathan's bridal, was absorbed by Mrs. Dearing in calls and afternoon drives, and in arranging those intricate trifles of the toilet which most women think the highest summit of recommendation to preferment in this world.

The hour having arrived, Eriginia Dearing descended into her parlor, surveyed her lithe form, rustling in silk and glittering in gems, in a superb pier glass. A smile of intense satisfaction swept as a sun-glean over her face as she turned from the mirrored type and sought her carriage. With a bound the spirited horses started from the elegant mansion near the park for one not less magnificent on South Broad street. Eriginia reclined comfortably upon the damask cushions of her costly equipage, giving way to the soothing witcheries of the loveliest moonlit night; forgetful of every surrounding, intent alone upon the coming triumph of vanity gratified.

As the superior vehicle swept by the old cemetery with its wealth, its living burden of hopes and joyous expectations, it formed a strange contrast to the silent deserted sleepers alone in their grim, solemn vaults, many of them broken open, and exhibiting the foul noxious remains of what was once beautiful and noble—as full of hope as the giddy passer, the one with no thought of the future, the other dust and decay, all alike awaiting the last signal trumpet to summon them to receive the reward of the just and unjust. As the carriage wheels quickened their revolutions to the festive scene, a figure shrouded in rags, a poor outcast, gaunt, miserable—a beggar and a thief—slunk like a guilty thing under the shade of an ailanthus tree near a time-worn mansion of the dead, the vault and it's corruption pointing to the end of man, the heavenly tree rearing its branches aloft to the mansion above, the hope of the blessed. The thief, oblivious to both phases, alive only to the nine pangs of hunger, skulked from observation.

Alas, such is life! The gay votary of pleasure, the vice-burdened outcast, the mouldering dead in their icy solitude, all meet at the same predestinated, unchangeable goal.

While the robber coward at the noisy whir of the coach wheels and sought the friendly shade, he crossed a little island of moonlight in the midst of shadow. For an instant he was visible to any observer. He was about to rejoice that his safety for the present when his terrors were renewed by the crackling of dry sticks which lay upon the earth. Cautiously turning his head he perceived a figure creeping along in a stooped posture. What if the police were upon his trail? At that moment the moonlight gleam upon the moving form showed the glittering buttons, the insignia of one of those bloodhounds of the law.

The thief felt that he was tracked. No was to be lost. Like a frightened hair he glided in the shadow to the shelter of a tall vault, wearing the proud (*unreadable phrase**) of the British lion, under which slept peacefully Sir Patrick Houston. Again he stopped and glanced furtively at his pursuer, who stood in the attitude of listening. The pause was only for a moment, then the policemen crept on in the direction of the outlaw. Flight or captivity lay before him. Keeping near the vault he moved slowly until he gained the further corner, where he must again cross the moonlight. At that moment the policeman was invisible, the friendly vault rested as a protecting shield between them. Darting forward, he gained the darkness, doubled, two or three tombs and crouched near the grave of King Tomochichi. This valiant Indian, the staunch friend of the white man in life, was faithful even in death. Poor, artless child of the forest by his own choice he rests beside his pale brothers of the east. Yea, he sleeps well by those who, holding out the right hand of fellowship, played the part of the ruthless despoiler and bereft the trusting savage of his birthright—the home of his fathers.

By this time the law's legate advanced into the light which the culprit had passed. Looking around he was about to give over the pursuit, when he heard a slight rustle among the leaves. With a bound he started forward, startling his victim from his cover. On they went between the tombs—one fleeing to save life, the other pursuing to destroy it.

The thief, weary with fright and with running, flagged in his speed, and was almost within the grasp of his enemy, when once more gaining the obscurity of a mansion of moldering mortality he stumbled, and the earth seemed to swallow him up. In pity the moon hid her face behind a veiling cloud, and the baffled officer, after vainly searching around, gave up the chase.

The thief was surprised at retaining consciousness in the suppose the bowels of the earth. Terror had suspended sense momentarily. Hearing no noise and feeling cramped and bruised from his sudden descent, he stretched his limbs, when oh horror! he touched something moist and slimy. A streak of moonlight at that moment displayed to his staring eyes, a human skull with hollow, glaring empty sockets.

The wretch blackened with guilt, hardened with crime, could not endure the skeletons proximity. His teeth chattered, a death-like frost nipped his vitality, his poltroon heart, alive only to fear, ceased it's beat, and physical as well as moral darkness and oblivion held vigils over his scarce animate body.

In another part of the city Christ Church, with its majestic pillars and it's ample steps stood invested in white, it's snowy purity increased by the sheeny lustre of the silver moonlight—mansion and emblem of Him who, while upon earth, characterized Himself as "a man of sorrows and acquainted with grief." From the stately windows gleamed the yellow light from the gas jets, sparkling like stars in the distance. The church, with its investiture of unblemished whiteness, and bespangled with gems, was as a maiden arrayed for her bridal; and, in truth, the expectant crowd within it's spacious portals awaited eagerly the coming of the votaries of Hymen. Why come they not? All things are waiting, and yet they tarry.

The scene shifts, and we must leave the sanctuary and cross the threshold of an elegant mansion—venturing even into the privacy of a young lady's chamber. There sits the bride, in wedding garments, alone, her brows knit, her hands locked, swayed by the ebb and flow of the mighty tide of doubt. What maiden has not felt all this dread of uncertainty as the hour approached to enter upon an unknown fate, and has not questioned whether or not it were too late to recede from a compact rendered indissoluble by vows at the altar until released by the emancipator death? In the endeavor to peer into the gloomy recesses of futurity, Miss Nathans became oblivious to all around her, and was only aroused from her trance by the approaching footfalls of attendants. Rising with an effort, with a mute prayer that all would be well in this venture, she slowly joins the waiting party, descends with the lover of her choice, is driven to the church where the vows are spoken which bind to hearts into one whole beyond reprieve. The pageant ended, the guests seek the festive board to sip the sparkling wine and offer congratulations to the happy pair.

CHAPTER IV.

Weeks fell from the gigantic tree of time, as leaves drop in autumn, ere Mr. Dearing was sufficiently recovered to stroll around the neighboring hills.

Mr. Portwood's rustic residence was situated upon an abrupt bluff hundred feet above the level of the river, short distance below two picturesque islands which divide the stream above into three channels. The bluff is made up wholly of limestone, arranged in thin strata, dipping to the southeast at an angle of about forty-five degrees. In this limestone is found fossil shells, both univalves and bivalves, small in size (not more than an inch in length), and occasionally a trilobite and an ammonite.

On the topmost pinnacle of this bluff, and within a dozen yards of the country house, are many Indian graves. The bodies were deposited in shallow cells which the natives countless ages ago, had excavated in this friable limestone; and each tomb was bordered by a hedging of thin stones set up edgewise marking its boundary. From some of these the bones of the nameless aborigines had been disinterred, and amid the small heaps of yellow clay and fragments of limestone, could be seen fossil shells of a million of years ago when an ocean rolled it's billows over the scene, and the shattered bits of human bones and here and there and undecayed human tooth of far more modern origin—probably only a thousand years of age.

Wherever the white man's axe had spared the native vegetation of this upheaval of limestone, a dense forest of cedars held complete possession of the earth's surface. These huge shrubs, sometimes rising to the dignity of trees, spread out they're stiff branches so low as almost a rest upon the ground, and rose in regular cones to a pointed apex of foliage occasionally thirty or forty feet in height. Beyond this narrow ridge of limestone an alluvial soil occupied the earth's surface. There the gigantic oak and hickory, and the still mightier or tulip trees which botanists, from its peculiar leaf, have aptly styled the Liriodendron, send far up toward heaven their lofty summits. Slender papaw trees put forth their delicate stems, sometimes burdened with golden fruit; and under all the soil is carpeted thickly with the fallen leaves of former years.

At this point of the Pellissippi river, just below the two islands alluded to, a small party of pioneers of European blood once crossed in pursuit of a body of Indians. It was in the same month of the year when the great Napoleon

Chapter IV. At this point of the Pellissippi river, just below the two islands alluded to, a small party of pioneers of European blood once crossed in pursuit of a body of Indians.

broke the power of the Mamelukes in the famous battle of the Pyramids. Here, in this far wilderness of the West, was a party of sturdy pioneers in pursuit of a marauding band of Cherokees who had invaded the "white settlements" near the present city of Knoxville. The "Children of Fire," as the Cherokees term themselves, had fled to the Northern mountains, now known by the inappropriate appellation of "Cumberland," with a fair and beautiful young woman as their captive. Below these islands, exactly opposite the cabin, Capt. John Gibbs had led his daring party across the stream by swimming.

One of Mr. Portwood's ancestors had figured on this occasion, and his simple descendants had allotted him an apotheosis for his prowess in Indian warfare.

It was the latter end of October. The air was mild and tempting, and the forest wore it many-hatted most gorgeous livery. As a dying man just previous to death becomes again lucid after prolonged delirium, and his senses gather a preternatural force to drink the last draught of the nature's beauties ere has soul wings its way through a halo of glory to the empyrean heaven, so earth, before being frozen in the winding sheet of ruthless winter, experiences most fully the expansion of her aesthetical elements, and adorns herself and all the imposing vividness of coloring which decorates God's arch of promise.

Mr. Dearing, accompanied by Hugh, had ridden in his carriage some distance up the river. Hugh proposed walking about near a handsome residence on a gentle ascent where a fine view of the country could be obtained.

Mr. Dearing was an enthusiast, and the site which burst upon his vision filled him with admiration too great for utterance.

Afar in the distant Northwest lay, against the horizon, a chain of dark blue mountains cleft between, where rose in royal isolation the grim "Pilot," its apex soaring like a mighty Pharos above its mates, wrapped in the majesty of its own sublimity. To the Southwest lay, the picturesque Lone Mountain, while nearer the undulating hills with their prismatic tinted foliage. Above hung the delicate blue sky, like a canopy, with here and there a film of luminous white cloud drifting slowly in an infinity of space, and dappling the earth with shadows a sorrow does the heart of man, yet reminding one of their pearl-like purity of the great white throne and Him that sitteth thereon. Beneath crept the murmuring river like a silver serpent losing itself among the distant hills.

"Lovely beyond description!" at last murmured Mr. Dearing, seemingly forgetful of Hugh, who had watched his very expression as he looked over the landscape. "How such a scene inspires man with the greatness of the Creator and his own insignificance!" he continued, turning to Hugh.

"I have felt this all my life," said the boy, "and yet I never tire of looking at the hills and mountains."

"Who owns this place, and what is it called?" inquired Mr. Dearing.

"It is called the 'Eagle Bend.' Here the river makes a circuit of many miles. I believe the place is for sale. I have forgotten who owned it. At any rate, someone who is involved and compelled to sell."

"I should like to have it for a summer retreat. Would you like me for a neighbor, Hugh?" he asked, turning the boy suddenly.

"For some things, yes sir. I believe I like to talk to you better than any one I ever met," and he ceased with an evident embarrassment.

Mr. Dearing's face colored. He was one of the most sensitive of men, and was unprepared for an answer qualified by reservations. He had suffered much of his natural reserve to rest during his intercourse with this country boy, unmistakably stamped by nature with nobility of soul uncommon among those reared in the middle of walks of life. Compressing his lips to check his vexation, he resumed: "I hoped to have built up a friendship between us strong as the gray rocks that so abound in this country, and that you had been rejoiced at the prospect of a continued intercourse."

"It would be presumption in me to have imagined you cared what I felt. In the course of things, if you lived here, there would be something to prevent our being much together. You are differently situated for me, Mr. Dearing, and while I am grateful for your interest in me I still will be the mountain farmer boy." As he said this his face was calm, even cold, in its expression.

Mr. Dearing was surprised at this acuteness of perception in Hugh. Although they had been much together for two months, and Mr. Dearing had observed many salient points of character in the youth, he had not thought of the exhibition of so much delicacy.

"The conventionalities of society where no doubt instituted for good purposes, although sometimes inconvenient. Happily, Hugh, we live in a democratic country, with no hereditary aristocracy. Merit can always rise to the highest level. I like the spirit you manifest. Fortune, in her caprice, may have made me in better circumstances than you are; but why need that divide us? I choose to claim you as my friend. If I lived in the sequestered paradise I see no barrier which can prevent our being together as we are now."

"Excuse me for my plain speaking," replied, Hugh. "I shall be proud indeed to claim friendship with you at all times. I did not like to be forward, although you were considerate."

"I must leave in a few days now. I can get about very well on crutches, besides I shall not need to walk much in going home, or have to reaching there. I have had a pleasant time, although one of suffering during my stay here."

"I am afraid you will not care to come again," said Hugh.

"Business will compel me to return occasionally. I shall never forget this scene. I love the country. Were I to reside here I would turn author. Excuse me,

Hugh, but tell me what are your aspirations for the future? Do you mean to be a farmer or study a profession?"

"I scarcely know as yet what I shall determine. At present I wish and mean to get an education. I have read somewhere of Eugene Aram's learning all the languages by his own power of will, and without any aid becoming a scientific man. Can I do likewise?"

"Certainly, if you possess perseverance. What a paradox that character was! With strength of purpose sufficient to endure all toil for the attainment of learning—in that a very giant, and yet a dwarf in his capacity for resisting evil. Striking lesson of the uselessness of accomplishments unless combined with virtues! But I believe with Bacon, that we can learn as much from the errors as we can for the good traits of the great."

"I think so," replied Hugh; "but we must have a foundation laid in home training. A good mother is everything to give the start."

"How do you purpose going to college, Hugh? I presume that is what you mean by an education. You seem to me to have 'a foundation' now; "and Mr. Dearing smiled kindly as he looked on the face of the earnest boy and as homely garb.

"I think of teaching during the leisure months until I can lay up enough."

"Good. A slow process I imagine. How would you like to be a clerk?" asked the gentleman.

"I never was partial to merchants," replied Hugh. "They never struck me as liberal-minded men."

"Yet they earn money, and eventually amass riches, which is a potent clue to the avenue terminating in aristocracy."

"I like wealth combined with other things. To live for that alone is like the Children of Israel worshiping the golden calf. It ties us to closely to earth. We are idolaters, and the false god has no power to sound our names to distant time as authors of great deeds. I prefer instincts to riches," said Hugh

"I regret that you are not fond of merchants. I fear you will dislike me, as I come under that proscribed class," and Mr. Dearing laughed at Hugh's puzzled face.

"I would never have thought so. You seem to me so different from those I have seen—in fact unlike any one I have ever met."

"Thank you, Hugh, for the implied compliment. I am not a shop-keeper, such as you may have seen. Those petty dealers, him Cicero in his Ethics denominates as 'irretrievably base;' nor am I one of your merchant princes, but a commission factor. I am one of the snails that creep by slow and sure degrees after years of industry into a competency. I had been in search of a clerk for some months. Return to my home with me and enter my employment. Reflect upon this proposition, and giving your answer a week hence."

"I will, sir. In the meantime I thank you for your good opinion of me."

They had strolled some distance from the carriage, and were sitting on a gentle slope during this conversation.

Mr. Dearing rose, looked lingeringly and admiringly on the enchanting scene spread out around him, and went slowly toward the approaching vehicle.

CHAPTER V.

In an obscure village among the mountains of Northern Georgia, where the shrill scream of a steam engine was never heard, lay nestled amid environing trees, a small cottage. The place was in good repair, with neat white palings enclosing a front yard with well-trimmed shrubbery; and everything about it wore an indescribable aspect of wholesome comfort. The cottage was situated in the suburb of the town, and it's compact, well-kept exterior struck the beholder in strong contrast to the ruined buildings of the village.

Its residences, all of wood, bore marks of decay and general dilapidation. The church near the main square was gray and worn, and the few tombstones, visible in the neglected churchyard, were tottering and defaced by weather stains.

Enterprise had, apparently, long since deserted the village in despair. While art had bestowed little on this place even in its palmy days, nature with her lavish beneficence had given much.

A more beautiful spot for founding a city could scarcely have been selected. It seemed land-locked by mountains. From every point of the compass, as far as the eye could discern, lay an undulating line of mountains. Some near, dark, and lofty; others afar, almost beyond the reach of vision, dying dimly and swelling waves of blue, until finally they melted into a shadowy tint of limitless ether, losing the beholder in an infinity of grandeur and loveliness, dimly linking him with pre-historic ages reaching far into the twilight epoch of time.

The interior of the cottage was perhaps more comfortable and spacious than would have been imagined from its outward appearance. A wide hall divided its length, and on either side were rooms large and lofty, well aired and lighted by large windows reaching to the floor. In one of these chambers, upon a low lounge, reclined a man advanced in life. His face was emaciated and cadaverous. A broad, high forehead beetled over a small keen pair of eagle eyes. The nose was long and aquiline; mouth large and well shaped; and the chin massive and dimpled in the centre. Thin iron-gray hair covered a large head. There was an expression of intelligence that affection in the restless eyes of the invalid as they fell upon the face of a delicate young girl in a chair beside him.

The lady was fair to transparency, with soft-brown hair and large, dark, pensive blue eyes full of benevolence; and the countenance wore a tranquility

Chapter V. "Kiss me. God bless you!" and as she stooped and pressed a loving kiss upon the lips the last fleeting breath escaped, and Vinvela Gladwin was an orphan.

and meekness, which expressed at once contentment and purity of thought. She was not pretty; but there was a nameless something, a holiness in the face which attracted the beholder irresistibly. Upon her knee lay a translation of "Euripides" from which she had just ceased reading to her father from the "Alcestis."

"What a fine eulogy the conduct of 'Alcestis' is upon the fortitude and unselfishness of woman," exclaimed Mr. Gladwin. "There is a moral sublimity in the sacrificial capacity of your sex; so frail, yet, in self-abnegation, assuming gigantic proportion. The courage of man shrinks into lilliputian dimensions when compared with it. Thank you, Vinvela, for your patient reading. Listening to these tragedies takes me back to the dawn of manhood when ambition was high and hope seemed a staunch ally, instead of the fickle goddess I have since found her."

"You are extravagant in your praise, father. I see nothing great in the relinquishment of life for a beloved object. I think the sublimity of "Alcestis" conduct entirely lost by her boastful consciousness of her sacrifice. The effect would have been heightened could she have ignored self, and allowed others to sing a paean over her heroic deed."

Mr. Gladwin smiled kindly at his daughter's critical acumen.

"Perhaps there is some truth in your remarks; but the greatness of the nation still stands out, and the devotion of the young wife is a fine antithesis to the self-love of the aged parents to whom life ought to have had comparatively few claims."

"Shall I read no longer?"

"No. You are weary now, and can resume after a while. You are a good child, Vinvela, to nurse a peevish man unmurmuringly."

"I deserve no praise, dear father. It gives me pleasure to serve or amuse you. The tedious hours of a sick room are difficult to endure, and I wish to do all I can to make you forget them. Are you better, father?" continued Vinvela, gazing anxiously on the thin face of the man.

Mr. Gladwin looked pityingly upon his daughter. The pent-up feelings of his sorrowful heart rose to overflowing, and prevented utterance for a few moments. With an effort he pressed back the surging current of grief, and looking sadly upon the pleading countenance of his young daughter, he said:

"I am no stronger, but the fever is conquered."

"Then you will soon be better, I trust."

"Vinvela, there's another channel wherein the moral sublimity of human nature can show itself; that determination to submit to the will of God—to bear afflictions, over which we have no control, with fortitude and patience. I have long desired to talk to you of yourself. My poor child, it is cruel longer to deceive you. I feel that I cannot last many weeks."

"O, my father! then what shall become of me? Willingly would I die that you might live."

And the girl clasped her hands nervously in a mute essay to keep back the tide of sorrow which was fast flowing over her.

"That would never do. I am old and near the end of my journey. You are young, my daughter, and can enjoy life."

"Father!" exclaimed the girl, "what is the world to me? To me, a poor cripple? When you are gone my sun will have set in darkness forever."

"Not so. God will raise up others to love you. I would not have you forget me; but after a season you will grow calm. Happily the heart is formed to rebound from the pressure of affliction. Were it not so, it would burst, or our capacity for usefulness here would cease. Listen while I have strength to tell you. This house must be sold, for there are debts to liquidate. But there will be something left for my little one. Your mother had a cousin several years her junior to whom she was much attached. They were schoolmates, and, although Eriginia Dearing was worldly-minded and gay, she was kind and generous. Her husband is a noble-hearted fellow and will be a good friend to you. They will receive you as an inmate of their home. In view of my speedy end I wrote to them. Here are their letters. My only sister is too distant to come to me. I have written to her also, and her home will be yours eventually. Until you hear from her, you must remain with your cousin. I need not ask you to be discreet and useful; you are always that, my darling. But promise your dying father to cultivate cheerfulness and contentment in your new home. Let not affliction or misfortune break your heart's buoyancy or cast you down; and your father's loving spirit will hover near you always."

Vinvela clasped his hand and bowed her head. Her sorrow was too deep for words. The comfort of tears was denied her parched lids. We all have felt that there are times when the heart traverses a cycle of a century of woe in a few moments. Alas! where were the buoyant hopes of Vinvela Gladwin for the beloved patient? Gone like eddies of smoke before the passing breeze. Drink deep of the bitter water, poor Neophyte in the world's strife, as a preparation for what is to come upon thee as upon all of Eve's children.

Mr. Gladwin had removed to the obscure town of Cascade and early life and purchased a farm. As years fell away his gains increased and he gathered many comforts around a pleasant home. His parents had given him a fine education, and nature had bestowed an enlarged mind, and a love for intellectual expansion; and knowledge was the great magnet of attraction to him. He accumulated a fine library, and at twenty-five his mind was enriched by the gleanings from a wide field of literature, from an extended study of the best authors. For a while his love for learning absorbed his whole soul, and wisdom was his idol; but anon discontent and *ennui* crept in. His hearth was cold; his house was drear. He needed the benign influence of light to drive away the darkness and desolation of a lonely home. Nor was he slow and finding that light; and ere long that home was made cheerful by the presence of a young wife.

Several happy years, seemingly as brief as a beautiful dream, swept by, and the wife and her little ones were gathered by the reaper Death to swell the harvest of the tomb, and a midnight pall of darkness fell, with its murky folds, about the despoiled home of the bereaved man. His heart grew colder and harder than steel, and for a season he was a recluse and a misanthrope.

Grief seemed to shrivel up his youth as a scroll; and he, that was once happy and gay, looked stricken and old. Disease, with its vulture talons, fastened upon him, and his life was a breath which might be exhaled in a moment.

And old domestic, seeing her master brought thus low, summoned a widowed aunt, who came with her young daughter and ministered to the sick man's sufferings. In his delirium he fancied his cousin his lost wife; and none could soothe him as she. The touch of her soft hand on his parched forehead alone could exercise his madness. He, who had mourned so deeply, learned to love his fair young cousin. Very quietly they were married, and again happiness dwelt with him. The world was fierce in its denunciation against the fickleness of man, and the impropriety of joy treading on the heels of sorrow in such unseemly haste; but, reader, he who marries quickly pays the highest compliment to the worth of a lost wife; and in loving again he slights not the angel who had first taught him the value of home joys. He but testifies how dear to his heart was the joy he had lost.

Vinvela Gladwin was the sole child of the second marriage, and her birth bereft her father of his wife.

Again came the darkness thicker and more deep than before; but the child rose like a star above the gloomy horizon and shed its flickering light over his path.

Vinvela was delicate and lame, and her nurture was a constant draught upon the thoughts and time of the afflicted parent. As she grew her extreme tenderness became more apparent; and as if in contrast, her mind developed with much vigor. Her lameness rather increased, and she could only walk with a crutch. Her amiability and cheerfulness were remarkable, and the cross placed upon her by nature did not incline her, as it usually does others to make her fellow beings responsible for her misfortune. No; she was a natural lover of her race, and her heart was as full and fresh as an odorous rose.

She had been denied, by her poor health and her misfortune, from mingling with other young people, and engaging in the pleasures of the world. Hence her enjoyments were more solid and lasting—those gleaned from a well stored mind. Her father was her world, and that world was to be taken from her. No wonder she was prostrated with the might of the sorrow that she, with all her devotion, could not avert.

No wonder if in the depth of her isolation, she asked in the beautiful lines of Wordsworth:

> *"What good is given to men*
> *More solid than the gilded clouds of heaven?*
> *What Joy more lasting than the vernal flower?*
> *None!"*

> *"This was the better language of the heart."*

Mr. Gladwin had always managed to live comfortably. His wants were few; his daughter's tastes were simple, but mirrored reflection of his own. Like all bookish men he had small capacity for the coarser knowledge of gaining a penny and hoarding it, so that when the inevitable summons came he found his affairs in worse plight than he imagined, and his daughter left in her double affliction without a patrimony.

This knowledge caused him acute suffering and much humiliation. Vinvela, from her affliction and extreme delicacy of health, he had shielded from her every care. Of business practicalities she knew nothing, and it was gall and wormwood to him, as the twilight dews of death were gathering about his brow, to feel that his daughter would experience that excoriating shackles of dependence. He saw, with all the clear-sightedness of a man of enlarged mental vision, the narrowing tendencies of the life of pecuniary vassalage. It is a frost that nips the new-formed leaves of unrestrained thought and action in the young especially; and its chilling effect is perceptible through all the stages of existence. Gladly, in these last hours of despondence, could he have lived again his life, would he have thrown aside all the refining pleasures found in the peaceful paths of wisdom for the grosser faculties which secure the amassing of wealth; that efficacious oil which opens the hinges of entrance to all castes of the social fabric.

Amid all these dismal reflections one thought alone comfort him. His only sister, a maiden lady with a large mine and larger heart, was in good circumstances, and his daughter was legally her heir. This, could they be brought together, would place Vinvela beyond want, and, above all, out of the pail of charity; and he doubted not that her inherent loveliness of character would endear her to his sister.

For many days after the conversation referred to between Mr. Gladwin and his daughter, she felt the relentless pinch of the iron fingers of despair about her heart. Vainly she strove to loosen their grip—by religion, whether it's dove-like wooings; by cold philosophy, and by that lovely unselfishness which sought to ignore her sorrow rather than add to that of her parent. Mr. Gladwin, whatever were his private regrets, appeared cheerful in his daughter's presence. In truth, with that deceitful fickleness which often marks disease, his health seemed to rally wonderfully, and poor Vinvela, grasping at the shadow, hugged it as a reality. With the belief that the patient was improving came some of her buoyancy of spirit; and as the spring advance she hoped everything. How often when we look out on a flower-covered plain, or on the concave vault of a serene summer sky, are we standing upon the verge of a yawning chasm of woe, above which hangs clouds dark and laden with the lightnings and thunders of affliction!

A few weeks passed of mild, genial weather, when there came a cold change—a bleak north wind. Mr. Gladwin was seized with a chill long and alarming. Then followed a relapse of fever. Vinvela felt now that her hopes were delusive, and that her father could not long survive. No persuasion could tempt her to leave his side. She seemed gifted with superhuman endurance. No word of murmuring escaped her. She was mute in the might of her agony. When the doctor came her eyes followed him as he felt the patient's pulse with a sorrowing, despairing eagerness which made him, rendered almost callous by constant intercourse with misery, feel the tear of sympathy flow.

After days of delirium, in which her name felt constantly from the lips of the sick man, the icy deliverer came with is dismal wings to bear his victim over the cold Jordan. Vinvela prayed that once more she might hear the voice of her idolized father speak to her with his senses restored.

It was near sunset. A few clouds hung on the western horizon soon to hide the great luminary, as death was to shut up forever, the eyes of the invalid.

As Vinvela, with trembling, clammy fingers wiped the death dews from the brow of her beloved parent, he opened his eyes and for a moment gazed on her pallid, suffering young face.

"Is it you, darling? I thought it was your mother with her angel wings who touched me."

How her heart thrilled at the sound of the faint voice.

"Kiss me. God bless you!" and as she stooped and pressed a loving kiss upon the lips the last fleeting breath escaped, and Vinvela Gladwin was an orphan.

Chapter VI. "Forms uncouth of mightiest power; for admiration and mysterious awe" pervade the imagination. And Mr. Dearing left Tallulah with a sense of ungratified interest which could only be filled a long sojourn amid the chaotic wilds which encompass the spot.

CHAPTER VI.

After the funeral, Vinvela Gladwin spent a solitary month at her father's cottage in solemn commune with the voice of despair.

The Interment had been conducted in the imposing ritual of the Church of England, most calculated of all ceremonies to exalt the thoughts from "dust thou art, and unto dust shall thou return to him" who saith "I am the resurrection and the life yet such:" was the girl's petrification of feeling that to her it had seemed as singular a pageant as did the premature obscene equities of Charles the fifth of Spain celebrated at his own command in his presence at Yusto a few months previous to his demise.

The attendant physician had enclosed Mr Gladwin's obituary to Mr. Dearing who wrote Vinvela a kind letter of condolence and offered to go and escort her to his home.

By the advice of friends. This proffer as accepted and the time appointed a month ahead of her letter. She had many things to arrange, many mute friend to bid Adieu before she left her home forever.

This was indeed a harrowing undertaking. As she went over the silent chambers preparing the those things she did not need for sale. Each article seemed to dear but inanimate friend speaking volumes of the parent that had gone and they're well known shapes associated so forcibly with her buried happiness caused each wound to gape and bleed anew.

Still she faltered not in her self-imposed task. Occupation was better than inertness even under the most doleful aspect. The day before Mr Dearing's arrival, and after Vinvela had completed all her preparation, she sought her father's grave.

It was not a great distance from the cottage, and she walked there alone. It was afternoon. The spring had advanced with magical celerity as it ever does in mountainous regions, and the trees were invested with their fully expanded vernal dress. The lengthening shadows of the afternoon sun, as they fell between the leaves, dabbled the earth with ever varying combinations of light and shade.

Vinvela heeded, not the beauties of nature, to her the sun, the flowers, the living green, the spring teaming with newborn life, were a bitter mockery. She walked slowly in her black garments aided by her crutch, through the cemetery around the church. Not far from the gate, under the spreading boughs of a majestic oak, rose a simple upright slab of marble erected to the memory of her mother with her name and age. Beside this unpretending memento was a newly-formed heap of yellow earth: and this mound was the severance of the last link of love which had bound Vinvela to home, to life itself.

The girl sat down at the foot of the grave and endeavored to quell the rising rebellion of tumultuous regrets which filled her bosom.

Strange fashion of being his man, that a debt, which began at his creation is yet unsettled, should ever hang over him and horror. Everything frequent becomes trite and we grow callous to all that is inevitable, except the exactions of the King of Terrors. With each new comrade that goes to swell the ranks of the invisible army of spirit comes the same poignant sorrow, the same mysterious dread, the same indwelling regrets for unkind actions to the loss, to torture the hearts of those left behind. Something of all this Vinvela experienced as she sat near the cold clods of clay which held her all.

Her whole life came in successive images before her. In it nothing had arisen to disturb her pleasure, except ill health, and she regarded that as a trifle in comparison with the pure enjoyment of simple, solitary, every-day life with a sympathetic parent. Henceforth her career lay among strangers, and she shrunk from the ordeal she felt must be hers in unbuilding her thoughts and actions to seek those with whom she should be placed. She knew that no one could replace what was lost; but she trusted that her new friends would prove lenient to her peculiarities, so that she might fulfill her promise, of regaining her cheerfulness, made to her father, and now seeming a sacred trust. Vinvela sat long in this last hour of farewell to her father's tomb, making many resolves for the future, wasting numerous regrets over the unchangeable past, until the sinking sun warned her to return. Casting a long, fond glance on the lowly graves, she turned sadly away and retraced her steps toward home.

The ensuing day Mr. Dearing arrived. His greeting to his young cousin was kind and quietly sympathetic. Naturally reserved, he was not given to extravagant expletives either of condolence or compliment. But under all this dignified exterior, the young orphan instinctively felt there lay a noble heart beating with all the virtues which adorn the higher type of manhood.

Mr. Dearing appeared older by some years than he was when last seen in the cabin on the bank of the picture as Pellissippi. The lines of the face were sterner and more earnest, though the pathos of his dark-blue eyes remained the same. His mind had expanded under the influence of travel and intercourse with his fellows, with the still more beneficial aid of copious draughts from the great fountain of literature. If he had lost some of his youthfulness, his face and form were handsomer and more striking in maturity, and connoisseur would have pronounced him a remarkable specimen of manly beauty.

He remained several days in Cascade arranging Mr. Gladwin's affairs in such shape as to be disposed of to the best advantage for the daughter.

The magnificent scenery of the country delighted him.

"Miss Gladwin," he said, "you will think I exhibit the taste of a parvenu when I express the opinion that we have landscape views that our country which exceed in beauty those so much extolled by tourists in Europe."

"No, sir; I admire your candor. I have always believed that such was a fact. Why should nature lavish everything upon the eastern hemisphere? Distance and novelty lend a certain lustre to all things, and the very difficulty of obtaining views in Europe enhances their value and beauty."

"My summer residence is a lovely spot, but it is not comparable to this," said the gentleman.

"You should visit the neighboring falls in this region to be hold awful grandeur of God's handiwork. There are some places which show forth sublimity and the highest degree. I was at Tallulah when a child, and, even then, was inspired with thoughts unutterable."

"I should like to see these falls," said Mr. Dearing.

"Then remain a few days," replied Vinvela, "and go there. You may never chance to be in this neighborhood again, and I think you will be amply repaid."

It so happened that there was some delay in getting suitable transportation for reaching the railroad, and Mr. Dearing procured a horse and went to Tallulah.

At times the road wound around steep mountainous ascents presenting fairy visions of enchantment, and, after climbing a rugged slope and reaching the top, the "Ocean View" burst upon him with sudden and startling effect.

There lay wave upon wave of undulating hazys blue, limitless and extent, except where the seeming ocean had caught the clear cerulean vault above, and held it until they merged into one vanishing whole.

The deceptive image of the sea spread out before the gaze, is complete. Mr. Dearing would gladly have dwelt longer upon this ravishing scene, but time admonished him to hasten forward.

After many delays he finally reached the falls. Securing his horse he walked with a small boy, resident of a rude cabin near by, to the precipice which yawns over the thundering waters below some fifteen hundred feet.

The abrupt bluff of gray, rugged granite with its sparsely covered growth of gnarled and stunted shrubs, worn by the rains and snows of centuries, soaring high on the opposite side, called up the idea most forcibly that the rocks had been rent in twain in the convulsion of nature, when the incarnate son of God said, "It is finished!" bowed his head, and he yielded up the ghost.

In the mighty chasm below, the boiling, seething, foaming, angry waters, white as snowflakes, went dashing down in three successive leaps, uttering maddening, deafening roars in their raging haste to escape their rock-bound confines. The whole scene is terrific and majestically sublime. A sensation of grandeur springing from,

> *"Forms uncouth of mightiest power; for admiration and mysterious awe"*

pervade the imagination. And Mr. Dearing left Tallulah with a sense of ungratified interest which could only be filled a long sojourn amid the chaotic wilds which encompass the spot.

The day at length arrived for Vinvela Gladwin to leave the loved home of her life. Tearless she walked for the last time through the silent chambers; with no visible mark of inward suffering except the pallid face and compressed lip.

The journey over a root and hilly road was long and fatiguing. The hack was a dilapidated remnant of what it originally was, the horses slow to apathy, their fleshy investments shriveled and thin; each

> *"His strutting ribs on both sides show'd*
> *Like furrows he himself had plow'd."*

The driver, a savage-looking daredevil sort of a fellow, seemed utterly reckless in driving, and regardless; in his rapid career up the steeps and down the slopes, whether he overturned the rattling old vehicle or not.

Mr. Dearing began to anticipate a disaster similar to that which befell him years ago in Tennessee, and expostulated with the man that the young lady's life was at stake, and the wind of his steeds might be in danger by such fast driving.

"My critters is naterally fast trotters. Mister, and thinks nothin' of this yer drive. Yer see, I changes 'em every twenty mile. Never mind the lady, I'll put you down safe. I will."

And as if the merit of his horses had been seriously aspersed, the driver urged them on a more rapid gait than before.

Mr. Dearing found that as the old saying goes, the prudent holding of his tongue was the valorous course, and endeavored to enliven and divert Vinvela by conversation and anecdote, inwardly ejaculating thanks to his Maker for his safety at reaching the photo of each steep hill.

The sun stood at moment wrapped in luminous amber-colored clouds before sinking to sleep upon the star spangled couch of night, as Mr. Dearing and his young charge reached the railway station.

"Miss Gladwin," he asked, "are you much fatigued? I really felt a fear that our braggart driver would overturn us and fracture some of our limbs. We have reason to congratulate ourselves upon our safe exit from the stage."

"I am less tired than I anticipated," replied Vinvela in a soft, low voice. "My thoughts were too busy to make the alive to danger, if it existed."

"I presume the route was familiar to you?"

"No, sir. I never traveled it before. This is my first journey from home."

Vinvela said this with a quivering lip. The remark called to mind most forcibly her recent affliction.

The travelers were not long in waiting for the cars. Anon they came, roaring like a tornado, the iron horse breathing forth loud breaths of white curling steam.

Mr. Dearing found Vinvela a seat in a comfortable high-backed bench all to herself, that she might sleep if she wished, securing one for himself, not far distant.

This was Vinvela's first trip on a railway, and the novelty of watching the different people, as their heads went bobbing to and fro as if bowing their doomed necks to the merciless executioner. Time, and the thumping, rattling motion of the car's kept her awake a long time. Finally she slept, and in dreams was talking and reading to her father, when she was awakened by a cessation of motion. Several box cars were off the track near a high embankment, but no damage was done.

Mr. Dearing told Vinvela that they would be delayed for some hours where they were. There was a rude shanty nearby and many ladies crowded there to sit through the night in as much room as could be found to lie down and rest. Vinvela procured a seat on the lowly portico and thought herself fortunate to secure a position where she could lean against the wall.

It was a beautiful starlit night, and she occupied herself with thinking that each star was a light through a loop-hole of heaven from which angels looked down and kept guard over the destinies of the children of earth. Was not her father one of the celestial soldiers, and would it be his duty to shield her from harm? She loved to dwell on this thought, and singled out one star more luminous than others on as her particular guiding light. How comforting it is to the bruised heart to thus associate the spirits of the departed with the imperishable worlds which swing in space and feel that they glean brightly as signals to inspire us to greater deeds, holier lives, and an unfaltering trust in the Great "I Am."

Day was dawning, with its rosy veil of vapor, when the passengers reseated themselves in the coaches and sped away on their journey, which was prosecuted without other accidents.

At Knoxville, in Tennessee, Mr. Dearing procured seats on the stage for Clinton, his own carriage not being there to meet him, and in the afternoon the wayfarers had reached that village. It was almost night when they arrived at his home beside the beautiful Pellissippi river, where Mrs. Dearing and her young daughter were expecting them.

Vinvela was greeted most affectionately by her cousins.

"Dear papa," said Minona Dearing, clasping his hand, "I am glad indeed that you have come at last. Mother and I have been lonely to distraction since you left. The mountains looked scowling, the scenery tame, and I had to close my windows to shut out their frowns."

"I am duly complimented by your dutiful feelings and the respectful deportment of the mountains, my little flatterer."

"It is all true, is it not, Mother?" said Miss Dearing, turning to the lady.

Mrs. Dearing laughed and nodded her head and acquiescence, and left the room with Vinvela to prepare for supper.

Minona Dearing was an only child, at the age of all others most devoid of reason and less favorable to personal beauty in a girl that stage of passive development when a girl is too old to act as a child and not matured enough to be a woman. Yet she was good looking. Her features were regular, her eyes fine and her teeth perfect. Her form was slender and immature, her intellect precocious, her manners self-possessed. One could see at a glance she had been petted and humored, and the germ of beauty was apparent in her undeveloped exterior. She was sprightly, impulsive and impetuous as a

"White-robed waterfall."

Her temper was stormy, but she was open to reproof, and there was much that was noble and generous in her disposition. Her father was her oracle and his frown alone held her in awe. To others she was imperious and exacting.

"Minona," said Mr. Dearing, during the absence of his wife, "your cousin Vinvela has had a great sorrow in the death of her father. She is afflicted by nature with lameness, and is, doubtless, sensitive on that point. Her home will be with us for an indefinite period, and I request that you treat her always with great respect and consideration. I wish her to feel that she is among friends who love her and desire to make her home happy. Will you bear this in mind and be her friend?"

Minona looked up with her earnest eyes and answered unreservedly: "Yes, sir; I like her already, with her sweet, sad face."

"See that you keep my injunctions ever before you. It is not always easy to do right." And Mr. Dearing took up a paper and read until supper was announced.

Minona thought in this instance it would be a simple matter to act well, and considered her father's warning a piece of supererogation. She was a girl of remarkably quick perceptions, and had from her short interview with Miss Gladwin drawn her own conclusions. She felt that she would love Vinvela and could always be just to her. Impetuosity of temper is like a mill race, which sometimes breaks through the embankment, bearing down salutary obstructions in its rapid current; and Minona lived to know that she could not unflinchingly adhere to good resolutions at all times.

Chapter VII. Before leaving America he commissioned Hugh Portwood to purchase for him the residence known as the Eagle Bend, in Eastern Tennessee, and on his return he had thoroughly repaired and improved the place. It was now a charming spot, where Mr. Dearing insisted on spending each summer.

CHAPTER VII.

Fatigue and anxiety of mind, added to the strange feeling engendered by a situation so entirely new, prevented Vinvela from sleeping the night of her arrival until near the dawn, when she fell into an uneasy slumber. Mrs. Dearing would not permit her guest to be disturbed, and hence she was surprised to see the sunbeams through the half-closed shutters on awaking. Her head ached and she felt too ill to rise. The chamber was handsomely furnished, but to Vinvela's eye it did not present that air of comfort that her own room wore. Link upon link thought came unbidden to her mind—painful memories of home and of him who made that home so dear. She felt desolate amid the surrounding elegancies. A few tears fell like dew from the closed lids. Revery is unfit medicine for a sick mind.

It was fortunate that Vinvela was diverted from our unwholesome thoughts by a rap at her door, and in a few moments Minona entered.

"Cousin, mother sent me to inquire after you, and see if you would have your breakfast. She would not allow you to be disturbed earlier. Are you well?" and Minona stooped over and kissed Vinvela.

"No, I have a headache and feel too ill to get up just now."

"Can I bathe your head? I am the best nurse in the world, and I like to wait on sick people," and without pausing for a reply, Minona began passing her hand lightly and soothingly over the throbbing temples of the young lady. "You must have some coffee; I will get it for you in a few moments," and Minona left the room. She soon returned with a servant bearing a silver tray with breakfast.

Vinvela drank the coffee, but declined eating. Minona then resumed her post as nurse, this time bathing the head with cologne and water.

"May I bring mamma up to see you, cousin?" she asked. "She wishes to come and know for herself if anything can be done for you."

Miss Gladwin assented, and Minona again departed.

Mrs. Dearing was not long in appearing, and found her guest had fever.

"I must have a physician to see you, Vinvela. You seem too frail to bear illness."

"Oh, it is not necessary. I often have such attacks. They wear off after a few hours or days."

"You can do as you think best. This is home, Vinvela, and I desire you to act unreservedly. But if your ailment continues I must have medical aid. I will act toward you as I do to Minona, and hope, my dear girl, you will regard Clarek and myself as parents whom you made love and confide in. Your mother and myself were warm friends, and you are so much like her, I can scarcely believe she is not before me."

Vinvela did not speak. This kindness unvarnished by compliment, touched her more than high-sounding words of flattery. Her heart was too full for utterance and she only pressed her cousin's hand in token of appreciation. Mrs. Dearing arranged the shutters and adjusted the curtains so as to exclude the light. Again assuring Vinvela of her sympathy and leaving Minona in charge with injunctions to remain quiet, Mrs. Dearing quitted the apartment.

Minona, after her mother left, asked her cousin if she could serve her in any way, and receiving a negative response, she presented a book and began reading. Of all things inactivity to her energetic temperament was the most foreign. Silence without employment was oppressive.

The book contained sketches of some of the distinguished women of France, and Minona became wholly absorbed in an account of the heroic bearing of Madame Roland during her imprisonment in the Reign of Terror. Her farewell letter to her daughter, written from the gloomy cells of the Conciergerie, with its admonition touching the necessity of leading "A strict and busy life as the only preservatives against all dangers," impressed her forcibly. By nature Minona was industrious and ambitious, with a good memory. She studied vigorously her allotted task; but these did not occupy all of her time, and often she ardently wished for some employment which had an aim to render it's accomplishment desirable. As she reflected on the sentence which pleased her, she framed her thoughts in words.

"I wish I could lead 'a strict and busy life—the only preservative against all danger.' This suited very well a girl in the midst of the terrors of the French Revolution, but I have nothing to fear. What calamities could a girl in my sphere of life, with ample wealth, possibly suffer?"

"Who are you talking to, Minona?" asked Vinvela, who had been quite still for a long while.

Minona glanced up quickly, and beheld her cousin's eyes bent upon her. She replied with a blush:

"No one. It is only a childish habit I have of talking aloud when I am thinking. Since you are awake and heard my query, answer it."

"Then, I think you're being a girl of wealth in high life subjects you all the more to hazards. You will be exposed to many temptations of frivolity and extravagance. You know these are to be shunned by every well balanced character."

"Phsaw! I claim no balance at all, unless it be impulse, and that is as likely to take one the wrong way as the right. I wish I were a sensible young miss—one of your sober-sided people fit for a heroine. But mother said, I must be quiet or I would make you worse."

"No, talk; my head is better and I wish to make your acquaintance."

"Your face is still flushed, and I am a perfect magpie when I begin. If you get worse we shall have to bring our circulating dispensatory to find some remedy for your ailment."

"Do explain," said Vinvela, "what this circulating dispensatory is," and she smiled at Minona's quizzical expression.

"Nothing short of a young village physician, who scatters his drugs promiscuously at our bidding, and puts all sorts of diseases to rapid fight. Would you like to have him come here and scare yours away?"

"Yes, if he possesses such power for exorcising maladies as you ascribe to him he must indeed be a model doctor."

"He cures me quickly," answered Minona. "I must have Tartar blood in my veins—the name of physic relieves me. I approve of the plan the Thebetans have of writing the name of the particular medicine on paper and giving that to the patient in the form of pills. I have talked at your bidding, cousin. Tell me what you think of me," continued Minona, lifting her lustrous eyes, full of mirth, and looking direct at Vinvela, at the same time folding her hands over her bosom in mock humility.

"I think you are sprightly, full of mischief, and very good company, and can scare away dull ears as quickly as your model doctor does disease. I have obliged you, Minona; give your opinion of your patient."

"Thank you," said Minona, curtseying gracefully and low. "It well suits a sage little body like you to deliver such an opinion of a rattle-brained school girl, but it would ill become me to retort. Modesty exhorts me to respect my elders."

"This is unfair treatment. I beseech you to throw aside embarrassment as you would your cloak—it is superfluous between girl—and express your impression of your new cousin."

"If you are determined I shall make a speech I must yield, as I detest obstinacy. To begin then, I like you. You are sincere, truthful and affectionate, amiable and cheerful, and all the other adjectives which qualify ladies' virtues."

"I see," said Vinvela, "that you are a consummate flatterer. Tell me how you learned all this mere guess work at last."

"No, it is not. I read people by their ways after I had been with them for some little time, but I judge them at first sight by their method of shaking hands. Now, cousin, you have the genuine 'shakus rusticus,' which Sydney Smith says betokens warmth of heart and distance from the metropolis. You cannot gainsay such reverend authority, I am sure; but mercy! there is the dinner bell. My garrulity has increased your fever I know. I will do penance by holding my tongue for the space of five minutes, if I can, until mamma comes."

Minona resumed her seat demurely, and she closed her lips resolutely. Vinvela scanned her countenance as she sat quietly, her eyes cast down with a look of a martyr. She had been much diverted by their animated, playful conversation. Her opinion of Minona was favorable and she hoped would be lasting. Of a cautious disposition, she seldom trusted her confidence hastily to any one. She called to mind her father's request that she would cultivate cheerfulness; and inwardly she said that Minona would be a good helpmeet to carry out such resolution.

Minona's patience was not put to a long test ere Mrs. Dearing came in with inquiries as to the invalid's improvement.

"Are you better, Vinvela? I fear Minona has talked you into a state of delirium. She always does me so when I am ill."

"Oh, no. She is the very best of company, and could easily drive one into the delirium of laughter by her queer remarks. I feel much better and hope to be up tomorrow."

"Shall I send you dinner?"

"Yes, mamma, and mine too. I told you I was a better practitioner than you and could cure our cousin. See, I have got her to talking already."

"I am afraid you speak too much. Loquacity does not always show profundity. In truth, I think it more apt to display vacuity. Fine talkers are seldom great thinkers. The wisest men generally speak the least."

"I think I never will be wise then, dear mother; but surely ladies are exempt from such stringent rules. With motionless tongues they would resemble bodies without breath."

"I see," said Mrs. Dearing, laughing, "you are determined to be witty if not wise. I must tell Clarek of your brilliant sally. Vinvela, you must keep our petted girl in check. I will return after a time." So saying, she left the room.

The interval of some years occurring since last Mr. Dearing was noticed, passed rapidly with little worthy of remark to the reader, and will be referred to by a cursory glance. Hugh Portwood had acceded to the proposition of retaining him as a clerk, and accompanied his employer to Savannah. Mr. Dearing and gave him a fair salary, and Hugh, frugal and never tiring in labor, gained for himself the most valuable of all recommendations to a business man—those of being honest, trustworthy and prompt to a second in all his engagements. Hugh found Mr. Dearing a high-minded, considerate friend who felt an interest in his improvement mentally, morally and socially. For this favor the young man was grateful, and it inspired him to emulate all those higher qualifications that metamorphose man into his original moulding after the image of his Creator before the corroding disfiguration of sin was known.

Anxious that his mind should gain vigor by the stimulus of education, Hugh procured a private teacher to instruct him at night, and often pursued his lucubrations until long past the midnight hour, when the watchman's lonely cry of "All's well" sounded on the still air and warned him to seek rest.

The ensuing year after Hugh's advent into Savannah, Mr. Dearing had a large estate left him in Scotland, and spent several years traveling in Europe and in attention to his business in that quarter of the world. Mrs. Dearing and her daughter joined him the last year of his stay, but Minona was almost too young to profit much by the travel.

Before leaving America he commissioned Hugh Portwood to purchase for him the residence known as the Eagle Bend, in Eastern Tennessee, and on his return he had thoroughly repaired and improved the place. It was now a charming spot, where Mr. Dearing insisted on spending each summer. Eriginia had opposed such movement, but her husband was immovable, and she knew that when he once formed a resolve, after mature reflection, he was unchangeable. Reluctantly, she acquiesced. At first the monotony was unbearable. The absence of society affected her like a fit of starvation, but Clarek never restrained her in any reasonable amusement, and at length she learned to like the change.

Her health improved in the salubrious mountain climate, and she frequently entertained her Savannah friends at her new home.

The residence was commodious, built of brick, with a handsome veranda in front. It rested upon a gentle elevation and faced due east. On the south side, immediately upon entrance, was the family's sitting-room, which opened up into a spacious apartment elegantly fit it up as a library. Here were well-filled shelves of finely bound books from the pens of the best authors. The windows of the library extended to the floor and opened into a half octagon conservatory blooming with choice flowers, which exhaled rich perfume to increase the enjoyment of the student. This library was tastefully furnished with light summer adornments. The curtains and sofas were ornamented with blue, and Mrs. Dearing romantically designated it the blue room. The blue room then, was Mr. Dearing's favorite resort. During several hours of each morning Minona occupied it with her tutor as a schoolroom.

The grounds at the Eagle Bend were highly cultivated. The dwelling was enclosed by handsome, substantial iron railing, and the garden displayed every variety of rare roses, odorous flowers and nicely trimmed shrubs, interspersed with rustic benches, which combined beauty and utility. Picturesque roads led from the enclosure to the river, and to the village of Clinton. The stream crept along its bank about two or three hundred yards distant, where large bathing house had been erected.

All the luxuries that wealth could bestow were at Mrs. Dearing's command, and had her enjoyment been dependent upon the ideal and contemplative, or could she have garnered intellectual gems from the limitless mine of nature's handiwork, she would have experienced many moments of exquisite pleasure at her mountain home. But, unfortunately, like too many of her sex, her higher intellect remained in a serene state of repose, and her happiness arose from intercourse with fashionable society—that mighty pair of shears which usually clips off every newly expanded bud of knowledge that struggles to bloom in the mind of a woman.

Like a child, she wearied quickly of each toy wealth could give, and was constantly on the alert for some new gewgaw, which was no sooner gained than thrown aside in the ardent pursuit after other diversions.

Vinvela's arrival had thrown for a season, all other projects into total eclipse, and Mrs. Dearing anticipated much enjoyment and bringing her out the ensuing winter. Minona was almost too young as yet for such expectations to culminate in a round of brilliant parties where she would reign as the attracting star.

Mrs. Dearing intended very soon to invite a select few of her city favorites to pass the warm months of the summer with her, and felt delighted in the prospect, as she doubted not Vinvela would prove a willing coadjutor in all her plans. Her disappointment was very great that Miss Gladwin's illness should prove rather protracted, and her husband's arrangements consequent on this, at length defeated her well-formed projects.

Vinvela was seriously, but not alarmingly, ill for some days. The attack left her unable to quit her chamber for several weeks.

Mr. Dearing had in a rude hot-house a rare variety of grapes that he had been watching for sometime with interest. The bunches were well developed and almost ripe of a pale green color. His directions had been explicit to Jock Hethrington that no one should be permitted to touch them on pain of his extreme displeasure. It so happened that Minona, in roving through the grounds, espied the treasure, their tempting clusters gracefully pendant amid the leaves. What a treat a bunch would be to the sick Vinvela! To think was to execute with her, and in a moment she had placed herself on one of the projecting beams running along the wall. Just as she caught the grapes and was gathering her prize, a rude hand seized her arm, and the voice of Jock Hethrington exclaimed:

"The master left orders that these grapes must not be touched, and I cannot let you have 'em."

The hot blood was up in Minona's face in a moment. Her eyes scintillated with angry flashes, and she demanded in haughty accents:

"How dare you, sir, to interfere with my wishes? This is my home, and I can have what I please."

"That's all true, young miss, and I meant no offense; but your father's commands are strict. I must obey."

"I shall ask papa if I am to be rudely pushed aside by every churl and trampled on as if I were a serf."

"I am sorry to displease you, Miss Minona, but Mr. Dearing knows best, and you ought to know his word is law here."

The quiet apologetic tones of Jock, as he went on arranging the vine which had been displaced in the difficulty, aggravated Minona's excitement to a still higher pitch. In the midst of a more withering denunciation of the delinquent, while her voice was elevated to a loud key and her face flushed in scorn. Mr. Dearing appeared on the *tapis*. He asked in amazement:

"What can the matter be, Minona?"

If a bolt from heaven had fallen the young girl could not have been more startled. Indignation changed to mortification, that her father, whose good opinion she valued so greatly, should catch her thus in a rage with one of his domestics. She stood pale, but proudly defiant, with all her chagrin, and no word escaped her.

"I did not mean to vex the young lady, master Clarek, but your directions was partic'lar, and I could not help it."

"Very well, Jock, I will see you again. I am waiting, Minona. Will you walk?" and Mr. Dearing extended his hand to assist his daughter from the green house.

Without seeming to notice it, Minona sprang down from her position and walked quietly beside her father. He did not speak, and she became more under the shadow of embarrassment is she regained her wonted equanimity. Reason told her that the gardener was right in the premises. She wished her father would talk; then it would be easy to explain her behavior and place her conduct in a better light.

But Mr. Dearing had no notion of opening the conversation. He was much annoyed that his daughter should be founded in an altercation with domestic, and her manifestation of such a volcanic temper startled him. Besides, Minona had purposely slighted his offer to assist her thereby showing irritation at him. His reserve closed around him like an investiture of steel. They were some distance from the house. Lighting in another cigar from the remnant he held, he walked on toward the dwelling.

Minona would have given any treasure she had to have broken the disagreeable silence, growing more oppressive at each step. She could hear her heart beat. She resolved at every turn in the walk that she would begin an apology, and on reaching the limit, timidity fettered her tongue and paralyzed its utterance. On gaining the door, Mr. Dearing said coldly:

"Tell your mother I shall not be at dinner. I have business which will detain me at Clinton. I will dine there."

He turned away and went in an opposite direction. Minona's eyes filled with tears. She had angered her father, and the opportunity for making peace was lost for the present. Seeking her room she gave vent to a flood of tears.

CHAPTER VIII.

"Vinvela, I congratulate you on being with us at dinner. This is your first entrance into our family circle. How pale you look. Quite ethereal, but all the more charming, my dear," remarked Mrs. Dearing as Miss Gladwin joined her in the sitting-room a few days after the events of the foregoing chapter.

"Thank you. I rejoice to get out of my room. It is not agreeable to be an invalid, and the sick are generally very troublesome," replied Vinvela.

At this moment Mr. Dearing and Minona's preceptor joined them and they proceeded to the dining-room, where Minona awaited them. Mr. Dearing expressed his pleasure at seeing Miss Gladwin released from her long imprisonment, and presented her to the tutor.

This gentleman was a delicate, nervous little man; a clergyman whose health did not permit him to perform the onerous duties of a parish. He was a good scholar, with high credentials, and owned a most unexceptionable character. He was fair to transparency, with modest blue eyes, dark brows and long, sentimental lashes. The forehead was good, the mouth large, and he had a square chin, denoting firmness. His diffidence was almost as painful to beholders, as it evidently was of himself. He seldom ventured a remark unless spoken to. His habits were bookish, retiring and modest, and altogether he suited Mr. Dearing's idea of a teacher very well.

"Miss Gladwin, if you feel strong enough you must have a drive this afternoon. Eriginia, your cousin needs fresh air and diversion; if you have no other engagement will you ride in your phaeton? Otherwise I will give her an airing in my buggy."

"I am at your service, Clarek. I have nothing in the world to do. This country life is enough to exterminate one with *ennui.*"

"Then shall we go to Clinton?" I am obliged to be there for a few moments. I will ride my horse, but would like the society of fair ladies. Miss Gladwin," he said, turning to her, "we cannot boast of scenery such as you have looked upon almost daily, but there are fine views here which seem beautiful to an eye unaccustomed to better."

"I think the scene from my window handsome. We had no water visible at my home."

Chapter VIII. A short time previous Mrs. Mann had learned the use of the double triggers of a rifle. With singular presence of mind, and a courage often inspired in the bosoms of the weakest in a moment of danger, this intrepid woman shut the door and barred it, as well as she could, with benches and tables.

"Eriginia, I have a proposition which I hope will meet your approbation. I have wished for sometime to visit Lea's Springs, in Grainger county, and leisure just now to go. I desire your society. A change may restore your cousin to health."

Mrs. Dearing did not relish this proposal greatly. She asked how long her husband would remain.

"Two weeks, or three, at farthest. I may have to go on a dying journey to Savannah."

"Very well, then. We will go. Vinvela, I fear the desolation of these country springs will more likely increase your malady into confirmed ill health than restore your bloom."

Vinvela laughed, and assured Mrs. Dearing that she was inured to isolation and country obscurity, and would soon be quite well without any journey.

"My dear, you have yet to learn that obstinacy is one of the largest bumps phrenology boasts of in the head of man, and Clarek has one of no ordinary dimensions. When he forms a resolution fire, air, earth and water cannot check him."

"Thank you, Eriginia," said her husband, laughing, "you will inspire your cousin with an awe of such a stubborn being."

All the time Minona appeared absorbed in her own reflections, making an occasional remark to the minister.

Mr. Dearing seemed to have forgotten her presence, and the ladies were too much engrossed in their conversation to observe her.

After dinner the party went on the veranda. Vinvela then inquired of Minona:

"Why so gloomy? Where is the spirit of mischief that seemed to dwell with you on my first arrival?"

"Lost. I have been recently on a visit to the cave of Trophonius. Doubtless I left my little vixen there. I shall wear a longer and more sober face hereafter, and forever, than any of those persons Addison describes."

"Enough," retorted Miss Gladwin, "the 'vixen' has not escaped you yet. Tell me the name of your tutor. I did not hear it."

"Reverend Aaron Crews. He always reminds me of the widow's cruse. He is brim full of learning and overflowing with piety."

Again Vinvela laughed, and as Mrs. Dearing and her husband joined them Minona reassured her Trophonistic expression.

The ride to Clinton Vinvela enjoyed very much. Her native cheerfulness of disposition enabled her to drink draughts of pleasure from every occupation, and a genial smile always rewarded her friends for their efforts to amuse her.

Not for a moment has she forgotten her father. Her regrets had assumed the form of a holy solemnity, which came to her in the dark, still hours of the melancholy midnight, when her soul went out, as it were, into space to hold commune with the dead. The spiritual inhalation of a something that had put on immortality, strengthened her, sustained her and was a link in the fast forging chain which was drawing her to Heaven, these shackles to fall away when her pure spirit escaped from it's imprisoning bonds of flesh.

Minona had excused herself from joining the party on the plea of having a puzzling lesson to memorize. Several days had passed since her rencontre with the gardener. Her peace of mind had flown. It was the first serious displeasure her father had ever manifested toward her. Like all reserved, stern men he was intolerant of the absence of self-control—one of the most essential of all virtues to foster in our bosoms if we expect to lead exemplary lives, and the display of rage in a woman, the angelic attributes of whom poets have been prone to expatiate through all ages, Mr. Dearing disliked to witness His deportment to his daughter was distant and polite, which to her was more rebuking than words of censure. Minona desired reconciliation. She felt no hesitation in admitting her fault, but she wished to meet her father alone. As yet no opportunity had presented itself.

On going to the library after tea for a book, as she approached the door she inhaled the fragrant odor of a cigar, which told her Mr. Dearing was within. Here was the coveted moment to explain her conduct. Her hand grew cold and tremulous as it dwelt for a few moments on the slivered door knob. Her heart fluttered with emotion, but nerving herself to still the swelling excitement, she tapped lightly and asked in a low voice for admittance.

"Come in," said her father, who was sitting with his back to the door near a table with a magazine in his hand.

Minona walked rapidly forward with her eyes cast down. As she reached the chair, she placed her arms gently around her parent's neck and said in a subdued tone:

"Father, I am so sorry I offended you the other day. Forgive me and love me again." She looked up then and her beautiful eyes were suffused with tears.

Mr. Dearing's own eyes were moist as he clasped his child and kissed her brow.

"You are forgiven," he said; "but, my daughter, learn to restrain your temper hereafter. It is better for your own peace of mind. If you desire to make a good and great woman, you must practice justice to others, and acquire self-government."

If there be a time when man or woman assumes the aspect of an angel it is when dropping the tear of repentance over the committal of sin. It was the hearing of this pearl of penitence which ope'd the gates of paradise to the patient seeking Peri. It is this contrition

"Whose scent is the breath of Eternity"

Minona explained to her father that she was not aware of his interdict when she sought to gather the grapes for her sick cousin. There was nothing mean in her composition, as she would disdain to be guilty of appropriating what was another's, so she scorned the equal dishonesty of false excuses to palliate her error. Freely she admitted her fault of unmaidenly anger and truthfully she regretted its exhibition. Truly it has been said the first step towards improvement is a knowledge of the wrong. If we feel no guilt how can the desire for amendment come?

After a week of preparations, during which time Vinvela gained strength to prosecute the journey, the party started for Lea's Springs.

Mrs. Dearing, Vinvela, Minona and Mr. Crews went in the phaeton, while Mr. Dearing rode a spirited black steed. A handsomely formed man never appears so well as upon horseback, and our equestrian sat his horse as if a part of him.

Lea's Springs was then a quiet, obscure watering place, with rustic accommodations and pretty scenery. Our travelers passed a pleasant time. Vinvela, from her lameness, was unable to walk any considerable distance; but solitude to her was ever pleasant, and the daily rides were delightful. Her health improved. Her delicate cheeks wore a faint tint of carmine which had not been seen for months.

Minona, happy and joyous again since her reconciliation with her parent, had an exuberance of life that infected her friends. Even silent, diffident Mr. Crews displayed more animation, and ventured an occasional remark to Miss Gladwin.

Mr. Dearing, with his love of the beauties of earth and sky, went on long rambles with Minona, explaining patiently all her numerous questions about everything she saw. He delighted to gratify that curiosity which God implants in the minds of the young for their advancement in learning, but he never checked in his daughter that prying inquisitiveness into subjects which concerned the affairs of others, that intermeddling spirit, the mother of gossip, which blemishes the deportment of so many people.

Of all men, Mr. Dearing had the nicest perceptions of (*unreadable Latin phrase**), practically and theoretically, abstractly and concretely. He endeavored to guide his daughter in that channel through which she would emerge into womanhood with the greatest share of commendable excellencies.

Mrs. Dearing provided a good store of very light reading, and in that way suppressed in a measure the discontent and lassitude, which generally followed her. Her mind was too inane to have any true affinity with her husband. She loved him. She was proud of his talents; she was vain of his person, and she stood in awe of him; but there was little in common in their tastes.

Although Vinvela was so much Mrs. Dearing's junior, she was her superior in solid culture and substantial attainments, Eriginia was disappointed. While she admired and respected the girl, she felt regretful that her hope of a light companion had vanished. Frivolity was wanting.

Mrs. Dearing was a fine tactician in the art of flattery, but before Vinvela's simplicity, her serenity and sweetness of disposition, it was useless. The lady was left as before to see congeniality beyond her home circle.

On the return journey of the party the sky became much overcast, and the clouds increased so much that Mr. Dearing feared the ladies would get drenched with rain. This he knew would injure his wife and Vinvela looked too frail to stand the test of a storm.

Jock drove as rapidly as the roads would allow until they neared Beaver Creek.

"There is a country house near," Jock said to the gentlemen. "Will the ladies stop till the rain is over?"

"A good suggestion. My dear Eriginia, shall we not adopt Jock's idea to remain with these people if they will give a shelter?"

"Certainly, if you are confident it will rain."

"The sky looks threatening; it would be safer to stop," said her husband, "Jock, take my horse. Ride forward and ascertain if we can be received. I will sit here and hold the horses until you return."

The exchange was made, and Hethrington galloped off. A few angry flashes of lightning cleft the western sky, and thunder peals shook the surrounding hills, reverberating in guttural tones in the distance as the sounds died away.

Jock was not long absent, and the announcement was made speedily that the ladies and gentlemen will be welcome at the country house. The party had scarcely alighted before the rain fell in torrents. It was afternoon and there was little hope of a cessation of the storm that night in time to proceed on the journey. The country people consisted of a man, his wife and four children, with the addition of an old grandfather almost too infirm to walk. They were people of extremely limited education, but they were very kind. The very best as such as they had was offered to the impromptu guests. Just before sunset the clouds cleared slightly in the rain ceased.

Mr. Dearing walked out with the farmer to reconnoitre and learn if the weather would admit of their starting home. In the stroll they came upon some gray rocks at the foot of a hill between some of which gaped an opening.

"Is that the entrance to a cave?" asked Mr. Dearing of his companion.

"Yes, sir. I have hearn tell of a man dying thar in the Indian time."

"I should like to hear that account," said Mr. Dearing, approaching and peeping into the mouth of the cavern. "It seems to extend some distance, and would be a good hiding place."

"The old man kin tell you all about it. In happened in his day. Old folks is mighty forgetful 'bout things 'curring every day, but theys purty apt to be mindful of what's long past."

"Very true," replied the gentleman. "Will you ask the old man to tell us the story, if it will not fatigue him? I am fond of Indian legends."

"No danger of tiring him. He's jest like a child, and likes mightily to be allers a talkin'."

A few heavy drops of rain began to descend, and Mr. Dearing proposed returning to the house. The air had grown chilly and the good dame had lighted some faggots on the hearth.

Father Milman expressed a willingness to relate the story, and the ladies were delighted at the prospect of anything marvelous to divert the tedium of a night at a country farm house.

Supper was dispatched, and the family and guests gathered around the wide throated chimney with its cheery blaze. The aged narrator related the following tale, founded upon fact, which is rendered into more legible English than he employed, while the substance is carefully preserved:

"Early in the year 1796 this region was almost a wilderness. Few and far between were the cabins of the early settlers. The vast forests were occupied by wild beasts scarcely yet impressed with the power of civilized man, and afforded secure covert for the stealthy march and deadly ambuscade at the crafty Indian. The earliest white occupants of the soil were, in their habits, almost as hardy and nearly as savage as the Indians themselves. Indeed, the fierce and relentless hostility of the red man had compelled the resolute pioneer to adopt in great measure the same mode of life and style of warfare as those of their foes for their own preservation.

"Into the thickest and most dangerous of these wilds lived a man named George Mann. He had cleared a small lot of trees and undergrowth, and built a log cabin of the roughest architecture. A few necessary outbuildings were constructed and here Mr. Mann, with his wife and children, hoped to earn a living by diligence and frugality.

"Indian incursions were not uncommon, but as yet these simple people were left unmolested, and perhaps flattered themselves into the idea of peace and security, so easily are our fears lulled to rest when danger is unseen.

"So free had these simple-hearted pioneers been from disturbance that they had almost ceased to fear the savages. One night Mr. Mann heard a noise in his stable, and with his mind still in this state of calm safety, he stepped out to ascertain its cause. The Indians, lying in ambush, quickly placed themselves between the man and the door, and intercepted his return to the house. Seeing the situation Mann fled, but not before he was fired upon and wounded. He reached the cave, a quarter of a mile from his house, where he hoped to secrete himself and escape with life; but the foe pursued, dragged him, already weltering in his blood, from his place of concealment and murdered him!

"Having dispatched Mann, they returned to the house to tomahawk his wife and children. Mrs. Mann, unconscious of the fate of her husband, heard them talking to each other as they approached the house. Supposing them neighbors aroused by the firing and coming to her assistance, she felt elate with hope, but as they came nearer she perceived that the conversation was neither English or German, such as the neighbors used, but in an unknown language. She instantly inferred that they were strangers coming to attack her house.

"A short time previous Mrs. Mann had learned the use of the double triggers of a rifle. With singular presence of mind, and a courage often inspired in the bosoms of the weakest in a moment of danger, this intrepid woman shut the door and barred it, as well as she could, with benches and tables. Fortunately, her children were asleep, and with noiseless step she found her way to the spot where lay her husband's well-charged rifle. She grasped the trusty weapon, placed herself in the darkness directly opposite the aperture which would be made by forcing the door. Her husband came not, and she felt sure that he was slain. She was alone in the silence. Her poor babes were sleeping unconscious of danger. The yelling savages were without pressing the door from its hinges. The stillness, the darkness, the suspense was oppressive, but the woman was undaunted. She thought of her babes; she mutely appealed to her God and awaited the foe. They, pushing with great violence, gradually pressed the door open wide enough to enter. The body of one was thrust into the opening struggle for admittance, while two or three more, directly behind him, were forcing him forward.

"The woman, with the calmness of a heroine, set the trigger of her rifle, placed the muzzle near the body of the foremost savage, aiming her weapon so that the ball passing through him might penetrate those in the rear, and fired.

"The first Indian fell mortally wounded; the next uttered a scream of agony as the ball pierced his body. Seeing the policy of silence the women uttered no sound, and remained still on the spot near the door. The Indians, by these tokens, supposed the house full of armed men. Gathering up their wounded they withdrew, stealing three horses from the stables and setting it on fire.

"It was subsequently ascertained that Mrs. Mann had, by her intrepidity, saved herself and her children from the attack of twenty-five assailants.

"The country people called the cavern Mann's Cave, and for many years believed the spirits of the pioneer in his daring wife dwelt within it's gloomy depths."

So ended the venerable man's story.

The effect of the thrilling narrative and the listeners was different. To the heroic natures of Mr. Dearing and his daughter, the wild courage of the pioneer and his faithful wife was exalted in majestic proportion tempered by regretful tenderness over the man's tragic death. To Vinvela's gentle heart the self-immolation of true womanhood, exhibited in the devoted wife and mother, was the chiefest charm.

Blood and carnage, even when surrounded with the splendors of bravery, could not elicit her admiration or suppress her horror. Mr. Crews turned from the earthly sufferings of the unfortunate couple to the joys they experienced in Heaven, reached through the gates of death.

To Mrs. Dearing's lighter mental calibre the horrors of the murder set into keener life all the superstitions of a weak nature.

Mr. Dearing thanked the old man for his kindness in affording himself and the ladies such an entertaining legend, and expressed his desire to explore the cavern.

Mrs. Dearing declared she was fearful she might encounter the shades of Mr. and Mrs. Mann, and would defer deciding upon the proposition until day dawned. Her nerves were all in an aspen quiver.

As Vinvela and Minona rose to retire, Mr. Dearing offered to loan them his revolver.

"I feel convinced that you young ladies dread an Indian assault tonight. Would you not like to be prepared to repel it?" he asked laughing.

"I have sufficient daring, I hope, father," replied Minona, "without the assistance of weapons; and I can hear an attack from such fanciful quarters."

"And I," said Vinvela, "am calm to apathy, and feel as if I shall sleep too soundly to be disturbed even by a dream of the red man."

"There are various grades and shades of courage in this world, and I think that the most prominent and widely diffused is that which is loudly proclaimed when the foe is invisible, but flies rapidly as danger approaches. However, I shall require from each one of you a strict account of your sensations to-night after hearing so thrilling a tale," answered the gentlemen as he bade good-night to the girls.

The party then retired for the evening, and were up early the next morning, which was cool and as lovely as a beautiful naiad dripping with pellucid water-drops.

Now, young ladies," said Mr. Dearing, after the morning salutation, "imagine me your Father confessor, and make a clear shrill. Miss Gladwin I hope you slept well."

"My slumbers were somewhat disturbed by my young friend," she replied glancing mischievously at Minona, "who fancied she'd heard the stealthy tread of the blood-thirsty Indians, and saw the shadowy ghosts of the murdered pioneer and his faithful wife flit by in the moonlight."

"Unfortunately," said Minona, shrugging her shoulders, "my imagination is set upon such finely-tempered springs that the slightest touch of the tragic puts them in motion, and their vilnatory* action is very apt to jostle my proximate neighbors unpleasantly. But, father," she added, "I own that excellent sort of courage which shrinks aghast in expectation of danger, but when it comes I am as firm as a granite rock. I would make a second Mrs. Mann," she said, laughing.

"Very well. Perhaps I shall live to see this vaunted courage tested, my little girl."

"I shall be a heroine if you do," answered the laughing girl, in the same mocking tone of raillery. "Ask Vinvela how she slept; and mamma, she looks pale."

"Oh! I saw ghosts of the unfortunate couple, and the pursuing copper men too; but I slept quietly, and am safe and well this morning, as you see, Mr. Dearing," said Miss Gladwin.

"I must answer for Eriginia," said Mr Dearing, pretending to yawn. "She kept me up all night, declaring she saw Mr. Mann with his glazed eyes riveted on her."

"I will candidly admit that I am timid, and I felt the cold touch of the murdered man thrill with a shivering sensation every time I closed my eyes. Clarek, you will do penance for having this story related in my presence by many a sleepless night."

"We have not heard your account, Mr. Crews," said Vinvela, turning to the modest little gentleman.

Mr. Crews moved his hands nervously, then played with his watch chain, moved his head to one side, and with an effort, looked up at Miss Gladwin and replied in a timid voice:

"I dreamed of seeing a sprite; but she was not old. As she swept out of the window she turned, and the face was young and lovely, and her look filled me with beatitude past expression."

"You are a minister, Mr. Crews," remarked Minona. "It must have been an angel come to bear you to Heaven."

"I hope so," was the quiet reply.

"Do tell us who it was," again pleaded Minona, "and I will recite double lessons when I return home."

"Angels never give their names," and Mr. Crews blushed at the reflection that he had ventured to say more at one time than ever before.

"Clarek, you must relate your experience," said his wife. "As you bring our follies to light, yours must not remain in obscurity. I suspect your nerves are a little tremulous."

"Certainly, my dear; I am so sympathetic that your ailments generally affect me. Are you not a happy wife to exert so powerful an influence? But time flies; what decision have you made about visiting the cave?"

"I think it wiser to return home," answered Mrs. Dearing.

"Very well. I will remain a short time, as I really desire to explore the place, and Mr. Milman is prepared to go. I will overtake you."

This was agreed to, and Mr. Crews was left in charge of the ladies, who, after bidding kindly adieus to the family of Mr. Milman, pursued their homeward journey.

Chapter IX. At this remark, Minona rose from her seat. Her face was pale, her eyes glittered with a diamond brilliancy; her lips were firmly compressed, and she almost hissed through her set teeth. "Base villain! were I only armed, as you are, you would not ask a second time for our goods!" The robber looked up astonished, and an expression of admiration shot from his eye as he glanced at the undaunted girl confronting him.

CHAPTER IX.

It was in the early part of August,

"One of those heavenly days which cannot die,"

when the phaeton of Mrs. Dearing left the house of Mr. Milman and moved along the homeward road. The route lay beside picturesque knobs, selling hills, and undulating fields of grain. Vegetation seemed to dwell in a state of perfect repose. All vegetable growth had reached its plentitude of perfection.

"Nature, though full of life, was calm as death."

This beautiful verse, expressive of that living stagnation nature wears for a season of each summer—that period when the growth of spring and summer has ceased, and the death of autumn has not arrived, emanated from the pen of a gifted genius of the seacoast of Georgia—a man whose name yet remains to be sounded by the trumpet of fame; although he nobly acted his part in the great drama of life and now sleeps his last sleep beneath a tall shaft of Italian marble upon the ocean-washed shore of his native State.

The carriage reached a long "ridge" which sweeps through the valley of East Tennessee, and is known by the name of Copper Ridge. This is a misnomer, as the formation has no trace of copper within its depths, but bears upon its surface immense trees of oak and hickory which form a vast forest. The ridge is sparsely inhabited, and the road winds westward up a gentle ascent upon a ledge dug into the sides of the slope.

The carriage had reached the top of the ridge where the route lay upon comparatively level ground, bordered by occasional fields of maize, with its graceful pliant stalks uplifting the burden of fruitage, and its wavy leaves sporting like long, green ribbons in the soft-breathing wind.

Turning an abrupt curve brought it in sight of two men sitting by the wayside. One was a large, brawny mountaineer, with unshorn hair and beard of goodly length, and of a red hue. He wore a slouched hat somewhat shabby, and his clothing was course and soiled. Little of the face was visible through the mass of hair which surrounded it, and which was more like a lion's mane than a human ornament. The hat drawn low over the brow shaded the eyes from view. His companion was shorter and of stouter build. His head was bare; locks tangled and long, with a pair of glaring, daredevil eyes, which would have graced the head of a grave-digging hyena better than that of a man. He wore no jacket, and the unclosed shirt bosom and rolled-up sleeves displayed a massive chest and arms, tanned by exposure and strengthened by muscles resembling whip-chords. Altogether they were a savage, brigandish looking pair. Mrs. Dearing, constitutionally timid, felt her heart bound, and then by a revulsionary action, stop its motion a moment, and then beat on in a fluttering manner under the compression of fear.

As the vehicle arrived abreast of them, and she hoped her alarm was groundless, the hatless fellow called out in a harsh, coarse, manner:

"Hello, mister! what time o' day is it?"

The Rev. Crews, courteous at all times to great and small in worldly station, drew out a handsome gold chronometer with a heavy fob-chain. The clerical gentleman appeared to concentrate his love for the vanities of the world in the possession of a costly watch and its massive appendages.

In a distinct voice he told the hour, "ten o'clock."

"Much obliged, stranger," said the fellow with the hat, rising and staring at Mr. Crews.

There was an unmistakable cupidity in the glittering eye, which Minona caught a glimpse of as he passed his hand over his forehead slightly elevating his hat.

The carriage proceeded, winding around a long semicircle, leaving the wayfarers in the rear. Mrs. Dearing breathed freely, and said to Minona in a low voice:

"My love, I did not like the looks of those men. I wish Clarek would overtake us. Had they attacked us, we would have been in a sad plight with no weapons."

At the mention of her father, Minona blanched ghastly white. By a rapid flight of thought, she recalled the fate of the brave George Mann and his untimely fate, and imagination pictured her father seized unawares and murdered by these men whom she felt were highwaymen.

Her terrifying reflections were cut short by a sudden halt of the phaeton and a shriek from her mother. As they turned the curving road the hatless villain had grasped the bridle reins, throwing the horses back on their haunches in the violence of the jerk, while the taller one demanded of Mr. Crews the watch he had so plainly displayed.

Mr. Crews, far more timid in the presence of ladies than a bashful girl, appeared strangely composed, and replied to the robber, saying:

"I prefer keeping my watch for my own use, friend. By what right do you make so bold a request?"

"By this!" exclaimed he, with a blasphemous oath, drawing a large revolver and place it against the minister's breast.

"Yer money, ladies, I must have. Sorry to distress you, but need knows no laws, is a sayin'."

At this remark, Minona rose from her seat. Her face was pale, her eyes glittered with a diamond brilliancy; her lips were firmly compressed, and she almost hissed through her set teeth.

"Base villain! were I only armed, as you are, you would not ask a second time for our goods!"

The robber looked up astonished, and an expression of admiration shot from his eye as he glanced at the undaunted girl confronting him. His purpose seemed to waver for a moment; then, with another oath, grasped the minister's arm, again saying:

"Give up yer watch, or I'll shoot!"

"Fire then," said the man of God. "I fear not death."

Minona in an instant bent forward and struck the pistol aside, and the ball passed behind Mr. Crews, doing no damage.

The robber, deprived of his prey, glared at Minona, and, addressing Mr. Crews, he exclaimed:

"Give yer watch, or I'll shoot the girl!" at the same time aiming his pistol at her.

Mr. Crews, unyielding before when peril encompassed him alone, no sooner filtered extended to Miss Dearing than he exclaimed:

"Spare her! If the gold will leave her untouched, it is yours," and he slipped the watch into the robber's hand.

The villain had no notion of leaving Minona. Her bold bearing had inspired him with an admiration, and he determined to capture her as a part of the booty. But just at the moment he was about to drag her from the carriage, Jock Hethrington who had been surprised by the suddenness of the attack and the celerity of events, aroused from his torpor. Slipping from his seat he dealt the robber who held the horses a heavy blow with the whip-stock, causing him to cry out.

The hatted rogue ran to the rescue, and Hethrington would soon had been overpowered and sent "where the wicked cease from troubling" had not Mr. Dearing appeared on the scene. Seeing at a glance the state of things, he fired several successive shots, which puts the foe to flight. Springing from his horse, he darted in pursuit and soon overtook the taller fugitive who was wounded by one of the shots from his pistol. As Mr. Dearing approached, the outlaw, feeling that his strength was failing and having one load undischarged, fired his pistol in the hope of disabling his pursuer. The ball whizzed through Mr. Dearing's hat he as he returned the shot and brought the highwayman down.

Going up to him Mr. Dearing perceived blood gushing from his side and arm.

"Curses on you for meddlin' with my game!" he muttered through his set teeth.

"I could not see you murder my family, man. It is too late now for regrets. Can I do anything for you?"

Oaths and imprecations issued from the robber's stiffening lips, and a stare of hate and defiance shot from his glaring eye in response to this question.

Seeing that one outlaw was dying, and that the other had escaped, Mr. Dearing returned to the carriage to encourage and pacify his family. His wife, under Minona's remedies, was fast recovering. Miss Gladwin had looked on in silence during the action, and was now aiding Minona in restoring consciousness to her mother.

Mr. Crews had regained his watch, which had fallen in the rencontre between Jock and the brigands.

Not knowing but the escaped robber might return with other confederates, Mr. Dearing recharged his weapon and ordering Jock to drive rapidly, they continued their journey, and reached home in the afternoon.

Minona's boast of her courage was not idle.

"Mr. Dearing," said Vinvela, as he handed her out of the carriage. "I never witnessed or read of more intrepid conduct. She is indeed a heroine."

There was a film over Mr. Dearing's dark, pensive blue eyes at the description of his young daughter's bearing under peril. Lifting his wife from the phaeton he carried her to her room. She was ill from excitement for several days, and would scarce suffer her husband to leave her for a moment.

"Miss Gladwin," said Mr. Dearing, a few days after the exciting little episode had occurred, "I have a proposal to submit to you, but must prelude it by a question. Shall I proceed?"

"Yes, sir. Ask any questions you like, and I will respond to them with pleasure."

"Then, do you consider your education finished? In one sense the pursuit of learning should occupy us through life, as this existence is given us for progression and expansion; but I refer particularly to the academic course followed in early life."

"I do not feel that it is. I never went to school a day. My father," she added, with a slight quiver in her voice, "was my sole teacher."

"Will you join Minona in her studies? You are doubtless more advanced; but it will be advantageous to her, and may be beneficial to you."

"I will do as you propose with pleasure. There is a delight to me in mental investigations. They had been manna in the wilderness of otherwise dreary life, cut off as I am, by my infirmity, from the amusements of other young people."

Vinvela was standing in the veranda and she spoke, leaning on her crutch. There was no bitterness, no morbid sensitiveness as she alluded to her deformity. Her fair, young face and her dark eyes, made a deeper blue from the long, jetty lashes warrant expression of holy serenity and perfect amiability. No rude jeers, no unmannerly teasings had ever fretted her temper or wounded her feelings. She was eminently thankful for the blessings she enjoyed—contented with her situation, and experienced no desire to quarrel with mankind, or rebel against her Maker because of her disfiguring malformation.

It was this entire absence of misanthropy, more than her apparent superiority in other respects, that inspired Mr. Dearing with so much compassion for her misfortune. Man is never so sublime as when seen unbent by the weight of affliction! The great Napoleon in the zenith of his glory, when he shot forth in the political heaven a mighty star of the first magnitude, whose brilliant rays dazzled all Europe, and extinguish the sickly crown-lights of the Eastern continent, was never exalted to such a height of admiration; was never so grandly great as when a persecuted, insulted, tortured, yet unsubdued prisoner on the solitary rock of St. Helena, isolated from the world of life and of hope by the inky billows of a vast ocean. Had he escaped to America he might have found oblivion, St. Helena was his shrine for perpetual adoration; the towering shaft that elevated his statute to a sublime height above all other heroes.

Mr. Dearing continued:

"Eriginia intends having some company very soon. Unlike you, Miss Gladwin, they are giddy butterflies ever on the wing, who sip pleasure from cups of folly, and quaff draughts of emptiness all the days of their useless lives. These are to be accompanied by a full complement of shallow-pated coxcombs, whose occupations seem circumscribed to cultivating a handsome mustache, lisping pretty compliments to their delighted hearers, smoking fine cigars and killing time, that mighty Titan so frightfully oppressive to most people."

"You are severe," said Miss Gladwin, laughing heartily. "What would you have young people do? Wear cowls and go about executing deeds of charity?"

"Better that than decapitating all their best traits under the guillotine of frivolity and then losing soul itself. I could preach a homily against the abuses of society. But to answer your question. All reflective minds, all the greatest of philosophers, have recognized the need of recreation through all stages of existence. But let it be in moderation, not a monopoly. We must foster the Divine essence within us by graver deportment, improve it by energetic employment, to enable our souls to return perfected to the Divinity when called for."

"You are right, Mr. Dearing. I was reared in the belief of just such opinions as you express. How much I wish you could have met my excellent father! Your sentiments were his. And I remember, when a little child, of being inspired with a determination to live for some purpose. As yet I have attained nothing."

This allusion to her father and her own imperfection was uttered in a low, musical tone of pathos irresistible in its unmeant appeal for sympathy.

"We have digressed," said Mr. Dearing, "What I meant to say, specially, when I began our conversation, was that Minona is at the most irrepressible of all ages. She is pliant clay in the hands of the potter. Will you be the artificer to mould my daughter into the form which ought to adorn a true woman? I ask this because she will be more with you, and the young exert greater influence upon the shaping of each other's characters, than all the efforts of parental teachings. I would not have my child led astray by the giddy company she will soon meet. Exert some control over her during our visitors' stay, and you will obtain my lasting obligation. She is impulsive and stormy, and Eriginia and myself will be necessarily engaged with guests."

"I will do all I can for you," replied Vinvela.

"Thank you, Miss Gladwin. To-morrow Mr. Crews will be prepared for your installation as a pupil. Remember, I am a strict governor of school girls," he added, laughing, and bowing he walked in the direction of the stable, and was soon heard riding to Clinton.

Vinvela was musing over the mark of confidence just placed upon her, and the superior calibre of mind and heart Mr. Dearing must possess by the glimpse she had from their conversation, when a soft, jeweled hand touched her shoulder, and the voice of Mrs. Dearing accosted her.

"Why so sad, cousin? Has Clarek startled you by a list of his gloomy notions about propriety, and what ladies must live for?"

"No," answered Vinvela. "I do not think him gloomy. He proposed I should join Minona in her studies."

"I hope you refused, my dear. I shall offer you something far more agreeable to occupy you than conning, tiresome text books. Next week our house will be enlivened by some of the most charming, elegant and fashionable of young people from Savannah. Won't we have a gay time? Clarek promises to get a band of music from Clinton."

And the lady hummed a tune, and skipped through a few steps of dancing.

"I accepted his invitation, cousin. I am scarcely more than a school girl, although I never attended a school in my life."

"Nonsense, Vinvela! Are you going to waste your beauty on a small, sanctimonious, unappreciative parson? He would never see your beautiful eyes; for him they would be hidden as securely as a mole's. With your attractions, you can captivate Mr. Torrister, the greatest beau and best catch in Savannah. I cannot hear, my love, of your secluding yourself in this fashion."

"But, cousin. I have already promised your husband."

"Pshaw! fiddlesticks! Clarek is a monomaniac on some points. I invited this company as much for your diversion as my own. I expect to bring you out next winter, and the summer's campaign is the initiatory step. Come! ladies are privileged; tell Clarek you have changed your notion."

"Dear cousin," said Vinvela, "you forget my mourning and my misfortune will ill fit me to enter freely into society. I cannot recede from my promise. I will be with you between school hours and aid you to entertain your friends as well as I can."

"You are incorrigible—as great a prude as Clarek delights in and wishes to make Minona. I am really vexed," and the lady swept into the house.

The ensuing day Vinvela repaired at nine o'clock to the Blue Room. Mr. Crews was alone. She had not seen him, except at table, since the hour of peril when he had displayed so much courage to the robbers. At meals he was shy and silent. As she entered he looked up, rose, bade her good morning, handed her a chair, and with something of a ray of pleasure lighting his transparent face, expressed his satisfaction at the honor she conferred by becoming his pupil.

"I trust I may gain honors under your guidance by my diligence in my studies," modestly replied Miss Gladwin, seating herself in the proffered chair.

Minona soon appeared, and the morning orisons were repeated with a simple, heartfelt fervor which touched Miss Gladwin's heart deeply, prone, as it always was, to go up in adoration to her Maker. There was no reserve, no embarrassment; the soul seemed to soar aloft above all earthly entanglements when seeking the presence of the Great Creator.

While Minona pursued her task, Mr. Crews passed Vinvela through a cursory review of the books Minona was studying. In teaching he appeared to forget self as a member of society, and remember only his duty as instructor.

"I fear you find this sadly deficient," said Miss Gladwin. "Owing to ill health, my education has been of the most desultory character."

"Miss Dearing in a few studies is more advanced; but you are her superior in the majority. It would avoid complication and delay if you will consent to begin with her in all."

Vinvela agreed, and her lessons were set. Before the morning was over she was fairly embarked in her new character of a school girl. She liked it.

Soon after tea each night, Mr. Dearing passed an hour in the Blue Room to enjoy the luxury of a cigar, and at such times Minona was required to be present. Questions were asked on her lessons for the day, books discussed, and extracts read from any volume under investigation. These hours, in course of time, became a source of great but melancholy pleasure to Vinvela. They recalled most forcibly the days spent in commune with her father. There was something in the scope of intellect, and in the grasp of a subject when handled by Mr. Dearing, which cast a flood of light before her, opening out new glimpses of his character and expanding her views. After a while the little coterie was enlarged by the addition of Mr. Crews, who begged leave to join them; and before the close of summer it was swelled by yet another member.

Vinvela saw little of Mrs. Dearing during the week. She was busied with preparations for her expected guests who were sure arrive early the following week. When she did meet Vinvela there was a slight stiffness of manner which savored of resentment.

The eventful day at length came and the carriage and buggy were dispatched to Clinton. Everything had an air of excitement. Servants passed and repassed each other wearing mysterious looks portentous of some coming event of great importance. Mrs. Dearing, after seeing the finishing polish put in every department, retired to arrange her toilet for the reception of her guests. Dinner was postponed to a later hour than usual. Minona and Vinvela made a slight change in their dress and sauntered through the rooms on a tour of inspection.

"I do not much relish this influx of people, cousin," said Minona. "I had just began my studies under full headway, and here is this interruption. I do not believe papa likes it, either."

"Your father told me we were to continue our school, and we shall see comparatively little of the company."

"True, if you could but checkmate imagination and keep it motionless, one might gain some knowledge, but all the study under Heaven is useless with the brain dancing and giddy whirl after other things."

"Are you acquainted with your guests, Minona?"

"I believe I have seen them all, but never cared much to cultivate them last winter. Now, I feel differently. I shall soon be in society myself." And she elevated her form to its full height. "Dear me," she continued, "I am tanned browner than an Arab," as she caught a glimpse of her face in the opposite mirror.

"This is the germ of vanity," thought Vinvela, "which Mr. Dearing dreads developing."

The sound of carriage wheels put an end to reflection, and Mrs. Dearing called the girls to assist in welcoming the visitors.

First, Helen and Lucy Christie alighted from the phaeton. They were of such diminutive stature that they could with grace have joined in the festivities of Titania's court. Veritable fairies they looked, with their light curls and fair faces as the bounded over the sward with elastic step.

"Dear Mrs. Dearing, how we rejoice to see you! We thought we should never reach it here," they both exclaimed in a breath. "Is this Minona?" turning and kissing her. "Quite a young lady, I declare!" said Lucy, addressing Helen.

Then swept in Miss Edwiston; tall, stately, and with a hauteur which said emphatically: "I am an object worthy of all admiration, I exact it as a right." She greeted Mrs. Dearing with a slightly patronizing air, extended the tips of her gloved fingers in Rev. Sidney Smith's genuine "high official" manner of salutation to Minona, and bowed stiffly to Miss Gladwin, surveying her, crutch and all, with one sweep of her telescopic vision.

The imperious lady was followed by Miss Elmira Hollis, a young lady of fifty-five; short, stout, and good humored in appearance. She was much dressed. In a very strong light or shadow of a wrinkle might be seen or fancied on her face by an acute observer. She possessed a substratum of common sense under a superincumbent mass of levity. The latter is endurable, sometimes even agreeable, when it rests on the solid basis of the former.

She met Mrs. Dearing warmly, and spoke kindly to Minona and Vinvela.

This phalanx of feminine charms was accompanied by three gentlemen; Mr. Hogan, Mr. Neave, and Mr. Torrister. As this last ascended the step, Minona pulled Miss Gladwin's dress, saying:

"Mr. Torrister," in a low tone, "the Czar Kolokol, or Monarch beau of Savannah. He has an

'Eye like Mars, to threaten and command.'"

Mr. Torrister was tall, with limbs formed for agility, grace and strength. His head was large and finally set on his shoulders, and the dark hair was long, wavy, and thrown back, displaying a high forehead. The face was good, and the owner was well convinced of the fact.

He was presented to the young ladies, and acknowledge the acquaintance with a bow of the most precise conformity to the rules of polished etiquette.

Mr. Hogan and Mr. Neave were neither remarkable for personal appearance, but fair specimens of the elite in city circles.

The ladies were ushered into their apartments to prepare for dinner, and refresh themselves after their fatigue.

Miss Gladwin and Minona joined Mr. Dearing in the parlor, before the other guests appeared, previous to the announcement of dinner.

"Miss Dearing," said Mr. Torrister, approaching, "I did not recognize you when I saw you on the veranda. How much you have changed since last winter! You are quite a young lady. How do you exist shut up in these mountain dells?"

"I rise early; feast my eyes on the loveliest of scenery; expand my lungs with the purest air; then take a hearty repast from the toughest school books, and wind up by a dessert of light literature. After this, I ride or run through the hills for recreation; then an evening meal of substantial reading and sage conversation under the direction of a stern father. One day is an epitome of the summer. Do you like the programme?" asked the girl, laughing.

"No; my constitution is too delicate to bear such strong nutriment."

"I should judge so, Mr. Torrister, from your appearance," said the young lady, with a roguish twinkle of her beautiful eyes.

The gentleman did not know whether to regard this as a compliment or not.

"Sharp-witted as well as handsome—an heiress, too," he inwardly muttered, as the other ladies swept in as an avalanche glides down the Alps.

Then came the busy buzz of tongues, with intermingling chirrups of affected laughter, which was as confusing as the language of the Batel architects, or the Pigeon English of the Chinese. Happily the announcement of dinner put an extinguisher, for a season, upon the clatter, and the fair ladies had a period of rest from their lingual labors.

Mrs. Dearing's table, had it been animate, would have felt weary and the weight of dainties spread out for the delicate palates of her guests. The ladies' languishing eyes grew bright, and their rounded cheeks assumed a more vivid peach tint under the circulation of sparkling champagne. The quiet gloaming of evening drew near ere the party returned to the drawing-room.

Miss Edwiston was a fine performer on the piano. She handled the instrument as a monarch would his sceptre; and there was a tone of royalty in her music as there was a regal air in her every action. The sisters, Christie, played some simple duets, and saying sweetly in hummingbird tones.

Mr. Torrister devoted himself to Minona. While her satirical vein disconcerted him, and wounded slightly his ineffable self-love, the hope of delving eventually into her fortune, which he magnified into gold mine proportion, excited his cupidity, and cheered him as much as the expectation of gathering a golden harvest did the fainting followers of Cortez on the mountains of Mexico.

The new-comers bestowed very little notice on Miss Gladwin, and she found herself in close propinquity to Mr. Crews. He, after several ineffectual attempts, finally mustered enough resolution to address a few remarks to her. She was agreeably surprised at his conversation. Some of his painful diffidence was put to flight before her gentle, unassuming deportment.

"Are you fond of company?" he asked, his hands toying nervously with his fob-chain.

To diffident persons it is a real comfort and feeling of security to have the hands move in measured concert with the lips.

"I do not object to it, but prefer a life of seclusion. I believe with De Quincy that 'solitude is essential to man.'"

"It is like light, the mightiest of all agencies, for all that is holiest and best within us. I have experienced all the varying shades of solitude that author describes so magnificently," he said.

The tones of a guitar came floating through the open window, and a clear, plaintive voice began a touching little Spanish song, buenas noches.

Vinvela looked up and encountered the gaze of the unobtrusive, bashful little minister fixed ardently upon her. His face colored as if caught in some overt act of treason. Without apparent notice of this, Miss Gladwin inquired who was singing.

"Your cousin and schoolmate," answered Mr. Crews.

"I was not aware she played upon any instrument. Her voice is full, mellow, and musical."

A deep-toned bass joined in the melody as she spoke. The voices, the guitar accompaniment, the faint perfume of flowers, the starlit evening, and the distant euphony of the river murmuring at its fall over the old mill-dam, filled the soul of Miss Gladwin with harmony.

Very soon thereafter the party dispersed for the night, and silence for a brief season held reign throughout the mansion of the "Eagle Bend," coming "like a poultice"—to use the quaint simile of Thomas Hood—"to heal the blows of sound."

Chapter X. An excursion on the river was planned for the afternoon following Dr. Crandon's visit. Hugh Portwood, Miss Gladwin, the Misses Christie, Mr. Neave (devotee to Miss Lucy) and Mr. Hogan were in one boat. Mrs. Dearing, Miss Edwiston, Miss Hollis and Minona, attended by Mr. Dearing, Mr. Torrister and Mr. Crews, were in the larger craft.

CHAPTER X.

Although the stables on Mr. Dearing's farm did not wear the imposing exterior of a castle surrounded with walls, towers and a moat, as those of Lorenzo the magnificent did at his favorite villa, the Ambra, they held a goodly number of fine horses, and Mrs. Dearing and her guests were not slow in appropriating them to add to their amusement. Rides and drives through the surrounding country were projected daily, and Minona found, despite all her resolution to devote her mind each morning to study, that she was more often absent on excursions with her city friends.

This giddy round of gayety did not affect or attract Vinvela. She was less impulsive, and had her thoughts better trained to concentration upon the employment before her.

About a week after the arrival of the first guests, there came a fourth gentleman. This was Mr. Dearing's confidential clerk, or rather agent, who had just returned from Europe, where he had gone as supercargo to one of Mr. Dearing's large merchant vessels.

Mr. Hugh Portwood, at this stage, was in the springtime of manhood. He was large, symmetrically formed, and possessed a face wherein inherent nobility and great intellectual ability seemed stamped instead of the less to be prized beauty of features. His manners were self-possessed, unpretending, unobtrusive, courteous, and slightly reserved to all, except his employer. When alone with him there was a welling of affectionate, gratitude, and unreserved utterance of any thought which could be framed into words. "The sympathies of mind, like the laws of chemical affinity, are uniform;" and between these two men there was an irresistible attraction, although widely diverged in station, in knowledge, and in mental idiosyncrasies.

During the sojourn of so many visitors, Vinvela had resigned her chamber and occupied the adjacent small room with Minona.

This arrangement was pleasing to both girls, and was continued afterwards during the whole of Miss Gladwin's residence at her cousin's.

More frequent opportunities were offered to Vinvela for counteracting the influences operating to lead Minona away from the sober paths of knowledge and reason; and the overflowing mirth and mischief of the latter, kept at bay the monster melancholy, and prevented it from trespassing on the lame girl.

One afternoon Minona had completed her toilet, and while awaiting her cousin, stood idly gazing through the open window. The apartment was at the back of the house, and the side window overlooked the road leading to Clinton.

"I declare!" exclaimed Minona, "if there is not our walking dispensatory, Dr. Crandon, and his amiable sister, Isabel. Vinvela, adorn yourself in your most becoming habiliments, and assume your most angelic expression to welcome the twain. They told me last Sunday at church they would call, but I forgot to mention it."

"I do not suppose their visit is meant for me, specially. What kind of a lady is Miss Crandon?" asked Vinvela.

"She has the highest of recommendations to gentlemen that of been a prim, tidy housewife, 'only that and nothing more.' Personally, she is as antiquated as a belle as that which struck the hours in the clock sent by the famous Haroun al Raschid to Charlemagne in the ninth century."

"You are the most satiric commentator on personal beauty I ever listened to. I would not like to have you draw comparisons on my look," said Miss Gladwin, striving to look grave.

"Just withhold your ani-madversions on the enormity of my remarks. If you please, until you see the fair Isabel, and then commend me for an accurate observer," replied, Minona, demurely. "Are you ready? Let us go down," she continued, and they left the room.

They found the other ladies assembled and discussing the plan of attending a Methodist camp-meeting, which would take place at the Blowing Spring Camp Ground at the close of the week.

"My cousin, Miss Gladwin, Miss Crandon," said Minona, with the most accomplished grace; and the young ladies found seats in the circle.

Dr. Crandon brought a chair and placed himself near Vinvela.

"Glad to find that I had the honor of restoring your health, Miss Gladwin," he remarked, in measured cadence. "Yes, yes! I was fearful you would have a serious time–yes–ah."

This last "yes" seemed to be the grace note which concluded all Dr. Crandon's tongue performances, and acted as a kind of connecting link to his next remark, always.

Vinvela expressed her gratitude for her recovery in appropriate tones.

"Yes, yes; your febrile symptoms were strong; the afternoon exacerbation extreme–yes, extreme. I am glad to see you so robust. Yes, yes! completely convalescent now. Ah, yes!"

Vinvela was at a loss what reply to make, and, in looking around to address Miss Crandon, she encountered the roguish twinkle of Minona's eye, and almost gave way to her risibility.

Fortunately the doctor left very soon. Miss Crandon extended a warm invitation to the ladies on call.

Miss Isabel Crandon was genuinely worthy and polite in her deportment; but her costume was fashioned somewhat after the picturesque style of the antediluvians. Minona's comments were not far wrong.

Mr. Dearing still exacted one hour of each night from Miss Gladwin and his daughter, after which they were at liberty to mingle with the guests. He watched Minona's growing fondness for gayety with a jealous eye. He exhibited, of late fits of moodiness when observing her, which her pleasant raillery failed to divert and her questions could not penetrate. She had developed with surprising rapidity and was now a graceful, handsome girl with a regal expression of face. Her vivacity and wit were never ceasing, and she was attractive and irresistible in manner. Light-hearted and pursuing pleasure with an eagerness felt alone in youth, she was never too gay or too much occupied to perceive the slightest shade upon her father's brow, and at such times would leave others to endeavor to dispel the cloud. Hugh Portwood, still studious, gained permission to join the "Blue Room Club," as he termed it, and being a fine reader, his presence added to the interest of the meetings.

Mrs. Dearing inclined to Methodism in her religious worship, and it had been decided to attend the camp meeting. Miss Crandon sent an invitation to have the ladies occupy a part of her tent, which was commodious, and the invitation was accepted.

An excursion on the river was planned for the afternoon following Dr. Crandon's visit. Hugh Portwood, Miss Gladwin, the Misses Christie, Mr. Neave (devotee to Miss Lucy) and Mr. Hogan were in one boat. Mrs. Dearing, Miss Edwiston, Miss Hollis and Minona, attended by Mr. Dearing, Mr. Torrister and Mr. Crews, were in the larger craft. The gentlemen managed the oars, and much mirth was caused by the awkward attempts of the city gentleman at rowing. They went some distance up the stream, whose precipitous wooded shores, and the blue mountains, looming grandly in the distance, called forth enthusiastic admiration from Miss Helen and Miss Lucy, Vinvela sat near Mr. Portwood, and their conversation was diversified by many topics. The moon rose "round as the shield: of Ossian's "father's," and cast her weird in witching light upon the winding Pellissippi before their return.

Minona's guitar and the chorus of voices mingled in the liquid sighing of the stream as they glided down the current. Each light heart breathed a sigh of regret as they approached the shelving shore. The larger boat discharged its living cargo safely and some of the ladies from the other had disembarked. As Vinvela attempted to step from the boat it parted from the shore, and she was precipitated in the water. Mr. Portwood was handing her out and rescued her almost as quickly as she fell with slight damage. The Little Savannah fairies shrieked romantically and brought many of the party who were going to the house back to the spot. Throwing a shawl around Miss Gladwin, Mr. Portwood insisted upon bearing her to the house, and in truth she had received some injuries and a shock which would have prevented her from walking. Very gently Hugh bore his light burden into the house and placed her upon a lounge in the Blue Room. Soon afterward she was removed to her own apartment, and preventatives against cold were administered.

As Minona was getting some articles from the bureau she observed a handsome bouquet with a card upon which was traced in delicate characters Vinvela's name. She was about to hand it to her cousin when her eye fell upon a note addressed to herself, in the scrawling chirography of a new-beginner. Her attention was at that time needed by her cousin, and she slipped the mysterious note in her pocket with the bouquet, which also surprised her, she approached her cousin's bed.

"Here are your flowers, Vinvela," she said. "What devoted swain could have sent them?" and she looked directly at her cousin to detect her embarrassment.

"I do not know. I have received several in the same way, but supposed it was some of your mischief."

"I assure you I had nothing to do with it," answered Minona.

It was sometime before Miss Dearing had leisure to examine her note. The orthography was wretched, the writing blurred and crooked. It contained but a few sentences, and, when translated into good English, ran thus:

> *"Come to me at sunset to-morrow on the Cedar Bluff, at the Indian tombs. I will impart to you and mystery of vital importance, and deeply concerning your future destiny.*
>
> *A FRIEND."*

Minona's first impression was to hand the note to her father, but second thought determined her to remain silent, at least for a season, until she had time for mature reflection as to the probable source of the communication. With the exception of Dr. Crandon and his sister her acquaintance in the neighborhood was restricted to her own family. What friend could she have, and who knew any "mystery" that could affect her well-being and the remotest manner? Any clue upon the supposition that it emanated from either of the Crandons or her own family, was untenable. She set her brain to work to scrutinize if her conduct had ever been such as to make enemies. Again she was puzzled. She could not remember ever intentionally, or unintentionally, offending any one. Then rose the encounter with the robbers. She had thwarted one in his attempt to destroy the minister's life, but her father had told her it was the taller of the two who had been killed. The other man could have no malice against her, except to visit her father's acts upon her. Perhaps he wished to murder her by way of vengeance for the death of his comrade.

Miss Gladwin, to whom had been administered Dover's powder by Mrs. Dearing's advice, after her bath, was asleep, and no counsel could be obtained from her. Minona was naturally courageous and self-reliant, but the more she reflected on the mysterious note, the more she was lost in the labyrinth of doubt.

She had declined leaving her cousin for the evening. Many hours must elapse before the sun of another day would set, and she could read the riddle.

She was not sleepy. She began looking at a book mechanically. It was Sir David Brewster's Letters on Natural Magic. She was slightly tinctured with superstition, and she opened the book with a childish feeling that she was the victim of magic influences, and the work of the sage philosopher might explain them away. She became interested in its pages, though it opened no rifts in the clouds of speculation which enveloped her mind for the light of certainty to pour in.

At a late hour she retired to spend a restless night. Just before day she awaked with a start from a singular dream. In fancy, she was lying asleep, when the tolling of a funeral bell aroused her. She was in a strange cemetery, and while looking around espied a freshly dug grave. As she gazed bewildered upon it, a figure arose from within clad in the ghastly cerements of the tomb with a veiled face, and cried out in a sepulchral voice, "Hear your destiny. In your eighteenth year a new existence awaits you; in your twentieth you will meet your fate at the Indian graves!" The voice sounded distant and familiar, but she could not identify it; an icy chill seized her and she awoke trembling in every limb. Throwing a shawl around her shoulders she drew a chair near the window and watched the twinkling worlds above disappear one by one before the coming dawn

As the first faint glow of crimson tinged the east the shrill clarion note of Chanticleer's morning song of adoration and thankfulness rang out upon the solemn silence and not less joyous than the voice of the snowy bird that "salutes the ear of Allah each morning with his melodious chant, and awakes all creatures upon earth save man," in the visionary heaven seen by Mahomet when borne on the breast of Alborak.

The call began near her window and swelled on the air until, far away in the distance, an answering sound floated back and swept from beak to beak, and the welkin rang with a jubilant reveille to rouse the slothful sleepers of the neighboring dwellings. The clamor of the feathered songsters had a comforting effect on Minona, chilled and awed as she was by her mysterious note and the singular dream. The voice of the veiled spectre yet vibrated in her ear. What calamity will befall her in the short space of two years and culminate at her twentieth?

What link connected her with the Indian graves? The open grave and supernatural being she had seen, coupled with the closing prophecy at the tombs of the red man, must denote that she would fall a victim to the assassin's knife, which would end her career at twenty years.

Not for a moment did she waver from her determination to appear at the tryst and discover who was her unknown friend. Vinvela lay in profound slumber and Minona concluded to keep her secret. The ladies generally rode out each afternoon and Minona hoped she could frame some plausible excuse to remain at home, which would give her the opportunity of going unobserved on her mission. Her plan perfected, she arranged her toilet, and slipping noiselessly down stairs she sought the garden. The flowers were all bowed with a weight of diamond-like-dewdrops, which glittered and trembled beneath the sun's bright glances. A few handsome fall roses were in bloom and she walked along gathering some for her cousin, who was fond of flowers.

Coming suddenly upon a vine-plaited summer house, she saw Mr. Portwood within, putting the finishing touch to a bouquet.

She was full in view before she observed him. It was too late to retreat. The gentleman looked up, bowed and accosted her.

"I hope, Miss Dearing, your cousin is not ill this morning from her accident last evening. I should regret my carelessness doubly in that event."

"I cannot imagine for a moment," she replied, "that any blame could attach to you. My cousin was not awake when I left her room. She is very delicate, but I hope no ill effect will result from her fall."

"I trust your hopes may prove truths, Miss Dearing. I am somewhat of a self-torturing spirit and would not relish being the indirect means of entailing misfortune on a fair lady. Will you grant me a favor?" he said, looking at the handsome girl before him.

"Certainly, if it lie in my power."

"Then be the bearer of my bouquet and this note to your cousin, and excuse the liberty I take in making my request. Should the time ever arrive when you need a friend, call upon me and I shall not be found wanting."

For one moment the idea of showing Mr. Portwood the incomprehensible note presented itself before her, but then she reflected that he was her father's confidential friend and might dissuade her from complying with its desire. Extending her hand she received the bouquet and note and left the bower. On reaching her room she found her cousin already awake.

"Good morning," said Minona, kissing the transparent forehead. "I have brought you a peace offering from the recreant knight who came so near consigning you to a watery grave. Poor fellow! He looked wretched at the prospect of your illness, which I was careful to exaggerate into something serious."

"How could you be so cruel?" asked Vinvela, as she received the roses and the note, which expressed many regrets at her mishap and an invitation to ride out with the writer that afternoon. "I am really too much indisposed to go," said Miss Gladwin. "My head aches, and I fear I shall be consigned to seclusion all day."

"Then I shall remain with you and avoid the fatigue of rattling my tongue except at the behest of my tutor. By the way, Vinvela, you appear to have magnetized Mr. Crews. I never saw anyone more metamorphosed. He has received the gift of speech since you came."

Vinvela disavowed any agency in the changes manifest in the gentleman, and asking for her portfolio, replied to her note.

She did not see Minona again until the dinner hour.

Miss Dearing was strangely inattentive at her recitations during the morning, and caused no small exercise to her preceptor's patience. He seemed more than usually silent and grave, and had Minona's thoughts not been preoccupied by one absorbing theme, his moodiness might have provoked one of her lively smiles.

The afternoon proved interminable to the young lady's impatient spirit. Consulting her watch, after many such investigations, she found that she would barely have time to reach Cedar Bluff by sunset. Framing some excuse for a short absence to Vinvela, she proceeded down the private stairway.

Mrs. Dearing and her guests had gone on a decent drive, and Minona had heard her father say business would detain him until a late hour at Clinton. Her escaping observation seemed certain. She had no idea where the minister was, but she could easily elude him, or if she encountered him she could dispatch him on some mission which would divert his attention from her.

She avoided the direct road and went by a devious path leading to the ruins of a log cabin, near the grave, long since deserted, and the same in which Mr. Dearing had many years before been introduced to the reader.

She walked rapidly with a beating heart along the sequestered way, looking about her with a keen glance, and in a manner that would not betray fear to any skulking foe. As she emerged from some cedars, and in view of the log hut, she saw a woman, shabbily dressed, with a straw hat tied with a kerchief under the chin, come to the door of the ruined building. The person looked around carefully, and as her I fell upon Minona she waved her hand toward the Indian tombs and cautiously proceeded thither.

"This, then, is my friend," inwardly said Minona. "Some fortune teller who wishes to gain money through my credulity. She will find me a disbeliever in her jargon." She walked on and soon reached the designated spot.

The old woman was, apparently, desirous of keeping her face concealed from Minona, and as she spoke her voice seemed feigned. In a wiry key she said:

"It is well yer came, girl, at my bidding. I kin tell what will change your whole nater!"

"Speak quickly then, dame. I have but a short time to tarry."

"Come in the shade of them cedars, close in the graves. Dead man can't tell no tales I rekin."

Just as Minona followed and was about to sit on the rim of stones bordering one of the graves, Hugh Portwood rose from the ground near by, and from behind the concealing limb of cedar which branched low to the earth.

"Rachel Mulkey!" he said in a stern voice. "How dare you come here?"

"I dare go whar I choose," said the woman, surprised into her natural tone. "It isn't for such as ye, Hugh Portwood, to put on airs to yer equals. I will speak to the girl."

"Rachel, beware!" exclaimed the young man, in an angry manner. "Remember, I have you in my power."

With a look of undying hatred and a scowl of malicious vengeance, the woman disappeared, muttering as she went through the trees.

"Miss Dearing, allow me to escort you home. Your father would be very angry at your speaking to yon woman."

"I see nothing wrong in talking to an old acquaintance," replied Minona, haughtily. "What right have you to interfere with my actions?"

"None." said Hugh, with a flushed cheek. "My interference was accidental; but I do not regret it. I did you a service which you may live to thank me for. That woman has proven herself unworthy to hold converse with a pure young lady."

"I believe you, Mr. Portwood," replied Minona, regretting her hasty speech. "You said this morning you would oblige me when called upon. Grant a favor now. Say nothing to my father or to anyone of this little affair."

"I will do as you request; but let me advise, nay, beseech you, to have no intercourse with that depraved woman."

"It is not likely I shall be entrapped into such an act a second time, believe me. I sinned ignorantly."

The rest of the walk was pursued in silence and Miss Dearing sought her room to tranquilize her tumultuous conjectures.

Despite her natural vivacity of spirit, the occurrences of the last twenty-four hours depressed her greatly. She no longer doubted that some cloud hung around her that she could not penetrate. Indistinct vesper bells from the wide waste of the past sounded dimly in her ear, calling up phantoms of recollection which dissolved into thin air as she endeavored to grasp them. She had suddenly entered upon a new turn in the road of existence, which diverged from the sunlight of perfect happiness and coursed along the shadows of unseen troubles.

Vinvela was better on Minona's return and rallied her upon her gloomy face.

"Has Mr. Torrister played you false, Minona, and bestowed his gracious attentions upon Miss Lucy or Miss Helen? Cheer up. He has only testing you by neglect to make his triumph more certain. His smile to-night will make all right."

"Odious coxcomb!" exclaimed Minona, her lip curling with contempt. "He will find my heart is not as easily won by a smile as the kingdom of Persia was to Darius Hystaspes by the neigh of his horse."

"Come, Minona, admit that you are irritated by the gentleman's neglect. He is just the knight to captivate fair lady."

"Honestly, cousin, Mr. Torrister has nothing to do with my depression. It is caused by other matters altogether. I have never yet beheld the gentleman who could quicken my heart-throbs. I am as invincible as the great Achilles."

"Remember that he had a heel which received the mortal arrow at last," said Miss Gladwin, laughing.

"Are you going down to tea, Vinvela? If you remain invisible much longer you will destroy two hearts. Let me assist your toilet and place this white bud and your hair."

Vinvela reluctantly acquiesced and the cousins descended into the parlor.

Mr. Dearing and Mr. Portwood were present, and both warmly congratulated Miss Gladwin upon her return to the family circle.

Minona challenged her father for a promenade upon the veranda, declaring she must have him all to herself, as she had seen nothing of him all day.

"Miss Gladwin, there is no one to criticize; will you sing me that little song I heard at a distance from you a few days ago?" asked Hugh.

"I am but a novice in music and dislike to play for any one."

"I do not know a note, I assure you," replied the gentleman, "so imagine you are alone." and he escorted her to the instrument.

Her voice was sweet, low and plaintive, and there was an expression of feeling in her singing which touched the sympathies of her hearers.

" Are you going to the camp meeting with your cousin?" asked the young man.

"I had not thought of it, but I presumed so, if I am well enough. I was never at one, and have a desire to witness the ceremonies."

"Allow me the pleasure of accompanying you in a buggy."

Vinvela expressed her thanks and acceptance.

"One more song," he asked, in a low tone.

At the closing verse the ladies came in.

"I did not know you sang," said Miss Edwiston with a patronizing look. "Your voice is weak, but rather sweet," she continued condescendingly.

"I think it exceedingly melodious," remarked Hugh, looking directly at the haughty belle.

Miss Edwiston vouchsafed no reply, but a stare, which plainly said, "Who constituted you the champion of this insignificant lame girl?" which the gentleman did not notice as he handed Miss Gladwin to her seat.

The camp meeting was discussed, and it was arranged that the party should start the ensuing Saturday afternoon and remain until Monday's close. They would then be present at the most solemn and impressive exercises of the occasion. Dr. Crandon invited Miss Hollis to accompany him in his buggy, which the lady did with many smiles.

Mr. Torrister rode on horseback with Minona, to the disgust of Miss Edwiston, who wished to appropriate him to her own service. She was obliged to content herself with Mr. Hogan as escort.

The remainder were divided between Mrs. Dearing's phaeton and Miss Crandon's rockaway, that lady having preceded them to have her tent in readiness.

The Blowing Spring camp ground is picturesquely nestled between Black Oak Ridge and Pine Ridge, on the old Jacksboro stage road.

These ridges, though near together, are entirely different in their geologic formation, the former being limestone, the latter sandstone.

The narrow valley between these elevations is damp, with loose, rich soil growing immense oak, elm, and Liriodendron trees. Upon the north side of the Black Oak Ridge is a singular cavern, known by the name of the Blowing Cave, by reason of a constant current of air issuing from its aperture during the greater part of the year, strong enough to keep in motion the leaves of plants growing twelve or fifteen feet distant from it. About twenty feet from this cavern is a fine gushing fountain of limpid water, supplying unadulterated the purest drink to the pious "campers," who, many of them, had frequented this temporary place of worship for thirty or forty years.

As Minona was returning to the Sunday afternoon service, walking a little in the rear of her companions, some one pulled her dress, and a voice low and feigned said:

"Meet me at the Blowing Cave an hour hence."

Turning, she perceived the old woman she had met before disappearing among the crowd.

An undefined shill crept through her veins. Were her footsteps to be tracked daily? What could this woman wish? What dire secret could she know to divulge? Her vain attempts at conjecture were torturing. She had not promised Mr. Portwood to avoid even an interview with the woman, but her judgment told her that it was best she should not meet her alone. Ought she not to inform that gentleman of the woman's presence and get him to banish her? Then came a dread that the malice of the old beldame might, averted from her, be directed against her father. Hugh's conversation led her to think that the enmity existed between them. Abstractedly she followed the ladies to their tents, undecided what plan to adopt.

It lacked but fifteen minutes to the time specified for the meeting, and as yet Minona's mind oscillated in a state of doubt. What course should she pursue? She gazed dreamily through the tent door, expecting momentarily to see the form of her persecutor glide by; wishing to solve the mystery and hoping some turn of events would disclose the secret, yet dreading to become the agent of so doing herself.

She was about consoling herself with that convenient doctrine of the optimists, and reconciling her spirit to the determination of being blindly led by fate and doing nothing, passively awaiting events, when a clamor was raised in the tent next to Miss Crandon's. A small child of five or six years old was missing from his mother. Parties went about the ground, into every tent and wagon, in search of the missing child, but without success. As the evening shadows traced their gloomy hieroglyphics over the earth the anxiety of the aroused multitude grew intense, and the poor mother's fears made her frantic. The men, and some women, lighted flambeaus and went in quest of the little straggler. Shouts and cries floated upon the air, and were reverberated by the echoing hollows. The twilight deepened into darkness, and the twinkling worlds, which sleep not, and have kept sentry since the fourth day of time, when the Almighty maker hung them in space of earth, scintillated their modest light on the troubled camp ground. The milky way looked like a pearly pathway leading into unseen, untried eternity. Squad after squad of seekers came in bringing no glad tidings to the frenzied mother, only to start anew in their search. Hour after hour crept slowly, sorrowfully away from night and rosy dawn brought no relief. The meeting was broken up and the day, and the succeeding day, were consumed, until on the evening of the third day the child was found in a secluded ravine among some moss covered rocks in the state of partial stupor.

The sudden joy at the lost being found seemed to snap the cords which bound the senses, and the poor mother fell, at sight of her darling, into a long fearful swoon.

Thus ended the camp meeting. Minona's fears, her doubts and her desire to penetrate the ministries gathering around her, were put to flight for a season by the life tragedy of the lost child, to be renewed and developed into certainty at no distant period—in a cloud of consequences which even her busy imagination had never conceived.

Mrs. Dearing and her Savannah companions, ever on the wing for new amusements, projected a visit to Montvale Springs. It was near the close of the season, but it is oftentimes sweet to drain the dregs of what is pleasurable. This trip would be the winding up of an agreeable summer, and the beginning of a round of enjoyment for the winter in the city.

Mr. Dearing heard this new determination without with evident dissatisfaction. He saw how utterly impossible it was to keep Vinvela and Minona at study surrounded by such votaries of levity. There was but one alternative, and that he felt unwilling to adopt. Vinvela and Minona were both congenial and interesting to him. Were he reduced to the necessity of sending them to a boarding school, especially his beloved daughter, then indeed the light would be extinguished from his home and darkness would envelop it until her return. He never condescended to curtain lectures, but he knew how utterly worthless were remonstrances from him against his wife's whole time being devoted to gayety. She, well meaning and kind in her way, with an affection for her child, viewed things from a different standpoint, and regarded the idea of mental expansion to any great extent as ridiculous, unfeminine blue-stockingism.

Poor Minona was in this manner constantly subjected to positive and negative influences of sense and nonsense, which would have been destructive in toto, to a less self-reliant, courageous character, with the noble qualities preponderating. At this mobike* stage of her existence the hollow pleasures of the world, with their bright and seemingly kaleidoscopic changes, possessed a charm that all the efforts of her elegant, intellectual father could not entirely counteract

Montvale, then, was the goal upon which all eyes were directed next. For two weeks the ladies were closeted with their seamstresses, and scarce visible amid the heaps of dress materials, trimmings and artificialities of every description, preparing for the finale to the summer. Minona and Vinvela were still engaged during the morning hours. Mrs. Dearing and supervised their costumes, and the former entered into the schemes with ardor. Vinvela being in mourning, and caring little for such exterior recommendations, had no difficulty in fixing her attention on her lessons.

Mr. Crews was more reticent than ever, and a gloom appeared to his settled upon his placid face, which Minona's sallies and Vinvela's gentleness failed to remove.

The gentleman generally appeared under a cloud, except Mr. Neave, who was happy in the smiles of the fair Lucy. The "monarch beau" was a prey to discontent. He was proof against all the attempts of fascination held out by the haughty Miss Edwiston. His self-love had received a blow, which was not healed, from the wealthy Miss Dearing. During the ride homeward from the camp ground he had proposed to the young lady and met an unqualified refusal. He had not given up the chase. A few hundred thousand were worthy of longer perseverance on his part. He went upon the theory that young ladies are never in earnest when they say nay until the third time, the two first denials being induced solely from the inherent coquetry which belongs to the sex.

The eventful day for starting at length cane, Mr. Crews gave vacation for two weeks, which was the period designated for the sojourn at the springs. The ladies and the city gentlemen, with Mr. Portwood, left in the stage for Knoxville. Mr. Dearing and the minister were to follow in a few days. The jam in the swinging stage coach was anything but agreeable to the ladies, but after a series of thumps and jolts they reached Knoxville safely. There they remained a day or two awaiting Mr. Dearing and the waiting maids, these latter being quite indispensable.

The morning was clear and beautiful as the coaches crossed the river Holston in the ferry boat. The scene was lovely beyond description.

Life at a watering place is not conducive to deep or quiet reflection, and Minona found that amid the vortex of its time-consuming nothings, the unpleasant effects of the recent events thrust upon her, faded away. All her hours were occupied by walks, rides, changes of dress, chatting and dancing. Seriousness was entirely conquered by frivolity. The desire to see, to be seen and to look well, was the all-absorbing aim of thought and action. She, as an heiress and a handsome, dashing, slightly satiric girl, gathered a galaxy of parasites around her. Not withstanding all her sound sense, her head grew dizzy from the sudden height of her elevation. Mr. Hogan, hitherto in the background, now moved forward to assert his claims amid the other competitors for her favor. This gentlemen was small, good-looking and a perfect exquisite in dress. Not a hair was suffered to escape from the satiny folds it assumed around his conical head. His clothing was of the finest, every garment adjusted according to the strictest mathematical nicety. No stray fleck of dust would have had the audacity to alight upon his well-brushed coat, and his boots were glittering as mirrors in their polish. If the interior of his cranium could have been looked into the upper stratum would have been found rather light, but be carried about him a battery of flattery, and what he lacked in brains he compensated for by his oily tongue. He sung comic and sentimental songs, and, generally speaking, was very popular and much admired by the ladies. He possessed the greatest of all charms; he never failed to put his fair hearers in an ecstasy of delight over their beauty, their merit and their wit. So great is the credulity of human nature that it fancies itself imbued with every attribute of excellence under the potent tongue of flattery.

The gentleman's attentions and his compliments alike called forth Miss Dearing's raillery, but this was not discouraging to him. He accepted all as a mark of her favor, and bestowed an increased need of adulation upon her.

One evening Minona appeared arrayed for tea and encountered this modern D'Orsay in the passage leading to the parlor.

"How exquisite!" he ejaculated, his eyes glistening with admiration. "You are like a brilliant, blazing star."

"Take care, sir, you approach not too near or the rays may scorch your gossamer wings," answered the girl, adopting his grandiloquent style.

"The attraction is so great I cannot withdraw, even were I certain of being consumed by the flame. How beautiful, Miss Minona! More lovely than the ancient Cleopatra. Grant the happiness of dancing with me this evening? I shall be devoured by the pangs of jealousy if you dance even one quadrille, with any but myself."

"Then you will fall a victim to the green-eyed monster, as I am engaged for every cotillion to-night."

"Cruel queen, turn away from your inferiors and bestow your smile and your hand on your admirer, who can appreciate your beauty and your worth."

And Mr. Hogan looked devotion, admiration and self-merit all at once. After his inflated speech.

Minona surveyed the vein atom before her, with his precise attitude and elegant attire, with a keen glance of mirth, and burst into an uncontrollable fit of laughter. The interview appeared so supremely ridiculous that she could not restrain her hilarity.

"I regret," she said at last, "that I cannot favor your superior appreciatory powers, but most unfortunately, I am unequivocally engaged to your inferiors for the dance to-night. Conduct me to the parlor, if you please. This is the only countenance I can allow you."

A sentimental Lilliputian sigh escaped the dainty beau.

As the couple entered the parlor Minona perceived near the door a young gentleman several years her senior and of graver deportment than most men wear in early life. This young man had been introduced to her a few days before, and exhibited so many higher aspirations than she had perceived in others that it recalled to her mind a passage from a great author which says.

"He only seems to live and enjoy life who, intent upon some employment, seeks reputation from some ennobling enterprise or honorable pursuit."

She had been pleased with him. He appeared to be a looker on, not a participator in the gayeties. His fine face was pale and there were some stern lines around the well-turned mouth. His whole exterior indicated poor health, and Minona thought that his smile of greeting as she entered with a light-hearted Mr. Hogan wore an expression of sadness. Mr. Delbridge Meverill was a well educated, high-souled young man, with a small patrimony, and his life since maturity had been spent in struggles to add to an insufficient income to aid in supporting a widowed mother and a sister. His sister was now married and comfortably situated. His mother, recently dead, had been many years an invalid, and he rested under a cloud of great sorrow, which had made many inroads upon a delicate constitution worn away by constant labor and anxious cares. By persuasion of friends he was a visitor at Montvale for a few weeks of recreation. Dr. Crandon, who, with his sister, had joined Mrs. Dearing's party, was an acquaintance of Mr. Meverill, and had presented him to the ladies.

There was something in Minona's exuberance of vivacity that fascinated this grave young man. He singled her out, and her conversation convinced him that beneath her effervescent gayety there was much in her character that was solid and commendable. He observed her at times when she knew it not, and her cauterization of vain pretensions and just appreciation of genuine excellencies pleased him. Again her devotion to her father, and to her afflicted and lovely cousin, recommended her to his esteem. His attentions were neither persistent nor frequent, they were deferential, yet bulwarked by a certain rampart of reserve which is, of all others, the most gratifying and captivating to a lady. His conversation with Minona led her to reflect on better things than she saw around her, and there was something puzzling in his deportment which attracted her. Before she left Montvale she found that she regarded Mr. Meverill as a friend whose approbation pleased her, and whose clouded brow cast a shadow of sadness over her. Dangerous platform for a young lady to stand upon; sometimes safe, but more often as insecure to the whole condition of the heart as the trap door that precipitated the beautiful Amy Robsart into an inextricable position.

Mr. Portwood had been marked in his kindness to Miss Gladwin during the first few days at the Springs. This attention had begun after her fall into the water. At first the field was unobstructed; the lame girl was generally overlooked; but a singular actor had entered upon the arena as an aspirant to her society. This was no less a personage than the little minister, who embraced every opportunity of being near Miss Vinvela, and, in an unobtrusive way, of endeavoring to amuse her. She felt grateful for his consideration. Not for a moment imagining that his conduct sprung from other cause than a wish to divert her, she extended toward him a certain amount of cordiality.

Hugh was irritated, and in the heat of such feeling inwardly accused Miss Gladwin of coquetry. At first he kept aloof from her, but one evening, chancing to step out upon the piazza, he heard the voice of Mr. Crews, though the utterance was too low to distinguish the words; at the instant he turned to retrace his steps the musical voice of Vinvela said:

"I thank you for this undeserved mark of your regard."

The sentence froze Hugh's blood, he did not wait to hear the conclusion, but stepping from the piazza, he went on a hasty and lengthy walk in the darkness. His reflections were bitter. "A craven, sanctimonious little parson to make her captive! Well has it been said, 'Frailty, thy name is woman.' Fool that I was to waste a thought upon one of the false-hearted sex. I will cast love to the winds and start on our next ship to Europe, where, amid its sights and scenes, I will forget that I ever bestowed a thought upon one so fickle."

And the excited young man sped on, elevating his hat to cool his fevered brow. A walk of a mile or two acted as a sedative, and, retracing his steps, he reached his room at a late hour somewhat calmed.

In the morning Hugh purposefully delayed appearing at breakfast as his seat was near Miss Gladwin's. At dinner he went to the table with some gentleman friends; in the afternoon he was absent; and at night bestowed merely a cold bow upon Vinvela from a distance. The young lady was at a loss how to account for such vacillating demeanor. There was nothing in her conduct that she could remember as offensive. She admired Mr. Portwood, but his deportment was inexplicable, and, while it pained her gentle spirit, it let him down from the elevation he had held in her estimation. She determined to allow the young man to enjoy his course without interference or notice from her.

Several days previous to the departure of the party from Montvale, they walked to the spring. They were conversing cheerfully while partaking of the water, when Miss Lucy Christie gave two or three tragic little screams, pointing her finger to some unknown horror, and, almost simultaneously, Miss Hollis uttered a terrified shriek in a coarser key, at the same time grasping Dr. Crandon's arm, exclaiming:

"Oh, doctor, save us from the venomous reptile!"

The poor man, taken by assault, blushed and circulated two or three emphatic tears, looking wildly for the object of alarm. The gentleman closed in solid phalanx around the helpless creatures as ready as Don Quixote to do battle for the fair, when Mr. Dearing espied the object of terror in a large snake which was held by an Indian not far distant.

"Do not fear, ladies," he said; "the snake is dead, and can do no harm."

But Miss Hollis was of a nervous temperament, and had a faint touch of that interesting disorder known as hysterics.

Her tremor could not be assuaged except by the administration of some nervine from Dr. Crandon's own hand. Mr. Dearing proposed to the ladies to go to the spot where the Cherokees were standing under a tree, so as to get a nearer view of the reptile.

"Come, Minona, will you go?" he asked. "You have frequently desired to see Indians."

Miss Dearing stepped forward, and her more timid companions followed.

The snake was very large with many rattles, and had been brought in as a trophy by the Cherokees who came to the Springs with venison to sell. They still slay the wild deer in those mountain wilds, and as their fathers did in the ages of the past.

"I should hate to be bitten by one of those things," said exquisite Mr. Hogan, with a visible shudder. "No cure has ever been found for the bite; has it, doctor?"

"A popular and scientific writer has said, in reference to the cure of the bite of the rattlesnake, 'scarcely any substance can be named so inert as not to have been recommended, or so disgusting as not to have been employed.'"

"I have understood," said Mr. Dearing, "that the only sure remedy is the free use of ardent spirits which ought to be swallowed to intoxication."

"Yes—yes—that is quite a mistake," answered the doctor. "The venom of the rattlesnake, if mixed with alcohol and inoculated, produces death as unerringly and rapidly as if you used without the alcohol. The experiment, and many others, have frequently been tried on animals with the view of ascertaining the most reliable antidote for the use of man. Yes, not only that, but alcohol introduced into the stomachs of animals bitten by the rattlesnake hastens death. And many examples are on record of persons under intoxication suffering speedy death from bites of the rattlesnake."

"This fact destroys the most popular remedy of all. I have heard ammonia spoken of as a cure," said Mr. Dearing.

"Ammonia has been proven to hasten death. Yes; so with other remedies which have in turn been much lauded—such as oil of turpentine, and nitrate of silver in solution. Cupping glasses may retard the action, and even diminish it by removing a portion of the poison."

"Have the civilized successors to the red man of America never been able to penetrate the secret of the vegetable remedies for the bite of a rattlesnake the latter employ?" asked Mr. Dearing.

"No, sir. A species of the Liatris and many weeds have enjoyed reputations is Indian remedies—all have been tried. Yes, yes, all had been found worse than useless. It is still asserted that the American Indians possess specifics for the cure of bites of the rattlesnake; but if they do, they conceal the knowledge from the white man. Let us try this native of the forest on the subject."

Here Dr. Crandon called to the Indian, who was still displaying the huge snake and a little distance. He came quickly, expecting some perquisite for the sight; but on hearing and being made to understand the scientific and humanitarian question and the learned doctor, he merely grunted out:

"Ugh! me no und'tand," and all attempts to explain or to elicit any information from the reticent red-skin was a signal failure.

"And has nothing been discovered by scientific research to give relief in such cases?" asked Mr. Dearing.

"Yes. The solution of iodine and iodide of potassium in water possesses the power, when properly used, of invariably retarding death, if it does not prevent it."

"How has the iodine used? To learn an efficacious antidote would be very useful information to everyone," said Mr. Dearing.

"Yes, yes," answered the doctor, swelling with the importance of the opportunity of delivering himself of a learned and didactic speech. "I would suggest that my fair auditors take heed—yes—yes, very useful information to lay away in memory's store house. On receiving the bite of the reptile, first, wash the part with a solution of iodine and iodide of potassium, and apply a cupping glass over the wound, or place ligatures around the member so as to prevent absorption. If the wound be deep, or absorption has already taken place, inject the solution under the skin beneath the cupping glass, and disseminate it by friction about the wound. With this treatment, the internal use of alcoholic stimulants may be advantageously combined. My own experiments on inferior animals have demonstrated the beneficial effects of this practice in a very large number of instances."

"How scientific you are, doctor," said Miss Hollis, her rubicund face all smiles; "one would feel almost secure enough of life to consent to be bitten by a rattlesnake if he could engage you professionally."

The physician bowed low, uttering several ejaculatory monosyllables of the monotonous kind so common to him when agitated by any current of thought or feeling, and the ladies returned to the house.

CHAPTER XI.

Everything was excitement at the Springs preparatory to the fancy ball, the climax of the summer gayeties, after which the ladies would leave Montvale for their homes.

A jaunt to the summit of the Chilhowee Mountain had been projected, and many of the ladies were inclined to give it up on the plea of want of time, a commodity the lavish abundance of which appears to fatigue most people, yet the want of which seems to be universally grumbled at alike by the busy and the idle.

Minona had no notion of relinquishing the plan of ascending Chilhowee; and, through her urgings, the party consented to go early the following morning.

Accordingly, at sunrise, Minona, Miss Hollis and the Misses Christie, with Mr. Dearing, Dr. Crandon, who acted as guide to the party, Mr. Meverill and several other gentlemen were equipped for what Minona called their ascension.

The top of Chilhowee slept in a wreath of fog which melted before the sun's rays. The ladies were provided with impromptu staffs to aid in climbing, which process seemed tiresome to the delicate Lucy and Helen, who occasionally halted a few moments by some friendly rock or fallen tree. After much toil the summit of the mountain was reached, and Minona's delight burst forth in words:

"Glory beyond all glory ever seen!"

"You are an enthusiast," said Mr. Meverill, smiling at the girl standing rapt in admiration at the beautiful scene far below, the grand smoky mountains skirting the horizon, and the sunlight dappling the picture with patches of shifting shadow and light.

"In nature's grand exhibitions, certainly, I am," answered Minona. "If I could only have unfolded to my vision the 'Mighty City' Wordsworth so beautifully describes in his "Solitary," I should carry it with me through life as the aroma of this morning's sweet experience."

How well the ardent girl appeared, her hat fallen back, her jetty hair in luxurious coils around her well-turned head, her eyes radiant with unalloyed happiness, matching well with her delicate features and soft, pale complexion.

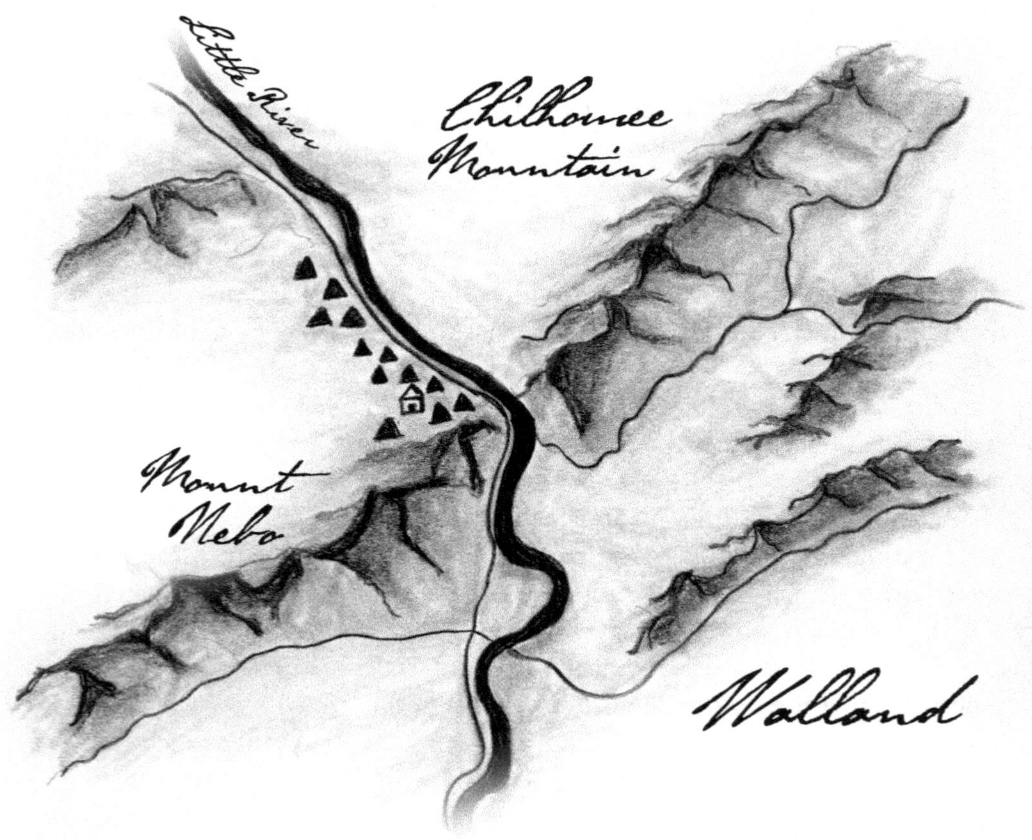

Chapter XI. A jaunt to the summit of the Chilhowee Mountain had been projected, and many of the ladies were inclined to give it up on the plea of want of time, a commodity the lavish abundance of which appears to fatigue most people, yet the want of which seems to be universally grumbled at alike by the busy and the idle.

The young man, as he looked on the peerless damsel before him, repeated slowly:

> *"Full many a spot*
> *Of hidden beauty have I chanced to espy*
> *Among the mountains; never one like this!"*

Minona turned, as he closed the quotation, to make some remark, and the look of admiration bent upon her called a faint tint of carmine to her habitually colorless face.

"Our companions seem to have forsaken us," she uttered, quickly. "Shall we seek them?"

"Let us wait their coming, Miss Dearing; I have had so little opportunity of conversing with you; and you are to leave in a day or two."

"Yes; we return to our East Tennessee home for a month or more, and then we shall go to Savannah for the winter."

"And I shall seek my Alabama home, desolated now by the hand of death; but I shall be in Savannah this winter to prosecute my profession. I have relatives there. I shall hope to meet you again."

"Doubtless you will, Mr. Meverill, and we will be pleased to renew your acquaintance."

"Thank you. In the meantime, may I dare ask a boon?" He paused a moment, and as she did not reply, he continued: "Will you correspond with me occasionally until we meet again?"

"I will reflect about it, Mr. Meverill, and answer you before I leave. I am but a school girl–a fledgling–and have not learned to fly well enough to test my skill at writing with an accomplished aeronaut in the literary sky like yourself."

"You mock me. Where did you learn that I attempted such flights as you describe?"

"Your friend, Dr. Crandon, showed me an article in a magazine from your pen, which he praised exceedingly."

"And your opinion?" he asked, with a mingled expression of sadness and gravity overshadowing his fine face.

"I liked it; but I can scarce be a judge yet of literary merit."

Mr. Dearing and his companions came up at this moment, and conversation became general as they began the descent of the mountain.

The fancy ball was a grand affair. The costumes were expensive and handsome.

Minona and Mr. Meverill promenaded the moonlit piazza conversing on a wide range of topics for sometime, when suddenly the gentleman said:

"You go to-morrow, and as yet have not replied to my request. Cut short my suspense by an affirmative answer."

"I believe I yet halt between two opinions. Twenty-four hours is short space for a lady to come to a conclusion. 'Mutability is her bane as well as nature's,' to paraphrase a line of one of my favorite poets."

"But you are more stable than most ladies," said the young man, seriously, with a grave look on his countenance, "and can surely terminate a state of uncertainty under which I present at rest. I have the best credentials to show that your confidence will not be misplaced."

"No doubt of that kind of deters me," answered Minona. "My hesitation arises solely, Mr. Meverill, from a diffidence in regard to my powers as a correspondent with a literary man like yourself."

Mr. Meverill laughed.

"I disclaim all pretension to being a literary character. I have as great an abhorrence to it as Christopher North of what he facetiously termed 'being made a lion et.' Regard me as I am, a commonplace mortal, and promise to reply to an occasionally friendly letter."

"It shall be as your desire," said Minona; "but close your eyes to imperfections. I abhor criticism as much as you can, Lionetizing," she added, laughing.

Supper was announced, and many were the glances of envy bestowed by the less fortunate gallants, as Mr. Meverill escorted the beautiful Miss Dearing into the dining hall.

Early on the following morning Mr. Dearing and family, and their Savannah friends, left Montvale with its gabled roof and gleaming white colonnades, it's cottages and tasteful grounds, reposing at the base of mist-cloaked Chilhowee; some of the party to behold it no more forever.

At Knoxville the Savannah belles and their attendant knights left on the E. T. and G. R. R. for their residence in the "Forest City." They parted from Mrs. Dearing with protestations of enduring friendship. The supercilious Miss Edwiston bestowed a bland farewell on Minona, feeling secure in the potency of her charms to captivate Mr. Torrister when she could monopolize his society. She even condescended to confer a complimentary remark on Miss Gladwin. Had she heard the parting assurance of Mr. Torrister to Minona that he would write, and some flattering speeches on her fair face, her humor would have been less sweet.

There was a slight tremulousness in Hugh Portwood's hand as he clasped that of Vinvela for a moment in bidding her adieu. Her face wore its usual expression of serenity and amiable cheerfulness and she wished him a safe journey to his home.

During the whole route her image dwelt with a young man, regretful, when too late, for his coldness to the innocent cause of his ire.

Mr. Dearing reached Eagle Bend in due season with his family. He did not intend removing to Savannah for the winter until the first of December. Mrs. Dearing's health, always delicate, was really much exhausted by the summer's campaign, and she felt quite willing to enjoy a few weeks of rest for recuperation.

Minona and Vinvela set to work in good earnest to study, and Mr. Crews, to all appearance, reposed under the effects of some happifying influence. He became less reserved, and at times was really agreeable.

Minona, receiving a new impetus from her intercourse with Mr. Delbridge Meverill, read with an avidity never felt previously. Her intellect expanded, and her imagination ranged in an infinity of thought never reached before. Fragments of music from memory's harp floated in melodious accents to her ear, but the keynote was wanting to reduce them into connected harmony. Vainly she strove to catch the euphony as it fell in broken tones upon her strained hearing. Quickly it swept by calling to mind a passage she often perused with delight,

> *"Our birth is but a sleep and a forgetting;*
> *The soul that rises with us, our life's afar,*
> *Hath had elsewhere its sitting*
> *And cometh from afar."*

A vague feeling that was undefinable haunted her ever that she had not always been what she now was. Where had she experienced these dim recollections which swept before her like some panorama seen through a semi-diaphanous curtain torturing it's indistinctness?

Coupled with these phantasmagoria of remembrance came the image of the old woman she had twice seen. All these reflections became in time so tormenting that Minona grew a prey to superstition. She felt averse to being left alone, or walking out, lest she should meet the unknown arbiter of her destiny in the shape of the woman.

One morning at breakfast, after Minona had passed an unquiet night of dreams, and looked unusually pale and lost in abstraction, her father startled her by asking:

> *"Why so sad?"*

He had been observing her for some time. As she did not answer, he took from his pocket and handed her a letter, saying:

> *"Perhaps this may prove a healer of all wounds."*

He scrutinized his daughter keenly as she received the letter and glanced at the address and postmark. Not a muscle of her face moved, nor did her color heighten. Looking up she smiled, saying:

"It is from the person I spoke to you of some weeks ago."

She turned the letter over in an absent manner, and resumed her breakfast.

"Too frank and indifferent for love to be her malady," thought her father, as he sipped his coffee.

"Eriginia, I expect a gentleman friend here in a few days; pray have a room ready for him."

Mrs. Dearing yawned in a lackadaisical manner, saying:

"I declare, Clarek! how inconsiderate men are! I am too unwell to entertain company after my long surfeit of society."

"Do not give yourself any trouble, my dear. Miss Gladwin or Minona will relieve you, and direct Genista what to do. He will make himself at home." So saying, he quitted the room.

On reaching Savannah Mr. Portwood's latent repentance began to assume the character of deep contrition, and he found it impossible to banish the face of the lame girl, which seemed to wear a clouded, pensive look. He regretted the hasty folly that led him away without securing the coveted prize. Never before had he felt attracted by any woman, and he had left her to the approaches of an admirer, who had every opportunity of ingratiating himself in her favor. At times he determined to make suspense a certainty; then, the sentence he overheard Vinvela utter to the minister would tauntingly drive him from his purpose. So engrossed was he by this master passion, that he made sad blunders in his books in the counting-room, and had often his work to repeat.

He was not aggrieved when a summons came from his employer to go up to Tennessee. It was but a short time until one of Mr. Dearing's ships would sail for Havre, and Hugh had been offered the opportunity of going or not in his old position.

"I will learn my fate before I decide," thought he, as he prepared to leave Savannah.

Miss Gladwin, naturally frail, caught a severe cold on the night she was immersed in the river. The malady had not yielded to treatment, and left her with a cough which grew troublesome with every exposure. Her father had been inclined to consumption, which had been kept away only by the most scrupulous care. Vinvela had always reflected on the probability of filling an early grave; and, since her beloved father's demise, she rather regarded it as a release from future suffering. Without being at all sensitive, her experience with Mrs. Dearing's company taught her that her infirmity, instead of exciting compassion, was regarded by the heartless world as a degradation. This awakening to a new phase of life did not embitter her. Her cheerfulness, her purity, her well-stored contemplative mind furnished her with an exhaustless fund of enjoyment that rendered her independent of society.

Perhaps her thoughts would not have retained this equanimity if she had met with harshness or inappreciation at home. But from Mr. Dearing she received always a chivalric deference and universal kindness; from her cousin, considerate, delicate regard, and from Minona, an exuberant affection and confidence.

She had never heard from her aunt, but Mr. Dearing had recently taken some steps what he thought would eventually lead to the discovery of her present place of residence.

When Mr. Portwood arrived it was quite late in the afternoon, and the weather was cold. Placing his valise in the custody of a merchant friend, he started to walk from Clinton to Eagle Bend. Thought whirled like boiling eddies through his mind. What reception would he meet from the lady of his love? Was she free, or trammeled by an unworthy engagement? He walked as far a wager until he approached the cabin on Cedar Bluff. Then he paused and seated upon the decayed step to collect himself and calm his throbbing pulses ere he gained the summit of the next hill where centered all his hope of joy.

Hugh had not been there long before he heard voices from behind some thick and low branching cedar trees. He was a good woodsman, with an Indian's tread. Creeping stealthily up near the trees he recognized the tones of Rachel Mulkey, but could not at first distinguish her words.

"Have ye told her?" asked the harsh voice of a man.

"No. I was kept from it by that thar upstart, Hugh Portwood."

"God curse him, and you too, and the feller that owns the big house!" said the man.

"Take care, man, how yer maddens me!" said Rachel; "or I'll let you whistle for revenge."

"Now, old coon, don't scare. We's good friens, yer know; 'Tice the gal out, an' I'll run off with her. She jist suits me. I wants money, too, worse than that time I fell in that ar grave in Savannah with them cussed police dogs arter me."

In Hugh's anxiety to get a glimpse of the male actor in this nefarious plot, he trod on a stick which broke with a cracking noise.

"Hist!" said the crone; "let's be off, Jake."

And she lowered her voice and glanced furtively around.

"Well, I like's not to tarry in graveyards. When night's a comin' them skulls allers is a grinnin' like that ar in the grave in Savannah. Meet me here a week from ter-day, an' be sure yet get the gal here."

The man ended this speech with an oath, and the two disappeared in the bushes in the opposite direction from Hugh.

"Wretch!" exclaimed the young man through his set teeth. "I thank my God that I shall yet be the means of baffling this villainous plot!"

He reached the house and was greeted kindly by Mrs. Dearing, who regarded him almost as one of her family. In answer to his inquiries after the health of the ladies, she reported Miss Gladwin as ill, having been in her room for several days. Mr. Dearing was in the village, she believed.

"I did not meet him as I passed through the village."

"He may have gone elsewhere," replied his wife. "I shall be engaged, but make yourself at home. If I can persuade Minona to tear herself from Vinvela's side, I will send her to welcome you."

"Not on my account, dear madam. I shall look in the library , and then walk out. I may meet Mr. Dearing."

Mrs. Dearing left, and Hugh went into the Blue Room. There was a fire there, and he set down. He felt the deepest dejection. Giant fears and doubts for the future loomed up gaunt and horrible for him. Danger menaced Mr. Dearing and his daughter. How could he avert it? Plan after plan suggested itself, but none appeared feasible. Then his lady-love ill! Was ever man in a more trying position? Rising, he walked a few turns up and down the room, his thumbs thrust in the arm-holes of his vest. Finally he sat down and penned a sympathetic note to Vinvela, expressing regrets at her illness and hopes of speedily seeing her. The only difficulty in this was to suppress the constant welling up of affection. Putting the billet in his breast pocket he left the room to stroll out, hoping to meet Mr. Dearing.

In the entryway he encountered Miss Dearing, and greeted her most warmly.

"Are you going on a walk?" he asked.

"I had not decided. I may do so," she replied.

Taking her hand and speaking with hasty energy, he said:

"Promise me, Minona, that you will not leave the house."

She looked at him in astonishment.

"Excuse me, Miss Dearing," he added. "I was led away by a feeling quite uncontrollable. Danger menaces you. I will inform you of it very shortly. In the meantime, grant my request."

"I will," she responded in an absent manner.

His thoughts had flown to the Indian tombs.

He recalled her by slipping his note in her hand, and asked its deliverance. He then left the house going on the road to Clinton as the probable one along which Mr. Dearing would return. He walked on until he neared a part of the route more densely wooded. He heard the clank of horses' feet on the hard ground, and then the discharge of a gun followed by the hissing sound of a bullet. The sun had sunken behind the hills, and darkness was fast approaching.

Onward Hugh darted in a ran until he was almost under Mr. Dearing's horses' feet.

"Is that you, Portwood? You go like a madman."

"Are you hurt, sir?" exclaimed Hugh, in an excited manner, not heeding the jocular question. "There is blood. In Heaven's name, answer!"

"A mere scratch. My left hand is grazed by a ball. Accidentally shot, I imagine."

Hugh begged his friend in a low tone to hasten on, and in short space they reached their swelling.

Mrs. Dearing turned sick almost to swooning when she saw blood on her husband's clothing and heard of his wound.

"My dear," he said, putting his arm around her, "do not be alarmed; it is a mere scratch."

"I shall feel terrified hereafter whenever you leave the house, Clarek."

"I presume it was the result of accident," he replied. "Remove these kerchiefs, and bandage my hand properly."

Mrs. Dearing procured some linen, but was so tremulous that she had to resign her intention to Hugh. Minona's alarm and apprehension were great when she heard of the event.

"Dear papa," she said, kissing his forehead, "I shall dread to see you leave the house. There is nothing more to be feared than the lurking assassin. Open enemies can be repelled; but cowards no man can allude. I am timid in what touches you."

"Quiet your terrors, my dear. There is no cause for them," and he kissed her cheek.

After tea Hugh recounted to his patron his doubts and suspicions, and what he had overheard at the tombs. Mr. Dearing's face blanched as he listened to the fiendish design of the ruffian against Minona.

"I shall bring the vagrants before the law yet," he muttered.

"The man, sir, I have no doubt is the author of your wound."

"What grudge can he owe me? I am not aware of ever having injured anyone in this community. Was he visible to you?"

"No, sir. I endeavored to get sight of the speakers, but, unfortunately, made a slight noise which attracted their attention. I am certain the woman was Rachel. I knew her voice; then her conversation alluded to things no one was aware of but herself. She spoke to her companion as Jake."

"I shall reflect what course to pursue. We shall remain here only a week or two longer, and I shall enjoin upon Minona not to leave the house without some gentleman friend."

"I promised to explain," said Mr. Portwood, "why I made so singular a request of her this afternoon. Shall I do so?"

"Certainly; but be prudent in your remarks."

"I will," replied Hugh; and he turned to admit the applicant at the door.

"Father," asked Minona, "may I come in? I felt so anxious about you I ran away from Vinvela to inquire how you are."

"I am not suffering much pain. Is your cousin improving? Sit down; I wish to speak to you."

Minona handed Hugh a card from Vinvela upon which she expressed her thanks for his inquiries after her health. It was formal and indifferent but kind in its tenor. Nothing else could be expected, yet it disappointed the receiver; so unreasonable is the heart surcharged with the rushing tide of love!

Mr. Dearing explained to Minona the necessity of her not leaving the premises for long rambles that she sometimes did; and, without going into detail, he informed her of the design of some secret enemies to injure her. She promised to be governed by his directions, and ere long returned to her room.

The next day Mr. Portwood recounted in full all the conversation he had overheard at the graves. This he could not do in Mr. Dearing's presence without violating his promise to Minona regarding her interview at the same spot with Rachel Mulkey.

"I believe your father received his wound from the unknown miscreant. He appeared to have some venom against him, which I could not understand from their short conversation."

"What name did she address the ruffian by?" asked Minona.

"Jake, I think, she called him."

Minona mused awhile, and said at last with a perplexed look:

"It is a link of the chain. I shall have them all some day."

"What do you mean?" asked Mr. Portwood.

"Nothing; only I have my suspicions. When I penetrate to realties, I will inform you. In the meantime, guard my beloved father's life, and you will ever claim me your debtor."

"I will," and he felt a yearning to confide to the girl before him his love for her cousin. Biting his lip he suppressed the inclination.

Suddenly, as Minona was leaving the parlor, she said:

"Vinvela will be down sometime before dinner. We will sit in the Blue Room with our sewing. Will you join us and read aloud?"

"With pleasure," answered Mr. Portwood.

And he was left alone to quell the agitating thoughts the prospect of meeting Miss Gladwin called up.

In an hour Genista appeared with an invitation from Minona that his presence in the library would be agreeable.

He entered the room after a short time, Minona and Vinvela were alone. The latter looked pale and interesting, with a light, black shawl thrown carelessly around her slight figure. Her rich chestnut hair was brushed and smooth folds from her snowy forehead, and her blue eyes looked almost black from the shade of the jetty lashes.

Her greeting was cordial to Mr. Portwood; but her hand trembled not in his clasp, nor did she betray any agitation at his presence.

"What shall Mr. Portwood read, Vinvela? As you are an invalid and must be petted, you shall select."

"Then I will have some poetry to-day. I wish to hear the 'Spectre Caravan,' and the 'Battle of Lake Regillus.'"

Hugh had a full-toned voice, and read poetry well. His utterance was clear and distinct as he began that gem from the German of Ferdinand Freiligrath translated in English by James Clarence Mangan:

"'Twas at midnight in the Desert, where we rested on the ground."

As he proceeded to the rising of the "Host of Shadows" Miss Gladwin's work fell from her hand, and she appeared transported in spirit to the sandy plains where the dead

"Rise by legions from the darkness of their prisons low and lone."

"Beautiful!" exclaimed both girls as the reader ceased.

"Do go on with the other. You will just have time before dinner," said Minona.

Again the sewing was forgotten, and thought sped far away to the time when Dictator Aulus, aided by the twin Gods

"Who fought so well for Rome."

put to flight the Latins and their mighty hosts on the margin of Lake Regillus, as graphically pen-painted in the famous "Lay" of Macaulay.

"I have heard persons assert that Macaulay was no poet," remarked Hugh, as he closed the book.

"I am perhaps no judge," said Miss Gladwin, "but I call that true poetry which causes the electric current to course like lightning through my veins, thrilling every nerve with an indescribable pleasure."

"I agree with you!" exclaimed Minona. "When I listen to the ring of the genuine poetic metal the sound causes my face to glow; my hands grow cold, and the spirit seems to soar as if disembodied amid infinite realms of rhythmic exaltation. The assertion you have heard, Mr. Portwood, is doubtless the opinion of poetasters, who after all their endeavors at contriving wings for poetic flights find, like Rasselas, their cumbrous machinery does but fetter them more securely to earth. I adore poetry at times; but too much is unwholesome.

It is the dessert in the feasts of literature. We need for health the substantial meat and bread of prose, in the main.”

“True,” answered Hugh, laughing; “but there is the summons to a still more substantial and needed feast.”

“Pshaw! how gross after reveling in such aerial flights. Come, Mr. Portwood, escort me to dinner. Vinvela is to play solitary during her meal to-day. We will join her after it;” and they left the room.

About three o’clock, after much conversation and reading and very little work, Minona arose, exclaiming:

“I must do penance for idling so beautifully to-day by writing a lengthy letter to a blue-stocking of the masculine gender. Give me some subject to discourse upon, can you not, Vinvela?”

“He would not thank me for my generosity. I am afflicted with absolute paucity of ideas this afternoon.”

“How illiberal! Mr. Portwood, I leave Miss Gladwin to your tender mercy, and under your special charge until my return. I shall hold you responsible for the trust;” and with a very quizzical expression Miss Dearing left the Blue Room.

Hugh continued reading snatches of fugitive pieces for a time. Finally he exclaimed:

“I am weary of reading. May I talk?”

“I shall endeavor to listen.”

He walked to the window and looked out; then about the room in an absent manner. At length he placed a chair near Vinvela, whose busy fingers drew the needle through a frill she was stitching.

He observed her for some moments, then asked abruptly:

“Are you happy, Miss Vinvela?”

“Yes. Why not?” she answered, looking up in some surprise.

“Because I am not; and I would have a reflex of my feelings in your bosom. Have you not suspected that I can never find happiness unless you grant me the right to call you mine? Speak to me, beloved Vinvela, and end my torture!”

“Mr. Portwood, I never had the vanity to suppose you, or any gentleman actuated by other motives than those of courtesy in your attentions to me. Debarred from society, and the performance of many duties by poor health and an infirmity, I have never thought of matrimony. Indeed,” she added, sadly, “from early childhood I have had a prescience of speedy death. My bridal shall be the tomb.”

“Do not terrify me by such forebodings. Let mine be the dear pleasure of nurturing you into length of life, and shielding you from every ill.”

“It cannot be. It would be ungenerous in me to accept your proffer, afflicted as I am. No; I thank you, honor you for a love which is noble and liberal; but it would be cruel in me to clog your usefulness in becoming, as I should, a burden on you."

"I am ambitious and filled with an abounding energy. If you will only surrender your sweet fate into my keeping, I feel that I can attain greater ends. If those mentioned are your only objections to our union, they are but trifles. Is your heart pre-engaged?"

"No."

"Then I may hope?"

"It is useless, Mr. Portwood, to continue a discussion which is more painful to me than to yourself. I admire and regard you as a friend. Be content with that."

"I will strive to obey; but let your admiration and regard ripen into love, and make me happy. You cannot rob me of hope until you become the bride of another."

He rose and left the room.

Vinvela burst into tears. Her unhappiness had dawned. The physical infirmity of the lame girl became her cross from that moment.

That night Mr. Portwood informed Mr. Dearing that he would accept his former position upon the next ship in which the gentleman was interested. The vessel was to sail for Havre in a week. Hugh had been rather undecided in his intention, and Mr. Dearing was somewhat surprised by a determination so sudden. He was not suspicious, nor very observing of the trifles that go to make the aggregate by which proximate incidents are weighed, else he might have known from what quarter the wind blew to waft his protégé in such a summary manner to a foreign land.

Minona, with a woman's needle-like penetration, had probed Mr. Portwood's secret long since, and she purposely designed offering him an opportunity for a declaration when she left the Blue Room to reply to her correspondent.

Her letter from Mr. Meverill was elegant in its diction, perfect in orthography, unexceptionable in punctuation, handsome in chirography, and, in short, an embodiment of the nicest rhetorical rules. She naturally felt some trepidation in replying to this august letter writer; and he assumed the magnitude which Johnson enjoyed, of being the great known of literature in her imagination. After several ineffectual efforts she determined to write off in her dashing, satiric style an epistle which she hoped would amuse and repay in that vein, what it lacked in profundity. In reading it over it did not sound as well as she wished.

"He knows I am a school girl," she uttered impatiently aloud, "and if wise men must have school girls write to them, they must read nonsense."

With this consolatory soliloquy she sealed and addressed the letter, and handed it to her father to post.

After tea Mr. Portwood asked Minona to promenade the veranda with him, and confided his disappointment to her.

"When I leave can I regard you as an ally, Miss Dearing? You have much influence in that quarter. Can I rely on your friendship to favor my suit?"

"As far as may lay in my power honorably to urge your claim, I will. But I abhor match-makers. In such affairs there ought to exist spontaneity. I would not value action which arose from intermeddling friends."

"You may be right; but drowning men are not often scrupulous as to the means of rescue. I am not hopeless; but my hope is of such slender dimension that I shall be miserable until it strengthens."

"Ladies are celebrated for their changeable feelings, and I believe in none are they so much so as in an affaire du coeur. Bear this in mind, and cheer up. A long face lengthens the distance between hope and the prize."

The next morning when Miss Gladwin and Minona appeared at breakfast, they learned that Mr. Portwood had left early that morning for Savannah thence to Europe. Mr. Crews was the only one present who heard these tidings with joy.

CHAPTER XII.

The sky was dark and lowering; gray leaden clouds curtained the vaulted arch of Heaven, weeping unceasingly fine, misty rain. It was early morning, and a young lady in a handsome dressing robe threw open the closed shutters have a window in the upper story of a brown stone mansion and looked below upon the sloppy street.

"Savannah, glorious city! where so many delightful days of my credulous, artless youth have been spent! City of all others! Most beautiful!"

Thus soliloquized the courted Minona Dearing, as she idly gazed from her window on the almost deserted street the morning after her arrival in Savannah.

Against Mr. Dearing's judgment his wife obstinately determined to usher her daughter, as well as Miss Gladwin, into society. Minona should be the star of the season, and Mrs. Dearing had caused her already elegant home to be refitted in the most superb style.

Minona did not experience the keen desire for a life of gayety she would have felt a few months before; and the prospect to Vinvela was absolutely distasteful.

Minona stood gazing through the window until Genista came and kindled a fire in the grate, and she heard her cousin's voice.

"How do you like the aspect of affairs?" asked Miss Dearing.

"If you allude to the weather, that is gloomy enough. Within, all is cheerful and promising. Do come away from the window; you will get cold," rejoined the orphan.

Minona walked to the fire.

"I refer neither to the weather within or without, but to the expectation of playing buffoon for the amusement of a score of simpering females, and a small legion of brainless men. If the intellects of a hundred of the latter were compressed into one, it would not acquire half the size of the great and glorious Daniel Webster's brain-power."

"I doubt, if it were possible to condense the capacities of the city's whole population, whether the would aggregate the proportion of that gigantic statesman's," answered Miss Gladwin, laughing at the odd manner in which Minona expressed herself.

Chapter XII. Mr. Dearing's house overlooked the Park. It was a large double building, ornamented with handsome balconies and an elaborate portico in front. The interior was most artistically finished, and fitted with the most super modern furniture.

"I wish mamma had remained in Tennessee. I love the mountains. We had such a quiet time with our books and the dear old school master. Poor fellow! what a dismal time he will have solitary 'monarch of all he surveys.'"

And something like a tear glistened in the eye of the impulsive girl.

"You will forget all in the whirlpool of gay company, dear Minona. When the sun shines, everything will wear a different look. My only fear is that you will love the world to well. We are all like pendulums; we swing as far one way as we do the other, as long as the main spring of youth keeps wound up."

"Well, I should like my pendulatory vibration to touch upon something sensible, at any rate. I believe I was placed here and given a soul for something better than to play the puppet upon the stage of fashion."

"So do I believe it; and I trust you will retain this same opinion at the end of the season. Let us hasten our toilet, or we shall be late for breakfast."

Mrs. Dearing rejoiced at the rain which continued unabated for several days. It gave her an opportunity of getting settled at home.

The very first afternoon which approximated to clear weather, Miss Hollis and Miss Lucy and Helen Christie called. The were profuse in kisses, smiles, and affectionate speeches.

"Oh, Minona! I am delighted that you have arrived! Your mamma has just been telling me she expects to bring you out. Her ball is to eclipse anything ever seen before!"

"Yes," said Helen, laughing, "how fortunate! So beautiful; so wealthy; so clever! I really envy you."

"We have a fine opera troupe in the city, and every accompaniment to make a pleasant winter," remarked Miss Hollis.

"How did you leave Miss Crandon? I felt much drawn to her."

"The doctor is as learned as ever, Miss Hollis, and looks thin and dejected. I think he contracted heart disease on that ride to the camp meeting," remarked Minona.

"Do you really think so, my dear?" said the lady smiling, with satisfaction. "I hope it is true; men need all the heartaches they can bear and more to keep them duly penitent for their continual sin of supreme selfishness."

"I imagine he experiences all you think he deserves; and that his penitence would gladly avail itself of your aid in bringing about a reform. He is very lonely just now. Miss Isabel has gone to Middle Tennessee on a visit to her mother. I wish we were at our home, and you could be with us, Miss Hollis," said Miss Dearing. "We might cheer him."

"One meets so few able professional men that they really command respect and admiration. Miss Gladwin, you do not look as well as when we last met."

Before Vinvela could reply, Miss Helen Christie remarked to Mrs. Dearing that Mrs. Horace Smith was a near neighbor, and one she would find most companionable.

"I did not know she claimed to be one of our circle. I doubt if she knows her multiplication table, or whatever we live in the Eastern or Western Hemisphere," said Mrs. Dearing.

"That was her status in the world's eye last winter, mamma, but I met Mrs. Smith several times. She was polished and as well informed as most ladies."

"Her husband is a relative of Sidney Smith," said Miss Hollis. "He has very distinguished relatives over the water."

"I should think his distinctions were a long time in crossing the Atlantic. They must have come in a sailing vessel," said Minona; "because last winter, gentle Mrs. Smith was in the depths of obscurity except to a few discerning, well-meaning ladies. What potent charm opened the eyes of the dozing world to the merit of Mrs. Horace Smith?"

"Cotton speculation," said Miss Hollis, with a knowing, important look. "He cleared a hundred thousand dollars last winter, and Mrs. Smith is one of the most charming little women I ever saw."

"She is perfectly lovely!" simpered Miss Helen. And Lucy declared she was beautiful and intellectual. "You will adore her irresistible manners, Miss Vinvela, when you meet her."

Minona smiled contemptuously. She knew positively that the admiring trio of worshipers had slighted Mrs. Smith the preceding season when she resided in a plain house without display. They seemed perfectly blind to the fact that they might be guilty of solecism by such inconsistency.

"Minona, you must join us in a promenade in the park as soon as the weather clears. Your appearance will cause many quakes and throbs among the hearts of the belles and the beaux. Adieu;" and the ladies left.

"How warm-hearted those little creatures are," said Mrs. Dearing. "How much more delightful it is to be here than shut up among the clay hills of Tennessee. Get ready girls, Horace will be around with a carriage directly. We must have a drive on the shell road."

Mrs. Dearing was in ecstasy during the ride. There were many carriages out, the weather having been inclement for days, the elite were obliged, at the first opportunity, "to air their gentility," and the ladies were overwhelmed with congratulations and flattery.

Minona declared she grew tired of nodding her head.

"We shall be suffocated with compliments. I wish to live, as I have a mission to fulfill before I leave the world."

"I should like to hear your vocation, daughter."

"Every whirligig has a certain number of gyrations before it stops. I have just begun my rotations, and do not wish to stop until I score somebody's heart to keep it with me in the sedentary stage of middle and old age."

"There comes Mr. Torrister," said Miss Gladwin. "Will his heart serve your purpose?"

"How exquisitely he rides!" exclaimed Mrs. Dearing, as the gentleman approached on an agile courser. "You could not make a more elegant selection, my dear."

The carriage was again halted, and warm greetings were exchanged. Minona had no time to reply to her mother, but her lips curled with contempt at the idea of such a choice.

"Miss Dearing, I am overpowered with joy at your return to the city. How long have you been here?"

And the handsome Mr. Torrister twirled his jetty moustache, made spiral by the free use of pomade.

"Three days. How is your friend, Miss Edwiston?" asked Minona.

"Three whole days and I did not know it!" exclaimed the beau, with a tragic little slap upon his knee. "I shall never forgive my negligence. I should have gone to your house the first evening of your arrival had I been aware of the fact."

"Then you would not have seen us, so spare your regrets and reply to my question."

"I believe Miss Edwiston is well. Let me see—I have not seen her in a week or two," he answered, slightly embarrassed.

"Your negligence, it seems, extends to more quarters than one," said Minona, laughing.

"Come to see us, Mr. Torrister. My house is always open to friends," remarked Mrs. Dearing, bowing, and her vehicle moved on, as the gentleman touched the rowels to his stead and galloped in the opposite direction.

"Is he not handsome!" said Mrs. Dearing. "And his polish is superb!"

"And his intelligence is so swift. It keeps a stupid girl constantly on the wing to catch up to it."

"You can afford to be satiric now, Minona, but it is not a safe weapon. Its blade often injures its possessor more than it does others."

"I never carry it among friends, dear mother, so do not feel at all uneasy about me."

"I regard Mr. Torrister as one of our peculiar friends."

Minona smiled, and very soon the ladies returned home.

The weather cleared bright and frosty. The door bell rang constantly, and Minona and Vinvela grew weary of entertaining visitors.

"I have had not a moment to devote to wholesome, sober reflection since I came here. My tongue is weary from much speaking, Vinvela. I am unsure if I remain until May I shall fall victim to bronchitis."

"You will grow accustomed to it after the first few weeks, and then you will not be in such constant requisition."

"Papa is going with us to the opera to-night. I am glad of this, on your account especially. He says the music is grand."

Vinvela answered in her quiet way that she would enjoy it. Fine music was a delight to her. There were many moments when she felt depressed in spirits. The image of her absent lover came dreamily to her, and awakened a tenderness that she did not attempt to control.

"I shall die young and be forgotten," she thought, "and why must I exclude even pleasant reflections?"

Minona, with a nice delicacy, never jested her about Mr. Portwood. She liked the young man. There was something in his integrity and promptitude of character, and his noble mind, which inspired trust and admiration, and Minona hoped Vinvela would waive her unselfish objections and receive the young man as her suitor. How immeasurably superior he was, in his poverty and unobtrusive manners, to all the young men she knew, except one!

The night came. The ladies were magnificently attired. Minona wore a cherry-colored merino with black facings, and her cousin a white dress of the same fabric, also trimmed in black. Crimson flowers gleaned in the jetty folds of Minona's glossy hair. She was radiantly beautiful, with her face colorless, except the rich tint of her lips.

As she and Vinvela appeared in the parlor Mr. Dearing thought he had never seen so superb a woman in his life as his charming daughter. His wife had been very handsome, and still wore the remains of beauty. A sensation of pain smote him as he looked on the unequaled child of his house. Beauty is a dangerous gift to a woman, and most generally saps all the adorning qualities she ought to wear when it fades. His own wife had yielded it the palm, and expected a successful career on its merits. Would his daughter do as she, or act wisely and place it among the poor, evanescent shows of life, cultivating the sterling virtues to carry along the battlefield of earth?

"Are you indisposed or gloomy to-night, dear papa?" she asked. "If so, let me remain at home with you. Vinvela and mamma can go with Mr. Torrister, who has invited himself to be of our coterie."

He pressed her soft hand.

"I am very well," he said, "and wish to see your enthusiasm and Miss Gladwin's when listening to soul enthralling music. But I thank you for this mark of your regard."

Very soon Mr. Torrister made his appearance, and the party set out for the theatre. As Minona was leaving the house she contrived to whisper to her father, and requested him to get Mr. Torrister seated by her mother. "Otherwise, the music will be drowned by his endless remarks."

Mr. Dearing laughingly acquiesced. On arriving at their destination, and entering the box, Mr. Dearing said:

"Eriginia, Mr. Torrister is under your care to-night. She will entertain you, sir," he continued, turning to the gentleman. "I claim the privilege of absorbing the spare attention of these two novices. I wish to study the effect produced upon the human soul when music casts her spell around it fully for the first time."

"You have two noble specimens to experiment upon. I envy you at least one," he added, inwardly.

"I must be selfish this time, Mr. Torrister. Married men are celebrated for this excellent virtue, you know."

The gentleman pocketed his disgust at the said virtue, and the virtues generally, with some mental expletives not very complimentary to crusty fathers, and resigned himself to the really more congenial society of the courted Mrs. Dearing. It would never do to appear oblivious to the favor conferred upon him by having her to entertain; so he began his remarks with several preparatory compliments. Mrs. Dearing owned a large stock of this very useful commodity, and there was a perfect hailstorm of fulsome flattery kept up for the evening. It is a very excellent and safe method, when a man has an eye to gaining the hand of a daughter, to march a few steps into the good graces of mamma. Wary Mr. Torrister understood the science, and like a good tactician, he advanced his forces to the very centre of attack, and in the end gained a victory in that quarter.

The orchestra struck up its prelude, as is usual, a short time previous to the lifting of the curtain. Then came noise and confusion from the impatient and expectant crowd, which died away into profound silence as the screen rolled up displaying the stage. The actors became visible, the music began, and the girls' whole souls were enthralled by the opera. Mr. Dearing watched Minona's expressive face which varied with every changing phase of the scene she witnessed. Miss Gladwin, less impulsive, sat quiet and listened with perfect abstraction to the full-swelling, undulating stream of harmony that seemed to float above, around and beneath her.

At the end of the first act Mr. Torrister, who had borrowed Mrs. Dearing's glass, exclaimed:

"There is my old friend Burleigh in the pit. I have not seen him since we left college. He has been traveling for years. Shall I present him to you?"

The lady expressed her willingness to see Mr. Burleigh, and in a short time he entered her box. He was a man of slight build, rather stooped in shoulders, very plain features, and his complexion somewhat tanned by exposure to the sun. His face had something of a scowl upon it, which plainly said, "The world has wronged me. I owe it nothing. I despise it." There was a defect in one of his feet which turned inward too much for symmetry, and it was elevated from the ground by a very thick cork sole to his boot. There was a scarce-perceptible lameness, yet the knowledge that the defect existed had embittered the whole life of its possessor. Mr. Burleigh was of an old English family, occupying the very best position in society. His education had been excellent, and his means, without being great, were adequate for all his reasonable wants.

He was introduced to the ladies, and seated himself near Miss Gladwin.

"How are you pleased with the performance?" he asked, scrutinizing her with one glance of his restless eye.

"Very much. I am no connoisseur, hence am easily gratified. Are you fond of music?"

"It depends on my mood. Sometimes it exerts a soothing influence, but more often it grates on my nerves excruciatingly. Such music as this is more calculated to exhaust than to exalt."

"I do not think so; but, as I said already, I am untaught, and this is my first introduction to the opera. I have been reminded here this evening, most forcibly, of the beautiful lines of Shelley on 'Music;' and these verses have been careering through my brain along with the operatic harmonies."

"Did you never observe the gradations of effect produced by the cultivation, or repetition even, of any subject? It takes away many of the pleasures felt, which, after all, are seldom real," said he.

"Yes. I have, but I do not think the result is always to detract from delightful sensations in either case. There are many things I like better the more frequently I see or hear them, and familiarity does but enable me the better to appreciate them."

"You, perhaps, speak from want of experience. As we grow older the scales of youth fall away from our eyes, and we behold the hollowness of the world as it is. I like to listen to the Æolian Harp. Its solemn wail, its dirge-like strains, tell of the bitterness of life, and possess a weird interest for me," said Mr Burleigh.

"I trust I may never gain that wisdom which will disenchant me with every simple pastime that should sweeten existence, Mr. Burleigh," replied Vinvela, looking at the gentleman with the whole depth of expression from her eyes.

"Miss Gladwin, it is refreshing to listen to your animated view of the world. You do not know it as I do. You, perhaps, were born to tread its flowery path, while I, as Sidney Smith so truthfully described it, came to walk rough shod through stony places."

"My lot, in some respects, Mr. Burleigh, has been by no means exempt from bitter experiences. The peculiar bearing they have upon our characters depends very greatly upon what kind of spectacles we look through."

"Credulity and gentleness are two very essential elements to enable us to get on smoothly. I confess that I own neither, and I regret it," he said.

"Perhaps I am as little blessed in these requisites as you," answered the girl.

The rising of the curtain prevented further remarks, but there was much of the gloss rubbed from the performance of the evening. Mr. Burleigh's conversation impressed her disagreeably. How often do the snarlings of a misanthrope cloud the prospect to even the largest hearted philanthropist?

Mr. Burleigh remained with the ladies through the opera. His enlightenment an observations on travel would have been captivating, but there was a bitterness of gall in his view of every subject which left its effect invariably upon his hearers.

At the conclusion of the opera he observed with surprise that Vinvela walked with a crutch, and that her lameness was quite apparent.

"Is it possible," thought he, "that one marked with a curse not less severe than that borne by Cain can know genuine happiness and regard mankind with lenity? I must watch this girl who is such an accomplished dissembler!"

And Akers Burleigh returned to his lodgings with something of a light heart to dream over the anomalous novelty he had seen that night.

A week before Christmas Minona would accomplish her seventeenth birthday, and her mother decided that, upon that day should occur her long projected party for bringing out into society to young ladies, and conferring upon them all the emoluments arising from such high privilege. It lacked but ten days of the time, and Mrs. Dearing was determined that no expense should be spared to render it the most brilliant affair of the season. The most thorough pastry cooks were engaged to supply and arrange the table with every delicacy the city could afford. Musicians were retained for the occasion, and invitations were sent a week previous to the important day. Mrs. Dearing's gift to her daughter was a costly white velvet robe elaborately trimmed. To Vinvela she presented a fine black satin. Her own dress was a claret colored velvet, which she had already worn.

The day at last dawned, and at breakfast Minona and Vinvela found upon their plates at the breakfast table each a casket from Mr. Dearing. That of the latter was a set of large pearls, and Minona a set of carbuncles and garnets. Mr. Dearing would hear of no thanks, which he expected to experience by seeing the girls wear his gifts that night, accompanied by bright eyes and smiling faces.

"I have another donation which I do not hesitate to assert will eclipse the other totally in the estimation of both of you," and with a quizzical look he handed each a note. "Confess that I am right in my premises."

"I believe I shall claim the privilege the ladies behold is inestimable—that of preserving a wise silence on so grave a question. Vinvela, you had better enlist under my banner. Father, though no lawyer, is very acute in penetration, and possesses in a remarkable degree like them that Euripidean faculty of reasoning sophistry into the similitude of truth."

"I think my daughter inherits some of my sharpness in the adroitness she displays in getting out of an embarrassing situation. Be more frank, Miss Gladwin, and confess; blushes are quite becoming to the fair."

"I am proof in that quarter," said Vinvela, laughing, "for I can neither blush nor decide on the relative value of the favors until I read my billet. I shall answer at a future season."

"I shall remind you of your promise. Will you make me a similar one, my dear?"

"I should not like to," answered Minona, and she and Vinvela disappeared to their room.

Minona's note was from Mr. Meverill, who had arrived the day before and requested the pleasure of calling upon her at 11 o'clock.

Miss Gladwin's note was from the absent Hugh. It was the exponent of a true heart, inspired with a boundless love for her, and wretched in the suspense of a passion that was not hopeless.

Locking the letter in her dressing case she decided to ponder over it a few days, and probably show it to Minona before coming to a final conclusion.

Eleven o'clock came speedily to Minona, who had been busy with Vinvela in assisting her mother to arrange the tables. Her visitor arrived punctually, and she descended to the parlor in her cherry-colored morning robe. Minona was fond of crimson. Harmony in colors is ever pleasing to the eye, and her faithful mirror taught her that she appeared never better than when attired in the rich hue of carmine.

Mr. Meverill extended a grave, earnest greeting to Minona's warm welcome. His appearance indicated less robust health than when Miss Dearing last saw him. She thought his deportment was more reserved and his smile played over his fine face more rarely. Life was no bubble to him, and those who combat its difficulties resolutely have little space to give to joy and mirth.

"You came to Savannah at the most auspicious moment, Mr. Meverill. Mother has a gathering of friends and we shall be happy to welcome you among them at 9 o'clock this evening."

"I thank you for the wish to have me present, but I seldom attend festive occasions."

"This is my birthday, and it will be gratifying to have all my friends with me."

"I shall certainly, in this case, do myself the honor of being present to offer you my congratulations." And he continued, "I must beg you to accept my thanks for your letter, which makes me laugh. You introduce sunshine wherever you are, and send forth rays of it even in your letters."

"I rejoice that the shimmer of mirth blinded you to its defects," said the gay girl, "because I sent it with much trepidation to such a profound thinker as yourself."

"You are disposed to ridicule, I see. However, you deserve the privilege after the benign favor you conferred upon me by writing. I regret I shall be in Savannah so long, because it deprives me of experiencing such favors again."

Mr. Meverill remained but a short time, and the rest of the day was consumed in putting the last touches to the preparations for the entertainment.

Mr. Dearing's house overlooked the Park. It was a large double building, ornamented with handsome balconies and an elaborate portico in front. The interior was most artistically finished, and fitted with the most super modern furniture. On the right of a large entrance hall were two ample parlors divided by sliding doors. On the left was a handsome sitting-room and dining-room adjoining. These two rooms were devoted to dancing on this occasion.

At half past nine in the rooms began to fill rapidly. Mr. and Mrs. Dearing stood at a convenient spot in the front room for receiving the congratulations of their friends who swept on, giving place to others in the rear. Minona appeared arrayed in her white velvet with her brooch and bracelets of garnets. She wore no ornaments in her hair. Its heavy coils almost covered her regal head. Her beauty was transcendent, and whispers passed between many, both envious and well meaning friends, of a complimentary nature.

Mr. Torrister filled the honorable position of escorting Miss Dearing through the rooms and dancing the first quadrille with her.

Dancing began early, and Miss Dearing found herself in requisition every set. Miss Gladwin, of course, did not dance, but it was diverting to her to observe the others and listen to the gushing strains of music. Very handsome she looked, her fair skin flushed into a warm glow, and her expressive eyes brightened by excitement.

After dancing several times, Minona found herself near Mr. Burleigh, who asked her to promenade.

"I had no opportunity of conversing with you, Miss Dearing, the night of my introduction. I had an interesting interview with your cousin, who appears to me to have far deeper reflective powers than most young ladies. She interests me. Her nature is a study to me; the antithesis of mine in most things."

"Then you believe in the philosophy of liking our opposites?"

"Yes, on the principle that extremes meet. This thing of what goes to make congeniality and accord between people, is a puzzling theme to me. All the discussions I have ever heard upon it failed to elucidate the subject. I have as often seen people of similar natures agree, as I have those of opposite elements; and vice versa."

"I never studied such theories on scientific principles, but I believe there must be some hidden affinity of mind to make any two persons really companionable, and likewise the same of heart to create love, and keep the current flowing smoothly. Suppose you take an acetic temper and unite it to one of alkaline predominance; do you not see that a tremendous effervescence would occur?" Mr. Burleigh laughed. "But," said he, "that effervescence subsides quickly, and then there is perfect repose, and people of your alkaline and acid formation would set out at the boiling point, and then lead the most placid existences of all others."

"Yes; if you could liquidate their whole tempers at once and confine them, that would be the most happy effect; but this quality only evolves a certain amount of material at any one period; then every time they come in contact a new ebullition takes place."

"You possess certainly a fine analytic mind, and have furnished a most philosophical illustration of the result, produced by the union of acids and alkalies. I am of the sour temperament. I shall henceforth be ever on the search for the opposite agency which I shall be careful to avoid, as I relish nothing stormy, and detest effervescences outside of a chemist laboratory."

At this moment the music began to discourse sweet strains, and the hand of Minona was claimed by some agile-footed gallant eager for the fantastic evolutions of the mazy dance.

Mr. Burleigh sought Miss Gladwin, and seated himself near her.

"You have a charming cousin, Miss Gladwin. Her intellect is as remarkable for beauty and sparkle as her imperial form and face."

"Yes; her presence brings a lustre to everything she approaches. She is the idol of her family, and more than that to me."

"I cannot see how that could be. Whilst she is very lonely, you seem to have resources enough within yourself to be independent."

"One wearies of ego; I am debarred, you see, by misfortune from engaging in the pursuits and recreations of other young people. We cannot follow any sole occupation continuously without fatigue. Man is essentially gregarious, and under all circumstances needs at times companionship. Now, Minona is my associate, friend, confidant, enjoyment, in short, everything I desire."

"You have summed up at perfect galaxy of nouns, each one a complimentary pearl of itself. You are fortunate in having such a friend, and she is to be envied for having inspired such a depth of affection in your heart. Will you pardon me, Miss Gladwin, if I ask you a few questions? They do not arise from impertinent curiosity, but from a desire to learn something which may benefit me."

"Certainly. I will reply to your queries, if in my power. I like to gain information, and should feel proud to think that I confer a similar benefit upon friends," she laughingly said.

"I am serious in what I am going to ask. Tell me, is your amiable love and toleration for the world genuine and heartfelt, or is it only a habit of mocking compliment that so many have when in company?"

"I express sincerely and truthfully what I feel in my words and actions."

"Have you no bitterness at the deriding, deceitful, wealth-worshiping, heartless throng one meets throughout the whole course of a life?"

"No; why should I? They may be all you say, but they never injured me. I have my defects, doubtless they have theirs also; but I mete out the measure I hope to have measured to me."

"Do you obtain it? You alluded just now to your misfortune, else I should not refer to it. Do you not receive slights and opprobrium, and wounds deep and never-healing which rankle forever"—and his voice trembled with emotion, and he continued after a pause—"from mankind; yes—even from those you have claims upon?"

Vinvela raised her dark, sympathetic eyes upon the gentleman, and replied:

"Slights from the gay, flippant pleasuresippers in society I have received; but they can never inflict wounds upon my spirit, because I value not their opinion, good or bad. It is a wind that sweeps by and is heard no more. God gave me my defect for a wise purpose, and I thank him for it, because it has made me strive for the attainment of better aspirations. My friends, Mr. Burleigh, are few! They are always considerate."

"How different are your sensations from mine! I, too, have my misfortune, entailed upon me by the carelessness of a heartless nurse. Looking upon one of my race as the author of a brand which pursues me as a curse that has darkened every prospect, embittered every joy, I have reached an altitude of hatred for mankind fearful to estimate. My sensitiveness has grown to that morbid excess, that I construe every act into slights, and while reason tells me they are often fancies, yet my rage and abhorrence have been none the less for it."

"Perhaps I might have felt something of what you described had my career have been different. I can see how I might have been brought to such a state had I been in contact with cruel, unsparing companions. But my whole life, up to the past year, was spent in sweet seclusion, with the best and most intellectual of fathers, who felt only compassion and love, and taught me, from my cradle, to estimate my own nature, and that of others, not by the exterior beauty of the casket, but by its contained jewels of heart and intellect. My cousins are of too noble a mould to be other than the most lenient of friends to me."

"I wish I could learn your philosophy, Miss Gladwin, and that is saying much, for never in all my life before have I met anyone who led me even to feel a desire to change."

"Then learn moral courage—that power which elevates man far above the poor, fleeting whims of his kind. It is the most sublime of all human attributes, for upon it hangs all the other virtues."

"Thank you. I will lay your suggestion to heart, and I hope you will place me in the catalogue of your friends."

Minona was conversing with a group of companions, who were watching the evolutions of the ever-shifting dance, and listening to their comments on the relative grace of the dancers.

"Minona," said Helen Christie. "Just look at Mr. Hogan. Is he not exquisite to-night? I never saw such a perfect dancer. He is symmetry itself. How can you resist his fascinations?"

"I do not pretend to escape them," she answered, with a derisive smile upon her proud lip. "As was said of the celebrated Duke of Marlborough, 'Every step he takes carries death in it;' though the gentleman resembles the great Churchill in nothing else."

Helen went off with a companion, and for a moment Miss Dearing was alone gazing at the dancers, but her thoughts apparently were far away. She was recalled by a deep voice behind her which seemed to construe what she was thinking of, as it quoted from the "Psalm of Life:"

> *"Life is short and time is fleeting,*
> *And our hearts though stout and brave;*
> *Stiff like muffled drums are beating.*
> *Funeral marches to the grave."*

"Will you walk, Miss Dearing? I had been observing you for some time, and your countenance expressed such a superlative contempt for the moving show before you that it suggested the beautiful stanza from Longfellow to me."

"Do you disapprove of dancing?" she asked, looking at him.

"No; but I think we were made for something better than to shuffle through life by a heel-and-toe movement."

Minona laughed.

"What an odd idea, Mr. Meverill! Your gravity makes me even afraid to smile in your presence."

"I regret," he said, "that I inspire so much fear. Do not withhold your smiles, they come like illuminating rays to my sorrowful heart. Did you know," he asked, changing the subject, "that we have a fine circulating library in the city? Will you go there someday soon with me?"

"Yes; join us in a drive, because I should like Vinvela to go, and she cannot walk such a distance. I was not aware of the existence of such a treasure and shall patronize it. Our fine library is in Tennessee. We spend but a few months of the year here."

The time was set for the ensuing Thursday morning at eleven o'clock, at which time Mr. Meverill promised to call.

"What have you been doing since I met you at Montvale?" asked the young man.

"It has not been very long, you know. While in Tennessee Vinvela and I went to recitations under a tutor each morning; and I read and walked, and discussed topics with my father whose conversation is always improving. Since coming to Savannah I have accomplished nothing intellectually."

Mr. Torrister now came to claim Miss Dearing's hand for the last cotillion before supper.

"Excuse me, sir," she said, "I must plead fatigue, and beg you to seek another partner. I shall dance no more to-night."

Involuntarily Mr. Meverill, upon whose arm her hand rested as they stopped in their promenade, pressed it slightly as she uttered her determination. A faint glow overspread Minona's face. They joined Vinvela until supper was announced, and Mr. Meverill escorted Minona into the dining-room.

"That will be a match; take my word for it, Mrs. Smith," said Miss Hollis, as Mr. Meverill passed with Minona. "Miss Dearing could do better than throw herself away upon a poor fortune-hunter. There is the elegant Mr. Torrister, his superior."

Quiet, gentle Mrs. Smith's face colored, and, with a look of perfect contempt, she said:

"Mr. Torrister may be a fortune-hunter, but Delbridge Meverill can be placed in no such list. He is as far above such dignities, as the Brobdingnags exceeded the Lilliputians in stature."

And with a distant bow Mrs. Smith accepted her husband's arm and left.

"Did you not know, Miss Elmira, that Mr. Meverill was related to Mrs. Smith?" asked Lucy Christie.

"No! I am overwhelmed with mortification, and must apologize. She is too rich to be slighted," she added inwardly, as she went into supper.

It was with indescribable exhaustion that Minona laid aside her elegant birthday costume as she retired for the night. Like all sensible people she could not contemplate with regret the hollowness of the pleasures she so constantly fed upon, and feel how utterly powerless they were to fill the unceasing cravings of soul to have the vacuum within filled by solid, wholesome nutriment. Although physically fatigued, her brain was restlessly active, and throwing on a wrapper and turning the gas jets almost to darkness, she seated herself at the window and watched the spangled canopy in the neutral-tinted arch of Heaven.

"Can you talk, Minona?" asked Vinvela, who had sought her couch. "I am perplexed, and wish your counsel. If you are not tired, I wish you could read the note from Mr. Portwood which your father handed to me this morning."

"No; I can read it, dear Vinvela, if it will gratify you. I wish to escape from self to-night, and can select no more gentle theme than you to dwell on."

She rose, and brightened the gas, she read the impassioned note.

"I knew you had refused him when I found he had gone to Europe, but such things are sacred from prying eyes. Why do you not recall him? Does your heart not plead for him?"

"Perhaps it does. I can scarce define my own sensations. But would I be right in marrying anyone? Would I not confer sorrow instead of happiness? If we love, the afflictions of the beloved render us wretched."

"In one aspect they do; but would not the gain of a beautiful companion repay immeasurably for any anxieties thereby called forth? Fears for a beloved object do but deepen the current of love. They vivify every joy in the same ratio as they increase each pain. I wish not to urge you upon a matter which you alone ought to decide, but if you love this young man—and I know none worthier—I would write to him, and give ease to his troubled spirit sorrowing in a strange land."

"I will reflect on your advice, dear Minona, and I thank you for all your tender kindness. Let us seek rest in the oblivion of sleep, and awake refreshed to the duties of the morrow."

CHAPTER XIII.

The next Thursday was lovely and clear, cheating one into the belief that spring had come with its vernal smiles to infuse new life into all creation. The trees overshadowed the smooth pavements with their warm, green foliage, and birds were on the wing, or sung a joyous carol amid the leafy boughs.

Mr. Meverill came and joined the ladies in their drive, and escorted them to the library. Many books were there which attracted Minona's attention, but she selected but one that morning, as she had received from Mr. Meverill the promised volume. These two books, lightly received, were to produce a great transmutation of the views and aims of their reader. How powerful is the spell cast around sensitive natures by the works of master minds, who have gone to swell the number of choristers in the mysterious eternity! Genius can never die; it lives forever to cheer each successive generation by its glorious revelations.

Mrs. Dearing delighted in light reading, and she provided herself with a novel not famous for its depth of learning. Vinvela selected one of Irving's sparkling volumes, with his easy flowing wit and quaint humor, that run like golden threads through almost every thought he ever penned.

The morning was consumed, and all concurred in the opinion that the ride was delightful.

"So much more agreeable, than to waste time in senseless discussions upon the fashions in the latest 'Godey's Lady's Book.' How do gentlemen escape ennui, Mr. Meverill?—a disorder exclusively feminine, I believe, and very annoying."

"You are mistaken, Miss Dearing. I think it afflicts both sexes. I can answer for myself. I escape it by seeking to keep this motto ever in view."

He withdrew from his finger a ring displaying a handsome bloodstone elegantly set in chased gold. Upon it was engraven a miniature temple of fame, with the device "Sapere aude" cut in old English letters.

"It was given to me," he said, handing it to her, "by a dear friend of my boyhood, now no more, who inspired me with the first throb of ambition I ever felt. I have regarded it as a sacred trust."

Minona had observed the ring upon his finger, and was familiar with it from having seen the impression upon the seal of her letter. After looking at the ring she returned it.

Chapter XIII. Mrs. Dearing delighted in light reading, and she provided herself with a novel not famous for its depth of learning. Vinvela selected one of Irving's sparkling volumes, with his easy flowing wit and quaint humor, that run like golden threads through almost every thought he ever penned.

"The remedy is worse than the disease, I think, Mr. Meverill," said Miss Dearing. "We purchase wisdom at too dear a price. I confess I have neither bodily strength nor mental capacity to undertake anything so grand. It would require as much power as Samson exerted in moving the gates of Gaza."

"O, dear mother! It depends on the temperament. To some people wisdom is a pleasure, and costs no effort."

"I am not one of the happy class, unfortunately," she added, with a slight sigh.

Mr. Meverill wondered how mother and daughter could be so very unlike. He was not, on reflection, surprised at Minona's brilliancy. Her father's example was sufficient inspiration, but how could the mother and wife be so antithetical? Strange anomaly that frequently occurs in every-day life, and puzzles more than this gentleman, who had wisdom and her luring happiness ever before him.

The Park was, as has been said, very near to Mr. Dearing's home. During the early morning it was generally deserted, except by a few nursery maids, who led out their infantile corps for airing and diversion. Often Minona and Vinvela would put on their hats and go there with their books to read under the lofty pines, seated on the rustic benches that temptingly offer rest to the weary promenaders. They generally read an hour, and then stroll to the fountain which graces the centre of the enclosure. Grim Triton sits securely upon his water couch in a state of stern repose in the mornings, but he blows unceasing jets of water through his shell trumpet during the long afternoons, when the place is crowded by pedestrians of all castes.

Minona and Vinvela delighted to walk and reflect in this spot in the quiet mornings better than in the quiet mornings better than in the bustling afternoons. It reminded them both of the serenity of life in the country, which is preferable to all persons of contemplative natures.

Minona plunged with delight into "Corrine." It's truthful descriptions of Rome pleased her, and enlightened her understanding, by their graphic power, into a vivid idea of the position of each memorable ruin of the "Eternal City." The weakness and faithlessness of Nelvil disgusted her; but Corinne, the enthusiastic, impassioned, improvisatrice of sunny Italy, with her undying and abounding love for her vacillating suitor, fired her imagination and swayed it with indescribable influence. The irrepressible genius of the beautiful Anglo-Italian wrought upon her fancy continuously. What was I made for? Can I not do something, pursue some course which will elevate me, and caused me to leave a name worthy of record? were questions felt rather than asked often in the midnight hour by the aspiring girl.

Mr. Meverill observed with delight, but in silence, that some change was being wrought in the beautiful being he admired against reason. She grew day by day more congenial—more assimilated to his vein of thinking. He pursued his legal studies with unremitted vigor, hoping to be admitted to the bar in early spring.

Christmas festivities came and passed. Minona went to few entertainments, and when she appeared she was courted, flattered, eulogized, and sought after. She could have counted her admirers by scores, but she determined that age should overtake her as Miss Dearing, unless she could be unequivocally convinced that her hand was sought for herself, with no thought of her wealth. After New Year's with its reception had gone, and comparative quiet reigned in the heart of society. Minona began reading the other book she got from the library. It was a rainy evening, and, glad of a respite from company, the girls had sought their room at an early hour. By a comfortable fire and the shaded gas, Minona sat, opened her book and began. She read; and read with a fascinating power over her that she could not resist. At eleven Vinvela begged her to retire, as she was going to rest.

"Only a little longer, until I complete this chapter," she said.

Again she became absorbed, and one, two, three, four o'clock sounded from the lonely watchman, and was echoed by his fellows in their night-long vigils over the sleeping city. Still she pursued her occupation with no sense of fatigue, totally insensible to the flying hours. The fire died down to a few embers in the grate, but she paused not in her eager, devouring haste to get to the end of her charming volume. As the first ray of dawn crept through the window, Minona closed her book. It was "De Quincy's Opium Confessions."

She bowed her head in her clasped hands on the table, and uttered in a low voice:

"O mighty child of Heaven-fledged genius! thy soul attuned with thousand strings of exquisite sensibility, vibrating beautiful music in the faintest touch. O rare De Quincy! I can not eulogize thee better than in thy own matchless language which thou dost apply to another: 'O, laureled scholar, sun-bright intellect foremost man of all of this world!'"

The girl ceased for some time, and when she rose and sought her couch, a tear glistened in her eyes.

Henceforth she had a new birth, lived another existence. De Quincy was the magic key which unlocked the chambers of her intellectual efforts. Life opened out a new vista paved with gold, that led to the jeweled gates of the temple of renown. Such it appeared to her. O deceitful fame! "It is a shuttlecock," says the great Johnson, "if struck at one end, it will soon fall to the ground; to keep it up, it must be struck at both ends."

The blows are made by fortuitous circumstances. Alas! how often are they wanting, and how much talent has slept in obscurity from the absence of these peculiar blows.

A great change came over this favorite child of nature. She had possessed a redundancy of life, an overflowing of wit and amusing satire, that rendered her a most delightful companion. Now, there was a reserve and apparent abstraction, with only occasional gleams of the old mischievous spirit. From being a talker, she became a thinker; restless, eager, dissatisfied. Thought as a scroll unrolled itself, displaying infinite fancies to her eager mind, which ever changed and fled away as she endeavored to catch them. All was chaotic splendor before her, and she a powerless artificer to bring order upon it. Her sleep was troubled; night and day the busy brain toiled with a confused mass which tortured it. She strove to banish ideas which acted only as a mocking fiends; but that were as impossible as it was for her to hush the winds in the howling storm.

One night, being unable to sleep, Minona rose, brightened the light and essayed to read. Thought is ever unruly, and cannot be broken to harness without much pains and trouble. Hers was of a peculiar, restive type, and could not be suddenly drilled into dray-horse service of patiently traveling a beaten road. She threw aside her volume in despair.

"I will keep a diary and transfer these multiform fragments of reflection to paper; eased of the burden. I may have moments of respite when my spirit will rebound with something of its old buoyancy, else I shall grow old before I am of age."

Minona, from a child, had this habit of shaping her meditations into words. She rose as she spoke, reached her portfolio, and wrote? No! As she took up her pen she asked herself what should she write. She mused awhile, then uttered in a low tone:

"I will recount the incidents of my life, beginning from my earliest recollection." But she had touched a spring which disclosed a vast, gloomy corridor filled with more confused cloud-masses than had yet been open to her vision. There seemed a link connecting her with Rachel Mulkey, and other dim shades flitting by in obscurity, which it was impossible to discern clearly.

No silken threads of thought offered themselves to her straining, eager, yearning mind.

She was not to be baffled. Her nature was too courageous and determined to be quelled or affrighted by shadows. If she could not write a connected narrative, she could photograph with her pen the detached masses that swept like summer clouds over her intellectual horizon; and in future it would be fitting occupation to study out the puzzle, and place each part in proper position.

Again she took her pen, and wrote now whatever offered itself to her versatile mind. These writings she termed "Dream Fragments of Early Years." Superstition is the offspring of the solitude and darkness of self-absorption, and there is more or less an inherent taint of it in every human being, though it assumes herculean proportion only when the blackness of ignorance adds its gloom to deepen the sombre colors. Minona had a slight tincture of this awe in her composition, that made itself known whenever she strove to exhume the recollections of the past, and connect them with her never to be forgotten dream, and the endeavors of the old woman to see her. That there was something hidden that ought to be revealed she was assured; but by what method she could begin to unravel the skein she was at a loss to determine.

Each night Minona rose quietly, and in the still hours devoted herself to her new employment. From beginning with a few desultory links, she soon found she could join them into a consecutive chain—not from babyhood and its attending years of childhood, that was hidden in an impenetrable mist, and she gave it up—going back only so far as she clearly remembered. Writing this delicious confessional, whereby one can silently, fully unburden the heavy-laden conscience and mind without dread of enforced penances, became a volatile essence which coursed through her nerves, infusing them with delights never before known.

Weeks moved on. The girl read and wrote her mental landscape, expanding day by day into new beauties which grade gratified for a season. But there came a stage—perhaps from overwork or from greater enlightenments—when all she composed seem trite, sickly efforts of a moonstruck miss. The mental pendulum swept in its lengthening oscillations far away into depths of increasing gloom, appearing in it's reverse vibration to dwell only a moment in the light, and then backward into the ever-deepening darkness again. Minona laid aside her diary and her composition, and began her studies. She read logic, poured over rhetoric, and all the treatises upon diction that she could find in the hub of elucidation and emancipation from the thralldom of the shadows. Vain delusion! Rhetorical rules to a writer are like the splints with which the body of a man, bruised all over, might be bound; the mind can neither move, think, nor act, without one of the rhetorical splints jostling rudely, or pressing painfully upon the abounding genius of the writer, who struggles vainly to escape the toils for awhile, and finally dies under the effects of a prolonged cramp.

Minona was in despair. She felt all this acutely. What could be done? Her father was much engrossed in business. He came home late, wearied, and she could not confide her girlish follies to him. Mr Meverill she shrunk from. Her sensitiveness flew to arms at the bare idea of avowing herself an authorling, even in secret, for her own diversion, to him. Mr. Burleigh? He was capable of aiding, but he was a cynic of the first magnitude, and one wag of his bitter tongue would crush out every aspiration. Mr. Portwood was in Europe, and the kind quiet little minister—ah! he might, in his mingled meekness and goodness, sympathize with her, but he was locked in the snows of her mountain home. Vinvela, then, was the only party who could be the escape valve to her pent-up troubles. Minona knew that her cousin suspected something of the kind. They were room-mates, and her actions could not be entirely secluded from observation. Of her cousin's sympathy she was assured by her knowledge of her cousin's nature; but could she help her? That was the puzzling query.

Vinvela, after a long conflict, had yielded to the dictates of her affectionate heart, and had written an acceptance to her absent lover. She was now the affiance of Hugh Portwood—separated from her by a vast and fathomless ocean. How quickly consent in such case changes the aspect of affairs! Now, not a wind sighed through the tree tops, but an echoing quiver coursed through the delicate frame of Vinvela, and a terror lest her lover might find a sepulchre in the wailing Atlantic and never reach her, took possession of her. Not very long after her hand was disposed of by promise, she received an offer from another quarter most unexpected to her.

One morning Minona and herself were, as usual, in the Park to enjoy the sunshine and balmy air soft as the infant spring. Minona availed herself of the opportunity to tell Vinvela of her nightly vigils and efforts, and an intention she had recently made of writing something anonymously for the press.

"May I read one of my silly effusions to you, cousin?" she asked. "And will you give your opinion truthfully without fear of offending me?"

"Yes. My father was in the habit, during his life, of writing articles and reading them to me before publication. It will seem like the good old 'long ago.'"

"You are accustomed to criticising then," joyfully exclaimed Minona, "and can aid me."

"No. I cannot do that; but I have my taste slightly improved, and can at least tell what I like, and what I think faulty."

Minona proposed returning to the house and bringing a few pages as a specimen. There was no fear of interruption at that early hour. Vinvela remained with her book. Her cousin had been absent but a short time ere she perceived Mr. Acres Burleigh approaching. He expressed his delight at meeting her in very warm terms. She had seen a great deal of him in the past two months, as he was a frequent visitor at Mr. Dearing's mansion.

"Are you alone, Miss Gladwin?" he asked. "I did not know you frequented the Park, or I should have been tempted to walk out hither more often."

Vinvela answered by saying that she was sometimes in the habit of strolling there with her cousin after breakfast to enjoy the sunlight and repose under the sighing pines, which reminded her of rural scenes she loved.

"My cousin left but a few moments ago, and will return shortly with a book we wished."

The gentleman seated himself beside the lady, and, with some slight embarrassment, unfolded his feelings and his hopes to her view.

"I have lived to reach thirty-two years. I have traveled in America, in Europe and Asia. I have been isolated among thousands, and thought my heart adamant, so stony were its bulwarks against all my kind until I met you. Your holiness your moral intrepidity, your meek, beautiful nature, the very antithesis of the misanthrope, have turned this rock into a quivering, beating heart, bounding with love for you. Complete your work, dear lady, and transform me into a rough similitude of your lovely character."

"Mr. Burleigh," she said, softly, sadly, "I have no heart to give. My hand is promised to another known long before I ever heard of you. You magnify my virtues. There are many far superior to me who could minister to you, and appreciate your good traits."

"I never saw one who approximated to you. Lady, I do not blame you. Cruel fate has pursued me from my cradle. I shall sink into a worse than Cimmerian darkness. Farewell!"

He wrung her hand, and was gone ere Minona returned. Vinvela never saw him again, but he mourned for her when she was no more as long as life's fitful fever agitated his frame.

She was the only star that had ever arisen over the night of misanthropy which had shrouded his life. Its beauteous light like a meteor swept athwart the horizon for a moment then disappeared, leaving a deeper darkness than before.

Minona appeared with her book. She submitted it to her cousin's judgment. Her effort displayed unmistakable talent. There was a profundity of thought, a terseness of expression, a graphic painting of scene which brought out the subject in a perspicacious manner, that left no room for the tangled mazes of doubt to dwell upon.

Vinvela expressed her admiration in unmeasured terms, and asked Minona what was her object in writing. Did she intend to become an author, or follow the beaten track of woman's true vocation?

"Vinvela," said the girl, "I have heard you say you a prescience of early death. I have not that, but I have an abiding indwelling knowledge that I am hurrying with rapid strides upon the verge of a yawning abyss—of what precise nature I cannot say. But, come a change there will. I feel it hour by hour, and I shall not long be as I am now. I am nearing the chasm with a velocity of a comet."

"You terrify me. What can you mean? Surrounded with every blessing imaginable, how can you be the victim of phantoms?"

"These are not mere phantoms. I believe Providence often opens rifts in the crapy fold which secretes furturity, and permits glimpses of what is to come, that we may prepare. A wise mariner furls his sails when the storm brews. There are soul-barometers."

"True; but what bearing can authorship have upon all this?" asked Miss Gladwin.

"The desire to scribble keeps up an irrepressible conflict within me. I can no more suppress it than I could change my spots were I a leopard. Now, suppose my father should fail, which is not an improbable circumstance to a mercantile man; if I were an authoress, in that event, I might be a worker, and not a drone as I am now."

"But authors are generally poor if they begin without a patrimony. You may gain fame if you show genius, and the wind sets fair; but I have heard it said that game in the form of golden eagles is generally wanting. Then, women who write are never, or seldom happy."

"I care not for that. Happiness is a myth, an imaginary something pursued by all, and has more hues than the Chameleon. Those are the happiest who ignore self, and confer the largest benefits upon their fellow-beings. Now, this term fellow-beings in one sense as a collective term, meaning vast crowds; but, in my application, comprises only those who surround or come in contact with us in our every-day walk, and the compass is small. If I could work and accumulate for a beloved father and mother in misfortune, thank you not I would be doing great good to my fellow-beings."

"Yes. But these are merely the restless imaginings of aspiring ambition emanating from a large heart. Cast them from you, and be content as you are. Do all the deeds of love you can in the situation you occupy, and bestow your affections upon some noble fellow who will appreciate them."

"This, then, is the true vocation," said Minona, contemptuously. "I have seen many inferiors, but, vain as I may appear, I have yet to behold my superior; until then I am destined to roam 'fancy free.' In the meantime, 'Satan finds mischief still' for idle women, and I must write to keep out of harm's way."

"Do so; but your health is failing under this constant tension of thought and loss of sleep. You will grow old and ugly and cross and unbearable," said Vinvela, smiling.

"I care not. I would yield all if I were only a genius, and could soar like the eagle to an everlasting eyrie of effulgent glory which would light the world for ages. Let us return home."

The rose and walked to the house.

Minona, after this conversation, toiled on, battling constantly against the fluctuations of hope and despair that alternately ruled her. She prepared a touching little story for a New England magazine, which advertise to pay for contributions on acceptance. The imbursement to her purse was nothing.

She entertained a vague thought that if she received remuneration it should be devoted to charity. In her letter to the publishing house of Messrs. Wise & Co., she was unintentionally ambiguous in her position regarding the mighty potentate, better known as the 'almighty dollar,' simply offering her manuscript for their inspection.

Horace, the coachman, was summoned, and the important manuscript dispatched, with a donation to him for silence and punctuality. Horace was a faithful, genteel mulatto, with manners more polished than many pretentious white men. He had been kind to Minona from her early childhood, and felt proud of the confidence reposed in him. He reported to his young mistress that he had placed her letter safely in the post office, and Minona was satisfied. She limited her expectation of an answer to four weeks, and devoted herself to writing this time, an autobiography. This course of life wrought a change in Miss Dearing. She lost the infantile roundness of form attending early youth, and that aimless expression of girlishness. Her face, always pale, became thinner and reflection with its unerring burin-traced lines indelible upon her face.

"Minona," asked her father, one day at breakfast, "what has come upon you? I never saw anyone change as you have since we left Tennessee. I have observed you for some time."

"Nothing," she said, smiling. "Human nature is progressive. I could not always remain a child."

"She is so morose, Clarek. I cannot get her to join in a single amusement. I think she must have lost her heart with that conceited Mr. Meverill."

"Dear mother, I did not intend to be morose. I have my heart yet with me in a perfectly whole state, I assure you, and I do not agree with you that Mr. Meverill is conceited. On the contrary, I never saw one of as great attainments appear so modest. I did not believe it possible."

"Then, if you are not changed, and not in love, why not go with me and enjoy your youth in these delightful amusements, which will be checked in a few months by a stupid country life?"

"Because I have a surfeit of sweets and am weary of discussing nothings. They do not amuse me."

"I cannot see how that is possible, Minona, and I must think you act from caprice and a desire to appear different from others," answered her mother, vexed at Minona's obstinacy.

A year before Minona's impetuosity would have led at once to one of her outbursts of temper, which would have made itself apparent, in a slight degree, even in her father's presence. No she smilingly replied:

"I do desire above all things, sincerely and truthfully, to differ from all the girls I know, except one; but in following this wish I regret deeply that I wound you," and a faltering was audible in her voice.

"And you do differ most widely from others, my daughter," uttered Mr. Dearing. "There exists something in you now that was not a few months ago. You will confide it to me, I fell assured, some day."

Minona raised her eyes, in which tears glistened, wondering to her father's face, and met his affectionate look full upon her. Had he penetrated her secret or had Horace betrayed her? She read no answer there, and silently finished her breakfast. Mr. Dearing handed Vinvela another letter as she was rising from the table, saying in a low tone:

"Our friend Hugh will be here in a month, much earlier than he at first intended."

Vinvela received her note and placed it in that friendly receptacle for ladies' secrets, the pockets of her dress. She did not blush or express joy at the announcement, so Mr. Dearing was disappointed if his remark was meant as a banter of discovery.

The time arrived when Minona could reasonably look for a reply to her communication, but Plymouth Rock reposed in ice bound silence. Week after week of suspense passed tauntingly before her and no tidings came.

She wrote with celerity, and very soon was near the completion of her small volume. She addressed a brief letter of inquiry to the celebrated publishers, Messrs. "Wary & Wirey," of New York, announcing the—to her—important fact that she had a book in MSS which she desired to offer for publication. She asked for explicit terms of publication. Ere long a polite reply came, without any specifications, saying that her production would be examined with pleasure. The girl was elated. The golden dome of renown's great temple loomed up brightly and grandly upon the near horizon. The MSS, was elegantly put up, officially tied with pink tape and sealed with crimson wax. The reticent Horace was summoned, paid and dispatched to the express office.

This done, there was a hiatus to care, quiescence after the gloomy oscillations that had long shaken her. Mrs. Dearing's health grew painfully delicate. Often she was compelled to remain for days in her room, and Minona devoted herself with unremitting tenderness to alleviate her sufferings and brighten the tedium of a sick chamber to her mother.

Vinvela had waited a moment of solitude to enjoy the contents of her letter from Hugh. Who shall pretend to describe the transports of feeling, the happiness that consumes a girl in perusing the first letter from her accepted lover? There are some brief moments in the life of each mortal when few droppings of delicious manna from heaven are richly experienced. God knows they are dispensed seldom enough in this world of care, and if it were not for their occasional showers, the poor, faltering travelers would perish from hunger and fatigue by the thorny wayside.

Mr. Portwood was coming. Has not every rose its thorn? Yes, and Vinvela had hers. This new dawn of happiness made her timid to excess. Her health grew more feeble, though she scarcely admitted it to herself, and often in moments of buoyancy by a sudden introversion, coffins and shrouds would intrude upon her with an appalling distinctness, which thrilled and chilled her for hours.

It was a cloudy afternoon, damp, cold, and cheerless. Minona and Miss Gladwin had been all day endeavoring to amuse Mrs. Dearing, who was suffering from one of her ill spells, when they were summoned to the drawing-room to entertain Mr. Meverill.

This gentleman was unusually cheerful.

"Congratulate me, young ladies; in a few days I shall pass my examination, and if I am successful I shall be launched fairly upon the sea of life."

"I hope you may have a most prosperous voyage," said Vinvela.

A shadow rested momentarily upon his fine face, and his eyes sought Minona as he uttered a response to the hope.

"Have you no good wishes for your friend in the trying ordeal of appearing before august judges and tremblingly awaiting their fiat?"

"Their name is legion, Mr. Meverill, and I cannot pretend to express them. You are fully aware that you have my warm sympathy."

"Thank you. Even were I sure, which I was not, it is pleasant, very pleasant, to be reminded of it."

"I dislike flattery," said Minona, rising. "It is a dark evening. Earth is in, what Hugh Miller calls, her dishabille. I will sing to you a martial air, Mr. Meverill, that may raise your courage to a proper point for the coming conflict."

Mr. Meverill smiled and handed her guitar, and Miss Dearing sang several inspiring solos.

"End with a tender, sentimental song, which will elevate the heart before you cease," he said.

"I thought you eschewed."

"I am mortal and like it sometimes."

"I am in a plaintive mood will sing 'Ave Sanctissima.'"

Most touchingly she sang, her rich, full voice swelling feelingly as it uttered the beautiful words from Mrs. Hemans' unequaled pen.

> *Ave, Sanctissima!*
> *'Tis nightfall on the sea;*
> *Ora pro nobis!*
> *Our souls rise to thee!*

Silence, unbroken, reigned a few moments in the room when Minona ceased. Melancholy brooded over all, wrought by the pensive strain.

"Thank you, when I am bowed with a weight of care and unrest I will call and ask you to exalt my soul, in pleasing transports, by that song."

Soon he left, and Minona ran up stairs to attend her mother. Vinvela stood near the piano, toying absently with the guitar, touching occasionally a faint chord. Her thoughts were on the wing over the distant deep. The words she had just heard resounded in her ears and she repeated to herself:

> *"Watch us while shadows lie*
> *O'er the dim water spread;*
> *Hear the heart's lonely sigh."*

Again she touched the strings, whose vibration seemed to echo her heart's desire. She gazed into space far away to discern the straining ship cutting its furrows on the crested deep, bearing her all on the treacherous elements. She heard no foot falls upon the velvet carpet. She was recalled by the embrace of her betrothed lover. She looked up and her eyes met those of Hugh Portwood beaming with happiness and tenderness.

He led her to a seat.

"You do not look so well as when I left. Have you been ill or have you pined for me?"

Vinvela blushed and said she had been in usual health.

"Why did you not apprise me of your coming?" she asked.

"Because surprise adds a double pleasure of reunion. I wished to test your joy at my coming, and walked here unannounced. I scarcely hoped to meet you alone. You must pardon a lover's impatience to behold his treasure after so long an absence."

He held her hand. He placed upon it the circle of betrothal; their plans, their hopes and his travels in Europe were all discussed, and Vinvela forgot her forebodings while listening to Hugh's conversation.

Mr. Dearing found Hugh in the parlor with Vinvela on his return. He greeted his protégé with warmth and his eyes began to open to the existing state of things, when Hugh, with his usual frankness, said:

"My friend, I have succeeded in winning the regard of this young lady. Pardon my temerity, and do not withhold your consent to our speedy union."

Hugh felt Vinvela's hand tremble in his clasp, and her face was bright with a rosy flush.

Mr. Dearing advanced, and taking both of their hands said, in a deep, low voice:

"Neither of you could have made a better selection. May the Triune God bless you."

Stooping he kissed Vinvela's cheek and left the room. And the lovers were happy that night—the cloud had vanished.

When hope had well-nigh expired Minona received a cumbrous envelope one day from Mr. Portwood, who usually brought the mail. She ran to her room and impatiently tore the coverings which contained her first literary effort, and an accompanying letter. This epistle had the august heading in printing letters "Editorial Rooms, Wise & Co., Publishers." The "reader," in grandiloquent style, proceeded to inform her that her story did not see the enlightened taste and needs of Plymouth Rock. They paid for first class literature a certain rate, but there was not, nor was there likely to be, any literary famine in New England; consequently, with heartfelt regret, he was obliged to return any third rate offerings.

Her MSS was scored by sundry pencil marks of correction. Some of them were good suggestions, but numbers merely hypercritical. Many of the figures of syntax were ignored. Any play upon the construction of words was carefully expunged. In truth, the dogmatism of the New England critic clipped close the feathery wings of fancy, and evidently nothing but the most common matter-of-fact style would be acceptable to the magazine readers of Messrs. Wise & Co.

Nothing daunted, though slightly discouraged, Minona awaited an answer from Wary & Wirey, New York. This time learning by experience that the printing of books did not work by telegraphic or steam celerity, she reposed in a state of non-expectation for six weeks, but these extended into months before she was gladdened by an ominous letter with book stores and advertisements printed upon the back.

Dr. Johnson has said "Booksellers are a liberal minded set of men," and Minona opened her letter with full fledged hopes. But booksellers have grown wiser since the great lexicographer's day and liberality is a rare fossil, seldom exhumed for the benefit of the present generation. Miss Dearing's letter from the publishers was ambiguous in the highest degree, but ended by asserting that her work would be put in press, with the eclat of Wary & Wirey's name affixed upon the receipt of a semi-score of hundreds of dollars. Messrs. Wary & Wirey presumed that the author cared for fame alone. Minona was aghast at this information. She could easily have commanded a thousand dollars by application to her father, but her delicacy and modesty forbade that. She could not make such a seemingly unreasonable request without avowing her design. Her father was the most exalted specimen of manhood in all respects she had ever seen, and she quailed at the bare idea of displaying her crude efforts to him. Had she been capable of purifying her writings by passing them through forty different processes, like the Cardinal Bembo did his, then, perhaps, they would have been prepared for display before so fine a scholar as Mr. Dearing.

She resolved a multiplicity of plans in her mind, but none struck her as feasible except one, and that was to prepare another work, and give one for the publication of the other.

This was a bright idea, and Minona determined to ask the gentleman who kept the circulating library something about publishers' rates, and if there was no way of coming to terms unless by the payment of a large sum.

Some days elapsed before she could execute her design, and then, without compromising herself or identifying herself as an author, she learned the rules of the business. The friendly gentleman advised against offering one work for another, and assured her that the delays and indefinite method of communication she had endured was only a means used to get her to pay for the volume.

Her book could be brought out at the booksellers' risk, with a very small percentage of net profits to herself. That was often done.

Her hopes rose as quickly as a thermometrical mercury before the rays of an August sun, and whispered a thousand pleasing fancies to her elated heart. She returned home, wrote a careful, eloquent letter to Messrs. Wary & Wirey explaining her situation and the impossibility of forwarding funds. Remembering Fanny Burney's experience in Cecilia, she hinted, if all other means failed, the plan of publishing by subscription, but mentioned her wish and urgent hope that her volume could be brought forward at the accustomed rates of publishers. She also stated what influence she could command to aid in the extensive circulation of her book. This time no doubt—cloud dappled the sun-sky of certainty. Her spirits resumed the elasticity of gayety, and she became again the light of the household.

She still wrote and read at nights with devouring avidity, and was pleased to discern the improvement in consecutiveness of ideas and their rapidity of conception. Thoughts were no longer nomadic, but dwelt upon whatever spot she chose to place them. Her pen became the magic wand that brought about action.

Thus winter, with its bleak winds and hoar frosts, retired to seek a more Southern clime under antarctic skies, when smiling spring returned from her sojourn across the equator. Vinvela had heard from her aunt in Kentucky, and expected to go to her after a few months. Mr. Portwood opposed this arrangement, promising to accompany her on a visit to her aunt in the following summer if she would consent to their nuptials very soon. Miss Gladwin appeared to think she could not agree to these terms without violating a promise to, or wish of, her father.

The time drew near to return to Tennessee. Minona and Vinvela hailed this prospect with pleasure, though not unadulterated. The former felt that it was the final glimpse of city life to her for a very long period, and even when we relinquish familiar scenes willingly, is it not human nature to experience a pang of regret when we remember we are saying farewell possibly for the last time? Vinvela would be severed from daily common with her lover, who was an inmate of Mr. Dearing's house. They're nature's blended most harmoniously and their engagement had been happy without alloy.

Minona had two causes of distress in leaving Savannah. Silence reigned for her over the postal service. She heard nothing from her book, and it would be very annoying to have matters indefinite when she dwelt in the country, where postal facilities were more rare. She ran much risk of her secret being discovered. There was a dernier resort she could adopt in case she did not hear. It wanted but two weeks of the day appointed for removal. There was occupation enough to divert her in paying farewell calls to a large circle of friends, in "packing up," and in purchasing articles for Vinvela's trousseau; still eagerly expected letter would intrude upon her thoughts, and each night came in new pang of disappointment in the announcement of no letter.

A week previous to Minona's departure Mr. Meverill called to bid her adieu. She had seen him and congratulated him on his successful admittance as a practicing lawyer, and he had been more agreeable and cheerful than ever before. The severance of this friendship was the second cause of disquiet.

At this interview there was a melancholy reserve. There was much to be said on both sides, but how to say it? that was the question. Several ineffectual efforts were made to keep the current of a sustained conversation. At length the gentleman said:

"Sing, Miss Dearing, it may be the very last time I shall ever have the pleasure of listening to your voice, which sways me with peculiar feelings. Nothing sentimental this morning. I cannot bear it."

Minona sang a cheerful little Scotch melody, but there was not much heart in it, her feelings were much too depressed. She was about to lay aside the guitar when he asked for the song she sang when he last heard her. She complied. It suited her mood, and there was a volume of pathos in the beautiful little air as she sung.

"Thank you; I shall never, never forget it," he rather mused, seeming to forget her presence as he uttered the words.

"How long will you remain in Tennessee, Miss Dearing?"

"Until November or December. I shall visit Kentucky in June to be present at my cousin's bridal, and then resume study under my old tutor. I regret, almost, that Vinvela ever came to us. Had I never seen her I should not be called upon to endure the pangs of separation."

"Will she reside in Kentucky?"

"No. I presume after a time her summer home will be with us. I hope so, and she will live in Savannah in the winter."

"Then you will not suffer the pangs of absence long," he said.

"But everything will be changed. She will no longer be heart-whole, and our sympathies will end when she contracts a nearer tie."

"And will you not follow her example?" he asked, with an unfathomable expression, in which fear, hope, doubt, and melancholy was apparent.

"Perhaps I may," she answered, laughing to cover a faint embarrassment. She was toying with a massive gold ring, which rolled upon the carpet as she spoke.

Mr. Meverill picked it up and placed it in his pocket, saying:

"I will return it to you at Montvale when we meet this summer."

"I prefer it now," she said. "I have no expectation of being there," she continued, with some feeling of annoyance.

"I will send it very soon. It will serve as a memento of this day's pleasant interview. Will you write, Miss Dearing, and tell me what effect a rustic life has upon you? The only bright gleam that glances over my departure from Savannah is the hope of resuming my correspondence with you?"

"I shall be closely employed at my studies all the summer and can have little leisure."

"But you will not forget old friends, or, I hope, not one, at least. The Scripture says, 'from him that would borrow turn not thou away.' Now I desire the loan of a few of your ideas as often as convenient, and will return an equal measure of mine. You cannot violate the injunctions of Holy Writ."

"You deserve a reward for the ingenuity displayed in framing your request," she said, laughing. "You will make a fine lawyer, Mr. Meverill. I will write occasionally if I have time, and if the mood for scribbling shall overtake me."

"I am greatly indebted, though I like not the 'ifs' that intervene between the promise and the performance."

He rose to go. He grasped her hand and pressed it with a look of overflowing friendship and regret, bade her a hasty farewell and was gone. His look and his tone dwelt with Minona for days. His conduct was variable and could not be construed in several ways, but Minona was not vain, and did not interpret every sigh into an utterance of love. Was her own heart yet impervious? We shall see.

Chapter XIV. *"RESPECTED LADY—Deign to listen kindly to the addresses of an humble follower of the cross. I have pined in secret for months with an over whelming affection for you. Consent to share the joys, the griefs and the labors of an unworthy missionary. May the good God bless you and turn your heart to me."*
— Aaron Crews

CHAPTER XIV.

Once again, Vinvela and Minona roved in the balmy air of a Tennessee spring. It was the close of April and the trees had just port put forth their tiniest leaves. Violets, "star-gleaming" anemones and liverworts, with their blue corollas, studded the earth, and heart-leaves, with their brown pitcher-like blossoms, lay thick under the dead leaves.

Vinvela, parted from Mr. Portwood, was a prey to foreboding, which attacked her with a greater force now that the future offered a happiness she had never dreamed of attaining. In a few weeks Hugh would accompany her to the residence of her aunt, where she would remain until June, when their bridal would be consummated.

Minona was a victim of melancholy at her cousin's approaching departure; her deferred expectations and a superstition which the constant gayeties of Savannah had kept at bay. She had confided to Mr. Portwood the fact of an important document being anticipated by her, and that she desired it forwarded to her under cover to Mr. Crews.

She had been at home about two weeks when it came with intelligence that crushed everything she had hoped. Messrs. Wary & Wirey with excessive urbanity, informed her that they could on no account "lock up" capital in an enterprise so precarious and slow in returning yields as the publication of a book from an obscure author.

"This, then, is the death of my effort. I will bring the literary corpse home and inter it in oblivion."

Like Pico of Mirandula, Goldsmith and others, she invoked the flames to form the funeral pyre. "I shall offer a holocaust to the idol ambition."

She remanded her MSS to the address of Mr. Portwood and ceased to remember the annoyance for a season.

The return of the family to Eagle Band was an event hailed with joy by the quiet, unobtrusive little minister, who had passed an isolated, dreary winter in the solitude of Mr. Dearing's mansion. This place was his headquarters. His residence there afforded him a home and gave protection to the mansion, although Jock Hethrington also remained there to overlook the farming interests. Mr. Crews occupied himself in the vocation of a pedestrian missionary during the winter. This for years had been his pursuit until engaged by Mr. Dearing to superintend the education of his daughter, which consumed only the summer months of each year. His salary was ample, his home agreeable, with the advantage of refined companions and a select library. He seemed to be alone in the world, never alluding to kindred ties. He had been a resident of Tennessee for years and bore an unimpeached character, which was sufficient recommendation. Vinvela and Minona had resumed their morning recitations to Mr. Crews, the former, from courtesy to her cousin, who lost to give up her schoolmate.

Some weeks after the girls had been studying, one day Minona returned to the Blue Room at noon for a book. She found Mr. Crews still there and writing at the table. She obtained the volume and was about retiring, when the gentleman asked her to remain, saying he wished to relate something to her. Minona sat down and he blushed, stammered, looked confused and handled his fob chain, a never-failing resource with him when embarrassed.

Minona could not imagine the cause of this singular deportment, and began to fear that she was the victim of her pastor's attachment, when he said with an effort:

"Miss Minona, I am going to China," again blushing.

"Mercy!" thought the girl, "I hope he does not intend to ask me to accompany him. I have no ambition to be Judsonized. I do not fancy a Celestial residence before I reach heaven!" Twisting her face into a look of demure gravity, she said:

"I thought you were going to stay with us and teach my ideas how to come into harness. They are erratic now and need training. What sudden freak lures you Celestial-ward?"

"I shall go thither in the autumn. Give this to your cousin, and bring an answer sub rosa," he continued, jerking the note nervously from his breast pocket.

Minona thought there was much ado about so simple a request, and wondering what China had to do with the note, at the same time much relieved that she had not been invited to accompany him, she received the note and left the room.

Vinvela was above stairs, and Minona sought her.

"I am officially sent to deliver this document into your safe keeping," she said, very seriously. "Read it; an answer is required."

Vinvela opened the envelope and read:

> *"RESPECTED LADY–Deign to listen kindly to the addresses of an humble follower of the cross. I have pined in secret for months with an over whelming affection for you. Consent to share the joys, the griefs and*

the labors of an unworthy missionary. May the good God bless you and turn your heart to me."
AARON CREWS.

Minona burst into a hearty fit of laughter.

"You are the most attractive young lady I ever met, cousin," she said. "Just reflect on the honor conferred upon you. You are to be carried to a Celestial paradise." And again she gave way for mirth.

"Do explain, Minona. This is some joke of yours that I am surprised at. How can you throw levity upon such a serious matter?"

"It is no jest, I assure you. Mr. Crews handed me the note and requested I should deliver it, and return him an answer. He announced with sundry grimaces that he would leave for China in the autumn, hence my supposition as to the style of home you would have."

"What am I to do?" exclaimed Vinvela, in despair.

"Discard Mr. Portwood and go to China. Learn to make birdnest puddings and wear wooden shoes, until you reach the dignity of being on of the 'golden lilies.' Your duty is as plain as the sunlight streaming through your window."

"We do not always perform our duty," said Miss Gladwin, laughing, "and in this instance I must shirk mine, I never was placed in a more disagreeable dilemma in my life. What could have possessed the gentleman to fancy me?"

"Your amiability and your piety, and your other elements of superb qualities that I have no time to mention. Reply to your letter. I am impatient to see the result."

Vinvela wrote a courteous and kind declination of the honor conferred upon her, stating that her hand was already disposed of, and Minona left with the fateful document for the Blue Room. Mr. Crews was still there, his eyes fixed upon a book.

She walked forward and handed the note, which was read.

"I never expected this," he said. "I thought she was free."

"I could have told you, if you had asked, or I had known the contents of your note. I regret it, Mr. Crews, but I cannot aid you."

"I know it. Do you remember the night we spent at the Milman cabin and recounted our dreams?"

"Yes," said Minona, wondering what that had to do with the present.

"I am a predestinarian. I saw her in my vision that night, and ever since considered her mine when I asked it. I believed the dream was a revelation."

"The wish gave rise to belief, Mr. Crews. I wish I could assist you. My cousin is to marry Mr. Portwood in June."

"God's will be done!" ejaculated Mr. Crews. "I will go on my mission solitary, but not alone."

He bowed his head on the table, the note fell on the floor, and Minona withdrew with her heart filled with genuine sympathy. Oh, glorious Christian faith that sustains in the sorest trials, spread thy brooding wings speedily over all the world.

A few days previous to that appointed for Mr. Portwood's arrival to accompany Vinvela to Kentucky for Mr. Dearing requested her presence in the Blue Room. She entered and he placed a chair for her.

"Miss Gladwin, I understand from Eriginia that you determined to leave us. I would be glad to dissuade you but for the fact that you would soon go to another home. You have never inquired into your business since you came here. Are you so indifferent to worldly advantage?"

"I never thought about my affairs. I knew they were in the most scrupulous hands. I felt that you would arrange them in the best manner, and presumed there was little or nothing left after the estate was wound up."

"I feel proud of your confidence in me, but it is not always wise to propose such unlimited trust in strangers. You're father's liabilities are all canceled, and here is the deed to his house, the home of your childhood. It is yours by inheritance, and will be a delightful summer resort."

Miss Gladwin looked up in surprise.

"How can this be?" she asked. "My father told me the place would have to be sold."

"It was found unnecessary. There were few debts, and those were liquidated without the sacrifice of the residence. It is just as you left it. I never mentioned it as long as you were silent and had no intention of changing your situation. I desired you always to live with us and be a companion for my daughter. You're intercourse has been a blessing, and I thank you for your benign influence in mellowing her character. Need I say that while I hope every happiness may attend one so pure as yourself, I regret that we must resign you to the charge of another, most worthy, most exalted in his moral rectitude though he surely is."

Tears blinded Vinvela as she thought of her beloved home, and the kindness of the man before her. She murmured her thanks in faltering accents, and she thought that while her betrothed was all that she could desire in excellence, yet before her stood one not less gifted in all that adorned the higher type of man.

Mr. Dearing, who, of all things; disliked to be overpowered with thanks to his upright actions, silently quitted the room. He felt and acted upon the principle that we deserve no praise for practicing virtues that all should strive to attain who desire to appear as just men made perfect in the sight of God. To all such souls the adulation, the falling compliments of sinful mortals are nothing— they seek a higher reward.

Hugh came, and with him the necessity to Vinvela of severing ties of iron tenacity. How inseparably intermingled are joy and sorrow! Under all circumstances they are indivisible. Mr. Portwood handed Minona her package privately, as she had requested, and for the present she hit it away in the obscurity of an unused trunk. Vinvela and herself roamed everywhere on the premises; every spot had to receive an individual farewell, so great are local attachments to the young and the tender-hearted.

The parting came at length. Mr. Crews had begged a few days respite, and absented himself to avoid this trial. It was a bright, cheerful day in early May, and the forest choristers chanted their most joyous jubilee. Busy insects were on the wing and the air was redolent with sweet odors. The trunks had been sent on and the phaeton was at the door. Mr. Dearing stood upon the veranda talking to Hugh, and awaiting the appearance of the ladies. They came; Mrs. Dearing weeping, Vinvela equipped in a grey traveling dress, her fair face looking pale and more ethereal than usual, and Minona, with her delicate lips compressed to drive back the rising flood-tide of distress at her cousin's departure. Hands were classed, kisses exchanged in silence. Mr. Dearing handed Vinvela in the vehicle, Hugh followed; the door was closed. Hearts were too full for words, and with a snap of the whip Jock drove on the restive horses. Those left behind returned to the desolation and darkness of the mansion. The May sun of that day, and many others, shone as a mocking contrast to the inmates of Eagle Bend, especially to Minona.

Mr. Portwood and Miss Gladwin reached Knoxville that afternoon, and that night left for Nashville, thence to Edmondson county, Kentucky. Most of the journey was by rail, and Vinvela, in the presence of her lover and the ever changing scenes, left much of her melancholy at parting with friends behind her. True is it that the journeyers cast their mantle of regret upon those who remain behind, and they, stationary martyrs, bear a double burden of sorrow.

The weather was propitious, the trip delightful and the travelers reached Brownsville safely. This is a pleasant little village, situated on Green River and about ten miles west of Mammoth Cave.

Miss Rebecca Gladwin was a nice, prim old lady, of tall and slender form, precise to a fraction, with a house comfortable in its arrangements, and exhibiting a neatness that rivaled successfully the city of Broek, or the "Dutch Paradise," immortalized by Washington Irving.

Though the frosts of age had dispelled the outward embellishments of youth her heart was warm, and she welcomed her niece affectionately, and bestowed a kind greeting upon Hugh.

In appearance she resembled her brother, and her voice recalled most forcibly to Vinvela, her beloved father.

Miss Rebecca was comfortably provided with property, sufficient to gratify all her needs and some of her fancies. She had been disappointed in love in early youth and had remained free and cheerful during a long and useful life.

Her house was a one-story building with six rooms, well furnished. Vinvela's chamber adjoined her own, and was adjusted as the old lady thought would please a girl.

Vinvela felt that she would be happy here, although separated from her cousins. She informed her aunt as soon as she could, concerning the relations existing between herself and Hugh.

"And I shall lose you almost as soon as found my child. I had hoped that I should have you with me to the close of life," she said, sadly. "But," she added, "the young man is prepossessing, and, I trust, worthy of you."

"He bears a character for the utmost integrity and the best business qualifications, dear aunt, and my cousin, Mr. Dearing, thinks I made the most unexceptionable selection."

"Well, we shall not dispute, my dear. All things wear bright tints to the young, and you are pardonable in your exalted opinion of your lover. May you be happy, is my earnest prayer. I regret I did not find you soon after my poor brother's decease."

"Mr. Dearing and I both wrote, and father told me he had done so."

"His letter never reached me. I had fallen into ill health and was persuaded to leave here two years ago and go to the North, where I have many kindred. There I was ill a long time. As soon as I was convalescent I went with an old friend to Canada and remained there some months. By some mismanagement your letters did not reach me until a few months ago."

"I should have felt much better coming to you, dear aunt, when I left North Georgia. I had a dread of going with strangers. I had never seen my cousin Eriginia, I had never even heard of her, but you I knew by reputation. Did you return South on my account?"

"Yes, mainly. I desired an excuse to come. Was your home agreeable at your cousin's?"

"Certainly, I could not have been more blessed than I was. They were noble, generous, considerate, and delicate beyond all expectation. I never was made to feel other than as an honored inmate, and I left them with heartfelt regret. They are wealthy and live luxuriously."

"The you will find my poor home lonely," said the lady, with a disappointed tone.

"Oh, no! dear aunt. I am the plainest person in my tastes, and my cousins, like all true aristocrats, put on no supercilious airs. Their deportment is as simple as the most retired could desire. You will see them, I hope, in six weeks, if I have your permission to invite them here."

"Of course, my child, any one who is your friend finds welcome from me."

"You will love Minona. She is beautiful, affectionate and full of life."

Hugh remained two days at the cottage, and felt glad to see Vinvela occupy so pleasant a place. He hoped her health would grow stronger by the change of climate.

"Are you really going to-morrow?" asked Miss Rebecca after tea as they sat in the parlor.

"I am obliged to go," he said, "and I start at dawn of day. But I shall come again in six weeks and spend some time. I suspect, dear madame, you will tire of my presence."

"Oh, no, but I must prepare you a lunch, and see to getting you an early breakfast," and the old lady left the lovers to bid adieu unobserved.

"Vinvela," said Hugh, "I shall be in worse despair at this separation than the last, you are so much farther from me now."

"I will write often. I have little else to do."

"Letters are a cold comfort to a warm heart."

"I shall be more lonely than you, because business cares press aside unwholesome repinings."

"You must be cheerful, my love, and acquire robust health. I would have your cheek lose its present delicacy. After all, six weeks is a short time and will soon fit away; then we shall meet to part no more until the Great Judge summons us to Him." He uttered this solemnly. After a pause he laughingly said: "You will be so pleasantly situated and have so much to divert you in forming new acquaintances that I shall grow jealous. You will forget your grief at parting."

"I never can. It is a thorn that robs both friendship and love of half their happiness."

Vinvela told Hugh of the deed Mr. Dearing handed her upon her departure.

"I am puzzled about it. I thought the place was sold."

"No. Mr. Dearing paid the debts himself, and the house is a gift from him. He sent me to superintend the arrangements, and told me you were so attached to the place he would reserve it and await your directions, though I did not know his intentions."

"Generous man! He did not tell me all this."

"Because I never saw any one so free from all ostentation in the conferring of benefits, and thanks oppress his proud heart."

"Keep this deed, Mr. Portwood. I give it to you. I am so inexperienced I know not what to do with it. It will revert to me again," she said, smiling as he was about to return it.

The parting hour struck.

"I shall not see you to-morrow. Promise to be cheerful, my love."

He kissed her and she sought her room.

At the earliest dawn he left the house, murmuring blessings and a prayer for safety upon the treasure left behind.

Minona, once more, plunged into a career of reading, devouring with avidity all the abstruse works that fell in her way. Her desire for knowledge was as insatiable as that of the Caliph Vathek, save she did not endeavor to penetrate into the occult sciences. Unlike most young ladies she had no taste for frivolous reading. Her mind was of a more elevated cast, and nothing common or light possessed any charm for her.

Pope, is said, after writing panegyrics on all the Princes of Europe, to have confessed that he "thought himself the greatest genius that ever was;" and Johnson adds that "self-confidence is the first requisite to great undertakings." This important helpmeet to success was precisely what Minona lacked. Her modesty was excessive, and she shrunk from placing her efforts as a writer in the hands of friends for comment. She fluctuated for several days in the trying maze of indecision whether she should carry out her first determination of wholesale destruction, and finally came to the conclusion that her literary efforts were about the ebullition of youthful folly. Had they been emanations from the pen of genius, they would undoubtedly have met with a different reception from those literary autocrats of the press. Quietly she kindled a fire in her bedroom, and consigned her work, piece by piece, to the devouring element; and, as the last leaf shriveled a blackened cinder, she heaved a deep sigh of mingled regret and relief. Thus ended this gifted girl's attempt at authorship. Have not thousands, whose names might have added new stars to the spangled banner of renown, remained forever hidden in obscurity from similar discouragements in early trials of skill?

At this time she received a visit from Mr. Torrister, who had secured Mrs. Dearing as his ally in the prosecution of his suit. Minona had less toleration for this young fop than ever, and did not pretend to conceal her contempt for him. His eagerness in pursuit of her fortune was mingled with a degree of malice at her evident disgust for his attentions, though his protestations of abiding love for her were fulsome and persistent.

"Minona," said her mother, a day or two before Mr. Torrister left for Savannah, "what are your intentions regarding our visitor? You have been a long time capricious, and I wish to know your decision."

"The gentleman learned my unalterable determination on his last summer's visit. He knows that I have not the most homeopathic dilution of an infinitesimal part of a drop of regard for him; and had he the spirit of a man, he would cease his pretensions and persecutions."

"Women are coy and fickle, and like to keep a suitor dangling at the end of a hook, and the poor fellow does not wish to yield what has been so long his idol. You cannot make a better selection, Minona; and I insist on your playing the coquette no longer."

"Mother," said Minona, in an indignant tone, "I am no coquette; and if other women like to show power by trifling with the affections offered them, I am not one of that stamp. Once more I assure you, as I have Mr. Torrister, that I never will marry him. He is utterly heartless, and my father's purse is his idol. This he cannot obtain without my incumbrance."

"You are mistaken and over suspicious. I insist on you not giving any such answer. He is the one of all others I have set my heart on as a son-in-law. I am determined to succeed," said Mrs. Dearing, in a vexed tone.

"Does father know of all this maneuvering to dispose of my hand? I shall ask him if I am to be forced into matrimony with an unworthy object against my consent."

"Your father has other affairs, and I am the most proper person to select a husband for you. My health is failing, and I desire to see you well settled before I die."

"I shall await his decision. Dear mother, rest assured that I do not desire to run counter to your happiness, but every feeling in me is repugnant to such a marriage."

Mrs. Dearing placed her handkerchief to her eyes, and, after a few moments' weeping, she said:

"Promise me, Minona, that you will say nothing to Clarek about this suit. It is the only reparation you can make for your ungrateful conduct to me."

And again she covered her eyes, determined to make an opening for a reconciliation.

"I promise," said Minona, proudly, "but only upon condition that the gentleman relieves me of his presence and persecution; otherwise, I shall ask my father's protection," and she left the room to quell in solitude her indignant feelings.

Vinvela, after the departure of Mr. Portwood, became quickly a favorite with her aunt and her new acquaintances. Some people are born to inspire perfect love and confidence, and she was one. None who knew her intimately could resist her amiable and affectionate nature. Her time was occupied in preparations for her bridal and deeds of kindness to her aunt, and to the absent loved ones in the shape of long letters. But there were many moments when a silent voice whispered to her that she would soon be at rest, and a sigh would escape her as she tried to exorcise the phantom.

Two weeks before the day appointed for her wedding, Vinvela reluctantly joined a party of young people on a visit to the Mammoth Cave. They started early on bright June morning, but had gone only about half the distance when the sky became overcast with ominous, leaden clouds. Distant thunder muttered, and streaks of lightning cleft the sky. The rain fell heavily. The vehicle was a light spring-wagon. Small umbrellas were carried to defy the sun, but were of little protection against rain. The party turned back, and reached Brownsville late in the day drenched with water.

Miss Rebecca felt very anxious, and gave her niece all sorts of remedies to keep off cold; but she was chilled and the mischief already done. In a day or two she was seized with fever, and confined to her bed. Her cough grew very troublesome, but Miss Rebecca did not apprehend a serious case of illness. Vinvela herself did not consider her condition critical, and anticipated being up in a few days to welcome Minona, who was expected a week before the marriage.

Miss Dearing arrived, having come under the care of some friends going to Louisville. She was surprised to see her cousin ill, with her cheeks flushed by a burning fever. Knowing Vinvela's delicacy, she was alarmed to learn that no physician was in attendance. She ventured to speak of it to Miss Rebecca.

"I was anxious to send for one; but Vinvela opposed it, Miss Dearing, telling me she was accustomed to such attacks. Do you think her in danger?"

"I do not know; but I never saw her with so much fever. She is very frail, and I think it safe to have a physician. I will assume the responsibility of disobeying her wishes, dear madam."

"I will summon one at once," said the old lady, thoroughly alarmed.

Dr. Bolton came; prescribed from some febrifuge, and relieved the ladies by assuring them that the patient would be restored in a few days, and their hopes were cheered by a diminution of the alarming symptoms. Vinvela was lively and enjoyed a reunion with her cousin very greatly. Their plans and prospects were discussed, and Minona afforded much mirth by her quaint satire of little things she had seen since her separation from Vinvela.

It wanted by three days to the bridal day. Mr. Portwood was expected the ensuing day; and that afternoon was brought to Vinvela a box containing her dresses and wedding garments. As Minona was displaying them to her, she said:

"Minona, I cannot divest myself of the idea that I am not to wear those beautiful robes. You may deem me silly, but it seems a fixed fact, that arises between me and my bridal whenever I contemplate it."

"I cannot see what can prevent. Your lover is true, and will be here to-morrow; and three days are a short space."

"We shall see. I shall not be well enough, and at best the time must be postponed."

"I hope not," said Minona. "You must not be superstitious, or you will infect me. Are you not better?"

"The doctor thinks I am."

"He ought to know, dear cousin."

And Minona kissed her fevered brow.

Vinvela's conversation affected Miss Dearing's spirits greatly, but she endeavored to rally and assume a cheerful exterior.

The ensuing day brought Mr. Portwood, and he was distressed to find Vinvela ill. Dr. Bolton assured him that her symptoms were favorable, and would yield to treatment in a few days. With this, Hugh was obliged to appear satisfied. His arrival had excited Miss Gladwin, and that night her fever was greatly increased, and was undiminished the next day.

"Minona," she said, "I believe I am growing worse, and my wedding must be postponed. Will you write to your father and mother to defer coming for a few weeks?"

"Yes," said Minona, "I will do anything you wish, if you will only grow better;" and she accordingly dispatched her letter.

Minona began to be really alarmed at her cousin's illness, and she felt no confidence in the attendant physician. Very reluctantly she consented to an interview between Miss Gladwin and Mr. Portwood. Vinvela had expressed a wish to grant his request to see her, and Minona dreaded excitement in his presence, or in her refusal to admit him.

Hugh entered the room mustering all the calmness he was master of. Vinvela reposed upon a low lounge. She had changed since he last saw her. Her brown hair was thrown back in thick masses from a lofty, fair forehead, in which the blue veins were traced visibly. The large blue eyes were deep-set, and glistening with a lustre fever only can bestow; while her cheeks and lips were of a deep coral hue, and her breathing was hurried. She held out her hand with a smile. Hugh took the hand and pressed it. It was sometime ere he could speak.

"Why did you not write to me that you were ill?" he asked, as he sat down.

"I did not think it was serious. I hoped to be well."

She looked at him long and sighed. Sighs are sentiments uttered but unexpressed, and often mean volumes.

Hugh did not speak. He only pressed her hand, for his heart was too full of dread to venture upon words.

"You must not look melancholy," at length said the girl, "or you will infect me. You and Minona must cheer me by your gayety, and comfort aunt Rebecca. She will be lonely when I am gone."

Did she mean that her end was near, or allude to her marriage? The sentence sounded as a knell to Hugh's excited feelings.

"I will come again," he said.

And he left the room, fearing lest his emotion should be visible.

By the afternoon Vinvela's symptoms grew much worse. At times she would awake and speak incoherently, then doze in a trance-like slumber. Night, with its dismal curtains, fell and brought two-fold darkness around the hearts of the inmates of the cottage. Dr. Bolton was again summoned, and administered some opiates, stating his belief that the case was not critical.

Minona prepared to watch through the night by her cousin, and Hugh, unable to rest, sat in the parlor wrestling with sorrow and fear through the slow, solemn, silent hours of that June night, so very different from his fond anticipations.

The opium induced, after a time, an unquiet slumber. Minona sat beside the ill girl ever and anon moistening her forehead with a damp napkin. How many fervent ejaculations she uttered during the tedious hours for the restoration of the pure girl beside her! Thought with ever-varying and multiplied images oppressed her; and she seemed to awake to the fearful uncertainty of human hopes and life as the moans of the sufferer cut through her tortured soul. If she felt thus acutely, what were the feelings of the lonely, afflicted lover?

Near day-dawn, Minona was renewing the cold cloth to Vinvela's brow, when she opened her large eyes upon her.

"Minona," she said, "I knew it would come. It is in vain we oppose fate."

"What, darling? You are better. Your fever is less."

"No; death is near. I feel it. It would have been sweet to live for him; but it is selfish; I would only have been a charge on his time and love."

"You must not speak in this strain, dear Vinvela. I see no cause. Must I call Mr. Portwood?"

"Yes; and when I am gone, dear Minona, be a friend to him, and help him to be reconciled to my loss."

Minona went for Hugh.

"Is she better?" he asked, in an agonized voice.

"There is change," she said, "and she asks for you. Come!"

She led the way, and placed a seat for him, returning to the window to hide her grief.

"Are you better?" asked Hugh, as he sat and took the girl's hand, alarmed at her appearance.

"I am in no pain," she said, in a low voice; "but I never shall be well again. It was selfish in me ever to have yielded to your love, because now you will grieve for me so deeply. It was cruel in me. I knew I should die young, and I ought to have resisted my own heart."

"I have known more happiness since our betrothal than in a whole lifetime before. You will not die and leave me!"

He bowed his head on the bed, and his frame shook; but no sound gave utterance to the mighty tumult which moved him.

"Dear, Hugh," said the dying girl, putting her hand on his head, "I always contemplated this summons as a thing that would relieve me of a lonely burden when my father left me. Since then, how many tendrils have clustered to make life dear! But God is the great Judge of all that is best for us. I should only have been a charge to your loving nature. Do not grieve so deeply, but sustain me in this last trying hour."

She ceased speaking, her own fleeting spirit bleeding and torn by the anguish of her betrothed.

"Do not forget me," she said again; "but be reconciled to my death. It is best for both of us, though it seemeth not so now to our troubled vision."

"My darling," said Hugh, "what will life be when you are gone? Tell me that it is not so! You will live to bless my lonely life. I cannot give you up so suddenly without a warning."

"Let not your heart be troubled," she sweetly uttered, and closed her eyes. Minona begged Hugh to leave the room and compose himself.

All day Vinvela tossed and moaned until late in the afternoon, when she fell into a kind of swoon. Her mind seemed wandering, and Minona and Miss Rebecca in alarm summoned Hugh. Vinvela had changed since morning. Her face had sharpened, and her eyes had a vacant, unsettled stare. Her breath was perplexed and fluttering. Hugh could scarce reach the bedside, so awful was the bursting grief that consumed him, though he uttered no moans; his affliction was too deep for tears.

He stood there, the hand of his dying bride clasped in his, looking upon the wreck of happiness on this, his wedding day, more like a sculpture of adamnant than a living, breathing man. At sunset when a solemn stillness reigned in the house and chamber of the expiring girl, and dark, brooding sorrow, the servant of Death held captive the friends around, Vinvela opened her eyes. They fell lovingly upon Hugh's agonized, stony face, and wandered to Minona and her aunt, then returned to her lover with a sweet smile. In broken, faint accents she said:

"Grieve not—be a friend to aunt. Minona, comfort Hugh; and meet me—" Utterance failed, and a pallor overspread her face.

"Lift her up, Mr. Portwood," said Miss Rebecca.

He raised her. Again she opened her eyes and smiled upon him. There was a slight quiver, a gasp, then stillness, and the girl's spirit had winged its way to Heaven.

Hugh pressed a kiss upon the pale forehead, and left his bride to mourn forever over this, his hapless wedding day.

And once more he saw her, arrayed in the snowy vestments of the tomb; and when the clods rattled upon the coffin's lid Hugh felt that for him they sounded an everlasting requiem of buried hopes and a broken heart. "O, deep is the ploughing of grief."

After the funeral he accompanied Minona to her home, and hastened thence to Savannah, where he endeavored to forget his own griefs in his close attentions to his patron's business.

CHAPTER XV.

The death of Vinvela Gladwin was the first that Minona had ever witnessed. It was the first grief, the first startling awakening into a new phase of existence, that taught her the painful heart-throbbings of giving up forever a beloved companion. Vinvela's was the most beautiful type of woman's nature she had ever seen; too pure and holy to remain long away from her place in Heaven. All this Minona experienced fully, and she would not have wished to recall the meek disenthralled spirit back to this world of woe; yet she could not refrain from grieving for the loss she sustained in the death of her lovely companion. She pursued her daily studies; she occupied herself in all the little trifles of home, and read; but not now with the interest before felt when her soul was untrammeled by affliction. Often, as her eye ran over the characters of some volume before her, her thoughts wandered far away into infinite space and saw commune with the spirit of her departed cousin, ever to return wearied and saddened with the vain endeavor to penetrate into cloud-mysteries wisely withheld. She lost much of her vivacity and loved to seek solitude and muse in natural but unwholesome repinings. The whole scene of her cousin's last illness and conversation would, in such moments, pass vividly before her; and again and again she lived through the trying ordeal full of affliction for herself, and deep sympathy for Hugh Portwood and the lonely aunt in Kentucky.

Minona wrote long letters of condolence to Miss Gladwin, but they did not relieve her own spirit of its gloom. They but kept the fire more ardent within. She heard occasionally from Mr. Meverill, who wrote cheerfully; but she did not reply punctually to these communications, reluctant to pen her gloomy thoughts in letters to her friend. There was one walk she was fond of, leading along the river shore. Often she sat there alone listening to the water tumble over the old mill dam, and idly dropping pebbles into the river. The hollow sound as they fell, the eddying circles and quick-disappearing bubbles that left the stream as placid as before, reminded her of the poor-fleeting shows and vanishing hopes of life; and she, the gifted, beautiful child of fortune, envied the light heart of the peasant girl who sang at the mountain's base beyond the river as she milked her cow, and who knew not the sorrow of mourning for a beloved friend.

Chapter XV. "Dear father, doubly mine by adoption and devotion, my duty is plain. You have every blessing this world can offer; and while I love you, honor you, and shall owe everlasting gratitude for all you have made me; yet, my natural parents are friendless and alone, and I owe a far greater debt to them. I can love you, see you, visit you."

One day, when in a peculiarly melancholy frame of mind, she was startled by a footstep, and looking up Rachel Mulkey stood before her. For one instant Minona's brave heart quailed, as the woman said:

"Met at last, Minona Portwood. You thinks yerself fine, but yer no better than yer neighbors."

"What do you mean, woman?" asked the girl, with a proud look.

"Don't woman me! I am as good as ye are, every bit. Yer think yers Mr. Dearing's fine darter; but yer no more that than I am. Listen! for I've long tried to tell yer. But for that sneaking brother of yourn—curse him—I could ha' telled yer long ago. Yer were born in that ar log hut by the Ingin tombs. When yer was four year old, Mr. Dearing got his foot hurtted and went to yer father's house. He stayed a long time, and took yer from them to Savannah. I went to nurse yer, and was paid to hold my tongue; but I wasn't paid enough; and besides, I doesn't like to see my equals puttin' on airs. Hugh was a smart lad, and went in Mr. Dearing's store. He held his tongue, 'case he liked to see his only sister dress fine and put on airs. But yer father is a drunkard, and your mother, Zelia Portwood, is a poor broken-hearted creature ever since yer was tuck from her."

And Rachel glanced a look full of malignity at the girl she hoped to crush.

"And where are my parents, Rachel?" asked Minona, in a husky voice.

"Out in the mountains. Mr. Dearing paid yer father 'nough for the hut to ha' supported him; but he's drunk it up. He's no count, and yer brothers is common backwoods fellers, 'ceptin' Hugh. He helps his mother, but that ar can't keep the family. Yer'll have a nice time, Minona Portwood, with common folks claimin' yer," and the hag laughed a loud, derisive laugh.

"Rachel, did I ever injure you, that you rejoice over my pain? I thought nurses loved children they had reared."

"Some does. Yer never harmed me yourself, Minona Portwood, but him yer call father did; and I hate them as is rich. I knowed it would cut ye both to the core to tell yer 'bout yer poor kin."

"I do not care," said Minona, proudly. "Birth is little if people have noble traits. I thank you, woman, for your tale, even if it is the offspring of malice. Leave me," she said, rising; "I would be alone."

Her imperious tone awed the hag in spite of her rude boldness.

"Remember, Minona Portwood, if yer tell Mr. Dearing who told yer this, and harm come to me, I'll have revenge. I'll see yer again."

And quickly she strode out of sight up the river.

Left alone, Minona endeavored to quell her emotion and disentangle thought which boiled as in a mighty cauldron through her brain. Was all this tale true, or a false story invented by the fiendish old woman to humiliate her? Then came Hugh Portwood's words; his acts and interference with her interview with Rachel and her father's request that she would not go out alone prior to her last visit to Savannah. Link by link she traced an imperfect chain, running far into the past wherein gloom of non-remembrance swallowed up the connection with early years. Her determination was taken, and she sought the house. Her father was out, and she went into her own room until summoned to tea, when she framed an excuse for not appearing. Mrs. Dearing was not well and Minona listened until she heard her retire to her chamber.

She then descended to the Blue Room, and knocked for admittance. Mr. Dearing was reading the last newspaper, and the girl walked near the mantelpiece and awaited his attention.

"Shall I read to you?" he asked.

"Father," said Minona, not heeding his remark, "I desire to ask you a question of particular moment. Will you give me a candid reply?"

"Certainly," he said, and looked up at her cold, calm face in surprise.

"Than, am I your daughter?"

Mr. Dearing's fine face blanched as he said:

"Of course. Why propound so simple an inquiry?"

"Yes; I am by adoption. But answer truthfully, frankly, is not Zelia Portwood my mother? and my true father a—" she closed her lips, not capable of repeating the words of the hag.

"Minona, who told you this? Why torture yourself and me with fables?"

"Your words confirm the tale. Father, is it generous to deceive me? I am no longer a child to be trifled with; and more depends on your words than you dream of. O, tell me, I beseech you, who am I?"

"My beautiful loved child by every right, except birth, and that is nothing."

Mr. Dearing's face was colorless as Parian marble, and the blue veins stood out like chords in his forehead as he asked:

"Speak, darling! What difference does it make that you are mine by adoption?"

"Much. You are noble, high-born, wealthy, and she that is my mother languishes in poverty and tears for her only daughter."

"And will you leave me?" he almost gasped, while his face paled yet more, and drops of moisture stood like beads upon his massive forehead.

"Dear father, doubly mine by adoption and devotion, my duty is plain. You have every blessing this world can offer; and while I love you, honor you, and shall owe everlasting gratitude for all you have made me; yet, my natural parents are friendless and alone, and I owe a far greater debt to them. I can love you, see you, visit you."

"Never!" exclaimed Mr. Dearing. "You must select between us. Was it for this I reared you?" he continued through his set teeth. "I must be your father or nothing. If you go to your parents, henceforth and forever all ties end between us. I shall be a stranger. Can you leave me and live a life of poverty among a set of groveling men?"

"They are my people; why should I scorn them? Oh, father, be yourself, and tempt me not to act contrary to your teachings of right."

"I do no wrong in wishing to claim my own. I have had you, cherished you from your babyhood, and your parents are strangers. You owe them no allegiance. Speak," he said, tenderly, "and tell me that you will not leave me desolate and mourning."

The tone called tears to Minona's beautiful eyes. Approaching, she threw her arms around her father's neck, saying:

"My trial is sore indeed; but God says 'Honor thy father and mother,' and I must go to mine. Let me be your child still. I can never forget you, or cease to love you."

"Never! Half measure can never suit me," he said, coldly, as he disengaged her arms. "Make your selection freely, fully, and eternally between us."

"I have made it," she said, in a low, sad voice.

"Then we are strangers from this night. I give you back your name, and return you to your people. But remember, my purpose is unalterable. When do you desire to leave for your new-found friends?"

"To-morrow. But let us not part in anger. Have mercy, and bid me adieu kindly. Let me bear into my obscurity one kind word or look to cheer me in my rough path."

Mr. Dearing heeded her not; and as she slowly left the room he bowed his head upon the table, exclaiming in agonized accents:

"My God, why hast thou forsaken me?"

All night Minona kept watch with the burning stars, unwavering in her determination to relinquish station, wealth, worldly adulations, to seek her lonely, tearful mother, sorrowing in her penury for her only one; henceforth to breathe,

> *"The keen, the wholesome air of poverty,*
> *And drinking from the well of homely life"*

beauties and graces of character, and laying up treasure in Heaven where neither mould or rust doth corrupt. She arranged a few articles of clothing, and several books—gifts from friends—leaving all her costly raiment and jewels. Near day-dawn she sat down and penned an eloquent and loving farewell to those she was to know no more as even friends.

She could not undergo the effort of bidding adieu to Mrs. Dearing in person. At sunrise Jock Hethrington tapped lightly at her door, saying:

"Miss Minona, I have the master's orders to drive you where you wish to go."

"Thank you, Jock. Bring this parcel, I am ready, and will be down in a few moments."

Once more along, she threw herself upon the sofa and gave vent to a burst of grief; not at going—that was her own choice—but at leaving beloved parents in their anger, and at the everlasting severance of ties binding her from babyhood.

Speaking a mute farewell to her happy home, and bathing her face she silently left the house, pausing in the garden to gather one rose steeped in dew.

With one fond glance at the beautiful home she was leaving forever, she entered the phaeton and bade Jock drive her to the house of Mrs. Portwood among the mountains.

"Yes, miss, I knows the road very well," respectfully replied Jock, wondering what had turned up to cause Minona to go to her own people, for he had been sworn to secrecy at the time of her adoption by his master, and faithfully had he kept the secret these many years.

Minona was silent, thoughtful, and unobservant during a drive of some hours. For her the glories of nature possessed no charm and that eventful morning, and the changing landscape passed unheeded before her eyes bent on retrospection and severe introspection. Always impulsive, and given to celerity of action, upright to a nicety not often found, she had contemplated only her duty to her forlorn mother as paramount over all other considerations. She had not paused to reflect on the reverse aspect, and now that she had more time to dwell upon her conduct, the question arose to her mind how her parents would receive her, and in what light they would regard her course. There can be little if any affinity between them and herself. She could not lay aside education, refinement, and high aspirations; nor could they rise to her standard; but she could accommodate herself to circumstances, and by patient, careful, kindly, and judicious endeavors she might elevate her parents and brothers above their present status. "Judgment comes by experience," says Johnson, and certainly impetuous courage is often the result of a want of full knowledge of existing affairs. Bravery is always tempered by experience, and Minona's stout heart, had she possessed this essential quality, would have qualified at the gigantic undertaking she proposed to herself as comparatively an easy task.

She had not succeeded in disentangling the heterogeneous mass of thought that lay in her brain, nor had she come to any definite conclusion about her mode of action, when the phaeton suddenly halted, and Jock announced that they had arrived at their destination. It was high noon. The resplendent raise of a July sun blazed upon the panting earth, and leaves drooped languidly as maiden's eyes "beneath their lover's gaze," when Minona was aroused from her confused meditations and looked around her. There stood a rude "log-cabin" in a deep gorge among the abrupt hills, with a few dilapidated out-buildings enclosed by a decaying fence. Mountains rested, hazily and lazily, with their purple faces, in the distance, and no sound trembled upon the silence to give a welcome, until chanticleer uttered his shrill noonday note to tell the passing hour, or perchance to offer gratulation to the new comer.

Jock, seeing no sign of approaching recognition, uttered a halloo, the customary method of introduction to country people under such circumstances. In a short time a middle-aged woman, coarsely dressed, was seen coming toward the house. She paused a moment on entering the dwelling, and then emerged to the fence, with an expression of mute astonishment upon her face at the spectacle of a fine equipage drawn up before her door.

Minona bounded lightly from the phaeton, and walking forward said:

"Mother, I have come home to you!"

The woman's eye shot forth one ray of pleasure; then settled into sorrow as she said:

"To laugh at my poverty and my rough ways?"

"No, dear mother, I have forsaken all to live with you always, and comfort and love you."

And the rude, unadorned woman at this appeal caught Minona in her arms, and sobbed convulsively. Poor creature! The pent-up woe of her large heart poured out its libation in this hour, when unannounced, unexpectedly God had restored the light of her household to her!

Jock silently placed Minona's articles over the fence, and touching his hat he drove off muttering to himself:

"Human nater's a strange thing."

Having delivered this sage remark, to the attentive universe at large, he fell to whistling as the best resort for companionship on his route homeward.

Mrs. Portwood was a good-looking woman, with a common education and a great deal of native intellect, and a most apt susceptibility. Her life had been one of disappointment and toil; and since the day her darling had been wrested from her she had groped her way in wretchedness and gloom. Hugh's occasional visits had been the only orient glimpses of satisfaction to her lonely, heart-broken life; nor could all his urgings and representations of the advantages reaped by her babe in the new home suppress her constant, motherly yearnings for her only daughter.

The year following Mr. Dearing's sojourn at Cedar Bluff he had purchased Eagle Bend, and in his journey thither had proposed to Mr. Portwood to adopt the little nameless cherub. Mr. Dearing had no children and his heart had craved the little girl ever since the night she had addressed him by the parental appellative. Mr. Portwood refused the proffer at first, for the little creature was endeared to him peculiarly by her winning ways; but subsequently when his inebriate habit became more public, and his affairs more ruinous, he had offered to sell his child for fifteen hundred dollars, and declared he would execute papers to Mr. Dearing binding him to abide by his contract.

Mr. Dearing's noble nature was horrified at this brutal disregard of the ties of consanguinity; nevertheless, he loved the child, and believed that by acquiescing he would rescue her from degradation or a worse fate. The deeds or bills of sale he knew would be invalid; but they would serve as a check upon any retraction or encroachment of Mr. Portwood.

The contract was made; the papers executed, and the money paid, with the stipulation on Mr. Portwood's part that the sale would ever remain a recondite matter between himself, Mr. Dearing, and the lawyer who prepared the writing.

He undertook to reconcile his wife and family to the ostensible adoption of his child by his rich neighbor.

Mr. Dearing on his side exacted, as a part of the contact, that Mr. Portwood should bind his family to inviolable silence on the subject of his adopting the child, and that he should remove to the mountains north of Clinton, where Mr. Dearing furnished him all the land he or his sons could cultivate for an indefinite number of years; and on no account was he to return to Cedar Bluff as long as Eagle Bend was the home of Mr. Dearing.

Mr. Dearing would have purchased the cabin at Cedar Bluff, but it belonged exclusively to Mrs. Portwood, and she was deaf to all entreaties for a sale of the spot.

The little nameless was called by her new parents Minona. Rachel Mulkey was retained for a few months as nurse until the child grew accustomed to her new friends, and then paid liberally to leave the country and hold her tongue.

Minona was small of her age, and for several years Mrs. Dearing passed her time at various watering places, traveling at the North and in Europe. On her return to Savannah, accompanied by her little daughter, no doubt arose among the discriminating and news-devouring public that Minona was other than a genuine Miss Dearing by birth and blood.

Minona found her obscure cottage home among the mountains sufficiently humble to have gratified the most enlarged anchoritic desires. It was antipodean in every respect to all she had left. There was much that was offensive and repugnant to her feelings of delicacy; nor could she ever become reconciled to seeing her father reel into the house in a state of intoxication. But with all the disadvantages she never regretted her step. To feel the sweet consciousness that we have acted right in the sight of the great God above, is a panoply against all ills that can encompass us.

Mrs. Portwood at first seemed timid, and fearful lest her fine daughter would feel scorn at her humble home and poor relations; but all this wore off in time when she saw her daughter cheerfully assist her in all duties, and exert her endeavors to improve the condition of things.

Mrs. Portwood had changed very little since her last introduction to the reader. She looked older; but her youth had departed then, and the sorrow over her husband's dissipation and thriftiness ways had at that time ploughed all the deep furrows that were visible upon her face, which sunk into a look of apathy after her little girl had been adopted and lost to her.

Mr. Portwood was not a constant imbiber of ardent spirits. His purse did not admit of that; hence he did not deserve one whit of commendation for abstinence. But whenever there was a lull in the business of farming, or any light excuse, he took advantage of it to go to some bar-room or village, and would sell anything for spirituous liquor enough to carry out a spree of many days. There was an evident distrust and aversion manifest in his deportment to Minona, which all her kindness failed to dispel. Many times would she retire to her own little shed-room to weep over this degradation, and the failure of all her efforts to gain her father's good will. She could not reprimand him for his sinful habit; only through affection did she hope for success, and that seemed to grow more remote every day. This, and one other trial she bore silently; the anger her beloved adopted father had shown at her forsaking him. She did not blame its exhibition, because she knew her conduct must appear basely ungrateful in his sight; but she hoped and prayed that time, the great soother, would mitigate the sorrow; and as years grew she might at least stand justified in his remembrance.

Weeks moved on and Minona, by sewing and homely housework, disposed of much of her time. She often told anecdotes of her past life to amuse her mother, and there had been a mutual explanation between them of the hiatus of years since they had parted, but all this did not occupy every moment. Her few books were perused until almost memorized, and she wished for more employment.

Her brothers, three, were at home. The two elder, William and James, were unmarried and lived in a distant county. Those with her regarded her as some exalted Princess, and did everything they could to gratify her tastes. They had only the rudiments of education. Could she not aid them and amuse herself by teaching them? Bright idea, as soon as conceived put into practice. She proposed to them that they should study together and recite at night. In this they gladly acquiesced, but often the difficulty of obtaining candles rose to defeat their plans. This at last was obviated by the young men providing the resinous wood of the mountain pine with some labor, and then study was pursued by the lambent light of a huge country fireside. Sometimes Minona's old mirth took possession of her, and she laughed heartily at the picture of the *ci-devant* Miss Dearing seated upon a low stool teaching a domestic fire-light school to three fine-looking, uncouth Tennessee mountaineers. Roy, the youngest of her brothers, was the brightest, and resembled most of all herself. She concluded their studies each night by reading, and ere long her hearers ventured to propound questions or express opinions of the subject, and she was rewarded by the certainty that her labors were not vain.

After Minona had dwelt some weeks in her new lodgings she wrote an affectionate letter to Mr. Dearing and his wife expressive of gratitude and deprecating their pleasure, but no reply came to lighten her distress, nor did her other epistles fare better.

Toward the autumn the monotony of the cabin life was varied by a visit from Hugh. He had been called by business to Eagle Bend, and was surprised not to meet Miss Dearing. The night following his arrival, after talking upon other subjects, he suddenly asked Mr. Dearing if his daughter was ill that she had not appeared.

Mr. Dearing's face instantly assumed a colorless hue as he said:

"You have gained a sister and I have lost a daughter. I presume Rachael Mulkey informed her of her parentage, and," he resumed, bitterly, "she forsook us to gain happiness with them."

"But she will return?"

"Never! All ties between us have ceased. I never could tolerate half measures. Henceforth I mourn as for a child removed from me by death. And she urged that my station and wealth would console for her loss."

"I regret it deeply, but I can influence her to return to you."

"No, the step is irrevocable. We will forget the subject, as she has ceased to remember me, and oblige me, Hugh, by never mentioning my name to her. Henceforth I desire oblivion to reign between us."

Vain boast, proud man! Daily, hourly the sweet face of the lost Minona rose before the desolate heart of Mr. Dearing, an ever-present, ever-torturing phantom, and there were moments when he would have given all his possessions for one bright glance from her beautiful eyes.

And Mrs. Dearing, with her growing ill health, repined each day at the absence of her brilliant daughter. In silence she bore her cross, because soon after Minona's sudden departure, when Mr. Dearing had explained all to her, he requested that the subject might never be alluded to in his presence. In all her sorrow Eriginia felt assured of his sympathy, full and overflowing, for his tenderness and care of her was greater than she had ever experienced.

Hugh's arrival at the home of his father was hailed with delight by all, and by none more than Minona. Him she had known during a long life of prosperity as a stranger, and now she could claim him as a brother, and unreservedly confide all her feelings to him. Besides, there was one powerful bond between them. They both grieved over one sorrow in the loss of a beloved friend, and this is a leveler of all conventionalities.

"Brother," said Minona, the first opportunity that offered for private conversation, "tell me of my beloved friends, now parents no longer. Are they well, and do they miss me and speak of me kindly?"

"I do not doubt that they feel your loss," said Hugh, with a pained expression, and reluctant to wound her feelings.

"But did they say nothing; send no kind word?"

"My dear sister, I had no conversation with Mrs. Dearing. Her health is wretched. I did not know of your absence until I asked Mr. Dearing for you."

"And what did he say?" she asked, eagerly.

Hugh did not reply, but turned over the pages of a book which lay on a chair near him. They were both sitting in the front room of the cabin, which was parlor, bed-room, dining-room, and often the kitchen.

"Tell me what my—Mr. Dearing said," pleaded the girl, and her voice sounded strange as she pronounced the formal name. "I wish to know the worst aspect, for suspense is a cancerous ulcer that eats away life by slow degrees."

"He feels your desertion bitterly, and asked me not to mention him to you. He desired to forget the subject and that oblivion might reign between you and him forever."

Minona's pale face blanched to a deathly whiteness, and grew finally rigid under these cruel words. She almost gasped for breath. After some moments she said, in a hollow voice:

"My God! it is hard to bear odium for our best actions, our holiest endeavors to do right; nevertheless, I must toil on, looking into futurity for my reward! Do you blame my course?" she asked, abruptly.

"It was hasty, but dictated by the promptings of a most noble soul. It restored to me a beloved sister that my heart has craved for long, weary years, and I do not regret it, though I should have prevented it if I had possessed the power. Dear sister, do not yield to the pressure of despondency. I know that Mr. Dearing's heart overflows with affection for you, and, finally, he will regard your course in its true light. It is natural that he should be angry now."

"I knew he was unrelenting, but I thought he would pardon me. He was never unjust, and always awarded to each an equitable judgment, even when contrary to his interest."

"And he will to you, in time, I have no doubt. In the meanwhile, patience is the safe rudder which steers us through the shoals and quicksands of life. Cheer our mother and repay her for her self-immolation in all these years," and he added, in a low, mournful voice, "influence our father to forsake the ways of sin, and be an honor to us."

"I can do nothing in that quarter. He distrusts me—hates me, I believe. My presence here is a disagreeable restraint upon him."

"Do not relinquish your efforts. Continual dropping weareth away stone. He cannot always resist kindness."

"I will do as you say. But I see no sunspots flecking the darkness which spreads drearily before us. I care not for poverty and toll. These develop the best gold from the mine of rubbish that exists in every individual. From my childhood I have craved action—to be of some essential use, to feel that I was created for some benign purpose."

"Work on. Success comes to those gifted with longest endurance, and often I have seen sunlight dispel the heaviest clouds. The moral horizon is like its prototype in nature," said Hugh.

Hugh's visit ended, and Minona was left again to her self imposed labors. Each day was a fac-simile of its predecessor, and resembled in blank monotony a long barren road, wherein there was no turn to vary the unpromising scene.

CHAPTER XVI.

Summer at length passed away, seeming longer and more dreary than any in the lives of the desolate inmates at Eagle Bend. Mrs. Dearing gladly welcomed the autumn, knowing that it would restore her to her city home, where she hoped to dispel her griefs at the loss of her cousin and daughter, by companionship with her metropolitan friends, and by the gayeties of city life.

Not very long before their removal Mr. Dearing was called to Knoxville by some bank transaction, wherein his Savannah house was largely interested. As he halted a few moments at the post office in Clinton to exchange some words with acquaintances, he observed an unusual throng of persons on the streets. The circuit court was in progress, and had been in session several days. The Sheriff came to the door of the small stone courthouse house near by, and exclaimed in a loud voice the names of parties whose presence was needed in the course of the proceedings.

Driving forward a little more than a hundred yards to the ferry across the Pellissippi river, Mr. Dearing's attention was attracted by the call of his name by some one approaching him from the rear. He caused his carriage to halt, when the Sheriff came alongside, holding a paper in his hand and exclaimed to Mr. Dearing

"You are my prisoner, sir!"

Mr. Dearing was thunderstruck. He did not quail—he was conscious of no guilt and could not imagine any particular or possible cause of arrest, but the summons disconcerted him. To be disconcerted on sudden arrest is no evidence of guilt, although sometimes cruelly misconstrued to that end on trials of criminals on circumstantial evidence. The suspicion of a joke flashed for an incident over the prisoner's mind, but the stern face of the officer dispelled it quickly. Mr. Dearing thought it a mistake.

"By what authority," he demanded, "do you arrest me?"

"By this," replied the Sheriff, opening the paper in his hand and handing it with an air of mingled sternness and compassion to Mr. Dearing.

A glance at the contents of the paper revealed to the gentleman the startling fact that he was under indictment for murder.

He accompanied the officer to the court room. As the Sheriff walked forward with his prisoner the attention of all eyes was concentrated upon

Chapter XVI. Her resolution was formed at once. She slept no more. The dawn of day found her far on her journey to Clinton. The wild March wind raved frightfully through the leafless trees, but the resolute girl pressed forward, and by ten o'clock she was entering, with intrepid step, the old stone court house.

them. The indictment had been known to but few persons previously, but now the buzz of undertone conversation, and the deep sensation legible on the countenances of the multitude, showed how quickly they comprehended the "situation."

The Judge of the court, having, by a rap of his walking cane on the bench as a signal, procured silence, proceeded to state to Mr. Dearing, in terms tremulously significant of his deep emotion, that it was necessary for him to be in the custody of the law until he was tried by a jury of the county, and that he was entitled to a speedy and impartial trial under the constitution.

The Judge was a slender man of medium height, about forty years of age, and of rare polish of manners that threw a charm over his pure and conscientious administration of justice.

Mr. Dearing remarked to the Judge that he was ignorant how to proceed, as he was not informed of the particular offense with which he was charged. Judge Alden directed that a copy of the indictment should be furnished him, which the clerk of the court commenced preparing. In this interval some other business of minor import was taken up by the court.

Seated near Mr. Dearing, within the bar of the court, was a gentleman of the legal profession, whom he had met occasionally before that time. He was short, thin, of fair complexion, with curly black hair, searching blue eyes, and a nose the end of which seemed to turn up in perpetual contempt of mankind. Mr. Maitland sat, the acknowledged equal if not the superior of every other practitioner at the bar. His tireless energy, his intimate acquaintance with all the minutiæ of his profession, his wonderful accuracy and his lightning velocity of mental action, made him justly one of the most brilliant and successful lawyers of his day.

Mr. Dearing at once requested the counsel and assistance of Mr. Maitland.

With the swift penetration of his mental nature, Mr. Maitland speedily mastered the character of the accusation, and under his wise counsel, after argument between him and the Solicitor, Mr. Dearing was allowed to enter into bonds for his appearance at a subsequent term of the court, and to proceed on his journey to Knoxville.

Mr. Dearing's firm nature was not proof against the shock of this unexpected stroke. He who is under indictment for a very serious charge, whose very life is dependent on the uncertain testimony of human witnesses and the fickle judgment of twelve capricious jurymen, may well quail. Who, if charged suddenly with the murder of someone he had never before heard of, would enjoy his dessert at dinner?

But Mr. Dearing had slain the man for whose death he was now held to answer the stern requirements of the law. He had killed him in defense of his person, his family and his property. The deceased was an outlaw and a highwayman. But could these facts be substantiated before the jury? That was the vital but dubious question.

But one witness saw the deed. It occurred a hundred yards from the road where Mr. Dearing's carriage was posted, in a dense thicket of shrubs and lofty trees clothed with mid-summer foliage. Could the only living witness, the accomplice of the robber, be found? He knew that Mr. Dearing shot his comrade in self-defense. Could he be compelled to testify, and, if so, would he speak the truth?

But upon whose testimony, and what testimony was the charge predicated? That puzzled him? Mr. Maitland had been able to glean this only—that the prosecutor, Jacob Eastman, was rumored to have been passing through the thicket just in time to see the fatal shot fired, that he lingered out of sight for fear of a similar fate, until Mr. Dearing had disappeared, and then had exerted himself to procure sepulchre for the unknown deceased. Such was the story in circulation, which grew as it flew from mouth to mouth of the devouring and insatiable public. A thousand sinister insinuations in regard to Mr. Dearing's character found ready credence in the popular mind.

How could Mr. Dearing establish the truth? Although his keenly sensitive mind had frequently suffered an intense though secret pain on account of having deprived a human being of life, yet he had always felt justified in the eye of God, conscious, as he was, that he had done nothing more than self-defense demanded.

The few months sped by and the date of the trial came. The unusual interest of the trial had brought a large crowd to the little town of Clinton. Mr. Dearing, pale but self-possessed, sat beside Mr. Maitland. Judge Alden, grave, oppressed at the seriousness of the occasion, sat on his tall judicial bench. Jurors were called, examined, and took their seats. They were sworn. The trial was reached, and yet Mr. Dearing had no witnesses who were enabled to speak of the immediate circumstances of the killing.

Mr. Crews was far away in a foreign land, and rumors had reached Savannah that he had terminated his labors and his life in his attempt to convert the souls of the earthly "Celestials" to the hope of a resurrection into a far more glorious kingdom. The gentle Vinvela, "after life's fitful fever," slept well. Mrs. Dearing was incompetent as a witness, and was purposely kept in blissful ignorance of the whole procedure. Minona! alas, where was Minona? Mr. Dearing thought of her as one lost, although her perch among the mountains was only a few miles distant. Would she hear in her eremitical seclusion of his trials? Would she fly to his rescue? Could she aid him if present? And, more than all, his pride, stronger than his love of life, forbade him to seek aid from her.

Jock Hethrington was there, in court, his only witness. He had remained at the carriage, and knew nothing of the circumstances in the thicket except the flight and pursuit, and the report of pistols heard there soon afterward. Whatever else he knew was known only by the statement of the accused on his return from the thicket, and was irrelevant and inadmissible.

The prosecutor was introduced as the principal witness on behalf of the state. He was an ill-favored man of about twenty-five years of age, coarse, ignorant, but with a native sharpness of intellect that cropped out continually. He testified that he was passing through the thicket on the Copper Ridge, when, a short distance from him, a report of a pistol attracted his attention; that soon afterward two men came running just in sight of him, pursued by the defendant at the bar, and that the defendant shot one of the fugitives, killing him almost instantly. The other fugitive disappeared, and the witness knew nothing more of him.

Mr. Maitland was unable, on a most searching and critical cross-examination, to shake the consistency of his story. The case looked almost hopeless for Mr. Dearing. Mr. Maitland's countenance darkened. Some of the jurors of the Coroner's inquest were called, and fully corroborated the witness so far as to establish the fact that a homicide had been committed.

To this unfavorable aspect of the case and Jock Hethrington's testimony afforded but slight relief. The attempt at robbery on the part of the deceased had been unsuccessful. The pursuit of the fugitives by the accused had been without apparent motive except revenge. He had not endeavored to arrest him for the offense of the attempted robbery. Killing for revenge, even on a sudden heat, was, at the eye of the law, a felony. Mr. Maitland was anxious, distressed. He entered keenly into the defense of his client, from his appreciation of the high honor and enlarged culture of the accused, his thorough conviction that there existed in fact no legal guilt, and perhaps from the potentiality of a very large fee, which stirs the sympathies of all of all lawyers to their profoundest depths.

The court adjourned until the following morning as night gathered gloomily into the narrow court room of the old stone house. The stars hid themselves beyond drifting masses of wintry clouds which swept across the sky, while the March winds howled afar among the lofty mountain summits.

Minona had recently suffered from a severe cold, and lay nervous and sleepless in her narrow little apartment and her mountain home. Her past life, like a strange dream, came up with the vividness of a painting before her vision. In the foreground stood the noble Mr. Dearing, once her "father!" How her heart yearned toward him! As she thus lay, along the dim road approaching the house, in the midnight blasts of winter, sometimes enlivened by eddying snow flakes, rode maudlin John Seiber. He had, in the uncommon darkness of the night, mistaken the way to his home only a mile distant.

"Hello!" yelled the mountain bacchanalian.

The call was quickly repeated by the impatient man, who had sobriety enough to see the dim figure of the dwelling, and to distinguish it from his own.

"Hello, if you want to keep a body from freezin' to death!" exclaimed Seiber.

Minona, in the deep darkness, threw open her window and asked who was there.

"Squire John Seiber!" was the reply, "and I wants to find out whar I am and how to get home!"

Minona informed him whose dwelling he had encountered. The "Squire" then explained how he had happened to wander so late, having an aversion to the idea that the beautiful Minona, whose voice he recognized, should suspect him of losing his way from tipsiness. Consciousness of guilt flies to falsehood, even if that falsehood implies a greater guilt. Strange cowardice!

The Squire told Minona that he had been detained by listening to the "big case for murder," as he expressed it. He then proceeded with maudlin garrulity to relate the nature of the murder case, and as Minona was closing the window he coupled the name of Mr. Dearing with the trial.

The window was quickly opened wide, an Minona, with eager interest, asked him what news he had of Clarek Dearing.

"He'll be hung for murder," exclaimed the tipsy man, "and I'm glad of it. I ain't for lettin' a rich man kill a poor one jest because he's rich, nary time!"

Minona's pulse almost ceased their beat, but by a great effort she inquired into the particulars, and learned enough, very soon, to comprehend the dreadful fate at that very moment impending over Mr. Dearing's head.

All his hauteur, his persistent silence, his unconquerable pride and resentment against herself became as nothing. Her resolution was formed at once. She slept no more. The dawn of day found her far on her journey to Clinton. The wild March wind raved frightfully through the leafless trees, but the resolute girl pressed forward, and by ten o'clock she was entering, with intrepid step, the old stone court house.

The dense throng opened to give her entrance, and in a moment, with pale but determined features, she stood in the presence of the actors of the dread drama of the day.

Mr. Maitland's face brightened as he learned who she was. Mr. Dearing with difficulty maintained his composure and seat in the culprit's box.

Minona, without approaching Mr. Dearing, turned to the Judge, and after respectful salutation, said:

"Hearing late last night of this proceeding I hastened hither, unbidden, to offer my testimony on the side of truth; for I feel sure that the accused is innocent of any crime."

The Attorney General muttered something indistinctly. The prosecutor hung down his head. He remembered that once he had felt the power of that dark, searching eye, calm even in danger, reading his very inmost soul.

Minona was quickly sworn and examined. The Attorney General objected, but as the Judge had not commenced to charge the jury he held the testimony admissible. She related in a clear and concise manner the events of the attempted robbery, which Jock Hethrington's stupidity had disabled him from presenting in an intelligible manner to the jury. Mr. Dearing's appearance on the scene, the flight of the robbers into the thicket, Mr. Dearing's pursuit, the explosion of firearms, the return of Mr. Dearing, and resumption of the journey.

"But did you see the fatal shot discharged?" asked the Attorney General, triumphantly.

"I did not," replied Minona.

The prosecutor raised his head. The Attorney General, whose feelings against the accused were always easily aroused, looked elated.

"Then why did the prisoner shoot and kill the deceased?"

"He did it in self-defense," answered Minona.

"How do you know that?" asked the Solicitor.

"He told me so on his return to the road," said Minona.

Her last words were drowned by the Attorney General's vociferous "Stop! Stop!" and appeals to the court to exclude the hearsay testimony.

Minona's dark eyes now rested for an instant on the face of the prosecutor. He quailed.

"There," said she, "is one who was in the thicket with the accused and the deceased."

All eyes turned in the direction indicated by her finger, and encountered the ghastly features of the prosecutor.

"How do you know that?" asked the Attorney General.

"He was the accomplice of the deceased in the attempted robbery, and the two fled together," said Minona.

The prosecutor whispered audibly:

"It is false!"

Minona quickly turning to the Judge exclaimed:

"I remember his face well. The scar over his left eye is unmistakable. Besides, if his collar shall be opened a deep scar, as if from a burn, will be perceived."

The prosecutor shrank in terror. The Judge directed him to open his collar. He began, several times, irresolutely, to comply, and as often desisted, when the

Judge ordered him to obey at once or be sent to jail. With the assistance of the
Sheriff the collar was opened and the scar met the eyes of the spectators.

On this exposure of the perjury and fraud of the prosecutor, and acquittal
was speedily declared by the jury, and the Attorney General at once ordered the
perjurer into the custody of the law.

Minona, unwilling to receive the thanks of her quandam father, or the
plaudits of the public, quickly left the court house and accompanied her
brother Roy to her home. She reached there late, exhausted by excitement and
fatigue, and with an increase of her malady by exposure to the bleak cold winds,
which searched through her frame at every gust during her journey in an open
wagon. For a week or two she labored with a severe and alarming illness, to
the terror of her mother and brothers, who regarded her with a worship little
short of idolatry. Even the stoical father manifested some anxiety, and, unasked,
went for Dr. Crandon, who exerted all his skill to restore the girl to health. He
brought the sympathetic Miss Isabella to assist in nursing her.

The doctor could not but admire the heroic nature of a girl brought up and
pampered in all the luxuries that wealth could lavish, thus voluntarily resigning
them for a life of privation in a miserable hovel, and this for a principle of duty
to parental claims.

In all the hours of illness, when parched by a burning fever and confined
for weeks to a coarse log room of ten feet square with no furniture save a
common bed, no murmurs escaped Minona's lips. Her deportment was gentle,
affectionate, grateful to her unpolished though loving mother and brothers.

"Yes! yes!" muttered the sapient Æsculapius, "she will make a noble wife.
Pity she forsook Dearing, but we shall see if we cannot better her condition."

Accordingly, he proposed to Isabella to insist upon Minona's going into
Clinton as soon as convalescent, and then spending some time with them.
Mrs. Portwood united with Miss Isabel in her request to Minona to accept the
invitation, and she went toward the close of March.

The past season's crops had been a total failure in many parts of the country,
and Mr. Portwood was one of the sufferers. His thriftless habits grew upon him
and ill-luck seemed to pursue every attempt made by the family to better their
fortune. Each year the farm proceeds were of necessity swallowed up by debts,
leaving an insufficient remainder to supply the family demands. There was no
alternative but to go again on credit to obtain necessaries, and this indebtedness
was increased still more than the addition of the old balance by Mr. Portwood's
inebriate propensities. The young men would have cut adrift from their
father's sinking condition save for their mother, and now they remained out
of deference to Minona's feelings. But no prospect held out any allurements
or hope of improvement. Minona had revolved all these dreadful and puzzling
questions in her mind, determined to assist, herself, in the building up of her

family; but no field for exertion was offered in the obscure position of their home. Teaching and stitching, never-failing weapons against want to the female sex, opened out the only resource to her, and to accomplish an end by either of these their location must be changed.

She consulted Miss Isabella, who assured her that she might do both if she was near Clinton. Dr. Crandon would exert himself to get her a school.

Minona passed three weeks with Miss Isabella, who treated her with the utmost consideration. Dr Crandon lived in an old-fashioned house, divested by time of every atom of paint that had ever adorned it. The exterior was unprepossessing. Within, everything was plain but comfortable; and while its complement of furniture might have seemed mean in the eye of a wealthy person accustomed to the grandeur of rosewood and damask sofas and chairs, and glittering mirrors—by contrast to Mr. Portwood's log house and deal tables it was luxurious. Minona's health improved very slowly, and whenever she appeared riding with Miss Crandon her presence excited much interest. Her conduct in the court room had gained her great eclat. How little she cared for this adulation, and how many times she sighed in secret for one kind word from her former father!

On Minona's return home she found Mr. Portwood in one of his worst fits of intoxication—very quarrelsome with his sons and brutal to her mother. She noticed him for days often leave the room, and after a time she followed him into a back shed where he kept his liquors. He had just poured out the last contents of a bottle into a tumbler that was three-fourths full of whisky, when she stepped forward and removed it from his hand, throwing its contents instantly upon the floor.

"Father," she said, "do not be angry, but I can no longer see you destroy your soul without an effort to save you."

The man was so astonished by her intrepidity that he had not thought of opposition. Her words recalled him. With an oath he said:

"What is it to you, proud girl, if a poor man the likes of me loves his dram?"

"Everything. You are my father, and if you are poor it makes no difference to me. You need not degrade yourself and us. Oh, father! be a man, upright and strong, and leave off this awful habit. It is killing my poor mother!"

Excited by liquor, though fully possessed of his senses, he said:

"Girl, I know you hates me, and came back to get after me for sellin' of you when you was a little child."

"What can you mean?" she asked, in astonishment.

"None of yer hypocritical cant. You knows full well that I sold you to that 'ere rich feller for fifteen hundred dollars."

"I never heard of it before," said Minona, oppressed with mortification of a man avowing his own brutality so shamelessly.

"I doesn't believe it. If Dearing never told you Zelia has, for women never keeps anything."

Overmastering her disgust, she said:

"Father, my lips have never uttered what is untrue, and once more I assure you that I never heard before what you now mentioned. And no matter if you did sell me, you are my father and I have voluntarily resumed all the ties that bound us before you severed them. I do not hate you. I wish you love me and to let me love you. Will you not forswear drinking from this night?"

He looked up at her in amazement, her eyes were full of tears. There was no pride, but perfect sorrow and compassion breathing in every feature. She, that regal, high-souled girl, born one of nature's nobles, forgetting all save the urgent desire to save the drunkard, threw her arms around the degraded, foul-breathing man, pleading with him to turn away from the paths of sin, wretchedness and utter destruction.

And he, the coarse, hardened, lost man, wept tears of contrition as he was locked in the arms of his heroic daughter. Her conquest was complete. From that night a light, steady, benign, elevating in its tendency, broke upon the soul of John Portwood, and he never touched intoxicating liquors again.

Minona was the star that reigned over his destiny, shedding its rays through that happy household with never-fading lustre.

Mr. Portwood and his sons went forward to Cedar Bluff, by Minona's wish, and began their farming. The old house was partially repaired. Business was conducted on a small scale from press of time and narrow means, but by June the family had removed to their old residence on the Pellissippi.

The Eagle Bend was deserted, save by Jock Hethrington, who had the care of it and still indulged in his "small glass" whenever he could obtain it.

Minona, by the kindness of Dr. Crandon, began teaching school in the village church. The building was some distance from Cedar Bluff, and afforded her a very agreeable walk each morning and afternoon. Her dinner or luncheon was always carried along with her, and in a few weeks she found herself safely embarked as a school mistress, with a score of pupils of all sizes and ages. Some people are born to command, and of these Minona was one. She seemed to have no difficulty in exacting respect, and preserving the most perfect discipline. There was a resolute, quiet dignity, a determination in her eyes, that suppressed incipient rebellion, and her winning deportment inspired affection. The duties of school-teaching are multiform as well as onerous. In some pupils the ideas or to be trained; in others created and then shaped. Again, among many, the germ of mentality has to be nurtured and encouraged into light; while, in a few, too full of self-conceit, a gently suppressing influence has to be judiciously used. It requires genius to understand all this and adapt it to a successful end. Minona, without effort, appeared intuitively to work skillfully upon all the raw material afforded to her by the village school. Even the most unpromising soil was made fruitful under her tillage, and she gave universal satisfaction.

At this time her heart was bowed by a weight of affliction. Soon after her father's removal to the Cedar Bluff she received a letter from Hugh informing her of the death of Mrs. Dearing, and of Mr. Dearing's departure for Europe.

It was bitter agony to Minona to know that one of her once adopted parents was removed beyond all possibility of a reconciliation, and the other embittered beyond hope of appeasement. One word to know that she had not been forgotten by Mrs. Dearing in her last moments, one kind line of condolence from Mr. Dearing, would have been of greater comfort and of more value than untold millions to her bruised spirit. Her grief was hopeless, and the more acute because secret. No one could appreciate it save Hugh, and he was seldom with her, and she was burdened by an incubus heavy enough, of his own without sharing hers.

She still taught her brothers at night, and Roy proposed entering as a pupil at her school, promising the most implicit obedience to her mandates.

"Sister," he said, "I can aid you as assistant corrector, if not teacher. Ladies are not strong enough to use the ferule."

"I allow no such implement in my little empire. I am autocrat there, and, what is best of all, I govern through love exclusively."

"Then I shall not be admitted into your dominion, as I shall be of no service," he replied, with an air of mock disappointment.

"I am fearful you will introduce disaffection, and I am too weak to cope with such powerful opponents," she said, looking admiringly on the symmetrical proportions of the handsome young man before her.

"I declare if you only give me six months probation, I will surpass Moses himself in meekness, and be your sworn ally in all the difficulties that may hereafter arise. Subjects and children tire of good behavior, as the latter do of eating candies. Say yes," he said, catching her around the waist. "I shall not let you go until you consent."

Laughingly she agreed, and in time her other brothers joined her school also in their leisure months. Roy could not attend college, but he had the offer of being aided in classical studies by Dr. Crandon, and he studied with Minona every day, reciting to the learned gentleman twice each week.

It may be asked, was Minona happy in her present existence? Yes, happy with a great grief! Strange paradox! She was happy in the sweet consciousness of acting well in the sight of her Creator, and happy in the knowledge of conferring blessings and conducing essentially to the pleasure and the benefit of others—the best of all elements of contentment and enjoyment in this life. But she sorrowed constantly and deeply over the decease of Mrs. Dearing; and yet more over the living grief ever present with her; the continued obduracy of Mr. Dearing. Never for a moment that she censure him, because he looked not to the cause, but dwelt upon the effect of her forsaking him. His embittered sentiments were natural, and she saw in their continuance how great had been his affection for her; yet she could not be reconciled.

Where was Delbridge Meverill during all these long months? Had he forgotten her? Often her heart pondered this query. She had disregarded his letters, that he was the most sensitive of her acquaintances in matters of etiquette. She knew his address, and owed him two letters, but time had lengthened since the indebtedness became due. Her station was changed now, and pride whispered for her to await the course of events.

Mr. Meverill had not forgotten Minona, but his pride was wounded, and he too was awaiting the course of time with a beating, restless heart—to continue how long? O, how long?

One day Minona had gone to school alone. It was a cloudless Indian summer day in November, that gloomy month that Hood so wittily characterizes by so many negatives; and its beauty was better appreciated by its rarity in this most churlish month of all the year. Just before the school was dismissed in the afternoon a buggy stopped at the door, and Dr. Crandon entered the church. Bowing, he walked to Minona, and in an undertone asked her to ride with him. She acquiesced. Dr. Crandon had been a staunch and valuable friend, and was so much her senior that she regarded him in the light of an elder relative to whom she could go for advice whenever needed.

The school was soon dismissed, and they started on their ride. Minona felt in fine spirits. There is always something exhilarating in a bright day after a succession of gloomy ones.

"Miss Minona, when are you to give vacation? Isabel is ailing, and she wishes you to help her play housekeeper for a few weeks. Yes, yes, she needs rest, and you do too. Your cheeks are pale, and your form has lost some of its roundness."

"I regret, doctor, Miss Isabel's indisposition; but I am such a novice in housekeeping I should give her more unrest by my blunders than would be desirable. I never have any color, and rest acts upon me as rust upon steel; it eats away all my bright qualities."

"That is impossible. Your traits are of that higher type beyond the corruption of rust. They will always shine resplendent. Yes, yes," and the doctor applied his whip to his already swift-moving steed in his enthusiastic encomiums upon his fair companion.

"I did not know before that you were a flatterer, doctor," said she, laughing. "Beware that you do not fall from grace in my opinion."

"I should lament that. By the way, Roy is a fine youth–brilliant as a new dollar–and yes, yes, very like his sister."

"I declare I shall begin to doubt the sincerity of your friendship if you continue your compliments. They do well in society, but among friends should be eschewed."

"Very well, Miss Minona, but you do not blame a man for the expression of his honest opinion? It will bubble up like a flowing spring; but I must try to suppress what is offensive. Yes, Isabel needs rest. I wish her to visit mother this winter. Yes."

"I did not know you had a mother living," said Minona, glad to change the subject from herself.

"Yes, yes! She is aged now, and lives in Middle Tennessee, the garden spot of all this world. I began life a poor lad. Father died when we, four of us, were young, and mother had us all to educate. I worked on the farm, yes, hard and steady, and went to school in the winter until I grew a raw, sturdy youth and felt a desire to enter college."

"Young ambition begins to bud in the breast of all, I believe, and is a powerful motor to drive us to great deeds!"

"Thank you, ma'am. Yes! I am not great, but I labored on and paid my own way through college. It would never have done for mother to have had that weight added to her others. Well, I studied my profession under a friend, and then attended a few lectures by his aid. Since then I have never wanted a dime, thank God! Yes, yes, and I have paid him long since all his advances. A friend in need is a great thing, and I practice the endeavor never to forget the admonition."

"I think you do, doctor, as I can testify most gratefully," said Minona, wondering what caused the gentleman to detail his history to her.

"I located here many years ago," continued the doctor, "and believe I formed the reputation of being an honest man, and a tolerably skillful practitioner."

"I never heard either impeached," said Minona.

"Yes, yes. Although my brother and I have had to support our mother and two sisters, I have prospered, and now own a comfortable property besides my profession. Yes, Isabella needs rest, and I need a wife; but the question is where to find one. Yes, yes," and again the doctor tapped his horse with the whip.

"I did not know that was a difficult matter," said Minona, without embarrassment, never dreaming that there was the slightest application to herself.

The gentleman cleared his throat, urged forward the willing steed, coughed, again cleared his throat and said:

"Yes, that's the question, Miss Minona, and you must solve it for me. You must make or remove all the obstacles for me; for I now offer you my fortune, myself, and my heart which has long been—yes, yes—long been yours. I need a wife. Come, and give poor Isabella the rest she needs."

If a thunderbolt had fallen, Minona could not have been struck more dumb than by this sudden denouement of an affection she had not the remotest suspicion of.

"I am very abrupt, Miss Minona. I am unused to the pretty ways of saying these things that very young men carry about with them as heart slayers. Yes, Isabel says I am a plain, matter-of-fact, one-idea man. If you need time for reflection, I can wait, only give me, yes, an unequivocal response in the end."

"Dr. Crandon," at last said Minona, "I hope there has been nothing in my conduct that led you to suppose I was luring you on to such a decision as this you have just unfolded. I do assure you that I never even dreamed of such a possibility. And as much as I regret to wound you, I must emphatically decline what I appreciate as the greatest honor you could proffer to me. I thank you sincerely for the compliment, but forget that it ever was made, and let us be as of yore esteemed friends. There are many other far more exemplary women, any of whom could assimilate with you as a wife far better than an erratic, inexperienced girl like myself."

"I know of none that can approximate to your unparalleled character. Let us be as before; but keep my good qualities in the foreground of your imagination; forget my peculiarities; and, if possible, in the future grant my request. In the meantime, if you ever need a friend call on Thomas Crandon. Yes, yes, come and spend some time with Isabella."

The ride ended, and Minona for days pondered over the singularity of the conquest she had made. Her opinion of her suitor was enhanced by his generous conduct and warm friendship for her and her brothers; but she felt that she never could, under any circumstances, entertain his proposition favorably. She refused Miss Isabella's invitation at first; but the lady was so urgent that she finally acquiesced and passed a week with her. Dr. Crandon's deportment was as if nothing had ever occurred between them. If anything, there was an increase of unobtrusive attentions to which the most fastidious could bring no objection, and she felt that her visits to Miss Isabel need not be curtailed or avoided.

Ere long Hugh made a flying visit to his mother, preparatory to the labors of a busy winter. Minona felt overjoyed at his appearance, and she hoped for tidings from the absent and the lost. Hugh could only assure her that Mr. Dearing was well and spending some time in Switzerland. His letters were infrequent and brief, and no exponent of his inner feelings. Hugh brought with him a case containing a handsome set of rare pearls that Mrs. Dearing had left for Minona.

"She told me to give you these with her blessing, sister, and that she had never forgotten you nor ceased to mourn your desertion; that you must always cherish her memory, and be kind to Mr. Dearing."

"I need no asking to remember her," said Minona, in faltering accents; "and Heaven knows how I long for an opportunity to fulfill the latter request; but I shall never have it. Did she suffer greatly?"

"Yes, and lingered long; and I never witnessed such a gentle, unselfish, untiring devotion as Mr. Dearing bestowed upon her. A man has a large overflowing heart when he can lay aside his nature and assume a woman's post by the bedside of a dying wife. Mrs. Dearing did not need friends, but he resigned his place to none, serving her to the very last moment."

"And, brother, did she ever ask for me? Cruel, that I was not summoned."

"Yes, she spoke to me of you, and desired to see you; but she thought such a request would be painful to Mr. Dearing. She became unconscious toward the last. I thought of you, but I could suggest what she shrank from proposing."

"You did well; but that does not lessen my regrets. An adverse fate pursues me. I lament deeply all this; yet I do not regret my course. I have cause for never-ceasing approval."

She then informed him of the change in their father's deportment, and they both united in the hope that his resolution would continue always fixed.

On Hugh's return to Savannah, a gentleman called one night at his lodgings, and introduced himself as Mr. Acres Burleigh.

"I have so frequently heard of you, Mr. Portwood, that I do not feel as a stranger. Knowing you to be a friend of the Dearings, I ventured to call and inquire them. Are they well?"

"Mr. Dearing was when I heard of him," said Hugh. "His life is lonely now, and Mrs. Dearing has passed to that sleep that knows no waking."

"Is Miss Dearing married?"

"No; she is in Tennessee," replied Hugh.

"What of Miss Gladwin?" asked the young man with his lips compressed, and agitation visible in every feature.

"She is dead," murmured Hugh, in a hollow voice.

Mr. Burleigh's face became convulsed and blanched in agony. Drooping his head upon a table near, he said solemnly:

"My God, help me to bear this blow! So young! so holy!"

"What was she to you?" asked Hugh, grasping his arm, and full of pity for his sorrow.

"Nothing! I was a rejected lover. But she was the only woman who ever called forth in me love, or a desire to forsake evil."

"And if you feel her loss so acutely, what must I endure who was her affianced lover, and saw her perish on our bridal eve?"

Audible sobs choked the haughty Acres Burleigh. He, that had so hated his kind, wept over the early tomb of the pure and holy girl who had first taught him the beatific inspiration of love.

Suppressing his grief by a mighty self-command, he rose and grasped Hugh's hand, saying, as he wrung it, in tremulous tones:

"God help you, as I trust he will me!"

He left; but henceforth there was a bond of union stronger than death between these two young men. The character of Hugh softened the harsh, bitter nature of Acres Burleigh, and taught him that there was much good yet left in the world; and Hugh, in his tender sympathy for the unfortunate young man, felt reminded of the lost Vinvela more vividly; for she had borne a like cross, but how differently! She with patience, cheerfulness and meekness, inspiring all with admiration; while he was morose and repellent, with a fierce, bounding heart scared and sorrowful within.

CHAPTER XVII.

Minona, whom fate seemed to single out as one constantly to figure actively in the great drama of life, was one day reading during the recess between school hours. It was a cool spring day, and she was seated upon a friendly rock and joined the genial rays of the bright sun. The pupils were some distance away; but she could hear the murmur of their joyous voices as they roamed among the trees engaged in some rompish games. Her book lay open before her, and her thoughts were on a far journey over the Atlantic when the voice of Rachel Mulkey accosted her.

"I told you when we last met that I'd see yer again. Yer not as fine, Minona Portwood, as when we last seed one an other. Yer as poor as any of us now."

"I do not mind it, as you see, Rachel. I am happy."

"I doesn't believe it. Yer heart craves riches this minit. And I can give 'em to yer, too."

"Excuse me, Rachel, but it is my turn to disbelieve you."

"I kin prove it."

She whistled, and from behind the church in the concealing trees emerged a man of about thirty years, attired in a worn, rusty suit of black clothes, with an ungainly figure and a sinister face; restless eyes that glanced furtively, always avoiding a direct look, which bespeak the want of honesty in any face.

"Mr. Easman, tell Minona Portwood what yer knows that kin bring her a fortin'."

Mr. Eastman touched his hat, cleared his throat, and unfolded that he was a lawyer of a neighboring place. Having occasion to overlook the records, he discovered that some of Mrs. Portwood's near ancestors had when he considered an indisputable claim to a large and valuable tract of land near Clinton, now owned by wealthy parties. That he could recover it, if well remunerated, for the benefit of minor children.

"Now, Minona Portwood, if yer's sensible yer'll recover this for yer and Roy, and can play the fine gal agin."

"I must hear more of the plans, and consult friends first," answered the girl.

"No! Mr. Easman must manage hisself, or he'll tell nothin' more."

"Well," said Minona, "is that all?"

"He must have good pay; but i rekin yer'll not quail 'bout that."

Chapter XVII. In imagination she beheld the wrecked ship with its living burden struggling amid the surging billows of an all devouring element. Again the pale features of her friend, locked in icy death, rose as the form floated on the crested waves as she had so often pictured it.

"Tell your plans, and name your price," said the girl. "I am in haste, as my time is almost out, and I must return to school."

"I rekin yer'll be after catchin' a husban', Minona Portwood. Now, Mr. Easman's a good, fust rate lawyer, and is willin' to tuk yer along with this yer claim."

"Yes," said the man, "I need a wife," with a half-sinister, half-amatory glance.

With a curl of her proud lip, Minona designed no answer to the condescension proffered her, but asked in quiet tones:

"What land it was that she had the claim to?"

"It's a place yer loves, for I've seen yer go there and weep, Minona Portwood, over yer poverty, and covet the rich man's goods. Now, be a good un, and consent to tuck up Mr. Easman's offer. It's a good chance for a poor gal like yer is, and he'll git back the Eagle Ben' from that ar cheatin' Dearing."

Minona's eyes blazed sparks of anger.

"How dare either of you couple his name with such words? Begone! If robbing Mr. Dearing is the only way for me to own property, I shall work my fingers to the bone first."

"Mighty fine eirs. I watched ye that ere day yer came, Miss Meddlesome, to the court house and had my son, Jake Easman, put in prison. This yer Easman is my brother-in-law, and we'll git yer both yet."

"Rachel, was it you who instigated that outlaw to prosecute my father?" said Minona. "He never injured you."

"He did! He killed my other son in cold blood, an' this yer one lives in prison fer yer both."

"I did not know they were your sons. I never before heard the prosecutor's name. But they were robbers, and Mr. Dearing killed the man in self-defense. I am sorry for you, but vengeance belongs to God."

"Yes, that's all yer fine folks ever comforts us poor uns with. Love of God don't fill us when we's hungry, or clothe us when we's bare."

"But 'though he slay me, yet will I trust in him,' says the Bible, Rachel, and he helps us all. Think of that, and forget revenge."

Minona rose as her pupils appeared, and the nefarious pair, baffled but not appeased, disappeared behind the trees.

The interview left a most disagreeable impression upon Minona. Her actions were watched, from the old woman's statement, and by parties with malignant natures thirsting for vengeance. She would go out hereafter, she resolved, only with her brothers; but then, might not the assassin's knife or bullet speed the work upon her or them? In the following winter she would complete the cycle of twenty years. The dream voice of the veiled spectre often sounded in her ears afar like some echo of a half-remembered vesper bell.

Would Rachel Mulkey and her vagrant son Jake, whose Christian name she had heard in childhood, figure in the closing scenes of her life?

Would she ever seen Mr. Dearing or Mr. Meverill again, and would they play a part in the drama? Unsolvable queries!

The spring leaped into the arms of golden summer, and Minona's life was a lengthened, busy monotony. She had all the diligence in her vocation that was said to characterize Pope in his pursuits, and her labors were regularly and unfalteringly performed. By the most scrupulous economy she was unable to lay aside some savings which, added to those furnished by Hugh, aided Roy to enter college in the autumn. Proud was the day to Minona when she saw her promising young brother leave home for Knoxville as a student of East Tennessee University. She would feel the loss of daily commune with one assimilating nature, but that nature would return more expanded, more fitted to cope with hers in new fields of thought and study.

Mr. Portwood began to taste the sweets of sobriety. This year his little farm yielded abundantly; his debts were liquidated, and a trifle left for household purposes, out of which he sent by Hugh for a birthday gift for his daughter. Hugh selected a lady's work-box with all the conveniences, adding a gold thimble from himself.

Mrs. Portwood was determined that her darling should have a dining upon her twentieth birthday, and that Dr. Crandon and his sister should partake of the celebration. Everything was nicely prepared; but Minona seemed to lose all her cheerfulness as the time drew near. Despite her strong will phantoms and weird shapes would rise in taunt her with unknown dread of a coming climax. Superstition is a cowardly foe; it hates the light, and skulks ever in mystery and darkness and gloom. At night Minona grew restless and nervous, and unable to drive away the fiends that mocked her. At length the day dawned in cold, bright December. She awoke early and bathed her face in icy water, attiring herself in a plain black dress, ever her costumes since Vinvela's death. She had changed little, except that her hair had grown into glossy black curls since her illness, and now fell in luxuriant soft clusters around her face, delicate in feature and in complexion. She sought her mother's bed-room, which also was the sitting-room. Everything was cheerful there, and neatly put to rights. Beside the fire sat John Portwood.

"Dear father," she said, "good morning. We have a fine day for our visitors."

He rose and kissed her.

"Here is a package, my child, to show a father's gratitude. God bless you, as you have blessed me."

She kissed him, and thanked him with a voice full of emotion. In that moment she was repaid a thousand fold for her noble self-sacrifice. She would not have exchanged the sweet consciousness of right for aught else on earth.

Her brothers, John and Thomas, each had some memento for her, and her mother looked happy and contented with her husband and sons, upright and sober, and her lovely daughter the light of all their hearts. The guests came. The good doctor and his sister had not forgotten her. A card case and a copy of Irving's works testified their appreciation of her merit.

It wanted only four days to Christmas, and her father, and brothers were going over a ravine into a field to arrange some matters pertaining to the farm. She had promised to spend a part of New Year's week with Miss Crandon. The day was cold, but she needed exercise, and she put on her hat and shawl to accompany them, with Irvin's "Alhambra" as her companion. The field was not very distant, and the nearest portion approximated the Indian graves. The ground was hard-frozen, and myriads of ice stalagmites reared their crooked and prismatic heads above the yellow clay, crackling crisply under their footsteps as they walked; and the sun shone as coldly.

The walk was enjoyed by Minona, who relished the frosty air. Her father and brothers began their fence-repairing, and she sat down on the outer edge of one of the Indian tombs and began her book. Ere long she became interested to perfect absorption, and did not perceive the onward movement of her protectors in their extending labors. She was alone; her spirit reveling in Irving's glowing descriptions of the beautiful Alhambra, with its arabesque ornaments, its fountains, its flowers, and its Andalusian sunshine. She forgot all else in her haste to read on through her charming volume, with its champagne sparkle emanating from every page, until a footfall arrested her imagination on the wing. She looked up expecting to see one of her brothers. She arose. Whose was that symmetrical form before her—Hugh's, or Mr. Meverill's? No! Mr. Dearing with his exalted face confronted her.

With the joyful exclamation she was about to spring forward, when all the past rose before her, and she knew not how to address him. The crimson flood surged to her face, and she buried it in her hands.

"Do you not welcome me, Minona, after such long separation?"

She did not speak, and he gently disengaged her hands from her embarrassed face.

"Are you still angry with me for never writing, and being so obdurate?"

"I never blamed you," she said. "Your resentment was most natural; but I hoped some day you would forgive me, and that my conduct would be palliated in your eyes, if not wholly justified and applauded."

"The hour has come. I have nothing to forgive, but must return you thanks for the worthless life you so generously saved. Why did you run away on that dreaded day when you came as a dove of rescue and of peace before I could express any obligations?"

"Because we deserve no commendations for simple actions of justice. I did nothing in comparison with the benefits I received from you." He spoke of Eriginia. "I never knew until after the end that she desired your presence, or I should have summoned you. Did you censure my seemingly heartless conduct?"

"Perhaps I did entertain a slight feeling of bitterness at first," she said, looking up at him with humid eyes for the first time. "But it has long since passed away. It was better I should have been saved the keen pangs of beholding another friend fall away from the circumscribed few that I can claim."

"Minona," he said, leading her to the seat she had vacated and sitting beside her, "have you never regretted the step you took so precipitately, and does your present life bring contentment?"

"I believe," she said, "I am as happy as generally falls to the lot of mortals to be. My life is calm and serene, and I find a useful field of occupation. I had but one regret in the action you deem hasty, and now that has passed away."

A shade of disappointment and almost of pain swept quickly over Mr. Dearing's face at her equanimity and avowal of contentment.

After some moments he asked:

"Are you glad to see me? You have expressed neither pleasure nor welcome yet at my return. I did not expect indifference from you."

"Nor do I feel it; and I did not look for reproach;" but still she did not answer the question.

"Minona," he said, "I came to ask you to make my home yours once more. I cannot live without your presence. Will you come?"

A radiant look of joy played over her face for an instant, then died out, leaving it pallid and pensive as before.

"I cannot," she said. "Duty claims me here."

"Are you to spend a lifetime in studying alone the good of others, or have you ceased to feel any affection for me? O, Minona, I did not anticipate ever to realize this pang."

And his face grew pale, stern and rigid as she had once before seen it.

Tears stood in her eyes as she uttered in faltering tones:

"I did not mean to wound you. Can we not be friends?"

"No," he said; "I came to test your feelings for me. I thank you now for leaving me, and inflicting a blow by forsaking me the most poignant I ever felt. I tried to bury your image in oblivion, to crush out memory, but I could not after my wife's death—your face went with me everywhere increasing in brilliancy. I have been lonely, and your decision must determine whether I continue so and again become a wanderer, or end my life in happiness. I cannot receive you as a child; but as I my wife you must come and grace my home. I have transformed my love into a dearer affection."

Laveter, the great physiognomist, would have been puzzled at the expression of Minona's face as she listened to Mr. Dearing's words. First, an ashy pallor overspread her quivering features, then slowly they seem touched by the finger of Medusa—so rigid they grew. She essayed to speak, but voice died in the vocal tube ere it reached her lips.

Mr. Dearing's glowing face caught the infection. It blanched as white as her own as he said:

"Speak to me."

His words recalled Minona. With a strong effort she said, with a shiver:

"Never can I be your wife!"

"Is this your unchanging determination?" he asked, coldly. "I am too late. You are betrothed to Mr. Meverill. Fool that I was to delay so long."

"Would that your words were true," uttered a deep, manly voice. At the same time Mr. Meverill stood before the equally astonished pair.

"Do you play the spy, sir?" asked Mr. Dearing, his eyes ablaze with anger as he stood up.

"I allow no insult, sir!" replied Mr. Meverill, with equal hauteur. "State your accusations at another time. Angry words are unsuited to the respect due a lady. Pardon my intrusion, Miss Minona. I called at your home. I was directed to seek you here. Unwillingly I heard Mr. Dearing's remark. I knew not we were rivals."

"Aye, rivals to the death," said Mr. Dearing through his closed teeth. "Minona, choose between us," he continued, his voice softening as he spoke to her.

"I sought you to lay all I possess at your feet, lady," said Mr. Meverill, sadly.

These two men were a study as they confronted the lady. Both fine specimens of symmetrical proportion. The one the favored child of fortune; noble, generous, with a heart brave and stern, or sympathetic and affectionate as an extrinsic circumstances demanded; endowed with the spirit as sensitive as the little flower which holds its leaves at the lightest touch. His dark-blue eyes shone with a depth of mingled emotions as he stood awaiting Minona's reply. Born to command, accustomed to deference, he awaited his sentence as a warrior with a calm exterior, while all within was tempestuous emotion. The other, equally noble, was the child of misfortune. The stern lines around the fine mouth, the pallid face, somewhat thinned by constant exertion, with its firm, self-reliant expression, indicated that he had scaled the rugged cliffs of life, and now awaited the decision of his lady-love as one who felt deeply, but whom disappointment could not daunt.

Minona remained silent for some time. Her face flushed and paled by turns, and she felt ill from the varied emotions which swelled within her heart.

As Mr. Dearing gazed upon the girl, and read the suffering revealed upon her face his heart grew gentle. He lost all sense of selfish emotion. Like a clairvoyant he seemed to trace every phase of feeling that rippled through the being before him, and sympathy alone impelled his words as he said:

"Minona, I came here to proffer you my heart and my home. Again I offer you my all. God knows how earnestly I desire you to acquiesce, but if it gives you pain I resign you. If there be misery let it fall on me rather than on you. Speak. Do you love this young man who sues for your hand? I desire no sacrifice on your part. If you love him, say so unreservedly."

"Speak, lady," said Mr. Meverill, in eager tones.

Minona's face flushed, then resumed its natural pallor. She rose, and with an unnatural calmness she said slowly:

"I cannot marry either. Best of friends," she continued, turning to Mr. Dearing, "why could we not have continued as formerly? Forgive me for again giving you pain."

Mr. Dearing's face quivered. Catching Minona in his arms he kissed her lips, murmured a farewell, and was gone before she could arrest him.

She sunk into her seat and buried her face in her hands. Tears fell through her fingers.

Mr. Meverill paced slowly the open space which so lately he had sought with such high hopes bounding in his breast. He had not calculated on defeat. What man ever does? Yet Mr. Meverill was not vain. He had heard, long since from his Savannah relative, of Minona's true parentage. He had not expected such a rival. Minona was his first love, her obscure origin held no weight with him.

He continued his walk until Minona appeared more tranquil, then he seated himself beside her.

"Forgive me," he said, "for urging my suit at so inopportune a moment. The hope of gaining you was my day-star all these years. You have declined, and I would not add to your emotion by further importunity. My love for you is unchanged. I shall bear it away as the guardian treasure of my life, and whether or not you ever return it, I desire you to use me as a disinterested friend whenever you need one."

"Thank you. Your conduct is blameless," said Minona.

"Shall I escort you home? You need repose."

Minona rose slowly, and in silence they walked through the winter sunshine which shone so brightly but a few hours since to her.

Mr. Meverill bade adieu to Minona at the door of her home. His walk along the river was in strong antithesis to that but an hour since.

Then hope, as a prismatic bow of promise, hung fair and alluring in his sky—now leaden clouds trails in their sombre banners and enveloped the bow in their dismal folds. Life was again a conflict unsweetened by affection; yet his heroic spirit did not quail. He returned to his home—plunged into study. Action is the great remedy for curing the ill of disappointed hopes.

Minona was stunned at the blow dealt her hoped-for happiness. All this weary time she had anticipated a reconciliation with her benefactor as the crowning event to form the sum of happiness. She had seen him; she had wounded him anew—they were parted probably forever. His words, his self-abnegation, often recurred to her, and each time gave acute pain. Does not apathy often creep in to occupy the gap made by disappointment in our hearts?

Minona experienced this want of interest in surrounding objects. She employed her time constantly, but the pulse which gives life to energy was stilled.

Months passed. One day Minona strolled up the river near the spot Rachel Mulkey had revealed her true parentage to her. It was a spot endeared by past memories, as well as the memorial of her greatest misfortune. She did not regret her restoration to her real parents. She realized that in resuming the ties to them she had reaped the truest and purest gratification life affords—that of doing real good and bestowing happiness on others. But had she never known these facts she would now have been free from suffering.

She felt peculiarly gloomy this spring afternoon. The flowers, the forest songsters, the flowing river, all oppressed her. Before her, on the distant horizon, rose the purple mountains, superb and hazy; their majestic outlines indicating strength and repose. She thought, as she threw herself upon the shore, the fever heat of man's ambition burns out; his eager pursuit after expected blessings which ever elude him are as nothing in the everlasting cycle of time. A little while and he is gone as a fleeting breath, while the grand fragments, flung from the hand of God to beautify creation, loom up immutable until time shall be no more, resistless of the elements—regardless of the sufferings of man—the almost conqueror of the elements in his God-like grasp upon science.

Minona had lost all consciousness of surrounding objects when a step recalled her. An exclamation of surprise escaped her as she saw Mr. Meverill almost before her. He held a parcel in his hand. He had changed since last she saw him. He looked older—sadder. The lines around the firm mouth were sterner, and there was a look of patient suffering mingled with the calm expression which unbending self-reliance always gives to the features.

"Excuse the intrusion, Miss Minona," he said, as he greeted her. "I came at the request of a friend to deliver a package to you."

He sat down near her.

Minona received the parcel. At the recognition of the characters upon the envelope she uttered a slight cry:

"Where did you get this?" she asked, eagerly.

"It was sent to me from New York. Here is the letter accompanying it. You will see that I was requested to deliver, in person, the parcel."

Minona perused the letter which contained but a few lines, then proceeded to open the parcel which was enclosed in an envelope. Within was the following letter:

> *"I desire you to be happy, Minona. Forget me and be happy with the estimable young man who is the bearer of the enclosed deed, which accept as a marriage portion—for both—from one who loved you too well to make you miserable. Farewell forever.*
> *C. D."*

The other paper was a deed to all of Mr. Dearing's lands in East Tennessee, including the Eagle Bend, beside bonds of considerable value.

"Are you acquainted with the contents of these papers?" asked Minona.

"I am not. I felt that I had been the supposed cause of the writer's unhappiness. For that reason, and urged by a desire to see you, I came hither," he scrutinized the face of the girl a few paces from him. She had changed too. There were traces of mental suffering upon her face. "Minona," he said, "do not send me away without hope. Consider how much I have endured—how long your image has been photographed upon my heart ere circumstances permitted me to disclose my sentiments to you."

She was silent a long time. At length, raising her eyes, she said:

"Mr. Meverill, strange as it may seem to you, I have never loved. Perhaps had I remained in the sphere in which you first saw me I might have loved you. Sorrow and care have left no room for gentler feelings."

"I can wait if you only bid me hope to claim you ultimately."

"Suspense is subtle poison which kills all the joys and destroys the ease of life. It would be unjust to doom you to such punishment," answered the girl, sadly.

"Not if I select it voluntarily," he replied. "Let me write to you. Leave these surroundings. Forget the past. I do not fear the test—in time you may regard me with less indifference."

"Were I to acquiesce, Mr. Meverill, you would have just cause of complaint. I have a mission to accomplish. A preoccupied heart is seldom open to the soft influences of love."

"May I write to you? Surely you can extend this favor without trespassing upon your ideas of justice. If I fail the consequences be on my own head. You shall be blameless."

Minona noticed the pained emotions traced vividly upon her companion's face. She thought of the mandate just received. Something was due to the years of affection Mr. Meverill had entertained for her unchanged by her changed fortune. She owed him some favor—then should she not endeavor to follow her benefactor's desire? Rising to return home, she said:

"You may write. I shall leave for New York next week to be absent for some time. I may find it necessary to go to Europe."

"May I not accompany you to New York? I have some business there later in the season. I can arrange it to go with you now."

"It is impossible. I have a mission. I may be obliged to visit Europe before it is accomplished."

"Minona," said Mr. Meverill, "you surely are not forming the insane idea of following Mr. Dearing. You have no clue to his whereabouts. It would be a fruitless journey."

"I have driven him from his home. Ought I not to endeavor to restore him to it?"

"He left before you had any agency in it."

"Had I never forsaken him he had not gone," she said, "I must make some effort to bring him back, else I shall know no repose."

"Send an agent or write. I will aid you in discovering his locality. You are too young, too inexperienced to go in search of him yourself."

"I must go as far as New York. Suspense is devouring my life. Death is preferable to continued uncertainty," she replied.

"If you discover him shall I be forsaken? Oh, Minona, how true are your last words. This uncertainty, borne in secret for years, is wearing my vital element. Answer me."

"I shall never marry where your question now implies. I can give you no hope. I must fulfill my purpose."

"I may write," he said, "and you will leave my fate an open question?"

"Yes," she replied, in an abstracted manner.

They had reached the house.

"Will you come in?" she asked.

"It is late. I must return to the village." He shook her hand and turned to the road leading to Clinton. The sun had set. His dying glow had well nigh burned out in the western sky, leaving the pearly gray gloaming more soothing to a heart preoccupied with melancholy. There is something withering in the vivid sunshine to those in affliction, but when night draws her starry veil across heaven's vaulted roof and the moon, like a chandelier, lights her ghostly lamp, there seems an influence that draws our spirits away from earth. They appear to soar upward and receive consolation in their flight.

Something of this fell over Mr. Meverill as he walked along the river shore after his interview with Minona. The faintest glimmer of hope folds the heart of man, as a nimbus, into the certain expectation of happiness. Ah! hope, thou art the Fata Morgana of life, yet the end is ever the same—disappointment—death!

Mr. Meverill returned to Alabama. He was comforted, if not joyous, by his visit to Minona. Yet the food she gave would not have saved the starving heart from perishing had reason held her sway.

> *"Oft in her absence mine fancy makes*
> *To imitate her, but misjoining shapes,*
> *Wild work produces oft."*

Minona's resolution was firm to go to New York, seek Mr. Dearing and persuade—nay, implore him, not to expatriate himself, but to return to his home and exert his talents in a public career. Thus she thought to make him forget the recent episode so painful to both. Thus was hope forming a mirage for her eyes also;

> *"A dancing shape,*
> *To haunt, to startle and waylay."*

She wrote to Hugh that important business made it necessary for her to visit New York, the nature of which she would disclose to him on her arrival in Savannah. She besought him to arrange his affairs so as to accompany her. He was startled at her altered appearance. She was obliged to delay in Savannah several days before he could arrange to leave his business. She informed him of her reasons for going to New York and showed him the deeds.

"I think your trip thither will be useless, sister. It has been several months since Mr. Dearing left here."

"Have you heard nothing from him?"

"Nothing," replied Hugh. "He bade me communicate with a certain firm in New York which had the control of his business. I should hear from him if occasion arose needing his immediate supervision."

"We can learn all about him from this firm," cried Minona, eagerly.

"I doubt it. It will be wise in you to let me write. I see that only disappointment awaits you."

"The fever of restlessness consumes me. I must go, dear Hugh. I must return these deeds and restore my benefactor to his home again. Otherwise, I shall continue wretched and fill an early grave. I know it."

There was an excited glow which burned in the poor girl's eyes, a hectic spot on her cheek that pained Hugh to observe. He objected no longer to Minona's wishes. Certain despair is far preferable to the tortures of suspense.

At length Minona began to feel that some steps were taken toward an ultimate result when she found herself steaming out of Savannah harbor. At any other time she would have delighted in a sea voyage. The human heart is subject to strange thermometrical changes not at all in accord with those of the atmosphere. There was a chill of despair which had frozen up even Minona's keen sense of the beautiful and sublime. She gazed absently on the grand old ocean, which, but comparatively a few months before, would have called forth loud encomiums from her. Now she murmured inwardly as she gaze from the deck on the swelling waves:

> *"The sleepless blows on the ocean's breast*
> *Break like a bursting heart, and die in foam,*
> *And thus at length find rest."*

The voyage was safe and speedy. Minona suffered little from that terror of travelers–seasickness. The bustle and confusion of New York elicited no comments. There are times when scenes pass before the eye, sinking insensibly and indelibly upon memory's palimpsest, which are brought vividly to view at some future time by the chemistry of outward events. Although Minona was a silent and apparently unobserved beholder, nothing she had seen was lost.

Hugh guided her to an elegant private boarding house, one at which he had been accustomed to lodge. He persuaded her to delay her investigations until the next day. She needed some hours' rest and he, through a mistaken kindness, wished to postpone what he knew would result in her disappointment to the latest possible moment.

At a late hour of the afternoon Hugh accompanied Minona on a short walk, if such elbowing and engineering through the sea of humanity can be so termed. This kind attempt for her diversion was fully appreciated, but still the hours crept slowly along. An unquiet night in a small unventilated room brought the morning. Minona, awakened long ere that time.

The restless hum of the never-resting population drove away sleep. What a strange sensation, to one accustomed to look upon the rural scenes, fresh from nature's hand, is the first sight of solid brick walls and the gray tiles of a mammoth city!

The work of God and man, both grand, yet how infinitely more beautiful the prospect, how much more exalting is the work of God than that of his creature, the one imperishable simplicity, the other massive mutability!

Minona rose in a state of feverish anxiety. Already there had been much delay, and, at best, she must wait some hours before she could learn any positive information. Breakfast was over finally, and Hugh, begging his sister to amuse herself and not give way to low spirits, left her to seek information of Mr. Dearing.

Minona occupied herself in glancing at the pedestrians and vehicles seen through her window. It required no mental concentration, yet it kept the mind from dwelling too seriously upon its own burden. Some hours passed; the girl wearied at length of this panoramic pastime.

She went into the reception-room and, having no book, took up some newspapers lying upon a table. These she glanced at superficially, until her eye fell upon a column headed "Terrible Marine Disaster!" She began reading, not much interested; then there was a start, an agonized stare, and a sickly pallor overspread the usually pale face. Clasping one hand over her heart the girl seemed transfixed—transformed into marble. The paper fell from her hand, and there she sat until Hugh found her on his return.

"Too late. I feared this," he said, as he looked at the girl. "Sister," he continued, "to speak to me."

She pointed to the paper. In that was the whole volume of her calamity. She did not faint. Hers was not a fainting temperament, but the blow was terribly stunning nevertheless, and there was a strange smothering in her heart.

"Sister, I would have spared you this. Let me conduct you to your room."

"Home," the girl gasped; "My mission is yet unended." Her voice was husky and strange, even to her own ears.

Hugh had not been absent long from Minona. The business house with some distance from his boarding place. He had just arrived there. The head of the firm was absent, but would return in a short time. A polite clerk handed him some papers to read while he waited. Why blanched that manly cheek? Under the caption of marine disasters was an account of the ship Hydra, lost off the coast of Ireland. Many were drowned, among them. Mr. Dearing.

Hugh felt dizzy as he rose, and left word he would call again. He feared his sister would see the account or hear of it without a warning, as he had. He dreaded the result to her in her present state of mental excitability. As his eye fell upon her stony face, when he entered the parlor, he needed no information to learn that shaft had sped.

It was late in the afternoon when the carriage wound its way along the road bordering the river to the cottage upon Cedar Bluff.

Minona's was not a weak nature. She resolutely combated the affliction which consumed her. She uttered no complaint, nor did she mention the cause of her distress. Go where she would, work as she might, her heart was folded in a winding sheet, which one moment floated upon the billows then was submerged beneath their surging rage. The form of her benefactor, in the ghastliness of death, ever rose before her, and she reproached herself as his murderess. When death robs us of our treasures, at every turn insensate objects seem to acquire voices to sing requiems over their loss, and keep their memories ever present with us. Everything about the Eagle Bend reproached Minona anew as the cause of the tragic end of her friend. She felt it would be better for her to change her residence to entirely new scenes, yet to regain her peace of mind seemed to her a sacrilege to the dead, so sensitive was her state.

A few weeks of misery went slowly into the past. Hugh had delayed during this time his journey to Savannah in the hope of consoling his sister by his presence. It was the last evening of his stay. The moon rose high in the heavens in all the beauty of maturity. Light luminous clouds drifted before a cool, soft breeze, and obstructed occasionally for a moment.

> *"The beat of her unseen feet*
> *Which only the angels hear."*

The swarming stars were all nestled to rest, leaving the mistress of night companionless with the exception of one or two bright and ambitious followers.

Minona and Hugh sat upon the doorsteps. The silence was almost oppressive. No sound disturbed the serenity of the night except the plash of the river upon the shore, and the distant dash of the waters over the old dam above. Suddenly Minona looked up, saying:

"Let us walk up the river shore, Hugh, I have something to say that I may never have the opportunity to mention again."

"I mean to return soon, sister," answered Hugh, with forced gayety; "but I shall be glad to walk, this charming night."

Hand in hand the twain walked slowly along. At length Minona began:

"I shall be more in despair after you leave than ever. I seem to grow more helpless as time passes. I cannot contend long with this consuming conflict."

"Sister, accompany me to Savannah. Remain there a short time, then I will travel with you until your health and spirits are restored."

"I cannot. Company or strange faces are odious to me."

"Solitude is not good for you. You ought not to yield to grief in this manner. Think, my dear sister, how it distresses us."

"I know it, and yet I cannot refrain. I seem a criminal in my own eyes. There is but one thing I can do, comply with the last request," this was said with an effort, yet not a tear fell from the eyes.

"Have you ever heard from him?" asked Hugh, understanding Minona's meaning.

"Frequently."

"Are you sure that you will consummate happiness by the step you propose?"

"I have never thought of that. I have never loved. My sentiments are only friendship, but I will fulfill the last request ever made by—" There was a pause, then she resumed: "I shall have more peace of mind by so doing. Were I sure of misery I should not hesitate to comply."

"Were our friend living, sister, he would be the first to object to a step that leaves the bear possibility of unhappiness to you. Reflect; wait until some sentiment beyond friendship fills your heart."

"I have determined. My peace of mind will be restored. Happiness for me has fled forever. I shall not trouble any one long."

His heart sank as he walked beside this fair girl in the morning of life, so hopeless, so changed from the sprightly, witty being he had known a few years before. Her words seemed prophetic as he looked at the slight form and pale face in the cold moonlight.

"Are you right, sister, to carry out your own selfish purpose and thereby confer wretchedness upon the object of your choice?" he said, gently.

"I shall not do that. The party does not require more than I can bestow. I shall be candid. It is a subject I desired to mention to you. I must act speedily. I shall not be long here. Oh, Hugh, think how happy I shall be when I go to rejoin Vinvela and the loved friends of yore."

She looked up as she spoke. A momentary enthusiasm pervaded her face as if a ray of light had been caught from the white moon, then it died out, leaving her countenance placid, pale as before.

The walk had brought the pair nearly opposite the mansion where Minona had passed so many days of peace and pleasure. Hugh had made no response to her last remarks. He was deeply pained and did not trust himself to speak; besides, what arguments could he offer. He was the victim of disappointed love, a sorrow sent by the hand of God, less bitter in its affliction than if the object had been false.

She was the victim of self-crimination, the most torturing of all sorrow. He was powerless to palliate or console, while his own painful experience enabled him to feel more acutely for her.

"Let us go to the house, Hugh," said Minona. "I should like to sit upon the steps and once more call forth the shadows of the past." The direction of her eye pointed where she meant.

"Is it not best to return home? It will be too painful."

"It will calm me. Let us go." She preceded him.

Hugh followed silently. He felt like one impelled by some luring fate to drift, the sport of the moment, yet whither was he tending?

The path curved gracefully. Minona opened the gate.

How dismal is a closed, untenanted house standing solemn and solitary in the cold moonlight. The girl walked slowly through the path, pausing here and there at some rosebush—then went on to the little summer house. She seemed to have forgotten Hugh's presence. Indeed, he had remained at the gate. With true delicacy he left his sister to her own reflections.

There he stood a long time leaning on the gate, watching the moon in her unceasing march in the earth's servitude. Some are born to rule, some to secondary places; yet those in servitude who fulfill faithfully all their trusts, shine as resplendent over the rulers as thou. Oh, moon, in thy peerless beauty giveth light to earth!

Hugh continued to follow the queen of night with his eyes. His thoughts soared away in a starry flight, striving to penetrate the unknown and commune with the spirits of the departed. Vain effort, and yet how natural to those who grieve. A rustle of some animal seeking covert in the rank undergrowth restored his wandering thoughts to the present.

Minona was still out of view. He walked through the grounds and was at length brought by the termination of a walk to the arbor. Minona sat upon the damp earth, her head resting upon the seat of the bower. Her eyes were closed. Hugh approached softly. He took her hand, it was cold and damp.

He spoke twice before she opened her eyes, looked vacantly and moaned, with her hand pressed to her heart.

"My dear sister, this will never do. You should have not come here."

He almost forced her to rise.

"I am better now," she said, with a sigh. "Let us go."

She took his proffered arm and walked slowly toward the gate. There she paused, cast a lingering look of affection, and with a smile said:

"Make me a promise, brother. Will you?"

"Yes, certainly."

"When I die bury me amid these roses. Beautiful spot. I would have my spirit walk here."

Hugh did not speak.

"You have not promised, Hugh. Say yes."

With a masterly effort at self-command Hugh forced himself to reply.

"I suspect you will outlive me, sister; but I will comply if I survive, provided you have me interred beside her."

"I promise," said Minona, grasping his hand. "It is a contract."

She seemed more composed. Spoke of his journey as they walked homeward. Arrived there Minona went into her own little shed room, lighted her candle and wrote Mr. Meverill an acceptance of his hand. Bowing her head in her hands she thanked God that her task was almost done.

She awakened early the ensuing day, and superintended all the essentials of comfort for Hugh's journey.

When he came out in the front room she greeted him with a smile like her old self.

"Here is my letter. Will you post it safely for me?"

"Yes; but is it not better for you to delay yet a while. This is a serious step, dear sister."

"I must act in this way. I have written to Mr. Meverill to come at once. After our bridal I shall leave this region until I am no more. Then remember your promise."

"Be it so," said the young man, hoarsely. "God grant I may go first," he said, almost in a whisper, as he busied himself strapping his trunk to hide his emotion.

Adieus were spoken. Hugh came back and again embraced a sister.

"Be cheerful for my sake, sister, while I am away. I shall return very soon."

"I shall strive to forget," she said, kindly. "Do not neglect to post my letter."

Some weeks after his departure, Dr. Crandon married an estimable lady. Mrs. Portwood felt anxious for her daughter to accompany her to the wedding, which occurred at the church.

On the day appointed Minona felt too unwell to go, but she prevailed upon her mother to attend the nuptials. When Roy came in to join them, he handed his sister a letter.

"Are you not going to the wedding?" he asked.

"No. I do not feel like so doing, as I am not well," she replied.

"Let us remain with you, my child," said her mother.

"By no means. Our friends will feel slighted if none of us go. I am only temporarily indisposed."

Thus answered, Mrs. Portwood and her son departed, leaving Minona in solitude, to enjoy her letter. Ever since the shock received by the tragic end to Mr. Dearing she had felt strange sensations about her heart. At times acute pains, then a smothered feeling, as if vitality would cease, again wild beating of the organ when any exercise or emotion swayed her. She was of an uncomplaining nature, and thought these symptoms only the result of mental distress. In New York and again on the night she visited the arbor at Eagle Bend, she experienced severe sensations, but these passed away, making no alarming impression on her. Soon after her mother left Minona, with her letter in hand, threw herself on a small lounge to peruse it.

The letter was kinder in its tone than usual, and, although Mr. Dearing's name was not mentioned, the writer evidently had heard of his death. This was not a reply to Minona's last letter, but it had an appeal to her to acquiesce to his proposal. The letter recalled all she had suffered, all she had lost. In imagination she beheld the wrecked ship with its living burden struggling amid the surging billows of an all devouring element. Again the pale features of her friend, locked in icy death, rose as the form floated on the crested waves as she had so often pictured it. The seeming reality froze her with horror. A sharp pain seized her in the heart region, rendering her face as pallid as that of a corpse. She clasped her hand over her heart, in the other was the letter. Oblivion came to cancel pain. Thus she lay like a marble statue, with closed eyes, in all the careless grace of youthful loveliness.

Mrs. Portwood returned quite late in the day. She approached her child thinking her asleep. The pale face of the sleeper alarmed her. She touched the hand, it was cold as stone. The woman uttered a piercing shriek. Ever does the noise of grief essay to disturb the silence of remorseless death. The woman sat upon the floor, the hand of the dead girl still clasped in her own, and at a still later hour was found in this situation by Mr. Portwood and Roy.

Restoratives were used with no effect. Dr. Crandon was summoned as soon as possible, and gave his opinion that Minona had perished of heart disease. Upon investigation he could learn of no former symptoms. Minona had never complained to any of her friends.

Mrs. Portwood appeared reduced to a state of imbecility by this last stroke, but friends were not wanting to aid in the funeral preparations.

Just before sunset on the following day, as the golden rays set the trees and the windows of the cottage ablaze with an almost celestial glory, a horseman rode to the cottage door. He threw the bridle over the gate post. There was an elastic, joyous spring in his foot falls as he coursed along the walk leading to the cottage. The door stood open. A human shape, under the ghastly white winding sheet, was stretched upon a low lounge in the centre of the room.

The stranger entered with a light, solemn step that each assumes by an inherent respect for the presence of death. He drew near. He lifted the pall. His bride had gone to God, before him lay the earthly casket, transformed into a stony sculpture by the artist Death. With a suppressed moan Mr. Meverill turned and fled as from the charmed house.

> *"What is youth?—a dancing billow,*
> *Winds behind and rocks before!"*

Happy they who pass from life's perils early in life.

The funeral awaited Hugh's arrival.

It was sunset on the ensuing day, the scene seemed lighted with burnished gold as the cortège wound slowly up the ascent to Eagle Bend. The light of the household had been extinguished. The shattered temple was lowered amid the roses in the garden of Eagle Bend.

A low slab was placed in the centre of the grave to mark the spot. Upon its polished surface was graven: "Minona, aged 20 years."

Two years past. The rumor went forth that Eagle Bend was haunted. Lights were seen sometimes at night. Some averred that a spirit went its ghostly round at the dead hours of night. Minona was said to walk among the roses.

The place was deserted. Rank weeds choked the rare flowers and covered the tasteful walks. One spot remained clear–that around the grave. A tall shaft of Italian marble usurped the place of the unpretending slab. It was supposed to be the work of Hugh. It created no remark. Few ever passed the isolated place. The poor were too superstitious–the rich concerned with other things. The dead are soon forgot.

It was a cold afternoon of a December day after the lapse of a year from the foregoing narration. The western sun had almost sunk behind

> *"Clouds of feathery gold,*
> *Shaded with deepest purple."*

when a pedestrian approached the garden gate of Eagle Bend. He was of low stature, somewhat stooped in form. The hair was iron gray. The face plain and serene. Upon his shoulders was slung a haversack.

As he neared the gate the white shaft gleamed in the growing shadows between the thick foliage.

He gazed in surprise. Opening the gate he traced his way to the monument. "So young!" he murmured. "Are they all gone?"

He turned with a sigh to the house. The windows were closed. The door was open. He stalked in, through the parlor into the Blue Room. Ashes were upon the hearth. A solitary chair stood vacant beside it. A low lounge revealed itself in the dim light. The man struck a match, lighted a candle which he found upon the mantel.

There lay a man upon the lounge. His eyes were half closed, his gray hair fell over the pillow in careless confusion. The face was careworn–prematurely old–sorrow had eaten deep lines upon the well turned features.

Mr. Crews lifted the candle, walked to the lounge and looked on the dead form of Clarek Dearing.

A year previous the former owner of Eagle Bend had been saved from the wreck, and had come home to witness the evidence of his self-abnegation in Minona's happiness. The house was vacant. Its mistress dwelt under the slab in the garden.

The sorrowing man existed in eremitic seclusion until Asrael bore him home to the bosom of his God.

THE END.